The elven race, driven from their age-old enclaves in the greenwoods, have crossed the Plains of Dust and harsh mountains into the distant land of Khur—the desert kingdom of sun, sand, and silence. Confined to a sprawling tent city under the walls of Khuri-Khan, they must forget past glories and fight to survive. But more than the hard-edged desert is against them. Shadowy forces inside Khur and out plot to destroy the elves. Some are ancient and familiar. Others are new and unknown.

At the head of the reunited Qualinesti and Silvanesti bands is Gilthas, now Speaker of the Sun and Stars. Though given a united rule, he has no crown, no throne, no marble hall—yet the blood of Kith-Kanan flows in his veins, and he's no longer the despised Puppet King. At his side, the fiery Kerianseray, bane of the Dark Knights, and known forever as the Lioness. To her falls the task of forging a new elven army, one that can safeguard the refugees and dream of taking back their lost homeland. But Kerianseray's chief opponent is not the legion of minotaurs plundering Silvanost, or the army of Dark Knights. Her true opponent is much closer to her head and her heart.

And so the battle lines are drawn, and the great game begins. Survival or death, glory or oblivion—these are the stakes. Gilthas and Kerianseray stake all on a forgotten map, faithful friends, and their unshakable faith in the greatness of the elven race.

ALSO BY PAUL B. THOMPSON & TONYA C. COOK

THE ERGOTH TRILOGY

VOLUME ONE
A WARRIOR'S JOURNEY

VOLUME TWO
THE WIZARD'S FATE

VOLUME THREE
A HERO'S JUSTICE

THE BARBARIANS

VOLUME ONE
CHILDREN OF THE PLAINS

VOLUME TWO
BROTHER OF THE DRAGON

VOLUME THREE
SISTER OF THE SWORD

SANCTUARY

ELVEN EXILES

VOLUME ONE

**PAUL B. THOMPSON &
TONYA C. COOK**

SANCTUARY

©2005 Wizards of the Coast, Inc.

Published by Wizards of the Coast, Inc. DRAGONLANCE, WIZARDS OF THE COAST, and their respective logos are trademarks of Wizards of the Coast, Inc., in the U.S.A. and other countries.

Printed in the U.S.A.

Cover art by Matt Stawicki
First Printing: October 2005
Library of Congress Catalog Card Number: 2004116919

9 8 7 6 5 4

ISBN: 978-0-7869-3817-9
620-95011740-001-EN

U.S., CANADA,
ASIA, PACIFIC, & LATIN AMERICA
Wizards of the Coast, Inc.
P.O. Box 707
Renton, WA 98057-0707
+1-800-324-6496

EUROPEAN HEADQUARTERS
Hasbro UK Ltd
Caswell Way
Newport, Gwent NP9 0YH
GREAT BRITAIN
Please keep this address for your records.

Visit our web site at **www.wizards.com**

DEDICATION

For Leon and Rita Cook.
— Tonya

SANCTUARY

ELVEN EXILES
BOOK I

There is a silence where hath been no sound,
There is a silence where no sound may be,
In the cold grave—under the deep deep sea,
Or in wide desert where no life is found.

—Thomas Hood, Silence

prologue

A flock of blackbirds took flight, screeching wildly. They were not used to strangers. The sight of so many figures, moving toward them, incited panic. In moments the birds were lost against the unbending glare of the sun, but the emptiness was soon filled by a long column of cavalry.

Dusty horses, heads low, trudged over coarse sand and loose stones, their riders dozing in the saddle. Stragglers limped along the column's flanks, shields hanging from spears borne on weary, bony shoulders. None lacked a wound—these ranged from stray cuts and bruises to missing limbs. More than a few were gray-faced, bearing the unmistakable mark of impending death.

All were elves, many of the Kagonesti strain, but fully half belonged either to the western, Qualinesti line or the Silvanesti, eldest among the ancient race.

At the head of this mournful procession walked Kerianseray, general of all the elven armies. Years in the desert had deepened her natural brown skin tone and given her eyes a penetrating squint. Just now, her eyes were fixed on her trudging feet, willing them to make one more step, and another, and another.

She was leading her griffon. Eagle Eye had come to her as a gift from Silvanesti lords grateful to have escaped their homeland ahead of the invading minotaur host. Kagonesti she might be, but the protocol-sensitive nobles insisted that Kerianseray should have the finest mount in the army, not only as the leader of the remaining elven host but as wife to Gilthas, the Speaker of the Sun and Stars. In skirmish after skirmish, Eagle Eye had proven his mettle, taking the measure of many a fierce minotaur and ushering numerous foes into the hereafter. But even under the guidance of his ferocious rider, he could not reverse the inevitable.

Kerianseray, known to friend and foe alike as the Lioness, had led ten thousand elves south through the desert of Khur, seeking some means of entering the despoiled kingdom of Silvanesti from the north. Her warrior band was united by an unquenchable desire to expel the invaders from the sacred sylvan fastness of that most ancient elven homeland. Half a thousand perished even before the border of Silvanesti was reached, lost to heat, tainted water, and poisonous reptiles. Where fine sand finally gave way to loamy soil, and stunted pines and twisted junipers to leaf-bearing trees, the minotaurs were waiting. Using their dreaded "dragontooth" tactics, they shredded the Lioness's force long before it reached Silvanesti land. Her grand plan to raise the common folk in revolt against their brutal overlords died before it could be born.

Repulsed at the border, the elves had shifted eastward, hoping to get around the wall of minotaurs. Everywhere they tried to enter Silvanesti, they were met by the swords and axes of the brawny bull-men. Food and water dwindling, the Lioness was forced to retreat. Failure in battle was one thing; she had known defeat before. Failure here, with nothing at their backs but three hundred miles of desert, was much worse. Annihilation stared every elf in the face. All they could do was return the way they had come, back across the scorching desert, hoping they would reach their temporary home—the tent settlement near Khuri-Khan—before they perished.

A rider was cantering through the slow-moving column, streams of dust rising behind him. Kerianseray heard the hoofbeats and halted, tugging on Eagle Eye's braided halter.

SANCTUARY

The griffon, unhappy to have his raptor's claws on broiling sand, arched his neck and clawed at the offending ground. The Lioness spoke briefly to him and he quieted.

The rider slewed to a halt. "General! I bring urgent word from the rear guard!"

She squinted up at him, wracking her sun-broiled memory for a name. Hytanthas, it was. Hytanthas Ambrodel. Two centuries ago his forefathers dwelled in the marbled halls of Qualinost, advisors to the Speaker of the Sun. Centuries before that, in Silvanost, his ancestors would have owned Kagonesti slaves. This dirty, disheveled young soldier was now among the last of his line.

His lips were so parched that he could hardly push the words out. After swallowing several times, he managed to rasp, "The enemy presses upon us! Lord Taranath says a regiment at least!"

A regiment. Two thousand minotaurs.

Exhaustion weighed on Kerian like a thick, heavy cloak. She still commanded almost eight thousand elves, but the enemy was well-supplied and fresh. Her elves were all but spent.

Her officers collected around her. She questioned Hytanthas openly, for everyone to hear. This was how the Lioness led, not from some lofty position, but as a comrade among equals. For this and other reasons, she was respected by her warriors almost to the point of adulation.

According to young Ambrodel the horned enemy was coming straight on, in battle array.

An elf, his sword arm in a sling, exclaimed, "Afoot? Perhaps we could just ride away from them!"

"Ride where?" said another injured officer. "The only thing in front of us is wasteland!"

"That's what they want," the Lioness said. Absently, she stroked Eagle Eye's feathered neck. "To drive us out and let the desert kill us."

"Let's stand and fight, then!" said the first elf. Others, despite their hurts, loudly seconded this declaration.

3

Kerian shook her head. Even if they managed to wipe out the attackers, they'd lose half their strength in the battle. Each and every warrior was precious these days. Expelled from their homelands, the elves had only the resources they'd been able to carry with them. Horses and trained fighters were more valuable than any amount of steel or precious jewels.

She scratched her head, dislodging a cascade of sand from her hair. The thick curls resisted her efforts to confine them in a braid, so she tied them back with a leather thong.

Her battered army was watching her, waiting for orders. No matter how gravely wounded, their heads were unbowed. If she ordered it, each and every one would fight—and most would die. Such an order was unthinkable. The preservation of the army was far more important than a fleeting gesture against the minotaurs.

She put a foot in the stirrup of Eagle Eye's slim saddle and swung onto the griffon's back. As she settled herself, the sea of expectant faces continued to regard her in silence.

"The army will march east, to the sea," she announced.

Some were openly stunned. While the coastline was less harsh than the deep desert, it was also subject to the watchful eyes of the minotaur fleet. Escaping detection would be impossible. The enemy could cruise along and land troops ahead of the retreating elves at any point.

Those who had served with the Lioness in her long campaign against the Knights of Neraka were not shocked, however. They knew she wasn't desperate or reckless, knew she must have some bold device in mind.

Quietly, she added, "I need volunteers." Although she didn't specify a duty, all present suddenly realized what she was about to say. The officers straightened to attention, volunteering one and all.

"I need a covering force to delay the minotaurs. To make a stand." She gestured to a slight rise among the gnarled junipers. "There, on that knoll."

Hytanthas Ambrodel opened his mouth, but before he

could speak, she waved a hand. "No, not you, Captain. I need you for something else."

He didn't recognize this for the kindly falsehood it was. The Lioness's weary face gave nothing away, but she wanted to spare the too young, too ardent captain this particular task. She had lost too many like him on this campaign.

A Silvanesti named Baranthalonus, a veteran, saluted. "General, allow me the honor."

She asked him why. His sunburned face turned south, hazel eyes growing distant, as if seeing the green land that still lay beyond the horizon. "I should like to die at least *close* to Silvanesti land," he said simply.

"Very well. Pick a band of five hundred, all good archers. Fix the enemy here for at least a day."

A tall order, but Baranthalonus nodded. "The five hundred should be Silvanesti."

None objected to the implicit gibe. Silvanesti were known for considering themselves superior to all races, including other elves. Ordinarily the Lioness would not have tolerated such a provocative statement, but these circumstances were hardly ordinary, and this elf had volunteered for death.

With a shrug, she said, "I wish you had Kith-Kanan himself."

"He was Qualinesti, General."

The jest elicited hoarse chuckles from the others. "Well, you'll have at least one in your company who's not of the star-born." She indicated herself.

Her officers protested. As commander of the army, she must not place herself in such peril.

"I'll do what I think is best for the army," she snapped, cutting off the protests.

Hytanthas was sent to bring Taranath forward. As the Lioness's second-in-command, he would lead in her absence.

Four other Silvanesti officers asked to join Baranthalonus, so he sent them through the ranks to pick five hundred warriors. In short order the covering force was assembled on the gravelly knoll. All of the army's remaining arrows were turned over to them. The archers chose their places with care, each surrounding himself with a hedge of arrows, points thrust into the coarse sand. One of the archers, the Lioness never knew which, yielded his food and waterskin to a comrade who was continuing the march. In rapid order, every elf in the covering force willingly surrendered his precious rations, then knelt to await the enemy's arrival.

Lord Taranath arrived. Formerly a commander in the royal guard of Qualinost, he was an unusually tall elf. This, together with his somewhat rounded ears, had always encouraged speculation about a mixed parentage. Taranath was renowned for coolness in battle, and such insults were the only things that stirred him to rage. Given his prowess with a sword, he was not often insulted.

"Lady," he said, saluting the Lioness. She didn't care for the honorific, but this was hardly the time to reprove her valiant friend. She delivered her orders with characteristic brevity.

"Take the army to the sea, Taran. Head north to Khuri-Khan, and present the army with my compliments to the Speaker."

Taranath raised an eyebrow. "The minotaur fleet—how will we avoid it?"

"Spring is nearly over. The Khurish nomads will be leaving the deep desert, before the summer heat sets in." Kerian grimaced; crazy to imagine this as spring, yet summer would indeed be much worse. "There'll be hundreds, thousands of them on the coastal route. Mix with them, join their caravans. The bull-men won't molest you while you ride amidst a pack of nomads." The king of the Khurish humans, Sahim-Khan, was known to be on friendly terms with the minotaurs.

"Is it honorable to skulk home," Taranath spoke quietly, "cloaked by hordes of ragged nomads?"

"War is not about honor. It's about survival—and victory." Since the latter had eluded them, the former was now paramount.

SANCTUARY

Flat horn blasts echoed across the sand. Kerianseray shaded her eyes. A thick, rising column of dust marked the oncoming enemy.

"Go," she said. "Tell the Speaker—" She stopped, a rare blush mantling her sunbrowned cheeks, as she failed to find the right words.

Taranath was deeply moved, but respected her privacy. "I know what to tell the Speaker, lady. Fare you well."

Like the tide retreating from jetsam on the shore, the elven army flowed away, leaving the small Silvanesti force alone on the stony knoll. Seventy-five hundred warriors, mounted and on foot, vanished among the pines and junipers. Despite weariness and heavy hearts, they made no more sound than the soughing of the wind. The volunteers watched them go.

The Lioness twisted around in Eagle Eye's saddle. From a long, leather-covered tube tied across the animal's hips, she withdrew three lengths of polished steel, each about four feet long. Screwing the threaded ends together, she soon had a formidable lance, a griffon-rider's deadliest weapon.

The archers lifted their heads. They heard a single voice, far deeper than any elf's, deeper even than a human's, roaring from across the distance. The minotaur commander was challenging his troops. Everyone looked to Baranthalonus. He in turn looked to the Lioness.

"I'll not rise yet," she said, tugging on mail gauntlets. Even though they were sewn of light-colored cloth to reflect the sun, donning them was like putting her hands into a hot frying pan. "No sense giving our position away."

The dust clouds grew thicker, spreading out in a semi-circle from south to north, fully encompassing the small hillock. Clanking and clattering, the great armored host of minotaurs drew nearer. Loose stones danced as the desert trembled under the tread of two thousand bull-men. Eagle Eye no longer shifted his clawed forefeet on the hot sand. The griffon stood unmoving, his golden-eyed gaze fixed upon the approaching enemy, alert for his rider's slightest command.

Kerianseray tightened the straps of her helmet beneath her chin. It wasn't a fighting helm, made of steel or iron, but a soft leather cap, designed chiefly to keep her thick golden hair out of her face while she was airborne. She shifted the steel lance off her knees and couched it under her arm. Thoughts crossed her mind: What a long way she'd come from the woods of Qualinesti. There she'd first fought the Nerakans with a simple leather sling. Now she commanded Silvanesti lords from griffonback, with a knightly weapon in her hand. A strange fate had led her here.

Fate—and her husband. Once despised as the "Puppet King," a tool of the Knights of Neraka, Gilthas had left a soft, comfortable life to lead the remnants of the elven nations across mountains and desert to find refuge in Khur. No one called him puppet now. The coalition of Qualinesti, Silvanesti, and Kagonesti who had abandoned their woodlands was six years old, and still as fragile as a hummingbird's egg. Holding them together was Gilthas, Speaker of the Sun and Stars.

The din of the minotaurs' approach was deafening. They marched in a series of tight triangular formations, apex forward, shaping their famed "dragontooth" attack. An enemy facing this battle line found itself squeezed into close combat on two sides. These minotaur dragonteeth chewed up and destroyed entire armies. But Kerianseray didn't intend to play the game their way today.

She looked to Baranthalonus and nodded. He gave the order. As one, five hundred Silvanesti archers—the best remaining in all the world—rose to their feet, nocked arrows, and loosed them into the air. Kerianseray closed her eyes for an instant and whispered one word.

"Gilthas."

1

For centuries Khur was thought of as an empty land, devoid of life or livelihood, containing only sand, stone, and sun. In truth the desert was home to many living things, each adapted to the stark environment. Beneath the sand dwelt creatures tenacious and frequently venomous. Above ground grew grass like wire, thorny vines, and waxen shrubs. By night the desert rose bloomed, source of the rarest perfume in the world. The scent was sweet, but the petals of the plant were deadly poison. Such was the life of the land of Khur.

The people of Khur were likewise shaped by their desert home. Most were nomads of hard mien and severe law, devoted to clan, tribe, and gods. Living on their own in a harsh land, they knew no master but the desert. Each tribe was its own nation, and every nomad his own lord. Ungovernable, they nonetheless had a king, the Khan of Khur, who dwelt in the city of Khuri-Khan.

The city had grown up in the east, where sea and sand met. Looted and sacked many times in the past (the last time by followers of the dread wyrm Malystryx), Khuri-Khan was rising again. Newly restored, the squat round towers and square dwellings once more thrust up from the endless sand. Scaffolds enfolded the shattered façade of the Khuri yl Nor—"the Palace of the Setting Sun"—and the city's outer wall was checkered with newly cut stone blocks, repairing the destruction wrought by the recent war. City dwellers had picked up the bricks and shattered timbers of their homes and set them in place. Noble and commoner alike had planted thousands of date palm seedlings throughout the city, alongside the towering ancients that still survived. Trade resumed and life went on in the noisy, contentious Khurish fashion.

New construction was not the only change in Khur. Outside the walls of Khuri-Khan sprawled a vast camp of multicolored tents. Miles across, the conglomeration of shelters clustered under the city wall like fungus clinging to a fallen log. Crowded into this makeshift metropolis were a hundred thousand elves, former residents of Qualinesti and Silvanesti. The camp of exiled elves was known to its inhabitants (not without irony) as "Khurinost," and to the people of Khuri-Khan as *Laddad-ihar*, the Elves' Anthill.

Laddad was an old word whose literal meaning—"those who walk on air"—was a reference to the griffon riders of ancient times. Now it meant simply "elves," encompassing Qualinesti, Silvanesti, and Kagonesti, since the Khurs made no distinction among the groups.

In the center of this great patchwork camp of tents was the home of the Speaker of the Sun and Stars. Gilthas, son of Tanis Half-Elven and Lauralanthalasa, was last of the line of Speakers great and ill, which stretched back to the founder of the Qualinesti nation, Kith-Kanan, and through him to the august Silvanos Goldeneye. On Gilthas had fallen the daunting task of leading his people out of their ruined homeland, abandoning it to the Knights of Neraka, mobs of wild goblins, and the bandit horde of Captain Samuval. The Qualinesti had fought their way across half a continent and come to rest here in this desolate desert. Thousands perished on the journey, felled by arrow and sword, as well as the less material but no less deadly menaces of heat, disease, exhaustion, and heartbreak. The sands of western Khur were littered with bones, broken carts, and abandoned possessions, and watered by the tears of an entire race.

SANCTUARY

When Gilthas first beheld the city of Khuri-Khan, a scant one thousand elves stood at his back. After the horrors of exile and the agonizing trek across the desert, the sun-baked capital of Khur seemed a dream of paradise, but the elves' ballad of woe wasn't done. As months passed, more refugees arrived, in groups of five or ten, as well as columns numbering in the thousands. From the far south came Silvanesti driven out of their forest glades and crystal halls by hordes of rampaging minotaurs. Fewer Silvanesti than Qualinesti abandoned their homeland, for no matter how wretched their existence, most could not bear to leave their sacred ancestral lands. Instead, they faded into the forest, there to dwell among the trees like their primeval ancestors. Those who had joined Gilthas were, for the most part, high officials, warriors, and nobles of the Silvanesti court. When Gilthas was proclaimed Speaker of the Stars by the abdicating Alhana Starbreeze, the exiled courtiers of Silvanost swallowed their outrage at having a Qualinesti (and one tainted with human blood!) as their ruler. If the race of elves was to survive, it needed a leader. The once-scorned "Puppet King" had proven himself capable. Elves of greater reputation had succumbed to death or, despairing, had given in to the enemy. Not Gilthas. The test of exile showed his true mettle, so the Silvanesti notables gathered around him, forming a tightly knit circle of advisors to the throne of the united elven nations.

Gone were the embroidered silk robes and soft finery worn in Qualinost and Silvanost. Living in the desert demanded more practical dress. The Speaker had taken to wearing Khurish attire, a sleeveless robe of white linen, called a *geb*, cinched in at the waist by the leather cord known as the *ghuf-fran*. Where once he had cultivated the distant air and pale complexion of a palace-dwelling poet, now Gilthas was lean, brown, and serious. The weight of the elven nation rested directly on his shoulders, and although he refused to let the strain break him, it occasionally bore him down. The Speaker rose early, worked all day, and lived as frugally now as once he had dwelt in aimless luxury.

11

This day began as most did, with Gilthas in his audience room, standing with hands clasped behind his back in the center of a round carpet. Wine-red with ocher curlicues radiating out from a central sun motif, the carpet had come from Sahim-Khan, monarch (but not master) of Khur. A gift, the Khan had said, to make the Speaker more comfortable, but Gilthas knew its true purpose: to serve as a mocking reminder of his lost throne.

"What word from Lady Kerianseray?"

The Speaker's question caused the assortment of courtiers and vassals to break off their various conversations. They were an odd-looking group, most in Khurish attire, but a stubborn few still persisting in the fashions of their homeland. A few feet from the Speaker, alertly watching, stood Planchet, Gilthas's longtime valet and bodyguard. Like his liege, he was dressed in the local style, but the sword at his waist was of pure Qualinesti design.

The crowd of onlookers parted to reveal a young elf, thin and hardened by sun, wind, and privation, who stiffened in salute. He doffed his Khurish-style cloth hat and said, "Lord Taranath sends his greetings, Great Speaker!"

The room grew silent. If Taranath, and not the Lioness, had dispatched this courier, it could only mean the Speaker's wife was no longer with the army.

"The army has returned from the southern expedition and is currently at Wadi Talaft," the messenger continued, naming a dry lake south of the city which was normally used by the nomads as a natural corral for their herds of horses and goats. "Lady Kerianseray"—the young courier swallowed—"is not with them, sire."

Before his assembled court, Gilthas would not parade his anxiety. As calmly as possible he inquired, "What happened, Captain?"

The courier reported the failure of Kerianseray's gamble in the south. At every turn, the army's entrance into Silvanesti was barred by minotaurs, and the bull-men's strength proved overwhelming. Pursued into the borderland between forest and desert, the Lioness and a handpicked band of archers had remained behind, making a stand so the rest of the beleaguered army could escape.

All eyes were on the Speaker as he digested this news. His perennial sunburn did not hide the sudden pallor of his face. Planchet took an involuntary step toward him, then halted. As much friend and trusted advisor as bodyguard, still Planchet could not allow his concern to breach the Speaker's dignity.

The courier reported that six thousand, eight hundred eighty-nine elves had made it to Wadi Talaft. This out of ten thousand. Murmurs swept the room.

While the Speaker's subjects whispered about the heavy losses, Planchet spoke privately to his master. Gilthas nodded once, and the valet slipped quietly from the room.

The Speaker raised a hand. In the ensuing silence, he declared, "Our adventure in the south is at an end. We cannot waste any more of our slender resources on such a hopeless cause." He then charged the courier to bid Lord Taranath return to Khurinost.

His words set the assemblage stirring anew. Captain Ambrodel saluted, but did not depart. "Great Speaker," he said, "pardon my boldness, but more can be done in the south! We can send small bands of fighters secretly across the Thon-Thalas, into the interior of Silvanesti—"

"To what purpose? Bands of twenty or thirty partisans can hardly prevail against the bull-men."

This came from a tall, elegant figure with shoulder-length, jet-black hair. He wore a heavy gold bracelet on each wrist and a silk robe the same color as his blue eyes.

"Lord Morillon is correct," Gilthas agreed evenly. "It is beyond our power to liberate our ancient homeland. More important now is finding a place we can put down roots and become a nation again."

The young captain glared at the haughty noble. Both were

Ambrodels. Hytanthas was of the younger line that had followed Kith-Kanan out of Silvanost more than twenty-five centuries earlier when he founded the Qualinesti nation. He had grown up in the Lioness's service. Slightly rounded ears and a thickening of his eyebrows betrayed the human blood in his ancestry, and his black hair was confined in a short, neat braid, as befit a soldier. Nevertheless, he bore a distinct resemblance to his distant Silvanesti cousin, elegant Lord Morillon Ambrodel.

The captain turned away from Morillon, pointedly addressing Gilthas. "Great Speaker, we were able to do much against the Knights back home. And they were greater in numbers than the minotaurs."

Morillon said, "Back home you were on familiar ground, with a friendly population to help you. Nothing in Khur is friendly—not the people, not the terrain, not the climate." He inclined his head to the Speaker. "Great Gilthas decides wisely."

Captain Ambrodel said no more, but his eyes blazed with frustration.

Other soldiers in the assembly took up his notion of raiding Silvanesti, and a brisk discussion ensued. Lord Morillon, his attention on the Speaker, saw the fleeting expression of pain that crossed his monarch's face. It was plain the Speaker's thoughts were on the fate of his dashing, dangerous wife. Sunrise was only an hour past, but the Speaker looked to have slept poorly. He was known sometimes to walk the narrow lanes of Khurinost late at night, his responsibilities weighing heavily on him.

The debate was becoming increasingly loud, but Morillon's cultured voice cut across it with practiced ease. "The Speaker is weary," he announced. "Let us withdraw."

Hytanthas would have lingered, but Morillon ushered him to the door, chiding the younger elf for taxing the Speaker's patience. The captain's frustration flared.

"We're not in Silvanost any longer, my lord! Our Speaker

has ears for all his subjects, not just the rich and titled!"

Cousin faced cousin: Morillon composed, indoor-pale; Hytanthas an inch taller, his suntanned visage red with anger. Yet the eyes were the same: the hard, unflinching blue of the sky arching over their tent city.

Hytanthas finally stalked away to carry the Speaker's orders to Lord Taranath. Lord Morillon watched his cousin until he was lost from sight in the maze of narrow passages that ran between the adjacent tents. Morillon was a longtime courtier, having begun in service to Queen Mother Alhana, and he had long ago mastered the art of keeping his expression bland, even when irritated. Upstart youngsters with no manners vexed him greatly. Cousin or no, he marked Hytanthas as one of the Lioness's hotheads and vowed to keep an eye on him.

Dismissing the young elf from his thoughts for now, Morillon approached the Speaker again. His coterie of Silvanesti lords followed closely.

"Sire, I have an audience with Sahim-Khan this afternoon. Are there any special messages you wish me to convey?" he asked.

"Tell him his climate is appalling." Seeing no change in the Silvanesti's expression, Gilthas added gently, "A joke, my lord."

Morillon inclined his head. "Yes, Great Speaker."

Gilthas sighed. "Assure the Khan of my goodwill and good wishes. As for the tribute—do what you think the situation supports."

For the privilege of remaining in the Khan's domain, the elves were required to pay Sahim-Khan a thousand steel pieces a day. This staggering sum came due every twenty days. Lord Morillon had been attempting to negotiate a lower price.

The noble acknowledged the Speaker's vague command with a bow and departed, the gaggle of silent Silvanesti trailing in his wake.

PAUL B. THOMPSON & TONYA C. COOK

Alone, Gilthas seated himself in the canvas cross-framed chair that now served as his throne, giving in to exhaustion and melancholy. As he rubbed his eyes, Planchet returned, entering through an opening in the far canvas wall. The valet paused at an imposing sideboard. Like most of the Speaker's furnishings, it was a vagabond's design, made of thin strips of wood and painted cloth. The skill of the painters had given it the look of polished wood and marble. Emptied of its contents, the cupboard could be collapsed in moments, put on a packhorse, and carried to the next night's camp. Gilthas found it a fitting metaphor for his entire life, for the life of every elf in the miserable tent-city.

Planchet filled a clay cup with white nectar and handed it to his master. Gilthas accepted the cup, but his attention was not on the drink. "Well?" he asked.

"I've spoken to the seers. Six of our people and two Khurs. They will try to ascertain Lady Kerianseray's whereabouts and . . . well-being."

"Assuming she's alive," Gilthas whispered, then flinched, as though saying the words would draw doom down upon his wife.

"Sire, you know as well as I, the lady in question is very difficult to kill. Have faith! If anyone can pull the minotaurs' tails and escape to boast about it, it's Kerianseray." He said it lightly, trying to coax a smile from Gilthas.

Planchet handed the Speaker a small bowl of dates, figs, and nuts, urging him to break his fast. Gilthas waved a hand, telling his valet not to fuss, that he would eat later.

"You say that every time I offer you food," Planchet complained. "You cannot rule a nation on an empty stomach."

His calm insistence—exactly the tone one might use with a recalcitrant child—coupled with a paternal demeanor, had the desired effect: Gilthas plucked a fig from the bowl and put it in his mouth.

"Happy?" he said, smiling slightly around a mouthful of fruit.

"Very happy, Great Speaker."

With that, the longtime valet and sometime general of the royal guard withdrew, a cheery, "Rest well, sire," floating over his shoulder as he disappeared.

Before the Battle of Sanction, when he'd put Planchet in charge of the Qualinesti troops, Gilthas had told him just how important he considered him to be. Friend, advis0r, father-figure, bodyguard, Planchet was all of that and more. Kerianseray was Gilthas's heart, his love, his life; Planchet, he'd come to realize, was his strength, the firm center in the swirling chaos of their lives.

Gilthas lifted the cup to his lips again. His hand trembled. Nettled by the sight, he drank quickly, draining the cup. The nectar was young and raw, inclining to sourness. No one could make good wine while in headlong flight. Nectar, like a nation, needed stability to reach its full potential.

He poured another measure. One had to make do with what one had. He drained the cup again, leaned back in the chair, and closed his eyes.

The world was turned on its head. Filthy goblins prowled Qualinost, despoiling the forested lanes of Kith-Kanan's city. Great blustering minotaurs inhabited the crystal halls of Silvanost. The bulky monsters could scarcely fit through a typical elven doorway—what use would they have for an entire city? To think such uncouth hands held the twin epitomes of grace, culture, and civilization! The images in his mind—or perhaps the raw wine—made sickness rise in Gilthas's throat. Coughing, he fought it down.

He chided himself for falling into that trap, thinking that places made a nation. Cities and towers, gardens and temples were only chattel. What really mattered was life, and the things that ensured life: food, water, simple shelter. Those essentials must be secured if the elven race was to survive.

And his people *would* survive. Gilthas was determined on that point. All else was mere vanity.

Gilthas had brought his people out of the conflagration

that engulfed Qualinesti, across the Plains of Dust, to the supposed sanctuary of Khur. Fate had delivered the throne of Silvanesti into his hands when his cousin Porthios, Speaker of the Stars, vanished. Porthios's son and successor, Silvanoshei, was slain at the end of the war. Queen Mother Alhana, grieving the death of her son, had gone on a desperate search for Porthios. Before leaving, she'd given into Gilthas's hands the crown of Silvanesti.

Out of the catastrophe of exile had come one of the greatest events in Gilthas's life, in any elf's life: the unification of two kingdoms sundered since the Kinslayer War. Alhana, a Silvanesti, and Porthios, a Qualinesti, had hoped their own marriage would bring the two nations together. Instead, it had driven them further apart. Now, against all odds, the two nations were one again, united in the person of Gilthas himself. Once sneered at as the "Puppet King" he was now known as Gilthas Pathfinder. It was up to him to find the path to a permanent home—wherever that might be.

Temporarily, pride could be sacrificed, honor dispensed with, treasure spent. To hold the ancient race of the Firstborn together, he would treat with whomever he must, even a rogue like Sahim-Khan, one of the most conniving, grasping humans he'd ever met.

In a royal line known for black hearts, Sahim's naked ambition and glowing greed stood out as exceptional. With half his capital in ruins, he dreamed of elven wealth flowing in to repair it. But if it took treasure to buy sanctuary, no matter how makeshift and uncomfortable, for his exiled people, then Gilthas would use every scrap of steel and gold his subjects could raise. Treasure, like buildings and land, was expendable. Life was not.

Once, he had measured his life by the fleeting moments spent with Kerian. Like a tempered blade, she was bright, sharp, and deadly, and must be handled with care. Not for her and Gilthas were quiet comfort and gently murmured vows of love. Theirs was a marriage of opposites. Planchet had said once—after a particularly rough day and too much potent nectar—that it was as if the gods had cleaved apart a single hero, creating strong, hot-headed Kerianseray and thoughtful, feeling Gilthas. Their marriage had joined the two halves together again, creating one person, one soul.

She lived. As certainly as he felt his own heart beat, Gilthas knew Kerian was not dead.

He hadn't realized he had fallen asleep until a noise suddenly jolted him awake. The empty nectar bottle lay next to his chair; the clay cup had fallen from his hand.

As he sat wondering how long he'd dozed and what had awakened him, the tent roof shook, sending motes of dust down onto his head. Shouts arose outside. A sirocco must have swept over the tent complex, upsetting some of the less stable dwellings.

The sound of ripping cloth put the lie to that notion and brought the elf to his feet. Sunlight poured through the roof into his face as a sword sawed through the ceiling panel. Head fuzzy from wine and sleep, Gilthas stared at the bright sword point, wondering how anyone could stand on the billowing roof. The tent poles and stays surely could not bear the weight.

More shouting, louder now, came to his ears, and the sword withdrew. A masked figure garbed in dirty white robes dropped through the hole, landing heavily but adroitly on fingers and toes. Beneath the figure's Khurish scarf a steel helmet gleamed.

At the same moment, Planchet burst through the tent flap, sword at the ready. Behind him came a swarm of the Speaker's householders, armed with everything from pikes to roasting spits. Gilthas held up a hand, halting his bodyguard on the threshold. He directed a wry look at the intruder.

"Lady, you've holed my roof."

Kerianseray, caked with dust and dried blood, straightened. She yanked the dust mask from the lower half of her face and shoved her sword back in its scabbard. Heedless of the astonished Planchet, and the gaping looks of the others, she leaned forward and kissed her consort warmly.

Drawing back, she exclaimed, "Those damned Silvanesti wouldn't let me in!" Lord Morillon and his cohorts, steeped in the court protocol of Silvanost, did their best to control access to the Speaker—even barring the Lioness when they could.

"How did you get past them?" Gilthas asked, amused. With one hand he cupped her smooth brown cheek, hollowed by travail.

"Eagle Eye."

He glanced up at the hole in the roof. The griffon flashed past as he circled overhead. Theirs was a remarkable relationship. With the Lioness the fierce creature was tame as a kitten, obeying her every word. Griffons usually bonded with a single rider from an early age and, should that rider be lost, never took kindly to another. Eagle Eye's original rider had perished fighting the minotaurs. Against all odds, the spirited beast had taken a liking to the Lioness—most probably because they were two of a kind, Gilthas thought.

The Speaker's would-be rescuers dispersed and Planchet went to fetch more nectar. In the meantime, Kerian helped herself to an orange, a fruit common to Khur's seaside gardens. She pulled off hood and helmet and raked a hand through her matted hair.

"Lord Taranath's messenger just left here"—Gilthas noted the angle of the sunlight—"less than an hour ago. After hearing his report, I feared for your safety."

His words seemed somehow to take away her joy at their reunion. Coughing the dust of Khur from her throat, she rasped, "Yet I am safe, and here I am."

When she said no more, he asked about the rear guard Hytanthas had mentioned, the five hundred archers with whom she had made a stand against the minotaurs. She answered, "They gave their lives for the rest of the army."

"No others survived? Only you?" asked Gilthas, mystified.

She crushed the orange slice she held. Juice ran between her fingers. "It was not my choice!"

Before she could explain this strange statement Planchet returned. She filled a cup and moved away from her husband, lapsing into sullen silence. Sensing the tension in the room, Planchet did not linger.

Gilthas went to stand behind his wife, close but not touching. He could almost feel the angry emotion radiating from her, like heat from the Khurish sun.

"I rejoice to see you, my love," he said softly.

"I'm not happy to be here, Gil! I should have fallen with my warriors!"

On the last word her voice broke, and he would have held her then. But she made no move toward him, did not turn, only drank deeply from her cup.

He asked what had happened, and still she was silent for a long time. At last, with an abrupt shake of her head, she said, "I don't want to talk about it. It's done. We must honor our dead by resuming the campaign. The bull-men will pay!"

She gripped her cup so tightly her knuckles showed white. Gilthas gave up the attempt to comfort her and returned to his chair, frowning. Somehow it was a little easier to say what he must while sitting in the royal throne. Raising his voice slightly, he forbade his wife to return south. The plan to invade Silvanesti, Gilthas declared, was over.

She whirled, a wild look in her eyes. "You're quitting the fight? Why?"

Gilthas kept his own voice even. "Again and again it's proven a waste of lives, battling the minotaurs. I have a more important task for you."

"What more important task is there than fighting our enemies?"

"Finding a home for our people."

Her laugh was sharp and dismissive. This was an old argument, one they were having more often these days. Kerianseray, her warriors, and many Silvanesti nobles among the exiles wanted to win back the lands lost to the invaders. Gilthas believed this a pointless dream. His people's only hope was to find a new homeland, one free of minotaurs, bandits, goblins, and greedy humans.

He stood and beckoned her to follow. To one side of the wide, circular room was an assortment of chests and cupboards containing official documents they'd saved from Qualinost. He unlocked a metal-strapped box and drew out a long, rolled parchment.

"One of my scribes found this in the Grand Souks. He paid eight steel for it."

A high price. Unrolled, the parchment proved to be a map, a drawing of Khur from the beaches of Balifor Bay to the wall of mountains stretching from Kern in the north to Blöde in the south. Kerian's disappointment was acute. Her husband possessed innumerable maps and charts. His scribes visited the souks every day, spending precious steel and asking about maps. Initially she had been encouraged by his efforts, assuming he was seeking information that would aid them in their quest to retake their homelands. But after months, when nothing useful had turned up, she lost interest.

As he spread the curling parchment with both hands, Gilthas told her eagerly that the scribe who'd found it had haggled the price down from fifteen steel. Such negotiation was the norm in Khurish souks; there would be loud discussion, much shaking of heads and gesticulating, the buyer pretending to walk away two or three times, before at last a price was settled, a deal struck.

"This isn't just any map," he assured her. "It's almost two hundred years old."

She considered the curled parchment more carefully. The detail on it was indeed amazing, with dry wadis and oases marked. In the lower right corner, where the cartographer would usually sign his work, was a peculiar sigil, a stylized bird with drooping wings drawn in black ink.

22

Kerian leaned in to study the map, and as she did so Gilthas felt the power, barely leashed, radiating from her, like body heat or the smell of her sweat. They were so often apart, he tended to forget how her presence overwhelmed him. Kerianseray was the most exciting woman he had ever known.

Their eyes met, and Gilthas saw again the brilliant, captivating warrior she'd been before defeat, exile, and privation had hollowed her face, hardened her views, and etched bitterness in her eyes. Despite their arguments, he loved her still. He regretted their growing estrangement. They disagreed constantly as the years went by—on policy, on strategy, seemingly on everything.

As his silent regard continued, Kerian opened her mouth to speak, but her words were interrupted. Planchet returned just then, to inquire whether they needed anything more.

Gilthas waved the valet inside and had him hold the right edge of the scroll. With his freed hand, Gilthas tapped a spot in the northern reaches of Khur, a place where the Khalkist Mountains split, enclosing a horseshoe-shaped valley. Although it was not distinguished in any way on the map, Gilthas smiled as his finger brushed this spot.

"This is the Valley of the Blue Sands," he said, lowering his voice, as though wary of eavesdroppers. "Called by Khurish nomads the 'Breath of the Gods.' "

Planchet's surprise was wordless. Not so the Lioness's.

"I've heard you talk of this place. I thought it only a legend! Where did you get this map?"

"I believe it came from a temple archive. When Khuri-Khan was sacked, many libraries were looted and their contents ended up in the souks." He tapped the spot again. "I am convinced the valley is real, and this is its true location."

The Valley of the Blue Sands was reputed to have a mild, balmy climate, quite unlike the rest of Khur. Annals from the libraries of Qualinost mentioned it, calling it *Inath-Wakenti*,

Vale of Silence. Shielded by mountains, it was said to be one of the few spots in the world unchanged since the First Cataclysm. Elven chronicles even mentioned it as a place where the gods once dwelled. Scholars disagreed on what this meant. Some took it as literal truth. Others contended it was metaphorical.

The people of Khur were just as divided in their opinions. In Khuri-Khan the Valley of the Blue Sands was regarded as nothing more than a myth, a strange place where the normal conditions they knew—heat, blazing sun, eternal drought—were turned upside down. Cityfolk used it as a setting for absurd bedtime stories for their children. In the valley, according to the stories, clouds clung to the ground instead of the sky. Stones grew like plants. Animals talked liked men. Khur's nomads, on the other hand, did not doubt the valley's existence. None had ever been there, but they believed the ancient tales fervently.

With great secrecy, Gilthas had been assembling information about the Inath-Wakenti for over a year. He believed it could be the future home of the elven nation.

Kerian asked, "What makes you think the valley is there?"

"I've collected six other maps of the region—Khurish, Nerakan, even some old Solamnic maps from the libraries of Qualinost. None of them shows this particular horse-shoe-shaped configuration of the mountains. I think I know why."

He paused as Planchet poured them both another measure of nectar. Kerian, despite her skepticism, found herself caught by his evident conviction. She waved off Planchet's offer of drink and urged her husband to continue.

"The other maps are all copies of copies of copies," Gilthas said. "This map is an original. The human who drew it knew of Inath-Wakenti because he'd been there himself!"

He could give no plausible explanation for why later copyists would omit the valley, saying only, "Everyone in

Khuri-Khan speaks of the place lightly. Even the city priests dismiss it as a legend—all but one. I don't know whether the spot is cursed or blessed, but I intend to find out."

Kerianseray suddenly realized what was coming. "You want me to go there," she said. He nodded, the smile returning to his face. Her next words chased it away again. "Gil," she said, "this valley is nothing more than a romantic fable. Even if it were real, it isn't our homeland, and never can be."

"The lands of our ancestors are lost. We do not have the strength to regain them—not yet. That time will come, my love, but for now, for the near future, we *must* dwell in a land of our own and not live by the grace of the Khurs. This forgotten valley could be our best hope!"

"It's a pretty dream, I admit, but nonetheless a complete waste of time. Give me twenty thousand warriors, and I will set the frontiers of our true homelands aflame! We can take back what is ours!"

His demeanor hardened, and it was the Speaker of the Sun and Stars, not her husband, who said firmly, "Preparations for an expedition have begun. I expect you to lead it, General."

"I see. As you command, Great Speaker."

The mocking words fell like lead weights at his feet. She would have continued arguing, but he cut her off.

"I've chosen Favaronas, one of the foremost historians in my service"—he'd almost said *in Qualinost*—"to accompany you. You will lead an escort of five hundred warriors."

She frowned, questioning the wisdom of sending so small a party. Gilthas reminded her that the mission was exploration, not conquest.

"Exploration?" she repeated. "This is a wild-goose chase. We should return to the Thon-Thalas and raise the people of Silvanesti against the minotaurs!"

"I have made my decision! The matter is closed!"

Planchet, devoutly wishing he were elsewhere, glanced from monarch to general, husband to wife. The burden of recent days was taking its toll. Never had he heard so open and bitter a breach between them.

"You are Speaker of the Sun and Stars. I will do my duty," the Lioness said at last. There was no sarcasm in her voice, but her tone was icy.

She made as if to go, but Gilthas, relaxing in the face of her agreement, forestalled her. "You need not begin the journey just yet. I have another task I wish you to undertake right away, one for which you are uniquely qualified."

She brightened, and in her expression he saw visions of daring raids on griffonback, the clash of steel on steel. The Speaker smiled benignly at his bold general.

"I need you to visit a priestess."

* * * * *

The bed trembled. Composed of rope netting stretched between four posts and topped by a thin, cotton-stuffed mattress, it tended to shake with little provocation. Gilthas, ever cautious, opened his eyes and silently took in the situation.

His private quarters were lit by the soft light of a blue bulls-eye lamp which hung from the tent post by the door. The simple canvas stools and chairs around the bed were empty. Kerianseray lay by his side, face down, rigid as a statue. Her hands, balled into hard fists, gripped the mattress. Every few seconds her whole body shook.

He touched her shoulder lightly, trying to ease her out of the dream. Her skin was dry and fever hot. She did not wake. He murmured her name several times, but still she did not rouse. When he laid his hand on her cheek, she sprang to life, rolling over so hard and fast she knocked him from the bed. He rolled out of the way as his wife fought unseen enemies. He heard the bedsheet tear in her hands.

"Kerian!" he yelled. "Wake up!"

She sat bolt upright, breathing hard. "Gil? You're here?" she said hoarsely, peering at him through the tangled curtain of her hair.

"You're in Khurinost, my love, in our bedchamber. You were dreaming."

At the head of the bed on Gilthas's side was a cupboard on which sat a jug of tepid water and a tin basin. Kerian sloshed water into the basin and bathed her face. Gilthas came up behind her, hesitated a second, then wrapped her in his arms. She leaned back, pressing her head into the hollow of his neck.

"Were you battling minotaurs?" he asked. She nodded, but didn't explain further. He suggested, "A burden shared is a burden lightened."

It took time, but eventually she gave in, telling a dreadful tale. Her pain was palpable in the darkened room, and Gilthas had to force himself to remain quiet, so as not to interrupt the flow of her story.

"It took the bull-men less than an hour to overrun us. We killed some, but it was like trying to halt an avalanche with arrows," she began. "What came after took much longer."

The elves who survived, grievously wounded or not, were bound hand and foot. Holes were dug, one for each captive, and the elves dropped in. Then the minotaurs fell to arguing amongst themselves. Some wanted to bury the elves facing their lost homeland; others thought it would be better to have them looking out into the wider desert, their backs perpetually turned to Silvanesti.

The latter faction won out. The minotaurs filled in the holes, leaving only the elves' heads exposed. Twenty-nine Silvanesti were left to die—of heat and thirst if they were lucky. If predators found them, their fate would be much more terrible.

Gilthas lowered his chin to her shoulder. "And you?" he murmured.

"They knew I commanded, but didn't know I was the Lioness of Qualinesti, wife of the Speaker of the Sun and Stars. Because I was the commander they tied my hands and feet and threw me onto Eagle Eye's back."

The minotaur warlord told Kerian to carry word to her people that Silvanesti was theirs no longer, and that should the elves come again they would find nothing but graves. With that, they whipped the griffon's flanks, sending him catapulting into the sky. Wisely, the bull-men had hobbled Eagle Eye's foreclaws and muzzled his beak with leather straps. All he could do was fly away with Kerian draped ingloriously over his back.

The griffon flew some distance before Kerian could work her gag free and convince him to alight. She tumbled off, rolling across the trackless sand. Loyal Eagle Eye clawed at her bonds until she could break free. In turn she tore off his restraints. They had little choice but to fly on. After midnight, they came to an oasis near the coast. Four of Taranath's warriors lay in the sand a hundred paces from the well. Wounded, they'd died of thirst within sight of water.

Kerian replenished her arms and armor from the fallen, rested Eagle Eye briefly at the oasis, and took wing once more. By the time day broke, she and her mount were within sight of Khurinost.

Gilthas's eyes closed in pain. Yet the litany of horror was not, quite, done.

"For a moment, I considered flying on," she said. "Past this stinking pile of tents, away from Khur, our pitiful people, and even you. I thought I would fly to the homeland of the minotaurs, find the palace of their king, and challenge him to single combat."

"You couldn't do that."

He meant she would never leave him or her people, but she misunderstood.

"No, his guards would cut me down long before I reached the king."

Burying his face in her hair, Gilthas said, "I'm glad you came back, wife."

She surprised him then. Breaking free of his loving embrace, she whirled to face him. "I should have died with my warriors!" she declared, voice trembling. "The bull-men shamed me! I wasn't even worth killing. They let me live just to spread their message of fear!"

He reminded her that while dead heroes were inspiring, only living leaders could save the elven race, could lead them to a new home. He tried to soothe her, whispering that Inath-Wakenti would be their sanctuary, a place where they could heal and grow strong against the day when they would again make their presence known in the world.

Once more his words had an unintended effect. Kerian made a sound of disgust and stomped away. "That damned valley again! Better to water the forests of Silvanesti in minotaur blood than chase your myth! Better to die as my brave archers did than flee yet again from our enemies!"

"Battering your head against a stone wall is foolish!" he snapped, then stopped, consciously mastering his anger. Seating himself on the edge of the bed, he said, "If fate is kind, our people will return to Silvanost and Qualinost. One day. But not today, and not tomorrow."

Gilthas had spies among Sahim-Khan's retainers, men with contacts in Delphon and other, smaller towns along the coast. Their reports told him that a day did not pass without minotaur ships rounding Habbakuk's Necklace, bound for the Silvanesti coast. Their holds groaned under the weight of armored troops, sent to reinforce the army already occupying the elves' homeland in a grip of steel. The Speaker could not hope to vanquish such foes, not now.

He told Kerian all these things, adding, "To all things there is an appointed time. The time to liberate our lost lands is not yet."

She circled the end of the bed and sank onto the other side of the mattress. "Instead, I go to the high priestess of the Temple of Elir-Sana and ask for her help in finding your mythical valley. Don't you ever tire of asking humans for favors? 'Give us land. Give us food. Give us water.' Is elven honor extinct?"

Seated back to back, their bed so narrow they were nearly touching, husband and wife stared in opposite directions. They might as well have been miles apart. The Lioness was flushed with fury, her hands clenched into fists; Gilthas's face, blurred by tiredness, was pale, his jaw stiff with tension.

He finally said, "No, lady, elven honor is not dead, merely stored, like the great archive of Qualinost, against the day when we can afford to display it again."

Both of them lay down. After a moment, Gilthas reached a hand out, but she edged away, curling up on the side of the bed, as far away as possible.

That was how they fell asleep—Kerian curled in on herself, facing away from her husband, and Gilthas, face up, one hand outstretched toward her stiff back.

2

Hard edges, that's where things is clearest. Where land and sky come together cleanly, with nothing in between. A man can see what's what, and who's who. Good and evil are obvious. They say the sea is like that. The desert is, too."

The guide, the very opposite of the usual taciturn nomad, folded his hands across his horse's neck and continued to expound his philosophy. His audience of one, riding a few steps behind, made no reply. Prince Shobbat of Khur was only half listening. Sunrise was an hour past and already the heat was intense. Shobbat adjusted the brim of his broad felt hat and told himself, for the hundredth time, that his goal was worth this suffering.

As far as Shobbat could see in all directions was sand, broken rock, and scattered boulders bleached to a uniform shade of tan by the unflinching sun. No color at all relieved the trail northwest from Khuri-Khan into the trackless wastes that made up most of the realm of Khur. No shade either. Only hard light by day and perfect, starry blackness at night.

Surveying the desolation around him, Shobbat wondered if there wasn't something to the windbag nomad's notions after all. Devoid of trees and buildings, the vista certainly was pristine.

"In green lands, there's trees, grass, and the like, sprouting out of the dirt to tie air and land together," his guide was saying. "Clouds in the sky are the breath of growing things, fogging the air. Underfoot there's nothing but corruption, worms, beetles, and rot, spreading over the land like a mantle of decay."

Shobbat grunted, eyes squinted nearly closed against the glare. "You're a poet."

"No, my lord. A nomad. I've known the hard edges all my life."

The guide's name was Wapah. So dry and leather-like was his face that he might have been any age from thirty to sixty. His beard was long, and the same flat brown color as the sand. Plaited into the hair on his head were thin reed staves that supported the light, cloth shade protecting his head and neck. Spiders were embroidered around the hem of the dirty linen cloth. The black-and-orange leaping sand spider was the symbol of Wapah's clan. A single bite from the creature could kill a man in minutes, or rot the leg off a healthy horse in a day.

Under brows so thick they were plaited into tiny braids, Wapah's eyes were pale gray. This was an unusual hue among Khurs, but not unknown in Wapah's clan. Gray-eyed nomads did not wear the perpetual squint of other desert-dwellers. Wide-eyed in a land of killing glare, the people of the Leaping Spider Clan seemed more intensely aware of their surroundings. Many were seers and given to visions, and for this reason nomads like Wapah were called "mirror-eyed."

Prince Shobbat, eldest son of Sahim, Khan of Khur, was not nearly so prepossessing. Past thirty, he was (as a court wit once said) "bearded and bland." He wore a loose linen tunic tucked into riding trousers of the same material, and tall, dark leather boots. The yellow and red sash at his middle did not, as he intended, hide his princely paunch but merely accentuated it. In the same vein, the beginnings of jowls were poorly concealed by his short black beard. When his father was Shobbat's age, he'd already been khan for ten years. All the prince had accomplished thus far was to eat a great deal, drink a great deal, and pursue a great many comely women. This journey represented his first significant foray beyond the walls of Khuri-Khan. It had been prompted by a broken wall and a cryptic stone tablet.

After the Vanishing of the Moons, the dragon Malystryx claimed and occupied Khur. Repeated attacks by the Red Overlord had left the Khuri yl Nor heavily damaged. After Malys was overthrown, Sahim-Khan gave his eldest son the task of overseeing repairs on the palace. It was a dull, thankless job until, one day, the laborers demolishing a cracked wall in the south wing had come upon a stone tablet hidden in a niche inside the blocks.

Shobbat immediately set a team of scholars to translating the tablet. It wasn't easy. The text was written in hieratic Istarian, a difficult, priestly script reserved for the theocratic elite of that lost land, but working in three teams of two, the six scholars completed the translation in a dozen days. Shobbat collected the translations, found they agreed, then had the scholars slain.

He regretted having to order their deaths, as he respected learning, but he could not risk anyone finding out what they had discovered. He'd seen to it their deaths were quick and painless. Scholars were always thirsty. To celebrate the completion of their work, he sent each of them a special vintage, doctored with arsenic. It slaked their thirsts, permanently. The deaths were attributed to cultists and soon forgotten.

In secrecy, the prince made plans. He sent trusted men to the Grand Souks to find a desert guide. Wapah was the result. Mirror-eyed nomads had a reputation as peerless navigators of the sands.

The nomad did not question why a pampered prince wished to travel to an obscure point more than two days' ride northwest of the city. For ten fine steel swords and a like number of stallions, handpicked from the Khan's own herd,

Wapah would have guided Prince Shobbat to the bottom of the Blood Sea.

"Hard edges," the guide repeated. "They make men strong and straight, allow them to see clear and to know what dwellers in green lands never know."

Shobbat obligingly asked what that might be.

"The will of Those on High."

Shobbat hid a smile, not wanting to antagonize a man on whom his life depended. Alone among all the peoples of the world, the desert nomads had never stopped worshiping their old gods. Sahim-Khan always said this was because the unfettered sun boiled away their few wits. Shobbat's father sneered at the nomads because he feared them. Nine times in the violent history of Khur the reigning khan had been slain in battles against his own desert-dwelling subjects. Sahim-Khan had no intention of being the tenth.

"The *laddad* came here from the green lands," Shobbat said. "It is written they drew forth the first life from the land, and their mages can make stone itself blossom."

"They do not make this land green."

Wapah's phrasing was ambiguous, but Shobbat did not ask him to explain. Their horses had topped a long, high dune sculpted by wind into the shape of a great curling wave, and a blast of southwesterly air flung grit in their faces. The prince coughed and spat, but his saliva never reached the ground. The dry air swallowed it.

Wapah cautioned him not to waste precious water. The nomad kicked the flanks of his short-legged pony and started down the windward face of the dune. Shobbat glared after him. He reached back and gave a reassuring pat to the skins of water lashed to the saddle under his gauzy cloak. The old nomad was just trying to frighten him. If they reached their destination in the time promised, they had plenty of water.

Wind rapidly erased Wapah's tracks in the soft sand. Shobbat urged his mount on. If he lost his guide, he was doomed.

The desert would swallow him as completely as it had his spit.

They had entered an area of sand dunes broken at intervals by intrusions of ancient rock. The rock was layered horizontally in shades of brown and tan. Shobbat grimaced. What a harsh, ugly land. He missed the teeming streets of Khuri-Khan, thick with the scents of cinnamon and cardamom, of sandalwood, and yes, of unwashed humanity. The emptiness of the desert made him feel small and unimportant. He was unaccustomed to such thoughts, and they frightened him. Fear made him angry.

Wapah had drawn a loosely woven scrap of cloth across his face to keep out the blowing dust. He returned to his earlier theme, explaining how the hard edges of the desert taught his people about truth and made them spiritually superior to outsiders. It was unclear whether he meant only those from outside Khur, or city-dwellers like the prince as well.

"We did not fear when the Vanishing came," the nomad declared. "Our gods were not points of light in the sky, but beings immortal and unchanging. They never left us. They guard us still."

Blown sand stung the exposed flesh of Shobbat's cheeks like a thousand shards of glass. He turned his face away. "Was everyone else in the world wrong when they thought the gods departed?" he asked testily.

Wapah shrugged one shoulder. "Who knows what godless barbarians think?"

On they rode, the nomad talking, the prince of Khur riding in uncomfortable silence. In spite of Wapah's talk of the desert's hard edges, the land had begun to look molten and soft to Shobbat. The terrific heat smelted the air itself, causing everything to shimmer and blur. Both horses grunted deep in their chests, resenting the task they were obliged to perform. Every two hundred steps, the duo paused for water. Two swallows for each beast and one for each man, as Wapah prescribed.

Once the sun climbed to its zenith, even the nomad fell silent. The air was too dry for speech. Shobbat's narrow, dark lips, so like his mother's, cracked. Smears of blood stained the gauze scarf covering his nose and mouth.

Just after midday they reached the first landmark on Wapah's itinerary, a shelf of stone rising out of the sand to a height greater than the mounted men. Pointed at one end and rounded at the other, the prominence was known as the Tear of Elir-Sana, named for the divine healer.

Unlike the monotonous sand or the unvarying hues of other rocks, the Tear of Elir-Sana presented a bold, colorful sight. It was composed of multicolored layers of rock; some were as orange as a sunset, others ash gray, blue-black, or creamy yellow. The eastern face was deeply grooved by generations of wind-borne sand. From tip to rounded end, the perfect teardrop was thirty feet in length. A spring bubbled from a cleft on the west side of the Tear. According to legend, the spring had been born from the tears of the goddess Elir-Sana, when she had collapsed here, half-dead from exhaustion.

Wapah announced they would refill their waterskins here. The water was said to have healing powers. Although it certainly slaked Shobbat's thirst, he found the taste nothing out of the ordinary.

After filling his two empty skins, the prince struggled back to his horse through the fine, drifted sand. His booted toe caught on something hidden just beneath the surface, and he fell forward. The full skins slung around his neck dragged him down. Cursing, he sat up and glared at the object that had tripped him. It was a skull. Clean, dry, and yellowed, it was not human.

"What unholy thing is this?"

Wapah leaned down from his saddle and peered at the find. "Dragon-man."

A draconian skull? Shobbat's annoyance vanished as he studied it more closely. The cranium was wide and triangular.

Fangs as long as Shobbat's thumb sprouted from the upper jaw, and there was a horny beak like that of a monstrous bird. The skull was half again as big as a human head, and on its rear were several parallel gouges—cuts from a blade, most likely.

"A warrior," the prince said, standing and dusting sand from his long coat.

"A scout in search of water. He found it, but never left. The desert takes no prisoners." Shobbat did not point out this draconian appeared to have died by the sword, not from exposure.

Mounted once more, Shobbat spotted something imbedded in a stratum of the Tear. He drew the dagger from his sash and jabbed at the rock. Fragments cascaded around his horse's hooves.

Wapah frowned at this wanton destruction but kept silent.

The prince had uncovered a yellow stone protruding from a layer of similarly colored sandstone. "Is this a shell?" he exclaimed. The object looked very like the top half of a clam.

Wapah shook his head. "Only a stone, shaped by chance. A jest of the gods."

The prince disagreed. He speculated the sea might once have covered this part of Khur. Wapah immediately dismissed this notion.

"It is told in the Song: the land of Khur is the oldest of the world, the first solid ground created by the gods," the nomad said flatly. "It has never been under water."

The Song was sacred to the nomads. A collection of legends from the distant past, it contained thousands of verses, too many for anyone to memorize entirely, so it was divided into eight cantos, each named for one of the great gods of the nomads: Kargath the Warrior, Rakaris the Hunter, Torghan the Avenger, Elir-Sana the Healer, Anthor the Hermit, Hab'rar the Messenger, Soro the Firemaker, and Ayyan the Deceiver. Wapah was a singer of the Anthor Canto.

The two men rode on. Progress became more difficult, as the horses had to plow through belly-deep sand. Wapah's short-legged gray animal, more accustomed to such terrain, kept a steady pace. Shobbat's elegant chestnut, its long legs meant for speed, floundered. As a result, sundown had come and gone by the time they reached their destination.

Like the Tear of Elir-Sana, Shobbat's goal was an island of stone in an ocean of moving sand. Rather than a single formation, it comprised a thick column of gray stone forty feet in height, ringed close around by four black granite towers only half as tall. The four angled inward, their tops touching the central column. Pale starlight gave the formation an eerie feel, like an ancient and forgotten temple.

The tablet found in the ruins of the Khuri yl Nor had spoken of this strange formation as an ancient oracle. It was said there were passages and a cave in the central spire. The cave was the prince's destination.

The wind died with the sunset. The air quickly lost the heat of day and grew cold, but warmth still radiated from the broiled sand. Shobbat dismounted and rummaged through his saddlebags. Knowing there would be no wood for torches, he'd brought a small brass lamp. He knelt and placed the lamp on the sand, then struck flint on steel to light the wick.

Wapah asked his intentions. When Shobbat said he planned to enter the formation, the nomad put heels to his horse's flanks and moved quickly to the crouching prince.

"Nothing was said of entering!" he said. "You must not! Do not disturb the spirits of this place!"

"I didn't come here just to view the sights. What I seek is within."

A cascade of sparks fell from his flint, and Shobbat concentrated on coaxing the flame to life. As he adjusted the wick, he heard a scrape of metal. Wapah had drawn his weapon, a narrow sword bare of crossguard, the style preferred by most nomads.

"You dare draw on me? I am your prince!"

Wapah was a motionless silhouette. The feeble lamplight did not reach his face, and his expression was hidden by the night. "If I rode away, what would you do? You'd never make it back to your city," he murmured.

For the first time, Shobbat felt a flicker of uncertainty. He quickly quashed it, falling back on all the arrogance and assurance of his privileged upbringing.

"My whereabouts are known, fool," he snapped. "If I do not return, for whatever reason, your entire clan will be hunted down and destroyed!"

This was a lie. No one in Khuri-Khan knew where Shobbat was. The prince didn't trust anyone enough for that.

For a long moment they gazed at each other, the pampered prince and the talkative nomad. Then Wapah sheathed his sword and bowed his head. "Let Those on High judge you. I shall not."

Shobbat picked up his lamp, his brief fear forgotten. Sentimentalists, that's what these nomads were. They'd ride to their deaths shouting for joy, but threaten their families and they crumbled. Exploiting that weakness allowed Shobbat's father to rule them. Sahim-Khan was the least sentimental man in the world.

The prince labored through the deep sand to the base of the formation. The central column seemed enormously high, rising tower-like against the starry sky. Around its base lay shards of black granite, shivered off the surrounding spires. Shobbat was grateful for the firmer footing they provided. The flickering light of his lamp showed no inscriptions, carvings, or any indication of intelligent handiwork, only rough, wind-worn granite.

Two-thirds of the way around from his starting point, he found an opening at ground level in the third black column. His heartbeat quickened. The roughly square entrance was partially blocked by drifted sand, and the prince had to drop to his knees to enter.

A passage rose into the column of stone. Steps had been

cut in the dense granite, spiraling around the wall. At last, evidence of an intelligent hand! The information on the tablet was again proven correct. Shobbat drew a jeweled dagger from his sash and started up the steps.

The dark air seemed to absorb the weak glow of his lamp. With his eyes adjusted to the dim light, the darkness beyond seemed even more intense. The dry, clean air of the desert outside had given way to a rank, fetid aroma that grew stronger as he climbed. The amber light showed gray splotches on the wall. Bat droppings and dried guano crunched beneath his boots. The presence of living creatures so deep in the desert was curious. What did they live on?

As he drew closer to the top, Shobbat saw that the ceiling of the hollow spire seemed to writhe. Thousands of bats were clustered tightly together across the rough-hewn surface. He could almost feel their tiny black eyes on him, glaring at the intruder who dared penetrate their abode. A few of the creatures dropped from their inverted perches and fluttered by his head. Shobbat pressed his back against the wall and covered his eyes with one arm, waiting for the bats to pass. The irregular steps on which he trod had become narrower as he ascended; here, near the top, they were deep enough only to accommodate the front half of his foot. A misstep, and he'd go crashing to the floor below.

He had encountered no landings or side chambers along the way, just a continuing inward spiral of rutted steps. Watching the bats circle away and vanish through a black crevice at the top of the steps, Shobbat had to smile. So there was an upper chamber!

Continuing upward, he reached an arched opening, low enough that he had to stoop to pass through. Outside, a breeze whistled around the tops of the spires. The air was remarkably cold, and it refreshed him like a draft of new wine after the rank odor of the interior.

From ground level it had appeared the tops of the four shorter spires touched the central column. In fact, there was a gap of some six feet between Shobbat's perch and the central column. Bridging the gap was a slab of black granite. It was barely wider than Shobbat's two feet, but he wobbled across, both arms held out to maintain his balance. He had not come so far to be stopped by his dislike of high places.

On the other side a round opening penetrated the central pinnacle. He halted at the opening and brought the lamp in close. Two lines of writing were chiseled into the gray rock, curving around the top edge of the entrance. Although the spelling was archaic, the words were in the Common tongue:

The roots of the Tree are deep. I shall live again.

It made little sense to Shobbat, but echoed what the scholars in Khuri-Khan had translated from the tablet.

He stepped through the opening and found himself in a large cave. The floor was paved with a polished black stone; the walls and distant ceiling were gray granite. As far as he could tell, the chamber was empty.

He shouted a few times, without visible result. Wind gusted against his back, sending his hat winging away and extinguishing his lamp. He wavered, off-balance in the sudden blackness.

"Enter, visitor."

Shobbat pivoted in a full circle, but could not find the source of the low voice. "Who's there?" he called.

"The one you came to find," said the voice, then added a lilting phrase in a language Shobbat did not understand.

Brilliant light flooded the cave, blinding the prince. With a cry, he dropped both knife and lamp and covered his aching eyes. A sound no desert-dweller could mistake came to his ears, the beguiling splash of water. He lowered his hands. Blinking, squinting, he beheld an impossible scene.

The cavern was lit as brightly as noonday in the desert, but the air was cool and fresh. Even more astonishing, a fine tree towered over Shobbat, its branches spreading to the high roof of the cave. Knowing only the palms and succulents of

Khur, the prince could not identify it. Its trunk was at least three feet in diameter, the bark gray-green and rough. Its dark green leaves were shaped like the shields carried by nomad warriors—long and narrow, rounded on one end and pointed on the other.

Shobbat stood staring dumbly upward. He had never seen such a tree before, and it was plainly impossible for its like to grow inside a closed cavern, shut off from the sun.

"No one has sought me out in an age. Your question must be grave."

Shobbat's gaze dropped from the magnificent tree to the old man sitting cross-legged at its base. He was thin, draped in linen rags the color of old parchment. White hair, fine as floss, hung to his shoulders. His skin was lined and darkened by time and the elements. He was obviously blind, his closed eyelids shriveled and sunken.

"Are you the Oracle of the Tree?" asked the prince.

Long, bony fingers gestured to the empty air. "There is no other."

A breeze set the tree's leaves to shivering. In the periphery of the cave, Shobbat saw movement, but when he turned to look in that direction, there was no one to be seen. Alarmed, he retrieved the dagger he had dropped and demanded to know who else was present.

The ancient turned his head slightly left and right, then shrugged. "We are alone." Shobbat insisted he'd seen movement. "Those are images of the past and future, not living beings."

The dismissive tone infuriated Shobbat. The haughty prince drew himself up, announcing his name and rank. The old man was not impressed.

"Makes no difference who you are. In any event, I've been expecting you."

"Expecting me? How?"

"I am not fixed in time like mortal men. I live equally in past, present, and future. Thus, I know you seek the throne of your father, Sahim-Khan of Khur."

Shobbat snorted. "What prince doesn't? Is that the extent of your augury?"

"You need do nothing to achieve your goal, Prince of Khur. Outlive your father, and the throne is yours."

"Bah! He intends to live forever!" Shobbat's petulant expression became harder, more resolute, and he added, "He treats with Nerakans, ogres, and minotaurs, seeking to enlarge his realm, and he allows foreigners to enter our country. All he sees is the gold and steel they bring, but his dalliances will destroy Khur. He does not deserve the throne!"

The prince again saw movement out of the corner of his eye. Again, when he looked directly at it, it vanished. He shifted from one foot to the other, gripping the hilt of his dagger nervously.

"My father has granted asylum to the exiled elves," he said. "He intends to use them as pawns to limit the influence of the Knights of Neraka. I need to know—will he succeed?"

"The Knights will not rule in Khur."

Shobbat blinked in surprise. He had expected a more cryptic response, but this was welcome clarity.

"Yet your house will not rule long, son of Sahim, if the children of Kith-Kanan are permitted to remain in Khur."

That too was plain-speaking, yet not so welcome.

Heedless of his audience's reaction, the oracle continued, "The elder race can win this land. Not with sword and fire, but by greening the desert." He opened his left hand, revealing a green shoot sprouting from his palm. "It is their peculiar gift to bring life to lifelessness."

Shobbat's dark eyes narrowed, a flush of fury mantling his face above his beard. "I will not allow it! Khur does not belong to the *laddad*. The throne will be mine!"

"So it will be, noble prince. For nine and ninety days. That will be the length of your reign."

Shobbat stalked forward, determined to wring a different fate from the scrawny old prophet. He reached out for the oracle's neck, then froze in horror. Before his eyes, the sage's skin became translucent. Muscle, bone, and vein stood out clearly. And the face was no longer human. The jaw had narrowed, grown pointed. The cheeks were hollow, the eye sockets high and arched. The prince recoiled from the ghastly sight, his anger freezing into fear.

"What are you, old seer?" he whispered.

The oracle ignored the question. Empty eye sockets turning to stare directly at the prince, he said, "Life has branches, like the Great Tree, and each choice represents a fork. You have one chance, Prince of Khur. It is vital that you keep the children of Kith-Kanan out of the Valley of the Blue Sands. If you do, their seed will wither in the wasteland."

Shobbat shook his head, wondering whether he had heard properly. The Valley of the Blue Sands was nothing more than a child's fable. What could such a myth have to do with the *laddad*, or with his success as khan? The burning need to know overcame his fear and he lifted his dagger, demanding an explanation.

"The word has been given. I will say no more," the oracle told him. "Go."

The final command echoed through the cavern as the sage vanished in a pulse of white light. When the glare subsided to a bearable level, the half-seen figures in the far edges of the cave solidified, and Shobbat could finally see them for what they were. Horrified, backing hastily away, he stabbed at them with his dagger. It was no use. They crowded in upon him, hands outstretched, claws gleaming, mouths agape. Shobbat screamed.

Outside, seated on the sand, Wapah heard the cry. A cloud of bats poured from one of the black granite towers. The horses snorted and pawed the ground. As the bats chittered overhead, weaving and dodging, debris fell around the nomad, landing lightly on the sand. Wapah picked up one of the fragments.

It was a leaf, dark and supple. Such leaves did not come from any tree Wapah had ever seen growing in Khur, yet the sand below the flying bats was littered with them, and more continued to flutter down like green rain.

Wapah pressed the leaf between his palms and begged Anthor the Hermit to protect him from the fell magic that obviously inhabited this place. A somber and solitary deity, Anthor nonetheless favored his desert children. They lived on the hard edges, where men and gods could see eye to eye.

* * * * *

The task Gilthas had given Kerian was straightforward enough: pay a call on Sa'ida, high priestess of the Temple of Elir-Sana in Khuri-Khan. However, his insistence that she leave Eagle Eye behind precipitated another argument. He didn't wish his wife to draw unnecessary attention to herself by arriving at the temple door astride a royal Silvanesti griffon. For her part, Kerian believed that the awe Eagle Eye inspired in humans prevented a lot of needless wrangling with guards and petty officials.

The bickering continued until Gilthas flatly ordered her to ride a horse. He seemed to be doing that a lot lately—ending their disagreements by issuing peremptory, royal commands. Tight-lipped, the Lioness obeyed.

She took as her sole companion Captain Hytanthas Ambrodel. Gilthas viewed this as yet another sign of her contrariness. He certainly did not expect her to go without an appropriate escort. Lord Taranath and the balance of the army had not yet returned to Khurinost, but a suitable complement could have been found. The Lioness refused, citing Gilthas's own stricture about not alarming the Khurs, and he could hardly argue against his own logic. Elves were generally accepted in Khuri-Khan (as was any cash customer). Lone elves sometimes earned glares, especially outside the broad-minded venues of the city markets, but nothing beyond that.

Gilthas had matters of state to attend to, but delayed long enough to watch his wife depart with young Ambrodel at her side. Clad in fresh tunic and trews, Kerian had disdained

Khurish attire, preferring her own Wilder garb over the more comfortable local fashion. Captain Ambrodel was more practical. He wore a white geb over fawn-colored Qualinesti trousers, carefully arranging the folds of the desert garment to conceal the hilt of his sword.

The midafternoon sun bathed Kerian's blonde head in a nimbus of white fire. As always, Gilthas could not help but be struck by her beauty, yet her grim expression was strikingly at odds with her loveliness. Her mood had grown worse since her return. It wasn't only their clashes that accounted for this. The loss of her command and her humiliation at the hands of the bull-men still gnawed at her. She'd not told anyone else what had happened, and rumors had begun to circulate in camp. The Lioness's courage was well known, but it could only be seen as odd that she had returned apparently unscathed from a battle in which all of her command had been lost.

Perhaps she was deep in thought, pondering the mission he'd given her, or perhaps she was concentrating on guiding her mount through the perils of the crowded tent city. Whatever the reason, although Gilthas waited, Kerian never glanced back at him. When, at last, she was lost to sight around a bend in the lane, he returned to his tent. Scouts from Taranath's command had arrived in advance of the main body of the army, and they had much news to impart.

As Kerian and her aide passed through the tumult of the tent city, each noticed very different things. Hytanthas saw courage—common people struggling to live in a hostile, foreign place, and beginning to succeed. The Lioness saw only injustice—the most ancient race in the world forced from their rightful homes and made to suffer ignominiously in this terrible wilderness.

Like the roots of a tree, the environs of Khurinost were tangled, having grown haphazardly according to the lay of the land and the whims of its builders. Sahim-Khan had given the elves permission to set up a camp outside his capital; he had given them little else. Exhausted, sick, sunburned, and parched, the elves cobbled together whatever shelter they could, making tents out of everything from silken cloth to horse blankets to canvas sails formerly used by ships plying the Bay of Balifor.

Desert winds and errant embers from cookfires had taken a steady toll on the makeshift habitations, but as days became months and months grew into years, the elves learned to do better. The flimsy tents acquired wooden doorways, brass fireboxes and chimneys, and carpets to cover the sand. Wide, central streets were left open to the broiling sun, to allow carts and mounted elves to pass and to bring in fresh air, but the rest, the miles of narrow, twisting passages between tents great and small, were roofed with rush mats woven from the knife-edged grass that grew along the seaside below the city. The result was a warren no stranger could hope to navigate, the very antithesis of the elven love of order and beauty. But the confusing maze of streets and passages also served as an effective defense against interlopers.

Ahead, some forty yards beyond the edge of Khurinost, the wall of Khuri-Khan rose, its western face washed by the afternoon sun. Kerian lifted her gaze from the tent-city and studied the wall.

Sahim-Khan's first priority after the fall of Malystryx was to rebuild his city's defenses. Until these were complete his capital was vulnerable. The northern and western sectors had been repaired first. In those directions lay the greatest threats: the Knights of Neraka and the ogres of Kern. The elves lived under Sahim's watchful eye, penned in by the city wall on one side and the pitiless desert on the other. The Lioness recognized Sahim-Khan's sanctuary as both a gift and a trap. If the elves' enemies moved against them now, there would be no escape for the Firstborn.

"Trapped," she muttered.

"General?" Hytanthas asked, but she only shook her head.

A sextet of heavily armed humans guarded the west gate. They wore broad-brimmed helmets styled after the sun hats worn by nomads, but wrought in iron. Their cuirasses, cuisses, and greaves were of Nerakan pattern. For many years, Khurish soldiers had hired themselves out as mercenaries to the Knights. The soldiers also wore a coiled dragon device on their breastplates, marking them as members of the Khur tribe.

Although the Khurs had given their name to the country, they were only one of the Seven Tribes of the desert, named for the seven sons of Keja, who had first united the desert-dwellers into a single nation. Centered on the natural fortress of Khuri-Khan, the Khur tribe had come to dominate the others both in war and trade. All the khans of Khur had begun as princes of the Khur tribe.

The guards had no trouble recognizing the elf general. Dressed in Kagonesti leathers, golden head bare to the brilliant sun, Kerianseray was hard to miss. The tallest Khur sketched an awkward salute. It was a Nerakan habit they had not fully mastered. Kerian acknowledged the gesture with a slight nod and kept moving, plunging into the heavy shadow of the gate. The gate was enormously thick, a full sixteen feet of stone. Compared to the blazing desert outside, the tunnel was black as a dragon's heart, and the Lioness blinked rapidly, her eyes adjusting to the sudden loss of light.

The Khurs had nothing with which to build but crumbly sandstone, and soft limestone from the cliffs overlooking the Bay of Balifor. To protect this weak stone they applied a veneer of large glazed tiles to the inner and outer surfaces of their walls. When maintained, this coating strengthened the stone and made it impervious to wind and rain. Many buildings were covered by tiles glazed in creamy or golden tones, but some were quite colorful, in bold primary hues or multicolored hues like patchwork quilts.

At the other end of the tunnel, the two elves were greeted by a riotous mix of colors, sounds, and smells that was utterly foreign. This was the Fabazz, or Lesser Souk, the city's market for spices, incense, and foodstuffs. Streams of smoke from charcoal grills mingled with the odors of freshly butchered meat, sizzling fat, and drying herbs. The aromas were not unpleasant, but to an elf, with senses far keener than any human's, the sensations of the Fabazz could be torturous.

The *soukats*, or merchants, converged on the newcomers, waving samples of their wares. The soukats of Khur had welcomed the elves even more than their khan. To them the world was divided into buyers and sellers; whether the buyer was elf or human concerned them not at all. All steel was equal, and equally sought.

Had they been on foot, Kerian and Hytanthas might easily have been overwhelmed. Khurish traders were not noted for their reticence, and in the Fabazz their approach was practically an attack. Most of the merchandise here was perishable. What wasn't sold today would have to be marked down for sale tomorrow (or worse, cast off).

"Great lady!" A soukat shoved a small bundle toward the Lioness, its smell so sharp that her horse sidestepped quickly. "Buy these spices! The burning they bring to the tongue will be matched by the burning they incite in the heart of the one you love!"

"Ignore him, lady!" boomed another soukat. "Mushra sells only street sweepings! Kandar has the best spices, oils, and resins in Khur! Buy from Kandar, who weighs his goods honestly!"

"Kandar is an infamous liar, noble lady! Only Teffik weighs truly, and handpicks his spices each morning from the Delphon caravans!"

When Kerian showed no sign of stopping, the soukats redoubled their efforts. Soon her horse was rendered immobile by the gesticulating merchants. Hytanthas could make no headway either.

A live chicken, squawking loudly and wings flapping, was suddenly thrust in Kerian's face. Recoiling, she planted a foot against the poulterer's chest and shoved with all her strength. The unlucky man was flung back against his fellows. All of them crashed into their carts and went down in a clatter of tin pans and a flurry of squawking chickens.

Wails of protest rose up from the soukats. This was not how things were done! In the Fabazz, a little shoving was commonplace, but nothing this rough. A number of soukats hefted pieces of the broken carts, waving the staves at the elves. The Lioness ostentatiously drew her sword. Reluctant but loyal, the captain did the same. The Khurs parted ranks and allowed the armed elves to pass.

By the time they emerged on the other side of the market, ascending the stepped street there, the Lioness's face wore a fierce grimace, and not for the altercation with the poulterer. That she had found rather invigorating. No, her distaste was for the stench that now saturated her clothing. The reek of the Fabazz seemed to permeate her very skin. She longed for a fountain so she might wash her hands and face, but this was a vain hope. Khuri-Khan did not waste water on such displays.

The closely packed houses, rebuilt after the depredations of Malys and her minions, looked bizarre to elven eyes. Some squat and square, others taller and round, they boasted a variety of tile patterns. In the wealthier districts, the more subdued shades of cream and gold predominated; here, alternating stripes of blue and white were common, but poorer householders used whatever leftover tiles they could scrounge. Their homes might be speckled with any color in the rainbow—orange, green, red, bright blue. In addition, since the people of Khuri-Khan were taxed according to the length and breadth of their home's foundation, most dwellings were wider at the top than at ground level. When the Lioness and Hytanthas reached the top of the narrow, winding street, only a thin strip of blue sky was visible between the overhanging eaves.

At this hour, most folks were at the souks. Aside from a

bony gray cat, the only sign of life was a faint chiming sound. Kerian led the way across to the lower end of the avenue called Temple Walk. All of the major shrines of the city were located along this street, which ran east-west. The Khurs were mad with religion, worshiping gods and demi-gods only vaguely familiar to outsiders. All through the Vanishing of the Gods, the Great War, and the fall of the dragons, the Khurs had clung to their faith.

Halfway down its length, the Temple Walk doglegged to the north, skirting the immovable center of Khuri-Khan, the great artesian well known as *Nak-Safal*. The name was difficult to translate. "Bottomless Pool" was the simplest rendering Kerian had heard.

Their trip did not take them that far. Only a short way down Temple Walk was their destination, and the source of the chiming: the Temple of Elir-Sana. A stone wall surrounded the sacred enclosure. Only five feet high, it was more decorative than defensive. Along its top was set a line of curved brass rods. From each hung thin disks of the same metal. When the air stirred, the disks clattered against the rods, creating a bright chorus of sound. It was meant to mimic the gurgle of falling water, but to Kerian and Hytanthas, born and raised in the green land of Qualinesti, there was little resemblance. Still, the sound was pretty, and mysterious. When the wall was out of sight, the chiming seemed to emanate from the very air.

The wall enclosed a large courtyard, paved with creamy limestone. At the center of the courtyard sat the Temple of Elir-Sana. It wasn't large, but Kerian thought it easily the most beautiful building in Khuri-Khan. It didn't compare to the great sanctuaries of Qualinost, of course, but it had a certain panache. Built of pure-white marble, the temple, like the courtyard, was partly in shadow now. When the sun was higher, the pale stone of temple and courtyard reflected the light with nearly unbearable brilliance.

The perfectly square temple was surrounded by a colonnade. The smooth, white columns were narrower at the base than at the top, echoing the odd construction of the city's houses. Capping the temple was a dome carved of a single block of palest blue marble, a rare color for such stone. At least thirty-five feet in diameter, the dome had been polished until it was no thicker than a fingernail. How the Khurs of old had made such a marvel, much less raised it atop the temple, was a question no one living could answer.

The metal gate was open, and the two elves rode into the courtyard and dismounted. Kerian gave her reins over to Hytanthas, telling him he'd have to wait for her outside. "Males are not allowed inside this temple," she said. "Neither are weapons, unfortunately."

She looped her sword belt over the pommel of her saddle and left her dagger, still sheathed, as well. Hytanthas reminded her that they must be out of the city by sunset. She nodded. That deadline was still hours away.

Sahim-Khan had decreed, ostensibly for the elves' own safety, that no *laddad* could remain within the city from sunset to sunrise. The Lioness had strong opinions about Sahim and his edicts, but before she could give voice to them, the scrape of iron caused her to whirl, instantly on the alert.

Four men in Khurish attire had darted into the courtyard through the only opening in the wall. Over their linen gebs each wore an *affre*—the hooded, ankle-length robe favored by nomads of the high desert. Scarves concealed their faces, leaving only their eyes visible. Each man held the nomad's favorite weapon: a long, narrow-bladed sword with no crossguard.

The Lioness had swiftly drawn her sword. "Keep off!" she warned them. "We've business with the holy priestess and no quarrel with you."

"We've a quarrel with you, *laddad*. Today your lives end!" said one of the men, his voice muffled by the scarf. Immediately, all four attacked.

Unlike the city guards at the gate, these humans seemed unfamiliar with their foes. Three of them went for Hytan-thas, thinking him the greater threat. Only one was left to engage the Lioness. Her sword flashed up, thrusting at the man's throat. With unexpected agility, the fellow parried her thrust and riposted. She turned aside his attack, but the slick surface of the limestone betrayed her. She slid—not far, but enough to throw off her balance. She felt the man's blade nick her left ear.

He chuckled. She distinctly heard him. Quickly, he at-tacked again, repeating the very same moves as before.

The Lioness's lip curled. He thought he was toying with her! A smart warrior would have taken advantage of her stumble to drive home a killing thrust. Instead, the nomad was content to repeat his previously successful attack, cut-ting her right ear this time. He obviously saw her as no real threat.

Fury engulfed her, not just for this stupid human's lucky hits, but for all the indignities and humiliations she and her people had suffered for six terrible years.

In a blur of motion, she lunged beyond the man, reversed her grip on her sword, and thrust it into his back. Steel punched easily through his desert garb, through skin and flesh, grating on bone. As he gave a shocked gasp, Kerian drove her blade in even further, burying it to its hilt.

Meanwhile Hytanthas had been forced to backpedal franti-cally, gaining time to draw his own sword. He was surrounded by flickering points and keen edges, all seeking his flesh. One foe landed a hit on his left arm, but the mail Hytanthas wore under his geb turned the blade. The elf made a wide, whirling slash at the men's faces—even the bravest fighter feared for his eyes—and his attackers drew back. All but one.

This man was too slow, and the elf's point scored a bloody line across his forehead. With a hoarse cry, the human clapped a hand to the wound. Blood coursed down, soaking the scarf over his face.

The other two men shoved their injured comrade aside and came on again. Hytanthas gave ground, then gave more, and still more, working hard to keep their blades at bay, until he found his back against the temple wall and could retreat no further.

While one masked man attacked, keeping Hytanthas busy, his comrade stooped, gathered a handful of fine sand, and flung it at the elf's face. Hytanthas had no warning. Suddenly, he found himself painfully blinded. He thrust out his sword in a desperate parry and waited for the feel of iron plunging into his body.

Retrieving her sword from her dead foe's back, the Lioness rushed to her aide's defense. By the time Hytanthas cleared his eyes, one of his attackers was dead and the other had fled. Hytanthas would have given chase, but a sharp command brought him up short.

"We have a prisoner." The Lioness pointed to the man Hytanthas had cut on the forehead. Face awash in gore, the human was groveling on the bloody ground, trying to crawl away unnoticed.

Kerian ordered him to his feet and, when he whined about his injury, growled, "Stand up, you coward, or I'll hamstring you!"

He made as if to rise, then rolled over abruptly, his hand shooting out to fling a short dagger. Kerian whipped her sword in a half-arc, deflecting the missile. The dagger flew back the way it had come, plunging into its owner's neck. The assassin gave a gurgling shriek and clamped a hand to the wound, blood pouring over his fingers.

Glaring up at the Lioness, his black eyes overflowing with hate, he groaned, "For Torghan!" Bloody froth bubbled from his lips, and his straining body went slack.

Hytanthas exclaimed over her amazing parry, but the Lioness, looking down at the dead nomad, denied any prowess. She rested her sword on her shoulder and said, "I didn't want him dead. He could have told us who sent him."

At her direction, Hytanthas rifled the dead men's clothes. He found nothing, no coins, no personal belongings, not even the fly whisk most city dwellers found essential. One odd fact: each man bore a scarlet tattoo on his left breast, of a crouching bird with wings folded and head curiously lowered. It seemed a bit familiar to Kerian, but she couldn't think where she might have seen it.

"What is that? An eagle?" Hytanthas asked.

"Condor."

The unknown voice brought both elves around. A woman stood in the shadows of the temple colonnade. Stepping into the sunlight, she approached slowly. Her voluminous robes were dazzlingly white. Her long hair was likewise white, braided, and woven through with azure ribbons and tiny brass bells. A wide, flat hat shaded her face, which was brown and smooth as polished wood. Her hands were folded into the sleeves of her robe.

The Lioness bowed her head, something few had seen her do, and sheathed her sword with unusual care, sliding the blade home silently.

"Holy Mistress Sa'ida?" she asked. The woman nodded, and the Lioness gestured at the two dead attackers. "Are these men known to you?"

"No man is known to me, but I recognize the mark they bear. It is the sign of Torghan the Avenger."

Torghan, Lord of the Wastes, was the Khurish god of vengeance, often represented as a giant vulture or condor. The elves knew him as Kinis, a malign deity not worshiped by their race. To his most devoted followers, the minotaurs, he was the great god Sargas. Kerian wondered if there might be a link between the Khurish cult of Torghan and the minotaurs who had invaded Silvanesti. It was not an alliance she liked to contemplate. In any event, she could not fathom why Torghanists of any stripe would attack her in broad daylight, in the supposedly safe confines of a holy temple.

The white-robed priestess regarded the dead man closest

to her in thoughtful silence, then remarked, "You stabbed him in the back."

Kerian's eyes narrowed, but the priestess's tone wasn't accusatory; she seemed merely to be stating a fact. The elf lifted a hand to one of her bloody ears, causing Hytanthas to exclaim at the injuries he only now noticed. She brushed aside his concern, reliving again the rush of fury she'd felt when the Torghanist cut her so casually.

"Let us retire within," the priestess said to her. "I will tend your injury."

Hytanthas could not enter the sacred precincts, but the priestess gave him leave to remain in the shaded colonnade. One of the temple acolytes, she said, would bring him refreshment. He went to tie their horses out of the sun before settling down to await his commander. Kerian followed the high priestess inside.

After the searing light of day, the stone-lined passages of the Temple of Elir-Sana were cool and dark. Only the scuff of the priestess's feet ahead gave Kerian any hint she was not alone. She had a general idea of the temple's layout and assumed the Holy Mistress was taking her to private chambers, located at the rear. However, halfway along a dark corridor, Sa'ida turned and parted a cloth doorflap on her right.

In the small, dimly lit chamber beyond, obviously waiting for them, stood an elder acolyte, dressed in a woman's geb of white linen, her hair covered by a matching turban. She held a small, silver tray on which rested various medicaments and a small roll of gauze. Kerian wondered how the high priestess had called for the medicines. Sa'ida had not been out of her sight since the battle with the Torghanists.

The acolyte cleaned the elf's wounds, but when the woman started to bandage her cuts, the high priestess stopped her, saying the injuries would heal more quickly if left open to the goddess's gaze. Although not especially pious, Kerian certainly had no desire to walk around with her ears wrapped in white gauze, so she agreed.

SANCTUARY

Sa'ida lifted another doorflap. Silhouetted against the light beyond, she turned and said to Kerian, "Come, seeker. We shall commune under the eyes of the goddess."

Kerian soon found herself in the temple's heart, the domed sanctuary. The pale blue stone of the high ceiling softened the harsh rays of the sun, bathing the great room in gentle light. Unlike the close, incense-laden interiors of most shrines, the air in the Temple of Elir-Sana was clean and fresh. Centered under the sky-colored dome, the sacred image of the goddess rested on a high pedestal. On the floor of the chamber, radiating out from the sacred image like the spokes of a wheel, were six lanes filled with sifted white sand, carefully raked to eliminate footprints. The paved floor between the wide lanes was dotted with stylized sculptures of trees, each six to eight feet tall. Slender tubes of copper or brass served as trunks and branches. Ovals of silver, hammered thin, formed the leaves, twinkling as they moved gently in the air.

Here and there in the white sand lanes, priestesses and acolytes performed their sacred rituals. Choosing an empty path, Sa'ida led the Lioness toward the image of the goddess. As she took in the sight, Kerian's steps slowed, then ceased.

The goddess was shown as a stout, broad-shouldered woman, her arms crossed over an ample bosom. Her hands, fingers spread, lay flat against her shoulders. Her hair, gathered into a single, heavy hank, was pulled forward over her left shoulder. Her chin was down, her eyes closed. Depicted in a typical Khurish gown, the great goddess Elir-Sana resembled nothing so much as a well-fed matron of Khuri-Khan—albeit one filled with a private melancholy. Unlike the temple itself, the image wasn't marble. In fact, it wasn't stone at all, but golden-yellow wood. Lovingly oiled over many years of devotion, the surface had a soft burnished sheen. The statue was the single largest piece of wood that Kerian had seen in Khur. In this barren land, fine wood was more esteemed than gold.

"She is a quiet god," Sa'ida said, her low voice sounding loud in the stillness. "A suffering god. She afflicts and heals, and laments both."

To the Lioness, the Khurish deity sounded like Quen, the Qualinesti goddess of healing. She almost mentioned this, but decided not to. It might provoke a sermon.

"Why is she so stout?" she asked.

"She is the bringer of plenty. How could she be lean?"

Several low, wide stools ringed the statue's pedestal. Sa'ida sat on one of these, spreading her many-layered gown like a fan until the stool vanished beneath it.

As the priestess settled herself, Kerian's attention was caught by the metal tree next to her. Its dangling silver foliage had been shaped to resemble aspen leaves. A memory flashed in Kerian's mind: the first light of sunrise catching on aspen leaves, the pinkish-orange blush tinting the trees' pale trunks. It was a sight she used to take for granted, rising every morning in the greenwood. Now, such memories brought only bitterness, reminding her how far she was from the leafy embrace of home.

The high priestess was regarding her curiously. Kerian realized she was still caressing the metal leaf. She let it go quickly, as if burned.

"Seeker, why have you come? To obtain the comfort and wisdom of the goddess?" Sa'ida asked.

"No, Holy Mistress. I do not seek the goddess, but her priestess."

"Why?"

The Lioness met bluntness with bluntness. "It is said you know of the Valley of the Blue Sands."

An emotion passed over Sa'ida's face, brief but intense, like a thunderstorm in the desert. Her lips flexed downward, and a furrow appeared between her eyes. As quickly as it had come, the expression was gone, replaced by her usual, serene mask.

"I know the legend, yes. But why does it interest you?"

"It doesn't," Kerian said flatly. "But it does interest my husband, the Speaker of the Sun and Stars. He has acquired a map he believes shows the location of the fabled valley. He desires to know what you know about this place."

The priestess was silent for so long that Kerian thought she would not answer. When she finally did, the words came slowly.

"It is said to be a place untouched by the world for more than two and a half thousand years. What does Gilthas Pathfinder want there?"

Out of habit, Kerian's hand moved to rest where her sword hilt should be, but was not. Feeling off-balance, she blurted, "He seeks a home for our people."

If Kerian had said Gilthas intended to move bag and baggage into the female-only precincts of the temple, Sa'ida could not have looked more shocked. "You enjoy the favor of Sahim-Khan," the priestess sputtered. "Would you trade that for a perilous journey to a land that may not even exist?"

This sentiment echoed the Lioness's own feelings on the subject, but she was ever practical. "The Speaker of the Sun and Stars believes our people cannot remain in Khur forever, even with Sahim-Khan's protection. This is not our country, nor our climate. Everyone knows the Khan covets the wealth we brought, and it may be that he hopes to harvest elven wisdom for his own ends. The Speaker is willing to trade treasure and knowledge for a little land and a little peace." Kerian shook her head. "I, however, see a darker future."

Sa'ida said nothing. Nettled, the Lioness spoke more candidly still. "I believe Sahim will sell us out. To Neraka, to the minotaurs, to anyone who meets his price. It's only a matter of time."

Her raised voice echoed through the chamber, ringing off the high, polished dome. Acolytes and priestesses glanced her way before resuming their prayers.

Sa'ida lowered her eyes, her posture echoing the goddess above her. "The seeker may be wise."

The elf general ground her teeth in frustration. "May be? Do you have definite knowledge of Sahim-Khan's treachery?"

A tiny shrug rippled across the priestess's shoulders. "The deserts of Khur are broad. No one can hope to hold every grain of sand. Even in the best-run homes, scorpions and spiders are found."

First bluntness, now maddening ambiguity. What in Chaos was the woman trying to say? That Sahim-Khan didn't rule unchallenged in Khur? That was hardly a revelation. Everyone knew the nomads beyond the city were an independent lot. Still, with the backing of his well-trained troops, Sahim kept peace among the tribes. But what if the trouble wasn't outside the city, in the larger desert—what if it was much closer? Kerian thought of the Torghanist assassins in the courtyard.

Even in the best-run homes—

"Are you saying it isn't the Khan I should be worrying about, but someone else in the city?"

The high priestess seemed to feel she'd already said too much. Abruptly she tucked her hands into her sleeves and bowed her head.

Kerian tried to persuade the priestess to reveal her thoughts. She strove to keep her voice level, but passion throbbed in every syllable. "Help us, Holy Mistress. Help *me!* I want to lead my people out of Khur, back to our ancestral lands, as soon as possible. We're defenseless here. I have tried to make the Speaker see this, but he will not."

"Yes, convince your king to leave Khur. That is the best course."

"He will not listen!" Kerian kicked the sand, sending a spray of white grains into the air. "He's tired of fighting and dreams of a new elven homeland in Khur, in that mythical valley!"

The priestess lifted her head abruptly, the tiny bells braided into her hair jangling discordantly. "The Valley of the Blue Sands does exist," she said quietly. "The analects of the goddess speak of it quite clearly. She calls it 'the refuge of the damned.'"

Kerian snorted. Maybe Gilthas was onto something. Who was more damned these days than elves? She pushed these thoughts aside and concentrated on fulfilling her mission. "The Speaker respectfully requests any documents you might have with information on the valley. Will you lend them, Holy Mistress?"

The priestess raised a hand, and a young acolyte appeared silently in answer. Sa'ida murmured to the girl, who bowed and left.

"I gladly dispense the wisdom of the great goddess," Sa'ida said. "I hope it will persuade your king to abandon this impossible notion."

Kerian nodded. "Holy Mistress, I agree with you. My people's future does not lie in Khur."

In moments, the acolyte returned, accompanied by three others. Each of the four bore a leather case about three feet long. Sa'ida checked the clay tags on the four cases and gave her permission for them to be turned over to the Lioness.

As Kerian took one, the priestess reached out, resting a hand on hers. "I entrust these sacred texts to you, Kerianseray," she said gravely. "By your word they must be safeguarded."

Equally grave, the Lioness accepted the charge. She asked whether the priestess would land in trouble with Sahim-Khan, or the Torghanists, for helping the elves.

"Why should I, a humble servant of the great goddess, fear the enmity of men?" asked the priestess.

Humble servant? The Lioness was amused. The old woman before her exerted enormous influence in Khuri-Khan, not only at court but among the people as well. In a fiercely patriarchal society, the healer-priestesses of Elir-Sana were accorded a respect and reverence given to no other women. This so-called humble servant was vital to the rule of Sahim-Khan. If the healers of Elir-Sana ever chose to withhold their skills from Sahim-Khan, his city would be in dire straits indeed.

Before leaving, Kerian offered a contribution to the temple's coffers. The high priestess gave her a severe look. "Alms are always welcome, but one cannot buy the favors of the goddess."

"I don't want the goddess's favor, just yours."

Sa'ida rose to her feet, face flushing. "You offend!"

"Forgive me, Holy Mistress. The cowardly attack on myself and my young aide distressed me. Please forget my unfortunate words."

Mention of the tattooed assassins had the desired effect. Sa'ida was plainly upset by the incident. In many ways, Torghan and Elir-Sana were polar opposites, even enemies. The god of the unforgiving desert, of revenge and rage, had little common ground with the goddess of healing, humility, and plenty.

Kerian bowed and turned to go, the three acolytes carrying the other leather cases trailing in her wake. However, Sa'ida called her back.

Stepping away from the Lioness, and turning to face the statue of Elir-Sana, the high priestess spread her hands and sank to her knees. She began to chant a rhythmic, unintelligible sentence. The three acolytes standing near Kerian bowed their heads immediately, but the elf general watched in wide-eyed fascination as the priestess reached out toward the statue's base. Her hand passed into the marble pedestal without hindrance. The Lioness blinked rapidly, suspecting a trick of the light.

On her feet again, Sa'ida held out a closed fist. "For your bravery, and to ease your suffering, the goddess presents you with a gift," she said.

This proved to be a smooth, heavy object. About the size of a goose egg, it resembled a giant opal, its white surface veined with pink, green, and gold. Pretty, but the Lioness couldn't begin to fathom its purpose. She asked, and Sa'ida gave a suitably cryptic answer.

"It will stop the killing—at least for a time. Keep it close by, seeker."

Their meeting was at an end. With Sa'ida in the lead and the three acolytes trailing behind, Kerian departed the sanctuary. The high priestess did not speak again until they reached the final portal, the double doors that would take Kerian outside. Sa'ida sent the three acolytes out, leaving her alone briefly with the Lioness.

"You and your people should depart Khur as soon as possible. No man in Khur is your friend—and only sorrow can come of your remaining here."

With that, the high priestess of Elir-Sana turned and walked back into her temple's shaded depths.

3

The Khuri yl Nor was a conglomeration of halls, corridors, and antechambers, all grouped around a central citadel, the great keep known as the Nor-Khan. As much a defensive position as the residence of the Khan, the Nor-Khan boasted thick walls of stone and brick, a massive roof, and absolutely no windows. The interior was always dark and cool, no matter the time of day.

The low light couldn't hide the magnificence of the Sapphire Throne of Khur. Torchlight only seemed to enhance its beauty. The six-foot-tall chair rested on a wide dais at one end of the throne room. Constructed of wood and covered with hammered gold, the throne was one of the few treasures successfully hidden from Malys and her minions. Its fan-shaped backrest contained two perfect star sapphires, the so-called Eyes of Kargath, the Khurish god of war. The flames of torches, reflecting in the gems, imparted an eerie appearance of life to them.

The Khan of All the Khurs, Sahim Zacca-Khur, was sitting in his impressive throne. He was richly attired in a trailing robe of sea-green silk slashed at the cuffs and hem with stripes of darker jade. Although he was past middle age, his black beard carried no hint of gray in its thick curls. Both chin and nose were proudly outthrust, like the prow of a ship. Heavy gold rings hung from his earlobes. On his head he wore the crown of Khur—a ten-inch-tall conical hat of stiff, red leather, its lower edge decorated by a band of hammered gold.

The Khan was staring pensively at the eleven men arrayed before him. The men were his *geel-khana*. Khuri-Khan was divided into eleven precincts, known as *geel*. Each had a commander of the guard, a *geel-khana*. Despite the moderate temperature of the room, they were sweating heavily.

After allowing the silence to lengthen sufficiently, Sahim-Khan finally spoke. His tone was calmly conversational; the expression in his dark eyes was anything but.

"Each day you report the streets of my city are calm. Yet the *laddad* queen was attacked by assassins at the doorway of one of our holiest temples. Who were the attackers?"

The eldest guard captain, like the Khan a member of the Khur tribe, replied, "Mighty One, they were followers of Torghan."

"From here in the city?" Sahim's voice rose.

"No, Great Khan. The two who were slain were nomads."

The Khan grunted. At least the assassins who'd dared test his sovereignty were not locals. Nomads were another matter. None could say what desert wanderers might do.

"The *laddad* have my permission to be here, and they have the privilege of my protection. Why were they attacked?"

"Mighty One, we have been told"—the captain laid heavy emphasis on the last word, so his lord would know this opinion was not his own—"that the Sons of the Crimson Vulture were driven to madness by the sight of so many foreigners in our city."

"It is I who decides who is welcome in Khuri-Khan. Only I!" Sahim declared coldly.

He stood and began pacing slowly across the dais. Even through the thick carpet and with his heavy scarlet slippers, he could feel the ruts in the stone, claw marks left by the great dragon. Rather than upsetting, Sahim found the sensation comforting. The formidable beast Malys was gone, and he, Sahim Zacca-Khur, stood in the monster's place.

Torchlight sent his distorted shadow rippling across the tapestries decorating the thick walls of the keep. The light also glittered on the design embroidered on his robe: two rampant golden dragons, the emblem of his line, faced each other across Sahim-Khan's broad chest. The design rose and fell as he halted, breathing deeply, pondering in silence. This worried his underlings. A shouting Khan was expending his bile. A silent Khan was hoarding it for a future explosion.

At last he spoke, his voice so low they could barely hear it, even though they were straining to catch every nuance.

"I shall have to apologize to the Speaker of the Sun and Stars. Can any of you imagine how likely I am to enjoy that?" Faces blanched, but no one spoke, and he bellowed, "Can you?"

"I see no need for you to apologize to anyone."

All eyes, including the Khan's, turned to the man who had spoken. Below the dais, on Sahim's left, was a tall, powerfully built man in foreign dress. He sat in a high-backed, western-style chair, the only person in the room, other than Sahim himself, allowed to sit. His face was clean shaven, his skin dark. His voice resembled the bellow of a bull, even in calm discourse.

"Lord Hengriff speaks truly," the eldest guardsman said quickly. "The Mighty Khan need not stoop to apologize to the *laddad*."

"That's not what I meant." Hengriff stood, letting his imposing bulk impress itself on the more numerous but shorter Khurs. His obsidian gaze briefly swept the assembly before fixing on Sahim. "Tell the elves their protection is an increasingly heavy drain on the royal coffers. Instead of apologizing, raise the fee you charge them for the right to remain here. Turn this misfortune into a fortune, Mighty One."

For the first time that day, Sahim-Khan smiled, a slow grin of delight. "You're a crafty rogue, my lord. Are you sure you aren't some part Khurish?"

SANCTUARY

No answering smile came to Hengriff's face. He merely sat down again, the heavy chair creaking under his weight.

Sahim ordered the high priest of the Temple of Torghan brought before him. Soldiers had already collected him, and soon he stood before his khan. A sharp-faced former nomad named Minok, the priest, like most Khurish clergy, was beardless and kept his hair cropped close to his scalp. Ritual tattoos were visible at the wrists and neck of his plain cotton geb. Alone among all the Khurs in the room, Minok showed no fear of Sahim-Khan. He made proper obeisance to his liege, but looked Sahim in the eye when he spoke and did not waver when the Khan denounced the devotees of the god for their attack on the elf queen.

"Men of the desert have noble souls, Great Khan," Minok said proudly. "It is too much to expect them to look the other way while foreigners multiply and flourish in our land. Give the word, Great Khan, and the Sons of the Crimson Vulture will sweep the *laddad* contagion from all of Khur!"

Sahim-Khan appeared to weigh this proposal with due care. Intimates of the palace knew better. The priesthoods commanded the loyalty of thousands, but Minok's followers had embarrassed the Khan. Whether or not he extorted a greater fee from the Speaker, Sahim did not take kindly to any challenge to his authority. Servants and guards in the throne room began quietly to wager on how long the priest of Torghan would live.

"Your patriotism and piety do you credit, holy one," Sahim said at last. "I will consider what you have said. In the meantime, it is the will of your khan that the *laddad* not be molested. Restrain your devotees, priest, or I will. Is that clear?"

All Minok could do was agree to the order. He was surrounded by the Khan's partisans. Sahim dismissed him, and the proud priest backed out of the room, bowing as he went. Once he disappeared through the double doors, Sahim nodded to soldiers waiting by the exit. They slipped out. Coins surreptitiously changed hands throughout the room. The priest of Torghan had even less time than most had thought.

Sahim sent the *geel-khana* on their way, too. As they departed, he realized the usual crowd at court was short by one—his eldest son, Shobbat, was not present. Curiously, this pleased Sahim. The heir to the throne of Khur was not known for offering sage counsel to his father (not that his father would have accepted any), so Sahim had placed him in charge of the repair work on the palace. He must be busy elsewhere in the sprawling, half-ruined complex. This new diligence was refreshing. Sahim would make a khan out of his wastrel son yet.

When most of the audience had gone, Sahim addressed Hengriff. "What do your people make of this new agitation, my lord?"

"You said it yourself, Mighty Khan. Patriotism and piety. The people of Khur tire of the elven pestilence."

Sahim shrugged. "A few fanatics. They will obey my decrees, or suffer the consequences."

"Hatred of the elves will spread, Great One. Mark my words."

Sahim had no doubt of that. He knew the Nerakan greased palms all over Khuri-Khan, buying goodwill for his Order and ill will for the elves. Slyly, he asked, "Should I loose Holy Minok and his followers then?"

Hengriff cleared his throat, the sound like a panther's snarl. "The zealous, once unleashed, are difficult to rein in."

His meaning was abundantly clear. If the Torghanists were allowed to rid Khur of the elves, they might not stop there. The Khan himself might not meet their standards of purity.

"Better you should expel them yourself, Great One," the Knight added. "The land would resound with your name for having rid it of their haughty presence."

Sahim thanked the Nerakan emissary for his insight.

Hengriff bowed low and departed, taking with him the trio of drably dressed men at his back. No amount of broadcloth or linen could disguise the breadth of their shoulders or the watchfulness in their eyes. Playing the game as he did, Hengriff never went anywhere without bodyguards.

Weary of the demands of court, the Khan withdrew to a small side chamber. The milling crowd of supplicants, lackeys, and sycophants bowed as he left.

The room he entered was lit by a single oil lamp; otherwise, it was dark as a crypt. Sahim shrugged off his heavy court robes, letting them fall to the floor, and scratched his sides. His ribs had been itching for an hour, but he could hardly sit on the throne of Khur and scratch like a mongrel dog. With more care he removed the crown of Khur and set it on a table, then applied his fingernails to his itching head.

As he poured himself a libation from an urn, something stirred in the room's darkest corner. Sahim didn't bother to look up. That distinctive, vaguely unpleasant odor could belong to only one person.

"Come forward. Don't skulk in the corner like a rat," he said, and drained his goblet.

A hunched figure limped toward the light. The figure was wrapped in a bulky brown robe whose deep hood hid its features completely. Long white fingers, the knuckles prominent, showed briefly before they vanished into the copious sleeves. Sahim eyed the ragged robes and shook his head.

"Don't you feel stifled in that garb, Faeterus?"

"On the contrary, Mighty One. I find it chilly here." The voice was dry, hoarse, and whispery with extreme age. "I first came to Khur for its climate, you know."

"And when was that, snow-for-blood?"

"Long before your time, Great Khan. Long before."

Sahim snorted. Even he, born and bred to the climate, thought it oppressive. This shuffling mage had been his hireling for a year, and Sahim still found it absurd that anyone could bear to go about so heavily dressed.

He poured another draft of wine. "You heard the audience?" The ancient nodded, a rustling movement of the layered hood. "So, what say you to Lord Hengriff's notion? Pretty justice, don't you think?"

Faeterus shifted from side to side, as though his crippled legs pained him. "Justice and money cannot exist together, Great Khan. Better to let the Sons of the Crimson Vulture wash their hands in elven blood. When all the *laddad* are dead, you can claim their treasure without further ado."

The golden goblet halted an inch from Sahim's lips. His black brows lifted. "What? You propose I exterminate your own people, the most ancient race in the world?"

A rasping sound, either laugh or cough, issued from the depths of the hood. "They are not my people. I am a race of one."

"Well, whatever you are, for now you're mine, bought and paid for. And I have a task for you: find out who attacked the elf queen, and why. Whether it's Minok and his Torghanists or Hengriff and Nerakan steel, I want to know." He set down his empty cup. "Is that clear?"

"Perfectly, Mighty One."

The wine had warmed Sahim's blood. Even in his sleeveless shift, he found the chamber too hot, too close. The smell emanating from his hired sorcerer was stronger now, musty and sour like the odor of the city's vast underground cistern where he lived. Sahim fought down a quick wave of nausea. A living body shouldn't smell like that. Faeterus stank not of flesh, but of old bones slowly disintegrating.

There was a knock on the chamber door. The muffled voice of a court lackey called for permission to enter. Even as Sahim replied, Faeterus faded into the shadows again.

The lackey delivered his news and departed quickly, knowing the word he brought would not be welcome. Minok had managed to evade the guards.

Sahim stepped into the elaborate puddle of his court robes. As he began to dress, he realized Faeterus had gone.

The room had another door, opposite the one Sahim and the lackey had used, but it was always kept locked. Of course, such impediments meant nothing to Faeterus. Locked doors, thick walls, deep chasms—nothing hindered him. He went where he willed.

Perhaps he should give Faeterus the task of silencing Minok, Sahim reflected as he settled the crown upon his head again. They both seemed to possess a talent for disappearing into thin air.

*   *   *   *   *

A blare of brass cornets heralded the arrival of the army of the elven nations. Although small advance parties had been in camp for a day, Lord Taranath and the main body now had been sighted. They were mustering at Khurinost's western edge, where the Speaker waited to welcome them home. A mere shadow of the hosts that once defended Qualinost and guarded the glades of the Speaker of the Stars, the entire army comprised thirty thousand warriors, all mounted. They did not always fight on horseback, but the survival of this slender force depended on mobility; there was no place for slower infantry. The soldiers came from every branch of elven society, from lifelong warriors of Silvanesti's House Protector to cunning Wilder elves from the forests of Qualinesti.

Dust-caked from their long, heartbreaking journey, the column of mounted elves slowed to a halt when the lead riders spotted the delegation arrayed to greet them. The Speaker, flanked by the Lioness on his right and Lord Morillon Ambrodel on his left, stood at the head of a mixed band of Qualinesti and Silvanesti. Behind them were the eight buglers who contributed the fanfare. Everyone squinted against the terrific glare, despite the sunshade Planchet had erected over the group.

The army had adopted desert wear over armor; the rays of the sun could cook flesh inside metal in a few hours. Foremost of the warriors was an unusually tall elf wearing a Khurish sun hat. Reining up, he pulled off his gauntlets and hailed the Speaker.

"Greetings to you, Lord Taranath." Gilthas extended a hand.

After clasping hands with his liege, the warrior looked beyond the Speaker to the Lioness. "General, I present the Army of the Elven Nations! You are once more in command," he said.

"Well done, Taran," she said warmly. "How was the journey up the coast?"

"Damned hot. And not only from the sun."

"Casualties?"

"Twenty-nine killed. Forty-four wounded."

"So many?" Gilthas asked. "To what cause?"

"The usual ones, sire: heat, thirst, dysentery, poisonous bites, and madness, all of which the desert provides in abundance. And one other travail." Taranath looked grave. "From the Cape of Kenderseen we were dogged for two days by nomads, who sniped at us from the dunes. They were armed with crossbows."

Desert tribesmen usually carried short recurved bows, lacking the materials and skill to make crossbows. Taranath's news caused the Speaker's entourage to shift and mutter among themselves.

"Where would nomads get crossbows?" asked Lord Morillon.

"You know where," the Lioness hissed. "Neraka!"

"There's no proof—"

"Give me three days and I'll bring you the proof—nomads and their bows!" she snapped, interrupting the noble.

None doubted that any nomads the Lioness brought would be dead upon arrival. Although several councilors, including Morillon, were made uncomfortable by her martial fervor, others obviously were not.

Still, the blazing sands were no place to debate policy. Gilthas ended the discussion by saying, "General Taranath, your Speaker and your people welcome you home. Lady Kerianseray will see you later with new orders. Maintain your normal patrols. The rest of your warriors may stand down. Food and drink await all."

Taranath saluted and signaled the column forward. With flankers and scouts on either side, the column extended a mile. It took some time for all the tired, discouraged warriors to file past him, but Gilthas remained where he was, welcoming every rider home. His gesture touched the warriors deeply. Though sweat began to stain his sky-blue robe, and the heavy circlet on his brow bore down hard on his matted hair, Gilthas never faltered, even when some around him swayed on their feet, dizzy from the heat. Each approaching warrior sat a little straighter and held his head a little higher when he saw the Speaker of the Sun and Stars, standing with great dignity to greet them.

His advisors chafed at the delay. Even the Lioness, proud though she was of her army, felt he was wasting precious time with this display. But not until the last blistered scout had entered the tent city did Gilthas depart. He turned and walked into the dust cloud raised by the passing riders. Kerian spoke again of the need to capture nomads, to obtain proof that their attacks were sponsored by Neraka. This rekindled the argument among Gilthas's entourage.

"The situation is most delicate," Morillon insisted. "We have the Khan's permission to be here, but if we go about abusing his subjects, we could lose our last safe haven!"

"You're the one who's delicate!" The Lioness coughed against the spreading plume of grit. "Look what happened yesterday—my captain and I set upon in broad daylight! You call this place safe?"

"A few firebrands. Regrettable, certainly, but—"

Kerian whirled on him. "Regrettable! Zealots lust for our blood and you call it regrettable!"

"Calm yourselves," the Speaker said. He did not raise his voice, but it was a command nonetheless. "The best path lies somewhere between the two extremes. We must take care to keep Sahim-Khan friendly, or at least neutral, toward us, but we cannot allow our people to be sniped at and murdered piecemeal." He halted at the edge of the hodgepodge of tents, adding, "We need alternatives, to this place and to the Khan's sufferance."

His glance at his wife was significant, reminding her of her upcoming mission, to conduct the archivist Favaronas and a small party of scholars to the Valley of the Blue Sands. Kerian was not altogether unhappy with the task. She still felt it nothing more than a kender's errand, pointless and time-wasting, but at least she would be out doing *something*. Court life wore on her nerves; added to this now were the convoluted intrigues Gilthas found necessary to deal with the human khan. Better to broil in the desert wastes than languish in Khurinost, strangled by protocol and hamstrung by tortuous diplomacy. The journey at least would provide an opportunity for information-gathering.

As the royal party moved through the narrow lanes, they passed tents with their flaps pinned back to admit any slight breezes. The wire-grass ceiling that covered the passage kept the sun's broiling light at bay, yet the very closeness of the area served to stifle breath. Despite this discomfort, Gilthas's steps slowed, awed anew by the ingenuity of his people.

Tents here had been turned over to workshops, where artisans used age-old skills to fashion metal and stone into objects not only useful but beautiful. Lacking large furnaces and forges, the elves were forced to buy raw materials in the city's souks. Ingots of crude brass were hammered thin as parchment, to be formed into everything from graceful urns to tiny, delicate earrings. In one shop, bales of silver wire were tightly wound into the bracelets and torques of which Khurs were so fond. One emaciated elf, seated with legs splayed wide on a coarse jute rug, polished a basket of semiprecious stones with a grinding wheel. It was the lapidary's ingenuity that caught the Speaker's attention. His tent's dim interior was brightened by sunlight, brought in by angled mirrors, and his wheel was attached to a small palm frond fan; as the elf toiled, the wheel's energy also served to cool his brow.

When the Speaker halted, he and his party interrupted the light that fell upon the lapidary's busy hands. The thin elf looked up, and when he saw his visitor, his lined face went slack in shock. He would've hurried to his feet, but the Speaker's raised hand and gentle voice kept him seated. Gilthas moved closer, reaching into the basket of stones and lifting a particularly beautiful amethyst. The deep purple gem was an inch square, and faceted with undeniable skill, despite the crude tools the lapidary was forced to use.

He made to return the stone to the basket. The lapidary begged him to keep it. Gilthas would've declined, not wishing to decrease the fellow's income, but Kerian whispered, "Take it, Gil. You'll disappoint him otherwise."

The old elf's eyes shone with pride as his Speaker thanked him most kindly for the gift. Gilthas's own eyes were suspiciously bright as he took his leave. Whenever he despaired of the task he faced, he would think of this poor, kind lapidary. What king dared fail such a people as these?

From outside the lapidary's rude shelter, Lord Morillon's prosaic voice ended the poignant interlude. "Before we came, the Khurs did not know how to facet a gem. Now, square-cut stones are popular in all the souks," he said.

"Well, that makes the journey here worthwhile," was Kerian's acid reply.

Gilthas said nothing. Fingers clenched around the amethyst gem, he moved on.

The winding route took him past scores of tents. Some were scarcely larger than the bedroll of their single occupant; others encompassed rooms, corridors, and antechambers laid out in considerable complexity. Everyone was hard at work. There was no place for sloth in Khurinost. Every scrap of food and clothing, every mouthful of water, must be purchased from wily traders.

Again, where one elf—Gilthas this time—saw triumph over adversity and courage in the face of privation, another saw only heartbreak. The Lioness could hardly bear this slow progression through the tent city. The pain that welled within her heart as she looked upon her people's plight was almost unendurable. Increasingly, she had been dealing with these strong emotions by growing angry. And of late, much of her anger was directed not only at her husband for not doing enough or at the invaders that had driven her people to these straits, but at *herself*, at her failure to best the bull-men and to convince her husband to support another foray against them.

"What about the documents I brought back from the city?" she asked.

Her whisper was harsh, louder than Gilthas would've liked. With a lowering of his eyes, he directed her to speak more discreetly.

"Favaronas has had them all day. We dine with him tonight to hear what he has made of them."

Gilthas saw that Lord Morillon, who did not know the reason behind the Lioness's visit to the Temple of Elir-Sana, was watching them closely. The noble had tried to pry the truth of that errand from Gilthas earlier, but without success. It wasn't that Gilthas didn't trust Morillon. He simply knew that in matters such as this, where lives hung in the balance, the fewer who knew his plans, the better.

The sun was low, nearly touching the western dunes, by the time the group arrived at the royal tent complex in the center of camp. The fiery sphere had changed from white-hot to blood-red, tinting the sky the color of polished copper. A rare breeze rolled in from the sea. It swept away the cloud of sand that had been raised by the returning army, as well as the perpetual fog of smoke which hung over Khurinost. Gilthas paused to inhale the refreshing sea air.

"If that wind would blow this time every day, I could happily stay here." Alarm showed on every face, and Gilthas couldn't help but smile. "Don't worry: we all know how rarely that wind rises."

The councilors chuckled at their Speaker's humor. The Lioness did not. Politely, she asked leave to depart, citing her need to go to her warriors. Gilthas assented, telling her he looked forward to their dinner together this evening.

Soon, the Lioness was back among her exhausted soldiers. They lived communally in large tents, clustered around the big stone-walled corrals that dotted the elven camp. Kerian busied herself choosing the five hundred who would make the journey north with her. She took hardy scouts and skillful riders rather than the best fighters. She told them little about the mission, the need for circumspection as strongly ingrained in her as in her husband. It wasn't only fear of Khurish treachery that prompted the Lioness's caution. Word of what Gilthas hoped to find could easily cause a stampede of desperate elves determined to escape Khurinost for the supposed haven of the fabled valley of mist and fog.

Taranath and her other officers were naturally curious. They speculated that the Lioness planned to cause trouble for the Knights of Neraka, whose homeland lay just on the other side of the mountains to which they were headed.

She only wished that were the case. Much as she hated the minotaurs, Kerian reserved a special dark place in her heart for the Knights and their hirelings. They were the enemies of her blood, and she knew how to fight them.

The attempt to invade Silvanesti had been a grave mistake: she knew that now. Each day that passed with elven lands in the foul grip of their oppressors was pure torment to her, and her impatience had caused the debacle in the south. Wars, she was learning, were not won by dash and fury. The Lioness was practicing patience.

Even so, Gilthas's fantasies about Inath-Wakenti were futile. Even if the valley existed and was habitable, it wasn't their home, she thought. The sacred lands of Silvanos and

Kith-Kanan were where the elven race belonged, and nowhere else. The Lioness felt that a better use of her fighting strength would be to mount small raids into the elven homeland, ambushing minotaur patrols, burning their depots, demolishing their bridges, and assassinating their leaders. By such methods she had all but retaken the Qualinesti countryside from the Knights of Neraka, although she was never strong enough to challenge their control of Qualinost, nor to attempt conclusions with the dragon Beryl.

To her curious officers she said, "The Speaker has a special purpose in sending us north. Fighting is not part of the plan. We'll be escorting"—she groped for the proper word—"librarians from the royal archives."

The warriors were uniformly startled. "Why send you, General? Any competent troop leader could handle such a simple mission," asked Taranath.

"I go because my Speaker commands it."

They nodded, acknowledging their obedience to their king. Kerian asked Taranath to tell her of the nomad attacks he'd suffered on the way back to Khuri-Khan.

He and the rest of the army had reached the coast without any problems, he said, thanks to the delaying action staged by the Lioness and her archers. The Qualinesti warrior had hoped his commander would explain how she survived, but she did not. He was too loyal and well-trained to question her about what had happened.

As the column moved up the coast, they encountered groups of nomads gathering dates and pine nuts from coastal groves. The nomads were driving their rangy cattle and goats to watering holes along the ancient seaside trail used by such herders for centuries. They gave the armed elves a wide berth, and there were no confrontations.

On the elves' second day riding up the coast, they noticed mounted humans observing them. Taranath hadn't paid them much attention at first because they were only a few and they were in front of the column, not behind. He logically assumed any pursuit from the Silvanesti border would appear from behind.

The first attack came when night fell. Heavy crossbow bolts flickered out of the high dunes on the elves' right. A few riders and horses were hit. Taranath sent out a patrol. They found no one, but there were plain signs in the sand that half a dozen men with horses had hidden in the dunes.

This pattern continued through the night and into the following days. Angered by the sniping, Taranath sent more and more flankers to rout out the crossbowmen. All to no avail. It was like chasing smoke. The snipers repeatedly fell back, loosing quarrels at the flankers.

"If their aim had been better, they could have emptied many saddles," Taranath said grimly. "As it is, their aim was too high."

The Lioness nodded. It was common for novice crossbowmen to overshoot a target. A crossbow lofted its missiles in an arc, unlike the flat flight of an arrow loosed from a bow. Obviously, the nomads weren't accustomed to the weapon.

The attacks ended only when the elves came in sight of Khuri-Khan. The elves never got close to the snipers, and their own archers never sighted a target long enough to draw a bead.

"One last thing, General," Taranath said. "Our foes seemed to be nomads by the way they knew and used the desert, but I believe they came from Khuri-Khan. The tracks from the ambush sites led north, always north; the last sets came directly to the city."

That made sense to Kerian. The men who had jumped her and Hytanthas on the Temple Walk were nomads, too, perhaps of the same band who'd harassed Taranath's column. They obviously were operating out of Khuri-Khan, but why? Nomads regarded cities and their diverse inhabitants with the same suspicion they felt for foreigners like the elves; and Khuri-Khan, as the largest Khurish city, was considered particularly vice-ridden.

The dinner hour was approaching. Kerian left her loyal officers to return to the Speaker's tent, and to attend her dinner with Gilthas and his archivist. Departing the officers' tent, she made a slight detour to visit Eagle Eye in his pen. The griffon had to be confined away from the horses; his presence unnerved them.

Eagle Eye stood like a statue by his feeding post. His head was hooded like a hunting falcon's, covered by green felt. This was the best way to keep him peaceful. When agitated, Eagle Eye uttered his shrill, gargling cry, and animals for miles around went into a panic.

Speaking softly to the creature, Kerian loosened the drawstrings and removed his hood. The griffon's golden eyes, each as big as a king's goblet, studied her intently.

"How are you, my friend?" she said. "Hungry? Of course you are."

She went to the far side of the pen, to a darkly stained wooden cask. It smelled strongly of old blood. She pulled out a sheep haunch, none too fresh, just the way the griffon liked it. The scent of blood reached Eagle Eye and he parted his beak, allowing his rod-like tongue to taste the air. His leonine tail twitched back and forth. He chuckled impatiently.

"Coming, coming," she said, amused.

She skewered the haunch on the hook hanging from the top of the feeding post. Eagle Eye waited until she'd stepped clear, then shuffled forward a few steps. He sank his hooked beak into the meat, ripping out a fist-sized bite, which he bolted down without swallowing. Many of her comrades couldn't bear to watch the griffon eat. Kerian found the process edifying.

In short order the metal hook had been thoroughly cleaned. The griffon flared his wings, bobbing his head in appreciation. She gave his feathered neck an affectionate pat, and he allowed her to hood him again. She bid him good night.

Twilight had fallen. The great vault of sky over Khurinost and the Khurish capital was purple, streaked on the western horizon with scarlet and rose pink. Here in the army's camp, there were few sunshades to block the view. Kerianseray lingered a moment, savoring the great expanse of sky and the cooling air that came with sunset.

Something flickered overhead. Birds were scarce in the desert, and she watched the movement curiously. Its shape and flight pattern seemed odd. After a moment, she recognized the darting flight of a bat. Strange. She hadn't seen one of the creatures since leaving the woodlands of Qualinesti.

It fluttered by, maybe twenty feet above her head. The flapping of its soft wings was faint but distinct, as was the chittering sound it made, like the squeak of leather rubbing against glass. Then it was gone, darting away among the low canvas roofs and rising smoke plumes of the tent city.

Kerian looked down and discovered she was gripping the hilt of her sword. She didn't know why, but the bat had alarmed her. Her heart was racing.

Lowering her gaze further, she saw something dark littering the sand beneath her feet. She knelt. The path was strewn with green leaves. Ash leaves. Yet, no such trees grew within three hundred miles of Khuri-Khan. More bizarre still, the leaves were green and supple.

* * * * *

Dinner with the Speaker of the Sun and Stars was an austere affair, at least as far as the menu went. Consigned to the magnificent past were banquets of twelve courses. Gone were dishes such as crystallized dew collected from the royal rose gardens, airy pastries, and delicate seasonings. Not only were such things out of reach, but the monarch of the elven nations did not condone pretentious luxuries.

Seated at a low, round table were the Speaker, Kerianseray, the senior surviving archivist of Qualinost, Favaronas Millanandor, and a Silvanesti cartographer named Sithelbathan, formerly personal mapmaker to Queen Mother Alhana Starbreeze. Attending the diners was Planchet, an amphora of wine in his hand and a slender dagger tucked into his sash.

Dinner consisted of fish, rice, roasted pine nuts, and an oily paste popular in Khur. Known as *feza*, it was a puree of seven vegetables, mixed with nut oil and garlic. On the table were clay pots containing Khurish stick bread, stiff rods of dough baked by sunlight until they were dark brown and nearly as hard as wood. Next to the Speaker's plate rested a white pottery pot and a tiny, matching cup. The pot contained *kefre*, the strong black beverage so beloved by Khurs. Gilthas was one of the few elves who had acquired a taste for it, and the only one who drank the bitter brew without the addition of sugar, cinnamon, or other flavorings.

"Ah, for some decent fruit," said Sithelbathan, eyeing his half-eaten fish. Khurish waters yielded many kinds of fish, all bony and strongly flavored.

Gilthas had finished his own small servings and was pouring himself a cup of kefre. "There are dates and figs for dessert," he said. "I'll have them brought in if you like."

The cartographer politely declined. He'd eaten enough of both to last a lifetime.

Small talk persisted a while, until the Lioness broached the subject that had brought them all together.

"So, Master Cartographer, what of this valley?"

Sithelbathan pushed his plate away. "There is undoubtedly a valley at the location on the Speaker's map, lady," he said.

Gilthas asked Favaronas, "The temple annals brought back by Lady Kerianseray—do they offer useful information?"

The archivist leaned back, clasping his hands across his belly. It was a rather prominent belly, for an elf, testimony to his habit of drinking the local beer and to his lavish eating habits. Unlike his choosy colleague, Favaronas had cleaned his plate and now munched on stick bread dipped in *feza*.

"Perhaps, Great Speaker," the archivist said, after swallowing. "They relate a tangled tale, full of allegory and legend. As a modern scholar, I hesitate to pass along such fables."

Making his rounds, Planchet leaned in, refilling the archivist's cup yet again. Favaronas thanked him, and lifted the cup to drink.

Tartly, Kerian said, "You're not here for the hospitality. Tell us what, if anything, you've learned."

Gilthas reproached her with a look, and she subsided, taking a stick of bread and biting into it with a snap. The Speaker regarded the archivist expectantly.

Favaronas said, "According to the temple chronicles, Inath-Wakenti was the first place on Krynn where the gods set foot in corporeal form. It became a kind of neutral retreat, where they could stand on solid soil and enjoy the world they had created. To keep their haven free of internecine strife, they agreed none were allowed to speak within its confines. Hence, the Vale of Silence.

"Whether that is true . . ." He finished the last bite of his bread, and shrugged. "But I can confirm that the area in question was part of the Silvanesti realm, prior to the First Cataclysm. Sithelbathan said the territory was part of a large grant of land given by Silvanos Goldeneye, first Speaker of the Stars, to his general and comrade Balif. It was mostly desert in those days, too. The plain south of the desert was infested with fierce nomadic human tribes, who were gradually driven out by Balif's legions. The furthest outpost of the elven kingdom was in or near the Vale of Silence, at a place called Teth-Balif—Balif's Gate."

"Fascinating," the Lioness drawled.

"Yes indeed!" her husband agreed, overlooking her ironic tone. "It may be that we have a legal claim on the Inath-Wakenti. If we could find remnants of Balif's stronghold, that would bolster our case!"

"This was all five thousand years ago," she said. "If anything remains, it would be rubble. I doubt Sahim-Khan will cede us land on the basis of a few ancient stones."

The diners debated the issue as the plates were cleared, and the dessert course was served. Favaronas helped himself to slices of fresh fig, licking the sticky juice from his fingers. Sithelbathan regarded his colleague with fastidious disapproval.

"There is one cautionary tale about the Vale," Favaronas said, now taking a handful of dates. "According to the priestesses of Elir-Sana, a powerful wizard was exiled there early in Speaker Sithas's reign. The temple records call him Wethdika."

Sithelbathan shook his head. "Barbarous name. Doesn't sound like any language I've ever heard."

Favaronas spat a date seed into his hand. "I am certain it is a corruption of Vedvedsica."

The Speaker, Planchet, and Sithelbathan looked at the archivist with new respect. Kerian, lacking their formal education, didn't recognize the name. Favaronas explained its significance.

"Vedvedsica was one of the earliest great mages of Silvanesti. In the beginning, he was an ally of the Speaker, and a vassal of Balif, but he committed a crime and was banished from the realm."

Balif was a name Kerian knew. He had been a great warrior, and a celebrated general. "What crime?" she asked.

Gilthas said, "No one knows. It was so awful, Speaker Sithas proscribed any mention of it in the annals of his reign. It fell to Balif to arrest the mage and consign him to a prison on the remote frontier."

"And in return, the vile sorcerer contrived his lord's ruin," Sithelbathan said grimly. "Balif, a fine, brave elf, was transformed into a twisted, shrunken, hideous creature. He vanished soon after, unable to dwell in Silvanesti ever again."

Silence fell. The long-ago fate of the elf general had a painful relevance for those around the table. Were they not also banished from their homelands? Perhaps they, too, might never be able to dwell there again.

The hour was late, the tent city quiet. The night wind

set the roof of the Speaker's tent to shivering, and the sound suddenly seemed an extra presence at the table. Unconsciously, Kerian edged closer to Gilthas. Ignoring protocol, he slipped an arm around her waist.

" 'Even the bones of wizards turn to dust,' " Favaronas muttered.

The quote from the bard Sevastithanas broke the gloomy moment. Planchet moved to refill their cups, and Favaronas recounted the later history of the Inath-Wakenti.

A kingpriest of Istar had received a prophecy, warning of a coming disaster. The only place on the entire continent that would not be changed by the catastrophe was the Valley of the Blue Sands, since where the gods once walked, nature held no sway. The Kingpriest sent an expedition to the valley; it was never heard from again. Later, dwarf prospectors from Thoradin found the valley and set up a mining operation. The project yielded rich placer deposits of silver, but was so bedeviled by accidents and serious injuries that the miners abandoned it after less than a year. During the bakali breeding migration in the days of the old Ergoth Empire, a band of human tribesmen stumbled on the valley and escaped marauding lizard-men by hiding there. For a time the humans flourished, sending trading parties to Istar and Silvanesti, but after a few years the trade diminished, then died out altogether.

The last mention of the valley in the temple archives was from a Knight of Solamnia who wandered through after the Cataclysm. He reported the valley untouched by the upheaval.

"And?" the Lioness prompted, when Favaronas paused to take a drink.

And nothing, lady," he replied, shrugging one shoulder. "That's the only information contained in that entry."

Since that time, he told them, the rise of the desert nomads had choked off contact with the Vale of Silence. Nomads who lived in the region regarded it as a forbidden place, while the rest of the tribes gradually forgot about it or, like the city-dwelling Khurs, relegated it to the realm of fable.

The oil lamps on the low table sputtered as their fuel ran low. Favaronas had finished his story, but added a final warning: "The temple annals are couched in the most vague and circuitous terms, Great Speaker, and required much interpolation and extrapolation on my part."

Gilthas was nodding thoughtfully. Kerian leaned close and nudged his cheek with her nose. "Well?" she said. "Do I go, or no?"

He smiled in his gentle, slightly sad way. "Of course. Master Favaronas, too. Our people must have a sanctuary. The Inath-Wakenti may be the place."

The archivist already had agreed to the journey, but when the Speaker asked Sithelbathan if he would like to go as well, the Silvanesti mapmaker quickly declined.

"Afraid of ghosts?" the Lioness teased.

The spare, neatly dressed elf drew his robe close around his neck. "Yes, lady," he said. "I am."

4

Water in a stone jug stays cool, even in the heat of day. If the jug is carved properly, of fine-grained soapstone with thick walls at the top and thinner walls near the bottom, water inside will stay as cool as the moment it was drawn from the well. Cool water is the first requirement for good bread. Not an easy requirement to meet in a desert. The east wind which rolled in from the distant sea hit the Pillars of Heaven (known to foreigners as the Khalkist Mountains) and dumped its snow on the peaks and its rain on the lower slopes. Purged of moisture, the wind then spread across the western desert, taking its dry heat to every corner of the land. Between the heat, blown sand, and flies, finding cool water and making bread for the family was no chore for the faint of heart.

Adala Fahim lifted the heavy soapstone jug and poured its contents into a brass bowl. Quickly, she stirred the water into the dry mixture of flour, salt, and soda. She never measured, except by eye. Twelve circuits of the wide, flat bowl with a wooden paddle and the dough was done. A shallow groove had been worn into the metal where her spoon circled. For thirty-two years she'd made bread in exactly the same way. For thirty-two years it had come out right, despite wind, weather, or war.

She spat on the iron griddle to test its temperature. At the right heat, a water drop danced in circles, growing smaller with every circuit until it vanished. When the griddle was ready, she poured a dollop of oil onto it. The oil ran to the edges, sheening the black surface. In the bowl, the dough was puffed up and bubbling from the soda. She tore off a piece, rolled it into a ball between her smooth brown palms, and laid it on the griddle. Sizzling, it flattened into a small round loaf.

Black shadows fell over Adala, cutting off the distant view of the gray mountains, but she didn't look up. The first loaf was the most important. How it baked told her whether the fire needed to be hotter or cooler.

The three men standing over her were nomads in the prime of life, men of the Weya-Lu tribe. Although none had gray eyes, they were of the Leaping Spider clan and Wapah's cousins.

"Wapah is back," said the one in the middle.

"I'll make an extra portion," Adala said, her attention still on the cooking loaf. She gave it a quick flip with her fingers. Other women used knives to turn their bread. Not Adala. One wrong stab and the frying dough would deflate; the loaf would be flat and tough as sandal leather.

"He has important news, Weyadan." Her title meant "Mother of the Weya-Lu." "Do you know who he was hired to guide from the city to the desert and back?"

She shrugged one shoulder, busy rolling a new ball of dough.

"Shobbat, son of Sahim Zacca-Khur!"

In quick succession, four new balls of dough hit the griddle, replacing the first, now done. "So the prince of Khur finally left the shaded halls of the city to visit the land of his ancestors. What is that to us?" she said.

"He went to the Oracle. The Hidden One."

The men were certain this news would bring Adala to her feet, dusting the flour from her hands. It did not. She removed the four freshly baked loaves from the griddle and put down four more.

SANCTUARY

"Weyadan, please," entreated the nomad. "You should hear what Wapah has to say!"

"And so I will. When the bread is done."

It took some time to cook forty loaves. Although the men shifted their feet impatiently once or twice, none complained.

When at last the baking was done, Adala left her fifth daughter, Chisi, to clean the bowl and griddle. Hitching up her black robes, the leader of the Weya-Lu left the shade of her tent and made for Wapah's dwelling across the stony ravine. It was just past noon, the hottest part of the day, and few nomads were moving about. Even the desert hounds the Weya-Lu were so adept at breeding were still, sleeping in whatever spots of shade they could find.

Adala entered Wapah's family tent and gave the customary greeting: "Those on High stand by us."

Wapah returned it. "And by you, Mother of the Weya-Lu."

He was seated facing the door. Other men of the clan formed a ring, their backs against the walls of the tent. Several of them had the gray eyes that stood out so boldly against swarthy faces and dark or tawny beards. Adala was the only woman present.

"I rejoice to see you," she said. "I hear you have a tale to tell."

"As grave as a plague, as loud as thunder. Take your ease."

She sat in the center of the male circle. As wife of the clan chief, Adala could not be touched by any man save her husband. Since Kasamir di Kyre had perished years before while fighting in the pay of the Knights of Neraka, she had become Weyadan, literally mother to everyone in the Weya-Lu tribe. She was just past her fortieth year, younger than some of her ostensible children.

Wapah began his tale. With the same patience she'd learned listening to her sons when they were toddlers,

Adala let the colorful torrent of words wash over her and focused on the important bits of information scattered throughout.

Prince Shobbat's men had come to the Grand Souks, looking for someone to guide their master on a journey through the desert. Wapah was selected because the gods knew him to be a humble man, a generous man, a man in whom the blood of endless generations of Weya-Lu flowed in a mighty, endless circle—

Adala frowned, closing her eyes to concentrate harder.

With no escort at all, Wapah and the Prince of Khur rode out of Khuri-Khan before dawn. They reached the Tear of Elir-Sana without incident. Although of no more use in the desert than a mewling babe, Shobbat insisted they press on without rest to reach his goal, the oracle of the high desert.

Wapah paused to sip buttered tea, and Bilath, Adala's brother by marriage and war chief of the Weya-Lu, asked, "The Hidden One? The keeper of bats?"

Wapah nodded solemnly. On his left, his cousin Etosh poured more tea into his crater.

They reached the oracle at night. No one in Wapah's memory had gone there, and he didn't know if the diviner still lived, but the ancient stone spires still stood, and the legendary bats flooded out when disturbed. Wapah, a righteous man, warned the prince he would not enter the sanctuary, so Shobbat went alone and stayed inside until nearly dawn.

Wapah was asleep between the horses when he heard a terrible scream. Rising valiantly, sword in hand, he braced himself to do battle against evil spirits. None appeared. Instead, Prince Shobbat stumbled out of the sanctuary, raving like a madman.

"Tell about his face!" Etosh urged him.

"The breath of the gods had fallen upon the prince," Wapah declaimed, spreading his arms wide, "stealing the manly color from his beard, brow, and hair! The stain was white as the scarves of the Khan's dancers!"

Adala looked down her long nose at him. "White is the color of light, of Eldin the Judge." This was the remote high god of the nomads, seldom spoken of and rarely invoked. "What evil can come from Eldin?"

A murmur went through the group, and Bilath said, "Then you believe it was a judgment, not a curse?"

Wapah did not wish to lose his audience in a theological discussion, so he continued quickly.

The tormented prince was not only ranting like one benighted, he was blind as well! He flailed his arms, crashing into the horses and Wapah. All the while he raved about trees growing in the desert, the coming of the elves, and how they would turn everything green unless stopped.

"I would like to see more green in this land," Adala commented, and the assembled men stared at her. "But not under the rule of foreigners."

Wapah had been forced to club Shobbat unconscious. After tying him onto his horse, the nomad started back to Khuri-Khan. When the prince awoke on the return journey, he was still crazed. Wapah questioned him, and Shobbat answered without guile, revealing everything, why he had come, what he'd hoped to gain, and what the oracle had said. But always, his talk returned to the elves and the danger they posed to Khur.

"He sought to depose his father," said Etosh, with a sage nod. "His madness is the judgment of the gods, punishment for plotting such blood betrayal!"

There was little love for Sahim-Khan among the Weya-Lu, but when sons conspired to murder their fathers, evil was truly loose in the world.

Wapah said it was not the prince's designs on the throne of Khur that consumed his disordered mind on the journey back to the city, but the oracle's revelation that the *laddad* might transform Khur into a green land and rule over it. Wapah's audience agreed with the maddened prince on that score. If that happened, the tribes of Khur would be lost. Everything they valued—families, traditions, loyalty to the gods—would be forfeit to foreign ways. Even the clean, beautiful emptiness of the land would be choked out by the vines and trees of the elves.

" 'If the elves find the Valley of the Blue Sands,' " Wapah said, quoting the prince, " 'then the people of Khur are lost!' "

Draining his crater of tea, Wapah was silent at last. His audience was thunderstruck. Even Adala had no comeback to this final revelation. Elves looking for the Valley of the Blue Sands? Why would they go there? No one went there. It was haunted by troubled, unholy spirits.

"You should have slit the Khur's throat," said Etosh, breaking the somber silence. "Left him in the desert to feed the vultures."

Several loud voices took issue with this statement. Such a betrayal of his charge would have brought ill luck down upon Wapah and his tribe. A Weya-Lu's word was a bond not only to the men to whom it had been given, but to Those on High as well.

For a time, they argued the merit of Wapah's decision to ferry the stricken prince back to Khur. As nothing useful emerged from their dispute, Adala finally cut them off.

"We must meet this storm and see if it is a true tempest or only the ravings of a sun-maddened prince," she said.

She stood. Extending her arm, she swept the circle, pointing to each man in turn. "We will go to the City by the Sea. We will see what the *laddad* are about. If they are quiet, and cleave to the will of the Khan, we will leave them in peace. But if they intend to invade the valley, we must stop them. The oracle said the *laddad* would not rule if they were kept from the Valley of the Blue Sands. By our blood, it is our duty to keep them out. The sacred land of Khur will endure."

She completed the circle, adding, "Your oaths on it, as men of Weya-Lu!"

Readily they swore, the burden of the oath light just now. No man present knew how heavy it might prove.

Messengers were sent out right away. Other tribes in the region would be told of this threat. If the elves moved toward the valley, it would mean war.

Some southern tribes freely raided elven caravans, picked off stray *laddad* riders, even attacked small camps. As a warrior people, they treated all strangers in their land thus. Over the years the elves had grown in number as more arrived in exile, and they showed no signs of leaving. Adala had even heard reports of elves in the Weya-Lu's ancestral city, Delphon. The city was a sinkhole of iniquity and vice (as all cities were), but it was the font of the Weya-Lu tribe. For foreigners—and not even human ones—to be there, contaminating the tombs and temples of the tribe's great ancestors, was a bitter draught to swallow. But as long as the *laddad* remained at Khuri-Khan and other cities, the nomads could ignore them. However, if Sahim-Khan allowed them to spread across the vastness of the open desert, then the people of the desert would rise up and proclaim a new khan.

And not the spoiled Shobbat; he was as wicked and godless as his father. A new dynasty must be established, a house of virtue and strength.

Such were Adala's thoughts as she crossed the blinding expanse of sand to her tent. Ducking under the flap, she flipped the sun veil back over her head and left such worldly concerns outside with the sun. Chisi had scoured the griddle and hung it from a tent pole to cool. The brass mixing bowl was rinsed clean.

With no more distracting thoughts of elves or cities or immoral monarchs, Adala dipped a hand in a basket of dried lentils. One, two, three handfuls clattered into the bowl. More water from the jug, to soak the stone-hard, brown seeds. Lentils went well with bread. She only hoped she had enough salt to season them properly.

*   *   *   *   *

Without fanfare, the Lioness led her small force out of Khurinost before sunrise.

If the Speaker's expensive map could be trusted, the Inath-Wakenti was more than two hundred miles away. The trip would take them across the High Plateau, some of the worst desert in Khur, with no wells, no oases, and no hospitable life for most of the way. According to Khurish records, rain had not fallen on the High Plateau in a hundred years, so every elf carried water, water, and more water. Spare arms and most armor were left behind, to allow the horses to bear a heavier burden of liquid. In consultation with Sithelbathan, Kerian had sketched out a route north by east, skirting the caravan trail to Kortal, which was rife with Nerakan spies. Each member of the expedition was provided with a copy of the map, so if he became separated from the main body, he would know where to go.

An experienced professional, Kerian completed her own preparations for the journey fairly quickly. This left her a few precious hours to spend as Gilthas's wife and not as the commander of his army. She puzzled anew over the seeming contradiction of her husband and king. He was both the gentlest person she'd ever known, and the toughest. Gilthas could give his last crust of bread to a hungry person in the street, then in the next breath, sentence a malefactor to death. He did not posture or preen as Speaker of the Sun and Stars, but honestly cared for every soul under his rule and for the long-range welfare of his realm.

Neither of them spoke of the task Kerian faced or her lack of faith in its purpose. Clad only in candlelight, they sat on their bed, facing each other, heads bowed, her forehead resting on her husband's shoulder.

Gilthas breathed deeply, inhaling the scent of her, striving to lock the memory firmly in his heart. Her unbound hair cascaded over them both. The feel of it curling against his shoulders was one of the sweetest sensations he had ever known.

"Will you take Eagle Eye?" he asked quietly.

She shook her head. The motion caused her hair to sweep slowly across his upper back. Gilthas shivered. "No, you know he frightens the horses. They will be nervous enough. And he drinks more water than a dragon."

Kerian felt her husband smile against her shoulder. "I have a salve for you," he said. "The apothecary Redinivis brought it. He said it will keep you from getting sunburned."

"And how many gallons of this salve are we supposed to carry with us?"

The smile became a low chuckle. "The stone jar he gave me is small enough to fit in the palm of your hand." She snorted, and Gilthas added, his voice pitched higher to mimic the apothecary, "However, to be efficacious, the balm must be applied quite liberally."

Husband and wife laughed together. Amusement grew into something deeper. This was their last night together for some time, and they made the most of it.

Before dawn, Kerian rose and dressed without disturbing her husband. It wasn't until she was in the outer room, ready to depart, that Gilthas appeared.

"Weren't you going to say goodbye?" he asked.

The sight of him thus, clad in a threadbare gown, long hair awry, brought an unexpected rush of tenderness, but she couldn't allow herself to give in to her feelings. She was departing on a risky mission. Her life and, more importantly, the lives of those she led, required all the skill and cunning of the Lioness, not the wifely sentiments of Kerianseray.

Striving for lightness, she said, "Think of your dignity, Gil! Should the Speaker of the Sun and Stars stand around outside, mooning like a lovesick maiden bidding goodbye to her swain?"

Matching her teasing tone, he replied, "I am Speaker. I'm only coddled like a maiden."

She grinned. They embraced, but too soon for Gilthas she released him and stepped back. A flash of a smile, and in the next heartbeat she was gone, out into the predawn stillness. For a long time, Gilthas remained where he was, standing, staring after her.

The west wind picked up as the column of riders left the tent-town. Robed and scarved against the flying sand, the elves rode in silence, unaccompanied by flying banners or flourishing pipers. Not like the old days, when the warriors of Silvanesti never stirred out of their capital city without a band of pipers, one thousand of their land's noblest youths. Or the army of Qualinesti, who marched and rode to the beat of massed drums, the golden sun standard of Kith-Kanan borne before them. No, the contingent of the exiles' army departed quietly, their horses' hooves making little noise in the soft, yielding sand.

Despite the discretion, their departure did not escape notice. In the saddle between two high dunes, a solitary figure lay prone, covered from nose to toes in a hooded robe the same color as the sea of sand. His eyesight was sharp as a falcon's. Neither distance nor the low light hampered him; he counted the double line of elven riders, and noted their course. Due north.

The spy slid backward through the sand until he was hidden from the elves by the intervening dune. Rising, he raced down the wind-shaped hill. At the bottom, two mounted men waited, one of them holding the reins of his horse.

He vaulted onto his pony. Snatching the reins, he hissed, "The *laddad* are going north! Five hundred, with sword and bow!"

The youngest of the three pulled his horse around in a half-circle until it faced west. "I ride to my chief!" he said. "The Tondoon will know of this!"

The watcher spoke to the third, older man. "I will take word to the Mikku tribe. Tell the Weyadan the warning was true: the foreigners are on the move."

The gray-eyed nomad nodded grimly. "By nightfall every tribe from the mountains to the sea will know the *laddad* are loose!"

They galloped away, each taking his own direction. Before they were out of sight of each other, the constant wind had erased their tracks from the sand.

The army of elves rode on. Dawn broke, and the sun quickly purged the chill of night. An hour after dawn the temperature was already hotter than ever was felt in Silvanesti. It would only increase.

Nomads did not travel by day unless sorely pressed. Like the serpents, lizards, and spiders of the desert, they preferred to lie still during the day and go out by night. Elves, accustomed to working by day, continued this habit even when the desert sun bore down full strength. This led to a new saying among nomads: Only fools, vultures, and *laddad* go abroad by day.

The Lioness rode at the head of the column, feeling the sweat run down inside her breastplate and pool in the small of her back. Her face remained dry. As soon as a bead of sweat formed on her forehead or neck, the insatiably thirsty air sucked it away.

She looked back over the elves following her and was struck by how unfamiliar they were—not just Gilthas's scholars, Favaronas and his two assistants—but the warriors, too. So many of her old comrades had fallen during the last days of Qualinost, the march into exile, and the brutal crossing of the Plains of Dust. Not all the losses were hard to take. Senator Palthainon, a slippery politician who made his name undermining Gilthas's policies, had vanished during the flight from Qualinesti. Whether dead or captured by Samuval's bandits, no one knew, but the Lioness felt either a suitable end for the troublesome rogue.

Someone in the column—a Kagonesti, by his accent— started to sing. Other riders took up the tune, a chorus of hoarse male voices. It was an old Wilder song, about being chased through the forest by unnamed enemies:

PAUL B. THOMPSON & TONYA C. COOK

Where I go I leave no trail, no trail,
But hang upon the sparrow's tail.
And fly as lightly as the wind, the wind,
For I was born of Wilder kin.

The words rang strange in this lifeless landscape, and after four verses the song died out. The air was too dry for singing anyway.

Flankers patrolled diligently ahead and behind the column, as well as a hundred yards on either side. An hour before noon, the scouts circled back to the main body for replacement. One rider did not appear. The Lioness halted the column and sent a pair of elves to find the missing rider. The pair did not return either.

She ordered the entire force to search for the missing. Spread out in a long double line, the elves descended the side of a north-facing dune. The tracks of the pair the Lioness had sent were still visible at the foot of the dune. Halfway up the next one, elves on the left side of the formation raised an alarm. Someone was moving atop the dune!

Swords sprouted from the line. Climbing through the heavy sand was hard work, and they labored uphill with horses gasping from the heat and effort. Within twenty yards of the crest, a dozen darkly wrapped figures popped up, bows in hand.

The Lioness shouted a warning as arrows daubed with red paint hissed toward her startled troops. One struck low on her breastplate and glanced off. She barked a command, and her own archers loosed into the line of snipers. One fell. The rest responded with more arrows, this time aimed low, at the elves' horses.

"Get those snakes!" the Lioness cried. On the right, two score riders swept forward, swords held high. The concealed bowmen couldn't rise up high enough to aim at them without exposing themselves to the elf archers. With elven arrows arcing over their heads, the Lioness and the bulk of the elves spurred hard up the hill. Just as they cleared the top, those on the right reached the flat ridge at the dune's crest and charged the enemy. There were only eleven: nine bow-armed nomads and two others minding their horses at the base of the dune. Faced on two sides by the foe, the nomads quit, racing for their ponies. Several were ridden down and sabered before the Lioness called for prisoners. The killing ceased, but not a single nomad escaped.

Four prisoners were herded to the Lioness. Three others, wounded and unable to walk, were carried forward and dumped at her feet.

"Who are you men? What tribe? What clan?" she asked. She had expected nomad interference, but not so soon, not such a pointless ambush. With a shiver she recalled a similar attack at the priestess's temple.

The nomads were silent. One of them knelt by a wounded comrade and began to chant a muted prayer.

Again, more calmly, the Lioness posed her questions, promising to spare all if they would answer. Not one of the captured humans said a word.

"Why do you fight us?" the Lioness demanded. Her exhausted horse picked up her anger and snorted, prancing in a tight circle. "We're not your enemies. We're nomads now, too, driven from our homes and forced to wander this desert. Tell me, are you bandits, or have you been paid to fight us?"

Nothing. Two of the humans sat on the sand and hugged their knees, eyes still fixed on the ground. The third continued to pray under his breath. The fourth, trembling from exhaustion and a wound on his upper thigh, remained on his feet, staring defiantly at her.

The Lioness glared back, frustrated by their silence. She had no time for this.

She allowed herself only a moment of indecision before snapping, "Captain!"

A Kagonesti veteran saluted his commander. "Search them," she said. "Anything unusual, bring to me. Take their swords and break their bows and arrows. Leave them food and water for two days. Their horses go with us."

The standing nomad opened his mouth to protest. Without horses, they were doomed. They would never reach a water source before their own supply gave out.

"You have something to say?" she asked sternly, yet her eyes were hopeful. The bearded man firmed his lips and said nothing. Hope vanished.

"Very well. Carry out my orders, Captain."

All the nomads, living and dead, were searched. The only thing of interest the searchers found was the small leather bag that each man wore on a string around his neck. One pouch was brought to Kerian. It was very light, containing a fetish, no doubt. She loosened the neck and upended the bag. A black and orange creature fell out, landing on the neck of her horse.

"Spider!" yelled the elf warrior who'd brought the bag. He swatted at it with his gauntlet. With astonishing power for so small a creature, it sprang from the horse and landed, legs spread, on the soldier's cheek.

The elf screamed. One of his comrades yanked the palm-sized spider from his face and flung it to the ground. He stamped it with his iron-shod boot.

Tragically, the evil already had been done. Two fang marks showed clearly on the elf's cheek. From the holes, red streaks were spreading even as the Lioness watched. The stricken elf went rigid, his eyes and mouth wide in agony. The Lioness shouted for a healer. The elf began to tremble, then convulse. Despite his comrades' strong arms, he went down, dragging them with him.

"What can we do?" the Lioness yelled at the nomad.

He shrugged, his face hard. "Iron's the only cure for him now." He drew a finger across his throat.

She turned away from him in disgust, and dismounted. The elf's face was dreadful, his mouth stretched wide in a scream he could not vent, and his face mottled by the red streaks that mapped the lightning-fast flow of poison through his blood.

Kerian knelt beside him. With a tenderness few could imagine, she touched his cheek. His skin was cold. What had been living flesh now felt like marble. His eyes, blue irises lost in a bloody sea, shifted toward her slightly.

In the heat of pursuit, with Knights of Neraka or worse baying at her heels, she'd had to use the iron cure before. She loathed it. It was all they could do for the dying elf now, to spare him needless suffering, but she hated it nonetheless.

Her free hand still resting on his face, she ended the elf's torment. His gaze remained fixed on her, grew unfocused, then empty. Kerian closed his eyelids.

"His name was Nafarallun," said one of the elves holding him. "Born a Qualinesti."

The remaining leather pouches were pounded flat, unopened. Stone-faced, the nomads awaited the same fate.

"Go home, men of the Leaping Spider clan," the Lioness said tersely, looking down at them from horseback. "We have not come to harm you, but if you make war on us, we will show you no mercy."

The elves formed up and rode away. Soon, the marooned nomads were only dark smudges against the blond sand, then they were lost from sight.

Around Khuri-Khan the desert was stony, with hills of sand piled up by contending winds from the mountains in the north and the sea in the east. The Khurish capital was set in a shallow depression, like a dry lakebed. All day the elves climbed out of this low-lying area. Stones became scarce, and the sand grew finer. There was no shade in sight anywhere. Each elf had donned eyeshades of the style worn by nomads, which looked very like bandages wrapping the head: stiff strips of hide held in place by thongs looped around the ears. The "bandage" had very thin horizontal openings, which admitted just enough light to see. Without the eyeshades, most of the elves would have gone blind in a day or two. Elves and horses were draped in white cloth, another nomad trick. The light color deflected the killing rays of the sun.

The column paused every few miles for water. Horses drank first, riders second. A warrior could persevere even when thirsty, but a horse would balk unless watered.

As the distance from Khuri-Khan increased, they found less and less evidence of intelligent life. They were too far east to encounter travelers on the caravan route to Alek-Khan and Kortal, and too far west to meet traders using the only paved road in Khur, the Khan's Way, which led to Delphon. Here, at its harsh edge, it was easy to see why even the hardiest nomads shunned the High Plateau.

The wind died. This spared them the stinging dust, but allowed the heat to grow. The entire column looked like a procession of phantoms, white-draped wraiths plodding slowly ahead through the calf-deep sand.

Under her stifling shroud, the Lioness fought against the lethargy that had her nodding in the saddle. She slipped a hand into one of the smaller saddlebags draped across the pommel of her saddle. Within, next to the smooth coolness of Sa'ida's enigmatic gift, she felt dry flakes. These were the leaves that had fallen on her during her last night in Khuri-nost. They had quickly dried in the desert air. She hadn't mentioned the odd occurrence to anyone, not even Gilthas. What could she say? A bat flew over and dropped ash leaves on me? Her husband would think she'd been sampling the Khurish homebrew. Yet, she was sure that the fallen leaves meant something.

Swaying in the saddle, the Lioness had plenty of time to consider what she knew about ash trees. The wood was hard and durable and made good tool handles, pike and lance shafts, and arrows. Eastern Silvanesti had a great many ash trees. So did the woodlands of Wayreth in Qualinesti. Had the leaves come from one of those places? Was the strange rain an omen, a sign that, one day, she was destined to return to one of the elven homelands?

If circumstance permitted, she would ask Favaronas about ash trees. Doubtless, the scholar knew all sorts of trivial lore about them. Perhaps she would find a clue in his knowledge.

Thinking of the archivist, she twisted in the saddle and looked for him in the line of draped riders. One of Favaronas's assistants had been killed by a stray nomad arrow during the set-to at the dune. The remaining two scholars were shorter than her warriors, and Favaronas especially was not an accomplished rider, making them easy to pick out. The archivist rode with knees stiff and feet pointed outward. From the bobbing motion of his head, she decided he was half asleep. Just as well. If she could afford the lapse in alertness, she'd doze, too. It would make the miles pass more swiftly.

When the horizon ahead lost all relief and became a monotonous line, the elves knew they had reached the high desert at last. Although flat, it did present strange features. The shallow sand beneath their horses' hooves was marked with swirls, squiggles, and converging lines, as if way markers had been drawn. These were the handiwork of the only living creatures sharing the landscape with the elves: serpents, sand crawlers, spiders, and lizards. The sky took on a silver color like polished iron, and mirages shimmered over the sand. To the elves at the rear of the column, the lead riders took on a fantastic aspect as the broiling air magnified them and their horses, making them look ten feet tall. The lead riders also seemed to be treading through water, their reflections perfect in the tantalizing, phantom lakes.

The sun reached its zenith. Breathing was labor, not only forcing Kerian's heavy chest to rise and fall, but having to take in the blistering air. She put a hand outside her white drapery. Even through her glove, it felt as though she'd plunged her hand into a campfire. Knotting her hand into a fist, she kept her arm aloft, signaling a halt.

Water was sipped sparingly. Favaronas asked for extra for his assistant, and Kerian allowed the elf—a Qualinesti named

Armentero—an extra swallow. Although younger than his master, Armentero did not look at all well, but he waved aside Favaronas's concern with a few brusque words.

Favaronas, face pink despite his sunshade, leaned close to Kerian and spoke. His mouth was too dry to manage more than a whisper. "The Speaker must be mad! Bring a hundred thousand elves through this inferno? And most on foot? Thousands would perish on the way!"

She gave a noncommittal shrug and took her turn with the water gourd. In truth, she didn't think Gilthas realized the enormity of the difficulties involved in shifting their people from Khuri-Khan to Inath-Wakenti, even if they found the valley of legend. Such a migration would make the journey to Khur across the Plains of Dust seem a pleasant parade. The Plains were larger than the Khurish desert, but the part the elves had crossed was not nearly so hot or dry as this. To reach the Vale of Silence, the Speaker could bypass some of the High Plateau by following the caravan trail northwest to Kortal, but that presented a different set of dangers. Kortal lay on the border with Neraka. Once the Dark Knights learned of Gilthas's scheme to save the elven race, they would stop at nothing to thwart it.

Kerian had agreed to undertake this expedition, but she believed that resettling the entire elven nation in the Vale of Silence was a preposterous idea. Favaronas was wrong. It wouldn't be thousands, but tens of thousands who would perish on the journey. Half of their people would die, surely.

"You disagree?" Favaronas said, seeing her shake her head.

"What?"

"I said, perhaps we could rest here awhile till the sun declines."

"Yes, we'll rest here a few hours."

The order was passed down the column, and the warriors dismounted, moving slowly in the breath-stealing heat.

Groups of warriors joined their sunshades together into a larger canopy, sheltering themselves and their horses. Beneath these, they cleared away the topmost, hottest layer of sand, spread canvas sheets on the ground, and took their ease. There was a little excitement when a nest of adders was uncovered, but the snakes were rapidly dispatched and everyone settled down. Soon, only the sentries were awake.

Feeling drunk with heat and weariness, Kerian muttered, "I hope the blasted valley is there, after all this effort."

Favaronas lay facing her, his head resting on the bundle of manuscripts he'd brought along. Equally drowsy, he replied, "It's there, General. The ancient chroniclers seldom lie."

She snorted. Seldom lying was not exactly the same as telling the truth.

When they arose two hours later, they could not wake Favaronas's assistant. Armentero was dead, his body rigid, skin blistering hot to the touch. Heat stroke, or "sun death" as the nomads called it. The inferno of the High Plateau had claimed its first elven victim.

5

The sun was not yet up when Planchet entered the Speaker's private chamber to wake him from a deep slumber. As he reached to rouse him, the loyal retainer noted how the hardships of ruling a people in exile had left their mark on the Speaker. He was a young elf, not yet touching middle years, but faint lines tracked the skin between his eyes and bracketed his mouth. His hair was lighter, due not only to the effects of the harsh Khurish sun, but to the silver-gray strands visible here and there. Despite this, in the dim light the sleeping ruler of the elven nations resembled a youth again, curled up in the bed linens, one arm outstretched over the emptiness where Kerianseray had been.

Planchet whispered, "Sire, wake up! Captain Ambrodel has returned!"

Gilthas opened one eye. "So soon?"

His valet nodded and held up a clean gown. Gilthas rose and slipped his arms in, tying the sash with a single brisk jerk.

Two days past, the evening of the day the Lioness had left Khurinost, Gilthas had sent Hytanthas Ambrodel into the nomad city disguised as a human. The captain's task was to glean information about who was responsible for the attack outside the Temple of Elir-Sana. The Khurs were attributing the assault to a robbery gone wrong. The story told by Kerian

106

and Hytanthas made that simplistic explanation unlikely. Gilthas had requested an audience with Sahim-Khan to make a formal appeal for an investigation, but he didn't intend to leave the matter entirely in Khurish hands.

As they left his quarters, Gilthas asked, "Did Hytanthas discover who was behind the attack?"

"No, sire," said Planchet, "but he says he has gleaned much information."

The Speaker's audience chamber was full of its usual inhabitants—Lord Morillon and his Silvanesti, various court functionaries, and Hamaramis, commander of the Speaker's private guard. They stood to one side, eyeing a disheveled Hytanthas Ambrodel. Planchet had ordered refreshment for him, and the young elf was making the most of it. He had a lamb chop in one hand and a slender silver urn of nectar in the other. He wore a thick, black wig cut in the style of a city-dwelling Khur, which concealed his upswept ears. His skin had been darkened with walnut juice. If Gilthas hadn't known better, he would have taken the captain for a scruffy denizen of Khuri-Khan.

Hastily lowering the urn from which he was drinking, Hytanthas bowed to the Speaker.

Gilthas looked him up and down and wrinkled his nose. "You smell like a chamber pot!"

Hytanthas ruefully agreed. "The places I've been were no garden, sire."

Although eager to know what the young elf might have learned, Gilthas first asked that the room be cleared of all but his closest advisors. As the courtiers departed, he seated himself on his throne and accepted a tiny cup of kefre from Planchet.

At last Hytanthas was free to relate his story. He began with the hostels he'd visited, looking for nomads with the vulture tattoo. Desert dwellers came and went from Khuri-Khan all the time, alone or in small groups, to trade, to work, and to sample the comparative luxuries of settled life. Hytanthas had found no Torghanists in the nicer hostels, and so worked his way down the ladder to the lowest flophouses. The Khurish he'd learned was flavored with the accent of the capital, so he pretended to be a city dweller dodging the Khan's justice. In the cellars and hovels where very poor travelers could rent a scrap of blanket for a few coppers, he let it be known he was available for rough work. This generated little response. He soon found out why.

The supply of thugs was already dominated by nomads, who toiled for next to nothing. Among the Khurs, revenge was seen not as a crime, but as a matter of honor, and it was considered only natural that devotees of the god of vengeance would make themselves available to assist others, weaker or fainter of heart, in obtaining the revenge they required. For Torghanists, this was a sacred duty. Hytanthas's attempts to find an assignment as an assassin offended them. When he continued his efforts, bragging on his skill with a blade, he was cornered by three hard-eyed nomads who warned him against trespassing in their domain. The three were devotees of Torghan.

Hytanthas had heard rumors of a benefactor to the Temple of Torghan. Someone was making rich gifts to the god—someone who expressed a strong dislike of elves. This was not lost on the Torghanists. Harassment and assaults on elves in Khuri-Khan were on the rise.

"So the attack on Kerianseray and yourself was part of a wider campaign of hatred?" Gilthas asked.

"No, Great Speaker. According to a conversation I overheard in a Khurish tavern, this benefactor actually paid to have General Kerianseray murdered, and he—the Khurs used the male pronoun—he was unhappy the attempt had been bungled."

The identity of the benefactor remained a mystery to Hytanthas, but he had made another discovery he considered of such importance that he had prematurely aborted his mission and returned to Khurinost. The discovery concerned one of Sahim-Khan's hired sorcerers.

SANCTUARY

The Khan had a variety of mages willing to do his bidding. One in particular, rumored to be a rogue wizard, was a secretive fellow about whom little was known.

"The very few who've seen him in the streets say he's rather nondescript. He wears ragged, heavy brown robes and walks with a limp. His name is Faeterus," Hytanthas said. "I believe he is an elf."

This statement left the Speaker and his advisors speechless for several seconds. Lord Morillon recovered first.

"What is the basis for this wild speculation?" he demanded.

The haughty tone annoyed the captain. "It isn't speculation. Well, not entirely."

Hytanthas admitted there were a great many stories about Faeterus. Gossip was rife about his antecedents, and the "experiments" he was said to conduct in his secret abode, and it was never said aloud that he was anything other than a human. However, one city-dweller, ancient by Khurish standards as he was more than eighty years old, had confided to Hytanthas his theory that the sorcerer was *laddad*.

"According to this human, Faeterus has been in the city since before he himself was born." Lord Morillon opened his mouth to protest, and Hytanthas rushed on. "The mind of this old human is still sharp and clear. The other Khurs are dismissive of him, but I found him extremely persuasive."

The name Faeterus was unknown to any in the room. Hamaramis noted it could be an assumed name, perhaps a corruption of the mage's true identity. The closest Silvanesti equivalent would be Faetheralas, and in Qualinesti, Fanterus.

"Could this sorcerer be the benefactor of the Torghanists?" asked the Speaker.

Hytanthas did not know, but all agreed that an elf who had so turned his back on his own kind that he could hire his services out to a tyrant like Sahim-Khan certainly was capable of anything.

"Make inquiries," the Speaker ordered. "Someone, somewhere, knows this Faeterus."

Planchet brought up the Nerakan emissary who had been seen skulking about the Khuri yl Nor. He asked Lord Morillon, who had been to the palace more often than anyone else, to describe the human in detail. As a lifelong courtier, the Silvanesti didn't miss much in his own milieu.

When Morillon finished, Planchet stood frowning, gnawing his lower lip in thought. Gilthas prompted him to speak.

"There was a man, a Nerakan, a vassal of that wretch Redlance," Planchet finally said. "He was dark, as you say, and had a very rough voice. It's been years since I thought of him, but I believe his name may have been Hengriff."

During the fight for Qualinesti liberty, a special group of Nerakan Knights was formed to track down the Lioness. Their leader, Lord Liveskill, stood high in the councils of Morham Targonne, master of the order. Liveskill left the dirty work of hunting the Lioness to a hardened warrior named Vytrad Redlance, who led a band of ninety-nine Knights. Their paths crossed Kerianseray's three times. The last time, Vytrad perished fighting her in single combat. Only a dozen or so Knights of this special band had survived, and they never returned to hunt the Lioness again. Given Targonne's lack of patience with failure, the remnants of Liveskill's band might easily have been dispatched on the least pleasant duties the Order could arrange—such as emissary to the desert wastes of Khur.

Vytrad's second-in-command at the time of his death was a brawny, bull-voiced fellow who chose to preserve his men rather than let them die trying to save the fanatical Redlance. Fighting his way out of the trap that cost Vytrad his life, Hengriff single-handedly killed four of the Lioness's best warriors. When he rode away with the survivors of Vytrad's command, Kerian was only too willing to let them go.

"So who is directing the Torghanists, Neraka or the renegade wizard?" Morillon wondered.

The Speaker shrugged. "In either case, we can't allow treachery to undermine our place here. Peace and goodwill are vital for our survival."

"Sahim-Khan is no friend of the sect of Torghan-worshipers, sire. If they challenge his authority, he will stamp them out most ruthlessly," Morillon said.

"Unless their efforts are part of some deeper intrigue between the Khan and the Knights," Planchet said. "He may be using them against the Knights—or perhaps the Knights are using the Torghanists against the Khan."

Hytanthas shook his head. "What murky times we live in."

"Every time is murky when you're in the midst of it," said Gilthas, smiling faintly. "In any event, the 'benefactor' of the Torghanists must be identified. So must the Khan's rogue mage."

What they would do with this knowledge once they had it was something the Speaker preferred not to worry about just now. For the moment, they would concentrate on uncovering their enemies.

A reward was considered. The Khurs were fond of elven steel, and the right price might buy more information. But the Speaker said such an offer would also raise a host of dubious opportunists. Hytanthas proclaimed his readiness to return to the city, and this Gilthas readily approved. The captain's persona as a human desperado might yet yield additional important leads.

"Find this benefactor, Captain Ambrodel, and bring him before me. Whether he wants to come or not."

Hytanthas saluted. When he departed, Planchet followed. Taking him aside, Planchet said, "Don't risk yourself with this blackguard, Captain. If possible, bring him in alive, but if circumstances require it, don't hesitate to kill him. Better this agitator should die than escape, or kill you."

Hytanthas nodded. For all his youth, he was a veteran, having fought the Knights in the woods of Qualinesti. In his very first skirmish, the Knights had surrounded a nearby village and threatened to destroy it unless the Lioness and her companions surrendered. She would not, so the Knights slaughtered everyone in the village, from elders down to babes in arms. Two hundred thirty souls. Hytanthas never forgot his brutal initiation to war as fought by the Knights of Neraka.

Standing in the open square outside the Speaker's great tent, valet and warrior were about to part when a commotion came to their ears. The byways of Khurinost were busy at this hour, and both elves strained fruitlessly to see beyond those thronging the paths, but it was obvious that the roar of voices was coming from the direction of Khuri-Khan.

"Sounds like a battle!" Hytanthas exclaimed.

"It's trouble all right, but not warfare."

Planchet borrowed a halberd from a guard standing watch outside the Speaker's tent, then bade Hytanthas accompany him. "Come, Captain. Let's see who makes such a noise on a hot morning. Maybe your mysterious sorcerer or the fell emissary of the Dark Order."

To the ignorant, Hytanthas's companion might have seemed a weak comrade to take into danger, but Planchet was no ordinary servant. He had commanded Qualinesti forces in the final battle to escape the collapsing kingdom, and his inspired leadership enabled thousands of elves to escape the net closing around Qualinost. Given a choice when confronting danger, Hytanthas would take Planchet over anyone else in the Speaker's entourage—save the Lioness herself of course.

The paths through camp quickly clogged up with frightened elves, clutching bundles of goods and struggling to put distance between themselves and the city. Planchet and Hytanthas made repeated attempts to ask what was happening, but no one stopped long enough to answer. At last Planchet turned his halberd sideways, blocking the footpath from tent to tent. Like water caught behind a dam, elves filled the passage, seeking other ways out.

"What's going on?" Planchet shouted as he struggled against the growing mob pushing against the shaft of his weapon.

"We were attacked in the Grand Souks!" an elf woman replied.

"They attacked everyone, or only elves?" asked Hytanthas.

"Only elves!"

Planchet moved out of the way, lifting the halberd. Refugees surged past. When the mob had thinned, Planchet and Hytanthas hurried on to the city.

The gate into Khuri-Khan was unguarded. The usual oddments of gear surrounding it—cloth sunshades for the soldiers, stools, and skins of wine and water hanging from posts—all had been knocked down and trampled. The gate itself stood open. A few steps inside they found a dead man, a Khurish guard. He'd been stabbed in the back.

The Lesser Souk had been sacked. Dozens of soukats, with their heads broken or worse, lay in the wreckage of their booths. Here and there, women and children tugged at the broken structures of cloth and lath, trying to find a lost husband or father, or to salvage the family inventory. Many of the beleaguered merchants stared with open hostility at Planchet as the two elves walked past. Hytanthas was still in his scruffy human disguise.

Whatever had happened was over in the Fabazz. Sounds of conflict echoed down the winding streets, growing fainter and farther away. The two elves had just decided to give up their search and return to Khurinost when a troop of the Khan's soldiers burst from a side street. Their articulated coats of plate armor and spiked helmets gave them the look of exotic insects, swarming from a hidden nest.

One of the Khurs spoke, pointing a finger at the ostensible human and his elf companion. The rest of the foot soldiers turned as one to stare at them.

"Not good," Planchet muttered, edging away. "I think I hear the Speaker calling."

Hytanthas agreed. They backed away, never taking their eyes off the soldiers. The Khurish officer, recognizable by the bronze sunburst on his helmet, shouted at them to stop.

"What language is that?" Planchet said, still sidling away.

"Can't understand a word he's saying."

The officer cut the air with his hand. Plates jangling, his soldiers ran at the elves. They trampled the already broken stalls, drawing protesting wails from the soukats and their kin.

"How many are there, do you reckon?" Hytanthas asked.

"Forty, fifty."

"No shame running from odds like that."

"None at all," Planchet said and dropped his borrowed halberd.

The two belted back the way they'd come, the shortest route to Khurinost. It would have been easy enough for two elves to outdistance a pack of burdened humans, but when Planchet and Hytanthas reached the street above the city gate they found that the portal was no longer abandoned. Worse, the iron portcullises were down, and the timber gates shut and barred.

The sounds of martial pursuit were growing closer. There was no time to bluff their way past the guards. Planchet, who knew Khuri-Khan best because of his frequent trips to buy supplies for the Speaker's household, led Hytanthas away from the gate to Har-Kufti Street, the paved lane that encircled the city just inside the wall.

"Where are we going?" asked Hytanthas.

Planchet panted, "Temple Walk. We might find sanctuary in the Temple of Elir-Sana!"

The captain had no better idea, so they turned off Har-Kufti onto a narrow lane that led to the center of the city.

They might have evaded the soldiers, laboring under the

twin handicaps of desert heat and bulky armor, but street urchins and doorway idlers obligingly shouted directions to the troops. Hytanthas cursed them in broken but effective Khurish.

The street suddenly ended on a square lined with ruined houses, destruction wrought by Malystryx and still not repaired. It wasn't the holy sanctuary, but at least it offered possibilities for concealment. Hytanthas tore the boards off an open doorway, and they squeezed inside. Flattened against the wall, they tried to calm their labored breathing. The ruined house bore no roof. All the palm wood beams had fallen in, and half the upper floor's tiles and bricks had tumbled to ground level. The place stank of fire and the peculiarly rank odor of the Red Marauder's breath.

The Khurish troops entered the square at a walking pace. They must have known the street was a dead end, and their quarry was trapped. Quietly, they fanned out, checking every ruin. It was only a matter of time before they reached the one in which Planchet and Hytanthas were hiding.

The Speaker's valet searched the rubble and drew out a reasonably stout length of timber, a crude weapon to supplement the sword he wore. When he straightened, he realized he was alone. Hytanthas was gone. A tap on his shoulder caused him to look up. Hytanthas was climbing the pyramid of charred rafters toward the nonexistent roof. He gestured urgently for Planchet to follow him; the searching soldiers were only yards away.

There was no way of knowing how much the beams had been weakened by fire. But they had no other options. Frowning mightily, feeling much too old for this sport, Planchet began to climb.

He was little more than six feet off the floor when a Khurish soldier shoved his head in the empty window opening below.

"Excellency!" he yelled. "Some of the boards are off the door here, but I don't see anyone!"

From a distance came the reply: "Look twice, fool! Our orders are to bring any *laddad* before the Khan! I have no desire to explain your failure in that duty!"

The Khur poked his head in again, looking left and right and cursing his commander with whispered eloquence. The two elves hardly dared breathe, so close was he. At last, he withdrew.

"No, Excellency. No one here!"

Planchet's legs shook with the release of tension. His foot had been a scant six inches above the soldier's helmet spike.

The valet hauled himself up beside Hytanthas, at the top of the crumbling wall. A forest of rooftops and brass flues greeted their eyes, spreading uphill to the center of the city. The Khuri yl Nor was clearly visible to their right, the palace rising beyond the heights of Temple Walk. Gleaming in the morning sun like a pale blue beacon was the dome of the Temple of Elir-Sana.

"Do you see it?" Hytanthas demanded. "We can reach the temple over the rooftops!"

Planchet grunted. To him it looked like a very long way to go, the terrain more than a little uncertain. Still, as with the climb itself, they had no choice.

The jump to the intact roof of the house next door was easy enough. Two more jumps, and they were out of the ruined district. Hytanthas would've discarded his thick black wig then, but Planchet cautioned against it. The captain's human guise might come in handy.

Wherever possible, they kept to the roof edges, creeping alongside the low parapets that rose up from the brick outer walls. Khurish roofs were made of palm fronds, plastered with mud, and wouldn't taken much weight. Although lighter than humans, the elves didn't want to risk breaking through.

After traversing six houses beyond the ruined district, the fleeing pair reached the more solid roof of a four-story building. They rested in the latticework lean-to that shaded one corner. It enclosed a rooftop garden filled with kefre shrubs, cardamom plants, and foliage neither elf recognized.

"Did you hear what the soldier said? They're arresting all elves in the city!" Hytanthas exclaimed. "What could've happened?"

"Perhaps Neraka or the minotaurs at last offered a price the Khan could not refuse."

"The Speaker must be told!"

Planchet looked at his sooty, scratched hands. "If we survive, he will be told."

*   *   *   *   *

Eight streets away from the pair of elves, the priest Minok also was hiding, huddled below a darkened stairway, gulping hot, dry air. For two days the Khan's men had been hunting him. He had escaped them originally, outside the palace, by the grace of his great god. A short distance from the Khuri yl Nor—far enough so his screams couldn't be heard at the palace—four soldiers ran at him with swords drawn. A nomad by birth and no coward, Minok could hardly stand his ground without a weapon. Arms were forbidden to priests, and he strictly adhered to the precepts of his order. So he fled.

Unfortunately, the wily guards split up, with two circling wide through back alleys to cut him off. Minok had no chance to gain the safety of his temple. His heart sank when he saw the glint of naked iron blades coming up on either side. He ducked down a familiar side street and ran for the front door of a large house at the rear of the square.

Then Torghan interceded. Before Minok reached the house, a powerful hand grabbed him by the back of his robe. Lifting him completely from his feet, it hauled him into a darkened outbuilding. He found himself thrust under a dusty brick staircase with nary a word spoken. He waited, sweating and shaking with fear, while soldiers tramped up and down the street outside, searching for him.

A skylight opened. The light that streamed down revealed

Minok's hiding place to be larger than he'd realized, and it illuminated a polished table at which sat Lord Hengriff. The servant who had opened the skylight retreated to the shadows.

"Come out," said Hengriff. In the stillness his voice boomed like a drum, and Minok flinched.

Minok emerged, stood stiffly, and tried to brush the dust of the streets from his priestly robe.

"Thank you," he said gravely. "I was sure I was done for out there."

"You're not done until I'm through with you. I've too much invested in you to let the Khan kill you out of pique."

Hengriff did not ask the priest to sit down. Papers and open scrolls covered the tabletop. A fresh sheet of foolscap lay under Hengriff's hand, with lines of black script neatly printed down half the page. Unlike most nomads, Minok could read, but Hengriff's writing made little sense to him. It was some sort of cipher, written for his superiors, no doubt.

"The attack today went well," Minok opined.

Hengriff's black eyes narrowed. "It did not. I told you to seek out elves, not the soukats of the Fabazz. No one in Khuri-Khan will blame the elves for what happened today. They know your nomads are responsible!"

Minok spread his hands. "My people are poor wanderers of the desert. When they saw the riches of the Lesser Souk spread before them, they lost their heads."

"You'll lose yours if you bungle again!"

Minok promised he would not fail a second time.

"Too late for that," Hengriff reminded him dryly. "Your assassins also failed to slay the Lioness outside the Temple of Elir-Sana."

Cautiously, Minok said, "Permit me to ask, Excellency, why you don't kill these *laddad* yourself. Why do you need the Sons of the Crimson Vulture to shed blood for you?"

"I'm trying to school a nation." Minok's look indicated he did not understand, so Hengriff added, "All your people, not just the followers of Torghan, need to learn how to deal with elves. If I kill them, it's foreign intervention. If Khurs kill them, it's a patriotic act."

Minok bowed. "You are most wise, Excellency." A sly expression crossed his narrow face. "It also discomfits the Khan, does it not?"

Hengriff made a fist. "There are lessons he must learn too."

He rang a small brass bell, summoning the servant who waited just outside the shaft of sunlight. A few words to the servant and the fellow scurried away, returning moments later with two large men. Hengriff gave orders that the men, two of his personal bodyguards, escort Minok back to the Temple of Torghan. He warned the priest not to show his face for a while, to give Sahim-Khan time to forget he'd sought Minok's death.

Minok did not thank him, only turned, head high, and started out. He and his protectors had gone only a few steps, when he staggered suddenly and clapped his hands over his ears.

"That ringing!" he cried. "Mercy, do you hear a great bell?"

The only bell in sight was the small brass instrument on Hengriff's table. But it sat silent. Neither Hengriff nor his bodyguards heard anything, as they stared in surprise at the priest of Torghan. Minok was in obvious pain.

"Something is being summoned! Something great and terrible!"

Minok's eyes rolled back in his head, his knees folded, and he dropped to the floor, unconscious. A thin stream of blood trickled from each ear.

Hengriff gestured at his men. The priest was not dead, but could not be revived. They covered him with a cloth to conceal him, and departed, carrying him back to his temple.

The Knight stared after them with a frown on his face.

Although he'd heard and felt nothing, he could not dismiss the sensations of an initiated priest. He made careful note of what Minok said, and when he said it, appending this to his next dispatch to the Order.

The report would soon be on its way to Jelek. Before the War of Souls, the Order's leader, Morham Targonne, had moved the knighthood's headquarters from Neraka to Jelek, some thirty miles northwest. Hengriff, himself from Neraka, had thought the move a singularly stupid one. Jelek was nothing more than a squalid little backwater, and the only reason Targonne had chosen it was because it carried the dubious (to Hengriff's mind) distinction of having birthed him.

Lord of the Night Targonne had been dead five years now, and the Order had been weakened by the events of the War of Souls: a great defeat at the Battle of Sanction and the disappearance of Targonne's successor, Mina, the self-proclaimed prophet of the One God. The Order's current leader, Lord Baltasar Rennold, was determined to restore its honor and sense of holy purpose. Rennold was nothing like Targonne, who had been a distinctly dishonorable man with the soul of a bookkeeper, yet Hengriff was uncertain what Rennold would make of this latest news. Rennold did not much care for him, holding against Hengriff the excesses and failures of his superiors, Lord Liveskill and Vytrad Redlance.

The Lord of the Night had set Hengriff three goals—the annexation of Khur, the final destruction of elven power, and the seizure of any remaining elven treasure. If he wanted these goals accomplished, he'd best heed every word in Hengriff's report.

*   *   *   *   *

The flat desert below the Pillars of Heaven rang with the clashing of swords and the pounding of many hooves. Dust swirled around maneuvering companies of riders. Over all, the sun shone down from a perfectly cloudless sky.

SANCTUARY

The enemy had fallen upon the elves just after dawn, before all the Lioness's warriors were in the saddle. A hundred nomads appeared out of the south, shouting tribal war cries and brandishing swords. The elves who were mounted rode straight at the oncoming horde, holding them off while their comrades readied themselves for battle. The Lioness led that first small force against fearful odds.

The nomads certainly were brave and bloodthirsty, but they had no formal training in arms. Once their initial surprise rush was spent, they found themselves at a severe disadvantage. They lacked any protective armor and most bore only a single weapon, a straight sword without a crossguard. Nomad archers used a short bow of cow horn and wicker laminated together. Deadly at short range, its effectiveness fell off sharply with distance. At two hundred yards—where elf bows were commonly used—nomad arrows merely bounced off elven armor. The iron-headed Silvanesti arrows went right through a nomad's chest at that range.

The Lioness organized her band into three sections: two hundred, two hundred, and one hundred riders. One of the companies of two hundred, armed with swords, held off fierce rushes by the nomads while the group of one hundred emptied Khurish saddles with precisely aimed arrows. The remaining two hundred riders circled northward, trying to surround the enemy, but the nomads would not be caught. They regrouped and charged at any vulnerable point that they saw. The desert around the tribesmen was littered with the fallen. Many were elves, but mixed in with them were the bodies of desert dwellers and their ponies.

After an hour of fruitless slaughter, the nomads began to lose heart. They had expected to stampede the elves, and when the Lioness's troops stood firm, nomad ardor waned. Without the discipline to carry on fighting all day, as the desert heat rose to its most incandescent the tribesmen rode away. The dust-caked elves gladly let them go. Kerian had no wish to pursue the foe. She didn't have the resources for a long chase across the desert, and more hostile nomads might be lurking beyond the horizon.

Fewer than twenty of her warriors had been killed; half that many more had notable injuries. The desert was dotted with a dozen slain nomads. As elves moved among the fallen, scavenging food and precious water, they noticed many of the humans bore the mark of the Leaping Spider clan, the dominant clan in the Weya-Lu tribe.

"Why did they fight us?" Favaronas wondered. "We've done nothing to them."

"We're foreigners in their land," Kerian replied grimly. It was a philosophy she understood. If armed Khurs had ridden through Qualinesti, her instinct would have been exactly the same: drive them out.

The scholar did not share her outlook. Shaking his head, he mumbled something about "live and let live." She had no patience with such feeble notions, but held her tongue. Since finding his assistant lying dead beside him, Favaronas had been somewhat shaken. He took to keeping as close to Kerian as possible. Still, he did not complain and did not hamper her or her warriors.

They buried the dead, elf and human, to discourage scavengers, with the Lioness urging speed and taking a turn at the digging herself. Their second day on the High Plateau was waning, and she wanted to put as much distance between her people and the scene of battle as possible.

The Khalkist range bulked larger on the horizon. The gray peaks resembled low-lying clouds at this distance. The terrain began to change. The thick layer of sand gave way to sand and rocks, then broken gravel. Animal life was seen, even if they were only small creatures, easily frightened lizards sunning themselves on the rocks, their emerald green and burnished gold hides sparkling in the bright light. Foliage reappeared: stunted cedars, creosote bushes, thorny creepers, and a type of grass so wiry that even their hungry horses wouldn't eat it. Still, the presence of plant life was a welcome change from the unrelieved sand of the High Plateau. They had passed out of the deep desert into the only slightly less hostile lowlands of the mountains.

Kerian sent an advance party forward to reconnoiter the way to the valley mouth. According to Gilthas's map, the lone entrance to the Inath-Wakenti was a nondescript pass that gave no hint of its importance. They had to find the right one, the exact one, or their journey would be in vain.

The troop topped a small rise, carpeted with shards of gray slate. A startlingly cool breeze struck their faces. The wind coming down the mountains hadn't yet acquired the desert's desiccating heat. The Lioness gave word to halt.

Water was dispensed. Kerian removed the bowl-like bottom from the gourd, poured water into it, and let her horse drink. Then she squatted in the shade cast by her mount and drank from the leather-wrapped gourd herself. The water inside was so warm that she could have brewed tea with it.

A distant, loud cracking sound rent the air. Everyone paused and looked to the mountains, the apparent source of the sound. Thunder? It had been a long time since any of them had seen rain.

Favaronas, resting like the Lioness in the shadow of his horse, asked, "Will we get a shower, do you think?"

It seemed wishful thinking; there wasn't a cloud in the sky. "Probably just a rockfall," she muttered.

Another boom echoed down from the gray peaks. Hearing it more clearly this time, the Lioness stood quickly, facing the desert. The sound actually was coming from the direction of the desert and echoing off the mountains. Yet all any of them could see was a stony landscape dotted with twisted cedars and spiky brown grass, and beyond that, a shimmering expanse of sand and mirage water.

When a third peal of thunder broke over the slate hill, Kerian ordered everyone to horse. The cooling wind had died away, and to the south a plume of dust rose straight into the air. The cloud was sizable and compact, indicating a tightly knit group of riders. The nomads were following them.

The Lioness sent Favaronas out of harm's way, over the crest of the hill, then distributed her weary warriors in a wide, crescent formation, with the tips facing the approaching dust cloud. From her place in the center of the formation, she shaded her eyes with one hand and stared south. The column of dust dispersed in the wind as it rose higher into the air.

The elves glimpsed movement at the bottom of the hill. Something burnished and bright flashed between the bushes. The Lioness squinted. It was a single object, larger than a man on horseback, and not a group of hard-riding nomads. She wondered what it could be.

The answer appeared the next second. In a blur of pre-ternatural motion, the approaching creature leaped from the foot of the hill and landed in front of the elves, barely a dozen yards away. Its rapid motion generated a sound like thunder. Horses reared, neighing shrilly in fright. Elves throughout the formation shouted with shock and dismay.

Standing before them was a terrifying apparition. It had four short powerful legs, a long tail studded with ivory barbs, a compact body four times larger than a bull, and a thick, upright neck. The creature's head caught every elf's attention. Long, angular, and covered with burnished green-gold scales, it was the head of a monstrous reptile.

"Dragon!" someone cried, but Kerian didn't think so. Squat and wingless, this was an earthbound creature. A crown of vertical horns encircled the monster's head from one earhole to the other, and a single thick horn erupted from its nose. Except for its unnatural size, it could have been a desert lizard.

"Archers!" the Lioness called. "Aim for its head!"

A hundred bowstrings twanged, and a hundred arrows arced through the air. The beast's eyelids slid over its slanting green eyes with an audible click, and the missiles bounced off its metallic hide. Eyes opening, the monster launched itself into the center of the elf formation.

Its speed was terrifying. With great sideways swings of its head, it mowed down horses and elves right and left, ripping them apart with its horns. When a horse fell directly in front of it, the creature opened its jaws and snapped the living animal in two.

"Break! Break formation!" the Lioness cried. Like quicksilver under the blows of a hammer, the elves flew apart. The monster dashed after the slowest riders, knocking them off their mounts with its horned snout. Several dismounted elves ran up on the creature's blind side and attacked it with swords. Their blows rang ineffectually against its hard scales.

At the Lioness's command, the bugler sounded retreat. She tried to restore some order to her ranks, but every time a sizable body of elves formed, the creature dashed at them, ripping them apart and trampling them under its clawed feet. In a quarter of an hour it slew more elves than the nomads had in a morning's combat.

Archers sniped at its eyes, and one succeeded in lodging a clothyard shaft in the right one. Grunting, the beast stuck out its blood-red tongue, snaked it around the offending arrow, and yanked. This procedure diverted the beast long enough to allow the elves to re-form and gallop for the crest of the slate hill. The monster caught up with them in two bounds.

The Lioness didn't see the beast coming. One moment she was astride her horse, the next, she lay sprawled on her back, sliding over the rough, stony ground. Her horse, decapitated by the creature's horns, was flung aside by one powerful clawed foot.

The beast advanced until it was standing over her. Dazed, she saw its wide, pale green belly blotting out the sky. She drew her dagger. With both hands, she rammed it into the creature's underside. It felt as if she was stabbing an anvil. Her point skidded off and the dagger twisted out of her grasp. The monster's right hind leg came forward, caught hold of Kerian's leg, and threw her several yards.

She rolled over and over, coming to a halt against the

carcass of her dead horse. Her hands and forearms sang with pain, and her head pounded. Around her, shouts and screams resounded, but sounded faint and far away. Even the searing light of the sun seemed dim.

Is this any way to fight?

The calm voice echoed in her head—her conscience, she supposed—sounding very like Gilthas. Why not? In most ways he was her conscience. She could see his face before her, his eyes full of disappointment. Get up, he told her. Don't just lie in the dirt beside your dead horse.

Laboriously, she pushed herself up on her hands, uttering an obscenity. Her leg ached where the creature had grabbed her, and she was certain she'd broken a rib.

The annoying voice in her head went on, telling her how stupid it was to fight such a beast with sword and bow. What else did they have?

It will stop the killing—at least for a time. Keep it close by, seeker.

This time the voice in Kerian's head belonged to Sa'ida, high priestess of Elir-Sana. Her words rang clear as mountain ice, cutting through the pain and the fog of exhaustion. She realized she had indeed been tossed back onto the body of her own horse. She tore open the small saddlebag, thanking the gods who live that the poor animal had fallen on its right side. Groping through the dried leaves, she drew out the odd stone.

Sa'ida's mysterious gift, the beautiful opal egg, lay heavy in her hand.

Now what? The priestess had given her no instructions, no explanation of how the gemstone was supposed to help her. Should she touch the monster with it? Daunting prospect! Perhaps if she tied it to an arrow and loosed it at the beast.

The elves had scattered, trying to keep out of the monster's reach. It made sudden, blindingly fast rushes at the small groups.

Her face scratched and bleeding, hair standing wildly

around her head, the Lioness stalked the creature. It saw her. Its eyelids clicked together, and the soulless reptilian visage never changed as it advanced. No dizzying rush this time. Instead, it came on slowly, raising one foot at a time like a prowling cat preparing to pounce. When it was ten yards away, the Lioness held up Sa'ida's gift.

"Here's a present for you, monster!" she shouted.

So saying, she leaned back and hurled the opal. Her aim was true. The orb hit the beast in the center of its chest, stuck there briefly, then fell to the ground. The creature's forward motion halted abruptly. It froze, one foreleg lifted off the ground, for the space of two seconds, then its legs unaccountably collapsed. It struck the ground so hard that the shock knocked the Lioness off her feet.

On horseback or on foot, the elves slowly converged on the fallen beast. It did not move. Kerian kept her sword in hand, ready to fight, but the monster was like a statue.

"Is it dead, General?" one of her warriors called.

Its breath washed over her feet. "No! Seems to be sleeping!"

Eight officers galloped up. Swinging out of their saddles, they ringed the monster's head. They struck the beast with their swords, but neither points nor blade edges would penetrate it. The swords merely bounced off the beast, doing no harm to its armored hide.

"Merciful Quen!" an elf exclaimed. "Can't we kill it?"

Kerian squatted by the beast. One eye, as big as her head, was half open. The bright green orb was as malign as ever and moved slightly to track her as she shifted position. She realized the creature could see her, but must be compelled by the power of the priestess's gift to lie quiescent. The question was, for how long?

The officers speculated what to do. As the discussion continued, the Lioness went and retrieved the opal egg. Its color had changed. Once glowingly white, it was now a dull ivory color, the pink and gold streaks on its surface faded.

She slipped it in her belt pouch. She owed Sa'ida a very large debt.

Favaronas come trotting over the crest of the hill. The archivist made his way to them, both hands clutching the pommel of his saddle, his attention fixed on the creature lying before them.

"Merciful gods and goddesses!" he exclaimed. "It's a sand beast!"

"You recognize this abomination?"

"After a fashion, General. Sand beasts dwell in the deepest, most desolate tracts of the desert. Sahim-Khan has the head of one preserved in his palace. They're very rare—"

"Not rare enough," she said dryly. Raising her voice, she ordered her elves to saddle.

A horse was brought to replace her slain mount. The wounded who could ride would double up with healthy riders. They would take their dead with them as well. The monster might revive, and the Lioness wouldn't risk leaving honorable warriors to its savage attentions.

The sand beast had slain fifty-two elves and wounded as many more. If Sa'ida's magic hadn't stopped it, the entire company likely would have perished.

They rode due north. Favaronas kept looking back over his shoulder, afraid the paralyzed creature might revive and be upon them again. Kerian had a different worry: Why had the sand beast attacked them in the first place? This mission was fraught with unexpected dangers, as though the desert was uniting against them, to stop the Speaker's search for the valley of legend.

The archivist couldn't help with her questions about the sand beast. From all he'd read, sand beasts were wild animals who, despite their ferocity, avoided contact with humans or elves.

Kerian's horse stumbled, jarring her. She coughed as new pain lanced through her side. Favaronas offered a handkerchief.

"There's blood on your face, General."

She wiped her chin, dismissing his concern. "I took a few whacks. I've had worse."

Day's end was magnificent. The sinking sun gilded the forward range of the mountains, changing them from slate gray to bronze and copper. Dust was much less a problem here, as the ground was more stone than sand, and they could see for miles in every direction.

Drained from their battles, the elves slumped in the saddle. Their horses walked slowly with heads hanging. Talk around the Lioness had turned to finding a campsite for the night, when a scout came cantering back with news.

She reined up and waited for the excited young Qualinesti to reach her. The scout, a recent recruit, almost fell from his horse when he jerked the reins too sharply and his foam-flecked animal skidded to a halt on its haunches.

"Calm yourself, lad," the Lioness said. "What is it?"

"A nomad camp, not a mile east of where we sit right now!"

Her officers crowded closer. The Lioness's fingers flexed around her reins. "How many?"

"Big. More than a hundred tents. Maybe two hundred!"

Too vague. He should've brought an exact number. "No one saw you?" she asked. The young scout shook his head decisively.

"We should take the initiative—attack!" said a Wilder elf named Avalyn, one of the Lioness's longtime followers.

"We don't know these people," Favaronas protested. "They may be one of the harmless tribes!"

"What difference does it make what tribe they are?" Avalyn retored. "Nomads are all the same!"

"That's ridiculous!"

The Lioness interceded. "We're not here to make war on every wandering desert clan."

"If they're hostile, we can't just pass them by, General," another officer put in. "They'll be behind us, between us and Khurinost."

This was true enough. Kerian decided to detour from their mission long enough to inspect the nomad camp. If the tribe seemed a peaceful one, the elves would pass on. But if the nomads were recognizable enemies, the Lioness would strike.

Weariness dragged at every warrior, but no one complained as the Lioness led them away. It would be dark soon—only the highest peaks of the mountains ahead were still touched by sunlight—and this aided their cause. Humans were hampered by darkness, whereas elves could see almost as well at night as in full daylight.

The Qualinesti scout led them over a series of alluvial hills, formed of soil and gravel washed down from the mountains over the eons. The sky darkened from sapphire to indigo, and the first stars appeared. A distinctly chilly wind teased the riders every time they climbed out of a hollow and topped a hill. The breeze brought the smell of smoke. Cookfires.

Holding up her hand, the Lioness halted the column in a shallow ravine. Wordlessly she indicated Favaronas and Avalyn should follow her. The rest of the company would remain here.

The three followed the dry streambed through the ravine, halting where it emptied onto open ground. There, spread out in a ring pattern typical of Khurish nomads, lay several hundred conical tents. The Lioness halted her horse behind a screen of cedars. Silently she and her two companions studied the scene.

In the center of the ring of tents, figures moved about, silhouetted against a dozen campfires. There were no men to be seen, only nomad women in their sand-colored gebs, making supper, and children darting among the tents or helping with the cooking.

Avalyn shifted in his saddle. "This must be the base camp of the band that attacked us! All the warrior-age men are missing!" he whispered loudly.

"Even so, we don't make war on unarmed women and children."

"General, they would slaughter our loved ones, if they had the chance!"

"You don't know that!" Favaronas said.

"It was done in Qualinesti!"

She silenced them both. "This is not Qualinesti. And we are not Dark Knights."

They returned to the waiting army. The Lioness gave the order to ride, and the elves faded into the night.

Theirs weren't the only eyes watching in the darkness. On the south side of the nomad camp, two yellow eyes stared at the ring of tents. The sand beast, recovered from the spell put on it by the opal of Elir-Sana, lay concealed by loose dirt and rocks. Its tongue flicked out, tasting the night air. Smoke smell was strong, as was human, but beneath that, the beast detected traces of elf.

The movement inside the ring of tents slowed and stopped. The humans settled into their shelters. The beast's tongue flicked out again. The human smell was enticing, though the elf tang was definitely present. The impetus in its blood burned like a fever: Find elves; kill them. The drive could not be denied. If humans were intermingled with its intended prey, they would die, too.

The beast rose from its hiding place, shaking off dirt and rocks. In four bounds it reached the outer line of tents. It bore straight into the first tent, rending the goatskin walls to tatters with a single swipe of its horns. Within slept three humans. The first two died without waking. The third had time to shriek once before she perished.

The tents did not impede the sand beast's progress. It raced through the camp. Tattered canvas and leather caught in its horns trailed through the banked cookfires, catching fire. One tent was set alight, then another, and another. Against the heightened glare, humans raced about, yelling. Methodically, the creature slew them all, in case they might be elves in disguise.

Barely twenty minutes after the beast's entrance into the camp, silence reigned. The only sound was the crackle and pop of the fires burning unchecked in three different places. Nothing remained alive, and the smell of blood was strong.

Too strong. The beast left the silent camp and circled upwind. A tantalizing whiff of elf came to it, borne on the cool night wind from the mountains. With uncharacteristic deliberation, the sand beast set out again and resumed trailing the pack of elves.

Near dawn the first riders of Adala's band reached a hilltop overlooking their camp. Horrified by what they saw, they sent for the Weyadan and her warmasters.

The nomad war party had passed the night in the saddle, trying to swing wide around the elves' path and outflank them. Unfortunately, they didn't know the foothills as well as they did their usual terrain, and too many of them became lost in the gullies and ravines. They'd finally assembled as the sky began to lighten, and Adala was taking them back to camp when word came of the terrible disaster.

White-faced, the Weyadan rode through the savaged camp. No one was alive. All those left behind—wives, children, old folk—had been ruthlessly slain. The tents and supplies that weren't burned had been shredded and trampled.

"Who could have done this?" asked Wapah, riding at Adala's elbow, the tears flowing unchecked down his face. This question was repeated over and over by the stricken men—and punctuated by harsh screams as one after another they found their butchered, burned families.

Outside her tent, Adala made her own dreadful discovery. Her two youngest children, the last remaining at home, lay dead on the blood-drenched ground. Brave, forthright Chisi lay atop Amalia as though she'd tried to shield her gentle sister from the horror that had found them. On her knees beside them, Adala wept, swaying from side to side as anguish buffeted her.

"The *laddad* did this," she finally said.

SANCTUARY

Wapah frowned. "No, Weyadan. However barbarous we find them, they are not such fiends. It is some fateful occurrence. Perhaps—"

"Fool! Can't you see with your own eyes?"

He stared at her—her own eyes were great bottomless holes of pain. "The *laddad* did this," she said fiercely, raising her voice to repeat her words for all the others. "The *laddad* did this!"

Bilath reported no broken elf weapons, no dead elves, and no dead elf horses, but Adala insisted the *laddad* had gleaned every item after the massacre, to hide their guilt.

Nothing Wapah or Bilath could say would dissuade her from this conviction. Then one of Bilath's men brought shocking news that stopped all speculation. In a nearby ravine were the prints of three horses. The prints bore the unmistakable mark of *laddad* smithery. More, they led down the ravine, away from this camp, and joined a mass of similar hoofprints. An army of *laddad* had indeed passed by.

"For these murders," Adala vowed, "they will pay."

Wapah, though unconvinced, said nothing.

The others shouted and wailed their anger.

No longer was this a war only to preserve the sacred land of Khur from foreigners. Now, cradling her daughters' torn bodies, her robe stiff with their blood, Adala of the Weya-Lu dedicated herself to Torghan, god of vengeance. No prisoners would be taken. No quarter would be given. This was a war to the death.

6

Planchet and Hytanthas remained in the rooftop lean-to for hours, watching as patrols tramped up and down the streets, hammered on doors, and bellowed at each other across the empty squares. Whatever the original disturbance, Sahim-Khan's soldiery had quelled it—no doubt with a heavy hand.

The need to remain under cover when they wished to be back with their Speaker tested their patience. The sun reached its zenith, then passed it, in the unbroken blue vault of the sky. The scents of cardamom pods and kefre bark in the little garden were as oppressive as the heat. Hytanthas gave up on his human disguise, pulling the black wig from his head and stuffing it behind a row of pots.

When a long period went by without sight of the patrols, Hytanthas slapped the older elf on the back, saying, "Let's go!" With a terse remark about respect due to elders, Planchet followed.

The Khurish habit of building houses wider at the top than at the base made the elves' trek much less difficult than it would have been elsewhere. And crossing Khuri-Khan by rooftop proved an edifying process. As the elves clambered over dwellings, they heard babies crying, laughter, shouted arguments, and lovemaking. A hundred different food smells vied with smoke, incense, and the stink of privies. The lives

134

of the ordinary people of the city were open to view as Hytanthas and Planchet passed above their heads, out of sight. Khuri-Khan was indubitably foreign, yet it was also vigorously, robustly alive.

Near the Temple Walk, the buildings grew higher and larger. These were no longer private homes, but government storehouses, granaries, and colleges for the priesthoods of the various temples. Sunset was well past when they finally found themselves overlooking the great promenade lined with holy shrines.

The entrance to each temple was illuminated by torches thrust into iron ring-frames. By the wavering light, Planchet and Hytanthas watched small bands of Khurish troops, with halberds on their shoulders, march back and forth. Other than these patrols, the broad lane was empty.

"There's the Temple of Elir-Sana," Hytanthas whispered, pointing to their right.

The temple's dome was lit from within and gave off a faint blue glow in the darkness. No acolytes or priestesses were visible in the courtyard. The chimes lining the low wall jingled in the night breeze.

The question now was how to get down. They were thirty feet above the road, atop a three-story, flat-roofed building. Its walls dropped smooth and straight to the pavement, offering no likely footholds for a safe descent.

A careful search of the roof revealed the solution: a trapdoor secured from the inside. Hytanthas was able to slip his slender fingers under its edges and free it. Slowly, silently, they eased the cover up.

No one cried out below, so Hytanthas lay flat on the roof and looked through the opening while Planchet gripped his legs.

"It's a hall," Hytanthas whispered, head-down in the opening. "Lined with doors."

Planchet murmured a curse. No nice empty storehouse for them—they were trying to enter a priestly dormitory!

He started to haul Hytanthas back so they could try another building, but the wiry young elf lifted his feet, gripped the edge of the doorframe, and somersaulted through the opening. Catlike, he landed noiselessly. Lifting his hands, he urged Planchet to use him as a ladder to climb down.

"Insolent whelp," muttered the Speaker's valet. Although less agile than Hytanthas (who was a quarter his age), Planchet was no graybeard. He lowered himself through the opening, hung for a second, and let go. Unfortunately, Hytanthas, in his zeal to help, managed to trip him. The two elves went down in a tangle, hitting the wooden floor with a loud thump.

They froze, expecting sleepy priests to emerge from the rooms. None did. No light showed beneath the doors. The holy ones slept on, undisturbed.

The elves hastened down the hall, toward a stair landing. As Planchet rounded the top of the steps, he ran headlong into a woman. She was clad in a pale gray gown and turban, and carried no lamp. The two intruders, looming up suddenly in front of her, stole her breath, and Planchet's hand clamped over her mouth before she regained it. He pressed her against the wall, hoping to forestall any magic she might try to use against them.

"Curse it, we've entered a college of priestesses!" he hissed. "This isn't Sa'ida, by chance?"

Hytanthas shook his head and whispered, "Be silent, lady. We intend no harm. We are unjustly pursued by the Khan's soldiers and seek refuge in the Temple of Elir-Sana. Do you understand?"

She nodded, and he smiled. "We'll let you go, but you mustn't raise an alarm. Yes?" Again, a nod.

The elves exchanged a look. After a moment's hesitation, Planchet took his hand away. Immediately, the priestess hissed, "No men are allowed here! Ever!"

"Begging your pardon, holy lady, but we're not men," Planchet said reasonably, touching the tip of one pointed ear.

"Males! This is sacrilege!" Her voice was rising. "The Khan will hear of this violation!"

That was enough for Planchet. He snatched the scarf from her head, loosing a fall of gray hair, and gagged her with the cloth. She tried to yell, but only a thin gurgle emerged around the gag.

He took her by one arm, Hytanthas grabbed the other, and they propelled the priestess down the stairs. At the bottom, they found a small cupboard under the steps. Planchet pressed her inside. Whipping out his silk kerchief, he tied her ankles together. When he asked Hytanthas to surrender his own kerchief, the younger elf shrugged. He had none.

"What kind of uncouth stripling goes out without a kerchief?" Planchet snapped.

"A poor one, with no more possessions than he stands in!"

Planchet spun Hytanthas around and pulled off his geb, leaving him standing in leggings and low boots. The priestess's eyes grew wider still at the sight of the bare-chested elf. Planchet had to admit he was an odd-looking sight. The dye he'd used for his disguise had been applied only to arms, neck, and face. His torso was several shades lighter.

Planchet tore a strip from the geb's hem and used it to bind the woman's wrists, then tore another to bind her wrists to her ankles, hoping to delay her escape. He tossed the ruined garment back to Hytanthas.

"And what am I to do with this?" Hytanthas asked sarcastically.

"Make yourself some kerchiefs," Planchet rejoined.

The woman's eyes, incandescent with fury above the gag, followed them as they closed the cupboard door.

They exited the building through a side door, which put them in an alley. The gate in the wall surrounding the Temple of Elir-Sana was directly ahead, across the promenade; the iron portal stood open. The patrol had already passed by, and all was quiet. They stepped out of the alley's concealment and strode toward the temple gate.

As Hytanthas reached the gate, a deep voice rumbled behind them, "Stand where you are!"

Planchet hissed a soft curse. Both elves pivoted to face this new menace.

Hard leather heels thudded. A broad-shouldered, dark-skinned man strode forward. He was clad in leather trews and a short tunic, much like the attire worn by huntsmen in Qualinesti. The stranger's togs were not the green or brown of the forest, however. They were an unsettling shade of purplish red. His wide face was clean shaven, with brows thick and black. He was head and shoulders taller than the two elves. His identity was obvious to both of them. It was the Nerakan emissary, Hengriff.

"That's hardly proper attire for where you're going," he said, gesturing at Hytanthas's torn geb. His other hand rested on the pommel of a sheathed sword, a slender court blade.

"Your own garb is out of place, too," Planchet said wryly. "Don't you stifle in all that leather?"

"I'm accustomed to it. Besides, I prefer it to the local style. Too much like a woman's dress. Males are not allowed within this temple, you know."

While he talked, the elves desperately searched the darkness behind him. Hengriff seemed alone. Although a formidable-looking fighter, the Knight could hardly hope to best two agile, sword-armed elves. Still, he seemed supremely confident.

Hytanthas said, "We have business with the high priestess. We're known to her."

"Business? What business could elves have with a fusty old priestess?"

"Our own," Planchet said, then shoved Hytanthas through the open gate, shouting, "Go!" Unfortunately, the captain, taken by surprise, stumbled.

The Knight shouted a command. Suddenly, the night air was filled with a strange whirring sound.

SANCTUARY

Four lengths of rope, blackened by soot, hit the pavement in an arc behind Hengriff. Down each rope slid a brawny human dressed all in black—short black tunics, close-fitting trousers, and suede boots. In seconds, the men had landed silently and drawn swords. They sprinted toward the elves.

Planchet jerked Hytanthas to his feet, and the pair scrambled through the gate. The pursuing Nerakans did not try to crowd through the narrow opening, but vaulted the chest-high wall. It delayed them hardly at all. Hengriff approached with more deliberation, entering by the gate.

"I have questions and I want answers," he said firmly. "You'll come with us."

"Not today, Nerakan!"

Hengriff laughed at Hytanthas's defiant statement. Echoing like a bull's bellow, the sound filled the courtyard. It died abruptly when light flooded the scene. The double doors to the temple had opened. Silhouetted there, her long shadow reaching out from the colonnade, was a woman.

"Begone! Men of war, you cannot remain on sacred ground!"

Hengriff shouted across the distance, "You don't command me, Sa'ida, nor my men!"

The high priestess, followed by a handful of acolytes, appeared out of the light. She looked even more commanding than Hengriff. Stern and regal, she kept her eyes fixed on the Knight, and spread her arms wide as she approached. Her white robe seemed to gather the light, surrounding her with a bright, flowing aura.

Without looking away from her, Hengriff ordered his men to take the elves. The four warriors advanced, but when they were just five yards away, the swords suddenly flew from their hands. The Nerakans tried to keep coming, but a powerful force pushed against them. They bent forward at the waist, like men bucking a high wind, though the air was still.

Hengriff put a hand on the hilt of his own sword, but did not draw his weapon. In grim silence he watched his men shoved relentlessly backward across the courtyard and through the opening in the wall. Once in the street, however, they straightened, the unseen pressure no longer affecting them.

"You'll regret this, healer," Hengriff rumbled. "You've made an enemy."

"Death was always our enemy! Go!"

The Knight spared a glance at the elves. "This is not finished," he told them. He and his men departed, submerging into the darkness beyond the sacred enclosure.

For a moment, no one spoke. Then Sa'ida sent two acolytes to close the temple gates; the clang of iron broke through the elves' dazed immobility. Planchet got to his feet and straightened his clothing, brushing dust from his knees. He performed introductions in his most diplomatic manner. Sa'ida pursed her lips, frowning.

"I know who you are. This one"—she nodded at Hytanthas—"has been here before. But you cannot remain. It is forbidden."

"Yes, lady, I know, but we hoped you could provide sanctuary," Planchet replied. "The Khan's soldiers are in the streets, hunting elves."

"It's not the Khan you need fear, but the followers of Torghan."

She gestured at her followers. Two gray-haired acolytes approached, received quiet instructions, and departed.

Hytanthas, still dazed by events, found he had to clear his throat before he could speak. "Those men," he finally asked, "how did you repel them, holy lady?"

"Potent protective spells are woven around our sacred shrine. No one may bear weapons of war into the goddess's sanctuary." The two elves glanced down at the swords they wore. "Do not draw them," she warned. "If you do, you will be driven out, even as they were."

SANCTUARY

The gray-haired acolytes returned, each carrying a bundle of clothing. Khurish robes, mostly old and dingy, were laid at the elves' feet.

"Hengriff is intimate with the Khan. When word reaches him that you are here, soldiers will come. I am sorry, but I cannot offer you any hospitality. You must disguise yourselves and go," Sa'ida said.

Hytanthas started to object, but Planchet cut him off. The valet thanked the priestess politely and began sorting through the clothing. Reluctantly, his companion did the same, discarding the torn garment he still wore. They decked themselves in sleeveless gebs and trailing outer robes. A scarf wrapped around the head concealed their tell-tale ears. Thus swathed from head to foot, and with the added cloak of night, their disguises looked authentic.

Planchet tugged the sash tight around his waist, bowed slightly, and walked toward the iron gate. Hytanthas hovered briefly, torn between the need to go with his comrade and the desire to try and learn more about the Nerakan Knight. Sa'ida ended his conflict by turning and leading her followers into the temple. The doors closed, the bright light was cut off, and Hytanthas was left in darkness.

"Come, lad," Planchet called. "We've a long way to go."

The journey across the dark city was a nervous one, but they reached Khurinost without serious incident. Dawn was breaking as they approached their greatest challenge, the city gatehouse, but luck was with them. A horde of soukats milled outside, eager to get back to their stalls in the markets. The mayhem of the day before had not discouraged them. Indeed, some spoke about how good business ought to be today as curious crowds came out to see where so much blood had been shed. Beset by the noisy, pushy tradesmen, the guards on the gate didn't give the disguised elves a second glance.

Planchet headed straight for the Speaker's tent. Hytanthas followed, but more than once the valet had to double back and retrieve the wayward warrior, finding him standing idle, his

141

gaze distant, and him lost in thought. Planchet himself was bone-weary and ravenous. Neither he nor Hytanthas had eaten since yesterday morning, before this whole adventure began. He could only imagine how much worse the captain must feel, these events having come directly on the heels of the two tense days he'd spent disguised in the capital. But there could be neither rest nor food and drink until they'd reported to the Speaker.

A small group of court officials occupied the audience chamber, but the Speaker was not present. In his place, Morillon Ambrodel held court at the center of the disturbed crowd. As a result of the violence of yesterday morning, they quickly learned, a flood of Qualinesti and Silvanesti had returned from Khuri-Khan with stab wounds, broken heads, and worse. Forty-four elves were still missing. Planchet heard cries of "What are we to do?" and "The Speaker must protect us!"

His strong hands and penetrating voice parted the crowd. Pushing aside Qualinesti, Silvanesti, and Kagonesti alike, Planchet made his way to Morillon and asked where the Speaker could be found.

"Still abed, for aught I know. Rousing him is your job, I believe." The haughty noble eyed Planchet's scruffy human attire with distaste. "Where have you been anyway?"

The valet folded his arms and surveyed the assembly. Some of the elves were former senators of the Thalas-Enthia. Others were commoners, elevated by circumstance or the vote of their neighbors to become their representatives to the Speaker. Every face bore an expression of grave concern.

"I passed the night in the city, my lord, running and hiding from humans intent on cutting my throat," he said.

Gasps circled the chamber. "Is the Khan turning against us?" asked a frightened senator.

The valet held up placating hands. "Don't panic. The riot appears to have been started by followers of the Khurish god Torghan. When the Khan's troops arrived to put down the fighting, they were told elves started it. Calm has been restored in the city, but I must report these events to the Speaker. He and the Khan need to meet to clarify what happened."

"I must go to Sahim-Khan."

All heads turned. Gilthas stood in the passage leading to his private rooms. Lord Morillon swept up to him.

"Great Speaker, you should not wait upon a barbarian lord like Sahim! Let him come to you. You have precedence as ruler of the most ancient race—"

"It's his country, Morillon. I will go to Sahim-Khan as soon as he will receive me."

Everyone spoke at once, some supporting Morillon's attitude, others the Speaker's. Woven through the discussion was frightened speculation about the possibility of war with the Khan's army.

Hytanthas found his mind drifting. The debate raging around him sounded like the hum of bees disturbed in their hive. He was wrung out. He felt disconnected, distant. Then, unexpectedly, his gaze fell on a stranger.

Across the chamber, a stooped figure stood motionless amidst the milling elves. Covered in heavy layers of ragged brown robes, he was comically out of place, yet no one seemed to notice him. Senators moved around Hytanthas, bumping him occasionally, but they gave no sign of seeing the robed stranger. Hytanthas stared hard but could get no impression of a face, only a cowled darkness.

He called a warning. But the noise of the discussion had risen to such a level, he couldn't even hear his own shouted words. Nor did any of the others seem to hear him. He began shouldering his way through the crowd, intent on reaching the cowled intruder. Was he a spy in the pay of Sahim-Khan, or another tool of Neraka? Whatever he was, he should not be here listening to the elves' intimate councils.

As he reached the stranger, Hytanthas grabbed the dagger worn by a rugged-looking Kagonesti, the chosen representative of his tribe. Normally keenly aware, the Wilder elf didn't react at all to Hytanthas's theft of his weapon.

Closer now, he noted the stranger's face was hidden in the depths of his hood, his hands tucked into his sleeves. Hytanthas seized him by the wrist. Or he tried. His hand passed through the intruder's arm as though he was a ghost.

At last, the stranger took notice of him. The cowl turned toward Hytanthas and from it came a faint, startled query: "You see me? How is that possible?"

Hytanthas tried shouting again, "Great Speaker, a spy!"

He found his own wrist gripped. The stranger's hand was solid enough now, with long fingers and prominent joints. His hold was like the snap of a bear trap, swift and hard. Hytanthas protested and jerked his arm repeatedly, but couldn't free himself.

"You had better come with me," hissed the stranger.

Hytanthas finally caught a glimpse of the intruder's face. It was dark, like polished wood, with a beak of a nose, thin lips, and eyes like none the elf had ever seen before. His eyes were dark brown—nearly black—from corner to corner. Hytanthas cried out in horror, and the cry rose in pitch as he noticed something even worse. Hanging down behind the hooded figure was a tail, bushy brown and fully three feet long.

At that moment, Gilthas glanced away from his wrangling advisors and his eye fell upon Captain Ambrodel. Hytanthas's head was tilted back, his mouth slack. He held his left arm rigidly across his chest. Concerned, Gilthas called attention to the captain's distorted posture.

The Kagonesti senator standing in front of Hytanthas turned and spoke to the young elf as Gilthas made his way across the room. But Hytanthas did not respond; his eyes remained closed.

The Speaker arrived, laying a hand on Hytanthas's rigid arm. Instantly, the bizarre trance was broken. Hytanthas opened his eyes, staggered back, and fell unconscious to the floor.

Planchet knelt by him. "Fainted," he said, attributing the incident to a lack of food and the rigors of the past few days.

SANCTUARY

At the Speaker's direction, Planchet carried the unconscious elf to a spare room off of Gilthas's own bedchamber. Excusing himself, telling his subjects to continue their discussion during his brief absence, Gilthas followed.

Planchet had placed the captain on a cot and was removing his boots. He looked up as the Speaker entered.

"I don't think this was caused by simple weakness," Gilthas said quietly, his expression grave.

He gently lifted Hytanthas's left arm, the one the young elf had held so rigidly. The wrist bore red marks, as though strong fingers had held it in a crushing grip.

*   *   *   *   *

By strenuous riding through the night, the Weya-Lu band circled wide of the elves and got between them and the pass leading into the Valley of the Blue Sands. The normally empty foothills were alive with skulking scouts and reconnaissance parties from both sides, all feeling their way through unfamiliar territory with every nerve strained to detect the enemy. Adala had hoped to pick up reinforcements before meeting the Lioness again, but her messages to other tribes had gone unanswered. When the elven army was seen to be heading north from Khuri-Khan, the Tondoon and Mikku scouts had assured Adala's scout of their tribes' support. Unfortunately, those assurances had not yet generated anything of substance. No Tondoon or Mikku riders had arrived to bolster the Weyadan's force.

Adala disregarded advice from both Etosh and Bilath that they wait a while longer, to give other tribesmen time to join them. The *laddad* must be punished for their foul deeds. They must be stopped and prevented from entering the hidden valley. The prophecy of the Oracle clearly warned of grave upheavals if the elves claimed the spot. The leader of the Weya-Lu carried several titles, one of the lesser-known being "Protector of the Blue Sands." Until now, this had seemed only an ancient, ceremonial distinction. With the incursion

145

of the *laddad*, the title was gaining new significance. And overlaying everything else was the Weyadan's unswerving, white-hot need for vengeance. The murderous foreigners had to be brought to account for their massacre of the nomad camp.

Most of the Weya-Lu accepted their leader's judgment that the elves were responsible for the atrocity. A few, like Wapah and Bilath, were troubled by the lack of evidence linking the slaughter to the *laddad*, but even they had to admit there seemed no other explanation. Sahim-Khan certainly was ruthless enough, but he stood to gain nothing from the killing. Besides, his army was bottled up in the capital, watching the elven host and guarding against any sudden coup. Knights of Neraka or wayward bands of ogres or minotaurs might be responsible, but none were known to be in the area. The only foreigners in Khur were the elves, and elven cavalry had certainly been close by.

A council of war was called for late in the afternoon. The land hereabouts was not the best for battle. Bad for horses, the ground was uneven, covered by shelves of rock tumbled from the Pillars of Heaven long ago. Clumps of thorny creeper made the footing even more hazardous. Still, it would have to do. The council gathered on a great shelf of slate, settling into its traditional ranks. The outermost ring was composed of elder warriors, the middle ring of war chiefs, and the inner ring of clan chiefs.

Etosh wanted to divide the nomad force in two and hide one band on either side of the pass. When the *laddad* were firmly committed to the single track into the valley, the furious nomads would have them in a vise.

Adala listened silently to the plan. She was darning a rip in a horsehair poncho belonging to a Weya-Lu man who no longer had wife or sisters to do the task for him; all had died in the massacre. Turning the garment over, she tested the stitches with her thumbnail and found them strong. When Etosh finished speaking, she announced, "Your plan is wrong.

146

The Weya-Lu won't follow it."

He took her judgment in silence, but the clan chiefs asked why she'd vetoed the scheme. It had their approval.

"Never divide your forces in the face of the enemy," she said, "even if you are greater in number."

Leaning forward, she used a darning needle to draw a pair of lines in the sand. The lines were at right angles to each other. "This is how we'll take them. This part of the warband"—she indicated the north-south line—"will attack the *laddad* first from the side, while the others"—the east-west line—"will swing in behind them, cutting off their retreat."

"Like the jaws of a panther," said Wapah, seeing the deadliness of Adala's plan. Her strategy had the advantage of never separating the nomads, while still striking the elves on two sides.

Gwarali, an elder fighter, disagreed. Adala's battle plan left two routes for the elves to escape: westward through the foothills, and north into the valley.

"If they go in either direction, their doom is certain," Adala said. "West takes them farther away from their people at Khuri-Khan, and we can drive them into the Burning Sands of the south. There they perish." She folded the mended garment neatly, laying it over her lap. "If they go north, we'll have them in a bottle."

"Yes, but they'll be in the valley!" said Gwarali.

"And I will ask the gods to punish them for their blasphemy."

At this, some men not of the Leaping Spider Clan openly snickered. Adala's dark eyes flashed.

"You dare mock Them! Those on High have placed me here to do Their will, and do it I shall, unto death!"

Gwarali, a great, bear-like man with a reddish beard and broad belly, said soothingly, "Now sister, how can you say that? Have the High Ones appeared to you?"

"Not directly, but Their will is plain. My husband was

taken by death, placing me, the Weyadan, at the head of my people. My husband's blood cousin, Wapah, was chosen by the Prince of Khur to lead him to the Oracle, thereby warning us of the *laddad*'s intent to steal our land and usurp the gods. Why else would these things have happened except to place the defense of our sacred land in my hands?"

"*Maita.*"

The word, murmured by Wapah, meant "fate," but with the connotation of an outcome predestined by the gods, something no mortal could escape.

A few clan elders were still skeptical, but they took care to be polite about it. Gwarali tried to steer the discussion back to Etosh's plan to ambush the elves, but the Weyadan would not bend.

She stood abruptly. This usually signaled the end of a council, and the men around her were startled by her breech of manners.

"Stay where you are!" she commanded. "I will show you my maita."

She picked her way through the rings of chiefs and warriors. Standing on the rim of the gray slab of slate, she pointed northward. Three mountain peaks, known by the nomads as Torghan's Teeth, were aligned in a perfectly spaced row. Half a day's ride straight toward them led to the only pass into the Valley of the Blue Sands. So tall were the three that their tops were dusted with snow that never melted. The sky above the mountains, streaked by feathery clouds, seemed boundless as the sea. The sun was nearly gone behind the western range. The setting sun left the three mountains in shadow but touched the high clouds and the snowy tips of the Teeth with orange and crimson.

"Hear me, High Ones!" Adala cried. "The time has come for justice! If I am to be Your instrument, make it known to all! I care nothing for fame or glory, Mighty Gods, only for Your will and the rights of my people." She flung her arms wide. "Show me my maita. Show the world!"

SANCTUARY

Her last words rang over the harsh landscape, echoing against the faraway slopes of the Teeth.

For several long minutes there was silence, broken only by the muttered comments of several of the men behind her. Then out of the clear breadth of sky, thunder rolled.

The men stirred. They hadn't expected to hear or see anything. From his place behind Adala's seat, Wapah bowed his head. The Weyadan was the Weyadan; he would never doubt her again.

A second, louder clap of thunder boomed, caroming off the Pillars of Heaven for an endless time. By the time the echoes died, the entire council was on its feet.

Bilath shouted, "Those on High have spoken! Adala maita! Adala maita!" The others took up the cry, turning it into a chant.

Adala lowered her hands, crossing her arms and bringing her hands to rest on her chest. She was breathing heavily, with tears filling her eyes. She had believed in her fate, but this display of divine favor was overwhelming. That the gods would condescend to give so obvious a sign before the doubters of her own people—this was the greatest moment of her life.

Gwarali approached, halting respectfully three paces away. "Weyadan, we will follow you," he said simply.

Six miles away, the sand beast was scrambling over the rocky ledges when it caught the scent of the nomad army. Poised between two spires of stone, it slowly turned its angular head, tasting the breeze. Humans, many humans, but no hint of elves. The intervening foothills confused it, limiting its usual range of sight and smell. The beast had been paralleling the elves for two days, but must have gotten ahead of them during the night. It would have to double back.

Legs like coiled steel sent the monster vaulting from its perch, and it began to run. So rapidly did the beast move, it rent the air asunder, sending cracks of thunder ringing in its wake.

Some miles away the Lioness, leading her depleted troop, heard the thunder as well. She held up a hand to halt the column. Favaronas, plodding along a dozen yards back, trotted to her.

"Did you hear it?" he demanded. "Did you hear that thunder?"

They knew well what such a sound from a clear sky meant. She told her officers to send flankers out a hundred yards. "But make sure they keep in sight of the column," she cautioned.

She wet a kerchief with a few drops of water, then offered the gourd to Favaronas while she dabbed her face with the damp cloth.

"What can we do if the thing attacks again? Will the magical orb work a second time?" Favaronas asked.

She shrugged, tying her hair back with the damp kerchief. Her knowledge of magical artifacts was limited. She changed the subject. "Have you any idea why this creature should be following us so doggedly?" she asked.

The scholar didn't. He knew only what he'd told her earlier, that sand beasts were wild animals of the deep desert, and rare. Obviously the creature was a predator, but what sort of predator would follow armed and mounted warriors over several days and many miles?

"Only the two-legged kind," Kerian said dryly. "And that's who I think set this monster on our trail. A two-legged predator."

When the flanking riders were in place, watching for attack or ambush, she waved the column forward. They would reach the Inath-Wakenti in two days. More and more, she felt the foolishness of Gilthas's idea to send their people there. Even if the valley proved to have a temperate climate, it wasn't their natural home, and never would be. Witless nomads and bloodthirsty beasts were the only creatures suited to this harsh, terrible land. Elves needed the cool green woods of the lands that had given them birth and sustenance through the ages. Without them, would they not soon cease to be elves?

As always, thoughts of home made Kerian's blood burn. It required all her discipline to keep from reining about and galloping madly to Qualinesti, to try to free the land of its oppressors or die in the trying. They should not be in Khur! Whether desert or city or fabled valley, none of it was theirs. None of it! They should be attacking the enemies who'd dared invade their ancestral lands!

Gilthas believed life mattered more than land. Of course Gilthas worried more about life than land—he had been born into royalty. No matter where he dwelt, he was the Speaker of the Sun and Stars. He was a king—no matter where he was forced to locate his kingdom.

In all her life, Kerianseray had known no such luxury. She was a fighter for her country and her people. Without her country or her people, what was left? What was she then?

Favaronas watched curiously as the Lioness prodded her mount to a trot. Her back was straight and her chin outthrust. In the time he'd been with her, the archivist had come to know that posture, that look. She was controlling her anger. Only two things in the world could make her so furious, could reduce her lips to that tight, white line: the gnawing loss of Qualinesti to their enemies, and disagreement with the Speaker. He wondered which was consuming her now.

7

The afternoon repose of Khuri-Khan was first broken by the jangle of sistrums and the clash of cymbals. Housewives lifted the shades covering their window openings and peered outside to see what the noise was about. Soukats, taking a respite from the morning's trading, pushed back their hats or came out from under their awnings. Anticipating an event, wine merchants in the Grand Souks reopened their stands. The street dogs of Khuri-Khan, always alert, began barking.

The deep thump of a drum sounded, two slow beats followed by two quick. A quintet of guards appeared. Their helmets were askew, armor straps flapping, for they had been sleeping, too. They made a ragged line and ported arms, standing as much at attention as the Khan's soldiers ever did. Someone was coming—someone important.

The curious Khurs first saw a double line of elf maidens, twenty strong. Each wore a white, knee-length silk gown and, as a concession to the punishing sun, a matching scarf tied around her head. Golden girdles draping their slim hips sparkled, as did the garland of golden leaves twining their necks. They carried white baskets, strewing the contents on the street before them. At home, this would have been flower petals. Here in Khuri-Khan it was white sand, washed and polished until it glittered like silver.

SANCTUARY

Behind the twenty maidens came thirty young elf males, also clad in white. Hands, feet, and faces were browned by years of desert life, but arms and legs were still pale as the forest shade had made them. Each elf wore a broad belt made of jointed golden plates. In the center of each plate flashed an enormous flat jewel, peridot or aquamarine. Each of the thirty elves held aloft a pole, laminated with gold. Ten poles were topped with the golden sun symbol, and ten with a stylized silver star. Atop the poles of the final ten was a flat plaque of lapis lazuli on which appeared a gold sun and silver star of equal size. The Khurs couldn't know it, but the precious metal on these standards was only thin plating over common brass or copper. Still, they made an impressive display.

By now Khurs of all ages were spilling out of their houses to see this wondrous parade. For years, they'd sold meat, meal, cloth, and soap to the *laddad*, and nothing dispels mystery like such humble, practical transactions. The elves they'd met were nothing like the tales said. They were a somber people of few words, with reddened faces and dirty nails. Not so the glorious apparitions promenading down the street today. *These* were the elves of legend!

Trailing the elf maidens and standard bearers were musicians. Four pairs of tympani strode down the center of the road, flanked on either side by a dozen white-robed youths either shaking sistrums or clanging cymbals. The rhythm was insistent: two slow beats followed by two fast, again and again. On the heels of the drummers were twelve older, brown-skinned elves dressed in green. They were Kagonesti pipers, carrying twinned flutes of silver and brass. Not yet playing, they walked with proud precision, dark hair hanging loose below their shoulders, their heads covered by leather skullcaps.

The parade penetrated the wide Street of Salah-Khan, which ran along the western end of the Grand Souks, and the pipers raised their instruments. A trill of notes floated over the desert city. Elf voices answered, crying, "*Esh! Esh!*"—the ancient greeting elves made to the sun each morning. The thirty standards, of sun, of stars, and of the two conjoined, were lifted skyward.

After the pipers, Hamaramis and fifty warriors of the Speaker's guard marched into view. They were arrayed in their best armor, with plumed helmets and brilliant green mantles. Boors might have noted the scuffs and dents in the armor, and how some plumes were broken, but such imperfections did not detract from the spectacle. Each warrior's short sword was sheathed and slung over his back, a traditional method of indicating peaceful intent. Each soldier held a brass and iron buckler to his chest with his left hand, and in his right gripped a ceremonial mace made of ivory. The heads were shaped like a sun or a star.

In the last rank of these warriors marched a watchful Hytanthas. He'd been attached to the Speaker's guard so he could point out the phantom he'd seen in the Speaker's tent, should the creature make an appearance.

In the soldiers' wake came a delegation of Silvanesti, led by Lord Morillon Ambrodel. They were dressed as Silvanesti lords had been for centuries, in deeply pleated robes of sky blue, sun yellow, or star white. Disdaining to mar their ensembles with practical headgear, the Silvanesti went bareheaded. They would pay for their pride later with bouts of sunburn and prickly heat.

Last of all came the Speaker himself, on foot. He could have ridden, but with every horse precious to his army, he chose not to. The way wasn't long from Khurinost to the palace. Not nearly as long as from Qualinost to Khur.

He did not wear his best robes—the cloth-of-gold and fireknap in which he'd been crowned—but a simple white gown, with elbow-length sleeves, which brushed his ankles. A rope of woven gold strands was tied around his waist, a collar of lapis bars encircled his throat, and gold bracelets decorated each wrist. He also had chosen not to wear a crown, neither the sun diadem of Qualinesti, nor the star circlet of Silvanesti. He was a Speaker in exile. Wearing crowns while homeless seemed to Gilthas the height of hubris.

Four favored senators walked around him, carrying poles supporting a light linen canopy. This spare shade was his only protection from the sun. Planchet walked at his left elbow. Where his consort should have walked, Gilthas deliberately left an open spot, honoring Kerianseray.

The end of the parade was composed of dignitaries of all kinds. Each elf carried some sign of his or her office: a senator's baton, a courtier's medallion, a scholar's scroll, a healer's vial, and so forth.

Not all the Khurs watching the procession were charmed or dazzled. Some glowered, and a few shook fists at the elves, who marched solemnly ahead. Only once, as they were passing through the Grand Souks, was anything thrown. A few overripe fruits pelted the ceremonial guard. They never broke step, and the Khan's soldiers charged into the crowd. They found the young offenders and dragged them away, beating them with olivewood staves.

The most direct route from the elves' camp to the Khuri yl Nor was all narrow, winding alleys and shade-darkened lanes. Gilthas's grand parade deliberately took a different way, following the widest streets in the city to give scope to his faded grandeur. In the great days of Sithel or Kith-Kanan, a Speaker's royal procession would have numbered many thousands. Today it contained fewer than three hundred.

Only one other notable incident occurred during the elves' passage, near the great Nak-Safal artesian well. The Street of Salah-Khan crossed the Temple Walk by the well. In a very real sense, this was the true center of Khuri-Khan, more sacred than any temple, more vital than palace or granary. Never in the harsh history of Khur had the well gone dry. When Malystryx scourged the city, it was to the Nak-Safal that the poor and destitute ran, knowing that whatever else befell them, they would not lack for life-giving water. Vexed by this display of faith, the red dragon tore a boulder from the city wall and flung it into the well. The great rock had been swallowed up by the white sand at the bottom of the well, and only a single corner showed above the water's surface. The Nak-Safal overflowed for five days, gently washing the cobblestones of the square. Still imbedded in the sand, the boulder was known among city folk as *Malsh-mekkek*, Malys's Tooth.

As the Speaker's parade wound past the well, Hytanthas Ambrodel saw a hooded, rag-draped figure standing at its edge. The hood turned toward him, and the elf suddenly felt dizzy. Framed by moldering cloth was the face of the strange apparition he'd glimpsed in the Speaker's tent the night before. The bizarre, solidly brown eyes locked onto Hytanthas's own. His step faltered. Drums, pipes, and cymbals sounded far away. He felt a strange twisting sensation in his stomach, as though the ground had unexpectedly fallen away from his feet, and all at once he seemed to be standing outside his own body, watching himself walk shoulder to shoulder with the honor guard. The effect of seeing himself walking was utterly disorienting. Hytanthas began to fall.

A strong hand caught him by the back of the neck. "Steady, lad," Planchet said, holding him upright. "Remember where you are!"

"He's here!" Hytanthas gasped. "The ghostly spy I saw in the Speaker's tent! He's by the well, in the ragged brown robe!"

Planchet squinted against the glare. "But that's no ghost. I can see him myself. Are you certain?"

"That's him . . ."

As Hytanthas fixed his gaze on the ground, seeking to regain his balance, Planchet looked again at the scruffy figure in brown. He was still there, facing away from the valet. Then, seemingly from one heartbeat to the next, he vanished. Planchet blinked and stared, but the hunched fellow was gone. The valet shook his head. It took little imagination to think the fellow most likely a sorcerer or a mage. Perhaps even the mysterious Faeterus himself.

"Do you think so?" Hytanthas asked, looking more himself, and Planchet realized he'd voiced his speculation aloud.

"It's possible," the valet said, pushing Hytanthas back toward his place in the procession.

The parade of elves reached the square before the Khuri yl Nor and found Sahim-Khan's household guard awaiting them, turned out in full regalia. While they lacked the grace and style of the elves, the Khan's elite possessed a barbarous splendor of their own. Handpicked for height and physique, the guardsmen made an imposing show in their tall, spiked helmets, articulated breastplates, and panther-skin mantles. Arrayed outside the main gate of the citadel in two blocks, the guards struck the ground with their halberds, and shouted, "Sahim-Khan!"

The elves halted between the blocks of Khurish soldiers. The maidens and standard bearers stood aside, allowing the remainder of the procession to advance. Soon, Gilthas was being greeted at the palace gate by Sahim's vizier, Zunda. A relic from the days of the dragon, Zunda had retained his place as vizier by being the oiliest, most obsequious courtier in Khuri-Khan. The tightly curled hair which fell past his shoulders was an obvious wig, and the flat black color of his elaborately curled beard was just as obviously due to dye.

"Greetings, O Light of the Elven Nations!" Zunda intoned loudly, bowing as low as his belly allowed. "The Great Khan of All the Khurs, Lion of the Desert, Vanquisher of Dragons, Sahim, son of Salah, welcomes you!"

Gilthas lowered his eyes briefly in acknowledgment. At his gesture, Lord Morillon stepped forward and answered the vizier.

"The noble Speaker of the Sun and Stars, Gilthas, of fa-vored name, earnestly desires an audience with the Great

Khan." The Silvanesti would not be outdone by a mere Khur when it came to flowery speech.

"The glorious Sahim, Father of Khur and Fount of All Justice, has heard of your coming. He bids me, his most unworthy vizier, to convey you to his awesome presence."

All eyes but the Speaker's switched back to Morillon.

The Silvanesti pressed a hand to his chest and bowed his head, smiling with magnificent condescension. "Gracious Vizier, we are awed by the generosity of your Great Khan. I, Morillon Ambrodel, son of Kenthalantas Ambrodel and councilor to the Speaker of the Sun and Stars, beg you to lead on, and we shall enter with gratitude into the presence of your mighty lord."

Everyone looked back to Zunda. This was obviously a battle to the death.

"My heart overflows, noble Morillon! Should I perish at this moment, I would die in blissful content to have known the celebrated personages of my Great Khan, Sahim son of Salah, the Speaker of the Sun and Stars, and your most noble self! You have but to follow, and this auspicious audience shall commence!"

Immediately, Zunda backed away, bowing three times as he went. Hamaramis gave the command and the honor guard started after him.

As he passed the red-faced Morillon, Gilthas murmured, "I think he won."

The Khuri yl Nor was still in poor shape, though repairs continued day and night. The inner yard had been swept clean of debris, but the restored facades of the Nor-Khan and the Khanate (Sahim's private residence) still were marked by large sections of unglazed brick and raw timber. The banner of Khur, with its pair of rampant golden dragons, hung from the battlement of the Great Keep, flapping slowly in the hot breeze. It had been rent by Malys's claws, giving it the look of a pennon.

Straining guards opened the heavy bronze doors. Within

the keep, the air was pleasantly cool. On the seaward side of the palace, enormous canvas funnels channeled sea breezes inside. This cooled the palace and filled it with the scent of the ocean.

The Nor-Khan was a maze of broad, high-ceilinged halls and long, low-roofed corridors. In part this was intentional, to confuse intruders, but it also reflected the varied history of Khur. Khans with money built lavishly. Those who were poor did not. The result was a hodgepodge palace, which only experienced lackeys and courtiers like Zunda could navigate successfully.

During their journey through the hallways, Planchet realized they were passing beneath the same area of cracked ceiling plaster for a second time. He murmured, "Sire, they're leading us in circles."

Gilthas smiled. "Sahim-Khan needs time to prepare his welcome."

When at last Zunda conducted the elf delegation into the audience hall, Sahim was seated on the Sapphire Throne, waiting. He wore a splendid gown of dark blue silk; along its hem were embroidered dragons in red and gold. The red crown of Khur sat upon his head, and his beard had been combed and arranged in neat curls. He smiled broadly when Zunda announced the Speaker of the Sun and Stars.

"My brother!" he proclaimed, rising to his feet. "To what do I owe this inestimable honor?"

Gilthas halted at the foot of the throne dais. He did not bow. As heir to two of the oldest monarchies in the known world, he took precedence over an upstart like Sahim. However, protocol was not as important as diplomacy, so he found a way to pay homage to his host. With an outward sweep of his arm, Gilthas managed to convey the spirit of a bow without actually performing one.

"Great Khan, I have come to confer with you about the troublesome situation growing in your city," he said. As you know, my consort, Lady Kerianseray, was set upon in the

Temple Walk. Two days after that, a mob of Khurs rioted in the markets, seeking out elves to beat and kill."

"Ah, yes." Sahim sat back down. "The perpetrators are known to me, and are being rounded up for punishment even now."

Most of the elven delegation silently fumed at seeing their Speaker forced to stand before the Khan like an ordinary supplicant. For his part, Gilthas adopted the bland mask he'd worn for so long during Marshal Medan's occupation of Qualinost.

"Who are these people? Criminals?"

"They are now!" Sahim said, and laughed unpleasantly. "They're fanatics, religious fanatics."

"How have my people offended them?"

"Only by your existence, Great Speaker. Worshipers of Torghan love their country, but the presence of"—he almost said *laddad*—"elves in Khur is seen by them as an affront to the nation and their god."

The exchange between rulers, polite on its surface, went on, with the Speaker seeking assurances that no further attacks would be made on his people, while Sahim eluded any promises. Planchet used the time to study the inhabitants of the throne room, those he could see without turning his head. The most glaring absence was that of Sahim's heir. Prince Shobbat had not been glimpsed in public for some time. It was rumored he was quite ill. The walls of the room were lined with a motley collection of Khurs, city folk and nomads. Nobles from Delphon and Kortal were identifiable by their distinctive fashions: flat-topped, conical hats on the Delphonians and the western-style attire worn by those from Kortal, a territory situated near the border with Neraka.

"Some of the miscreants have in fact confessed," the Khan said, and Planchet's attention snapped back to him. Given the sort of persuasion meted out in the Khan's dungeon, his prisoners would confess to anything.

"To a man they insist the trouble began when elves paid for goods using debased coinage."

The soft background chatter ceased throughout the hall. Sahim had just accused the elves of passing coins made of inferior mixtures of metal rather than pure steel, gold, silver, or copper. The Speaker's slender brows drew together. Those who knew him well recognized the stirring of anger.

"I know nothing of this," he said tersely.

Sahim leaned forward, his expression one of concern. "Traders in the Souks are shrewd, but many live on the knife-edge of ruin. A day's wages lost in bad coinage can mean starvation for their families. I am told that word of the false coins reached the Sons of the Crimson Vulture, and they sought to make the offending elves pay in genuine metal." He leaned back again, spreading his hands expansively. "Alas! They could not tell the guilty from the innocent, and waylaid all elves they found. But be assured, Great Speaker, the matter is resolved. The offenders will pay with their heads."

He announced this with the same casual air another man might adopt when promising a simple favor. The Speaker's entourage wore grim expressions. Sahim, while vowing to punish the rioters, plainly blamed the elves for the trouble and was daring the Speaker to contradict him.

A faint smile crossed Gilthas's lips. "The Mighty Khan's justice be done," he said, inclining his head slightly. "Might I make an offer, in the interest of good relations between our peoples?" Grandly, the Khan waved for him to continue. "Let me repay those vendors who lost money, and the families of the men who face your judgment. This I will do out of my own treasury."

The humans filling the edges of the hall shifted, murmuring among themselves. They had not expected this.

Sahim-Khan, on the other hand, could not stop the grin that split his face. He beamed, saying the Speaker's generosity would not be wasted.

Polite robbery! thought Hytanthas. From his place with the honor guard, he seethed at the injustice of the gesture that the Speaker should pay for a riot not of the elves' making. Sahim was stealing just as surely as if he held the Speaker at the point of a knife and demanded his purse! And Hytanthas had no doubt every steel piece of the so-called indemnity would end in the Khan's pockets.

To distract himself from his anger, Hytanthas let his gaze wander. The honor guard was divided into two lines, each facing inward toward the Speaker. Hytanthas was on the Speaker's right, looking toward the Khurs on Sahim's right, those crowded along the north wall of the hall.

As he scanned the Khurs, he hoped to see the rag-draped man among them, but he did not. He did spot Lord Hengriff. Although draped in civilian dress, the Nerakan was unmistakable. Standing behind him were four more large humans. Like him they were clean-shaven and dressed in civilian finery. Hytanthas had no trouble recognizing them for what they were—the Knight's personal bodyguard and most probably the same men who had tried to take Hytanthas and Planchet at the Temple of Elir-Sana last night.

Hamaramis suddenly barked an order. The honor guard made a quarter-turn, facing away from the throne. The Speaker bowed slightly as the Khan slipped away. His audience was over.

The elves went out with proud dignity, but every heart burned with shame, and every jaw was clenched tight. Only the Speaker appeared calm. He spoke a few words to his valet. Planchet's angry color lessened. He nodded obediently, and drifted away from the Speaker's side.

Outside, musicians, courtiers, and standard bearers began to form up again. Hytanthas took his place at the rear of the honor guard, but was pulled aside.

Planchet pushed a Khurish robe at him and hissed, "Shed your armor, and don this. You're staying in the city."

The captain knew why: to look for Faeterus. Unbuckling

his breastplate under cover of his milling countrymen, he whispered, "What do I do if I find him?"

"Send word. We'll take care of the rest." Planchet added, "The word is 'Eagle Eye.' That will mean you've found the sorcerer."

Hytanthas pulled the robe over his head. It smelled as though it had just come off its previous owner. With a sun hat pulled down over his ears and his chin down to hide his hairless cheeks, he slipped away from his comrades.

An investigation of the robe's pockets yielded a purse containing twenty steel, a sizable sum. It ought to be enough to buy the information he needed.

* * * * *

One of the forward scouts came galloping back, his horse's hooves clattering loudly on the stony soil. Kerian reined up, halting the column. Although the Qualinesti said nothing until he'd halted his mount before her, she could tell by his face that he'd been successful.

"I found the pass, General! The entrance to the valley!"

He confirmed the identifying landmarks Kerian had memorized from Gilthas's map. The three peaks, snow-capped, were there, lined up abreast. No tracks went in or out of the pass.

Kerian was relieved. She didn't imagine the nomads were done with them yet, but at least they hadn't reached the pass first. The sand beast, too, haunted her thoughts. There was no telling when the creature might turn up again.

While the scout and his panting horse quenched their thirsts, she turned to another important task. It was time to apprise Gilthas of their progress. The sun was low in the late afternoon sky, but she didn't want to wait until morning to dispatch a courier.

She chose a rugged Kagonesti named Redhawk to return to Khurinost with the reports she'd composed. The sealed letters went into a leather pouch, which the Kagonesti looped around his neck. She handed him one last missive, a flat parcel wrapped in oilskin and sealed with wax.

"This," she said, "is for the Speaker personally. No one else. The other dispatches may be handed to Planchet or Hamaramis, but this goes into no hands but Gilthas Pathfinder's."

Redhawk swore to carry out the mission exactly. Laying a blue-tattooed hand on the pouch around his neck, he vowed, "This will not leave me so long as I live." None knew better than she the seriousness of a Wilder pledge.

When Redhawk had diminished to a smudge of dust on the horizon, she turned her attention back to the Qualinesti scout.

"Lead us to the entrance into the pass. We'll camp there for the night."

With the Qualinesti in the lead, the column moved out.

The three mountain peaks loomed ahead, blotting out all sight of the way beyond. Kerian stared in amazement at their snowy tops. She couldn't even remember the last time she'd seen snow.

As the column entered the mouth of the pass, the last fingernail slice of sun vanished below the western range to their left. With the light gone, the temperature plummeted, leaving shivering riders to don long-unused cloaks. It really wasn't so cold, but compared to the blast furnace of the High Plateau, the air felt frigid indeed.

The pass was a silent place. The wind, which had swirled around the elves since the Khalkist mountains first came in view, died away. Although there were more plants about—scrub pines and gnarled junipers, thorny greasebushes and spiky aloe—the area seemed oddly lifeless. The only sound to be heard was the clink of their horses' hooves on the pebbly soil. No birds chattered from the trees, no insects buzzed.

Color was returning. To elven eyes, the desert was dull, all tans, browns, and grays surmounted always by a blue sky that, cloudless, seemed oddly flat. At the mouth of the Inath-Wakenti, subtle shadings were restored to the landscape's palette. The mountainsides were softly washed in purple and blue. Dark green pines stood over dwarf junipers in lighter greens. Moss and lichen mottled the rocks in silvery gray, or a green as bright as the limes popular in Khuri-Khan.

Kerian did not like it. When the valley had been nothing more than a spot on a map, she'd had many reasons for not wanting to come here, much less to live here. Now that it was real, now that she was here, her objections only increased. The very feel of the place was wrong. Tainted somehow.

She wasn't the only one to notice this. Favaronas had drawn his cape close around his shoulders. "Feels like a graveyard," he muttered, his eyes darting left and right.

Unconsciously, the elves slowed their pace. They'd come through the fiery crucible of the High Plateau, losing many of their number to nomads, the sand beast, and heat stroke, and they had reached their goal at last, yet no one felt any joy. No one smiled. Like Favaronas, all were looking around uncertainly, not drinking in the sight of their fabled destination, but regarding it with suspicion. Talk ceased. Every face reflected the same thought: What sort of place have we come to?

"General! Tracks!"

Kerian shook off the tomblike mood and urged her mount into a trot. The vanguard riders had found an area of prints. Horses had crossed the elves' intended path, from left and right. Kerian dismounted and joined one of the scouts, kneeling to study the prints.

"Small hooves. Unshod," she observed.

"Nomad ponies," agreed the Wilder scout. "Many."

"How long ago?"

He put his sun-darkened face scant inches from the prints, then lifted a handful of trampled dirt, crushed it, and let it fall from his fingers. "Half a day or less, but more than an hour," he reckoned.

So much for having beaten the nomads to the pass, she thought unhappily. Kerian rose. Favaronas arrived leading his horse. He asked what they had found.

"Nomads," she said. "Probably the same ones we've fought twice before."

"Why? We aren't in their desert anymore," the archivist said, exasperated.

"To keep us out of the valley." Dusk had come and gone. Stars were appearing overhead. Kerian realized that even she, with her keen eyesight, found it difficult to penetrate the shadows ahead. A sudden shiver chased itself down her spine, and she muttered, "I almost wish they would."

The howl of a wolf pierced the air. Immediately it was answered by others both ahead and behind the elves. Kerian's gloomy mood shattered.

"Stand to horse!" she cried, drawing her sword.

Favaronas did as she ordered, but didn't see the need for such alarm. Surely even a large pack of wolves wouldn't attack a column of armed elves.

The Lioness glowered at him. "Those aren't wolves, librarian! The enemy is upon us!"

Her officers came cantering up, the balance of the company following.

"Deploy your riders, now!" she ordered.

Favaronas's uncertainty evaporated abruptly as a hail of arrows fell out of the darkened sky. The wolf cry was a nomad signal.

With a hundred riders, the Lioness moved down the slight slope to the east, seeking the hidden archers. The ground was broken by deep gullies cut during winter rains. Nomads skulked in these crevices, raising their heads long enough to loose an arrow, then ducking under cover again. The mounted elves were forced to bend low to saber the enemy, but in a few minutes they put the archers to rout. Whooping with victory, they would've chased the fleeing humans, but the Lioness called them back.

Returned to the main body of warriors, she sat motionless in the saddle, her head up, straining to hear the slightest sound. She divided her attention between north and south. From one direction or the other, the main attack would come. She was beginning to understand nomad thinking. Feint into ambush was practically their only tactic. Wolf calls and a burst of arrows were intended to strike fear, to fix the enemy's attention in one direction, while the main assault came from elsewhere. The pass here was too wide for a strike from the west; it would come from the north, directly ahead, or the south.

"Keep alert," she called. "Watch the shadows."

From the north came the rumble of approaching horses. The Lioness spread out her small band in skirmishing order, each rider seven or eight feet from his neighbor. By the sound of the enemy's approach, she estimated she faced a force slightly greater in size than her own.

Others in the line had made the same mental calculation. An anxious voice asked, "Should we sit still and receive their charge?"

"Unless you want to die tonight," the Lioness replied. She was certain this was yet another feint. The main attack still had not shown itself.

A dark mass of riders appeared out of the north. The nomads were strung out in a long, thin line, stretching beyond the limits of the elves' small formation. Fortunately, the rough ground prevented the Khurs from charging at full speed. They had to pick their way around broken ground and small trees, then climb through steep gullies in small groups. Under the Lioness's steady hand, the elves waited. When the first nomads reached level ground, she ordered half her command to charge. A brisk melee began, with the elves battling the Khurs as they arrived, piecemeal. This effectively destroyed the nomads' numerical advantage.

The battle continued, Khurs and elves wheeling and turning on the ground as the stars overhead performed their own slow, stately march between the high peaks. A rider made his way to the Lioness. He reported large numbers of nomads coming up from the south.

She felt a kind of relief. At least the waiting was over. "How many?" she asked.

"Difficult to say, General. Three hundred, maybe more."

She sent him back to his comrades. Three hundred nomads against fewer than one hundred of her soldiers, awaiting their charge. Even with the advantage of darkness, those were daunting odds.

The elves around her watched her in silence. The veterans, with her since the days of rebellion in Qualinesti, sat as motionless as she. Younger warriors shifted nervously. Since she was the Lioness—admired just short of worship, yet first among equals—one spoke up, asking what her orders were.

She turned a thoughtful look on him. "Who carries our fire?" she asked.

Certain elves in the warband were detailed to carry live coals in clay pots. From these each night's campfires were lit. The young elf couldn't fathom why the Lioness would ask about this now, but he replied after only a brief, confused pause: "Sergeant Vitianthus has our fire, General."

She knew Vitianthus. A Silvanesti volunteer, he was a former horse trainer and an elegant rider.

"Tell the sergeant I want fire—lots of it." Twisting in the saddle, she pointed to a copse of cedars forty yards distant, on their right flank. "Have him set fire to those trees."

The young elf saluted and galloped away.

"Everyone is to remain where they are," Kerian commanded. At her order, swords were drawn and rested on shoulders.

Sergeant Vitianthus and a contingent broke off from the band and galloped to the cedar copse. For a long interval nothing could be seen, then sharp elven eyesight noted smoke rising, nearly invisible in the night air. The sweet cedar smoke drifted back over the motionless warriors. An orange flame leaped up. Then another.

To the main body of nomads, advancing steadily from the south, the sight of fire was a shock. The leading elements of Adala's tribe faltered, uncertain what was happening. Adala, mounted on her donkey, saw the flickering flames and shrugged.

"So much the better. A fire will make it easier to see the *laddad* and kill them."

Gwarali, who had begged for the honor of leading the attack, agreed with her. The burning trees clearly showed him elves on horseback waving fiery brands. It seemed a futile gesture. The trees were too few to make a blaze large enough to ward off the nomad warband. All the desperate elves were doing was illuminating their own destruction.

He drew his sword and uttered the new war cry—"Adala maita!"

Hundreds echoed him, as he led the men forward. Wisely, they did not gallop toward the foe, but rode at a fast trot. They saw the elves who'd started the fire retreating from the burning copse, and naturally went for the enemy they could see.

As the nomads skirted the blaze, the crackle of burning wood and snap of boiling sap masked other sounds. The Weya-Lu never heard the hail of arrows that emptied a score of their saddles.

"Where are they coming from?" Gwarali shouted. The firestarters were still in view, galloping away to the north.

No one could answer him. Another wave of arrows fell. These weren't random volleys, lofted in the general direction of the Khurs. Every missile found a target; the arrows were well aimed. Even nomads farther from the fire and not illuminated by its light were being hit.

The answer hit Gwarali like a bolt of lightning: *Laddad* could see in the dark!

He shouted a warning. It was echoed back through the ranks, and the Weya-Lu faltered. Gwarali roared, "They can die in the dark, too! Up swords!"

More arrows came, scything across the starlit landscape, each wave bringing down men and horses. Gwarali pulled his horse up short, causing the pony to rear on its hind legs. He bellowed, "Will you leave your murdered families unavenged? Did your fathers and brothers die in battle for nothing? Are you men?"

Backs straightened, blood surged anew. The Weya-Lu lifted swords high and prepared to charge.

"Believe in your maita, sons of the sand! Follow me! For your gods! For—"

A perfectly aimed arrow cut off Gwarali's rallying cry. The point took him in the left eye, burying itself deep. The nomad chief was dead even as he toppled backward off his horse.

The Lioness watched with satisfaction as the Weya-Lu attack melted away. The fire had worked even better than she'd hoped. By lighting it on their right flank, the elves drew the nomads to that point. The flames weren't enough to light the battlefield for the humans—in fact, their proximity to it served to ruin what little night sight they had—but the elves, with their keener vision, could clearly see the nomad riders.

There was no time to celebrate. The fire was dying out. Stung by the elves' arrows, the nomads would probably return with everything they had. It was time to go. She and the archers rejoined the northern half of her army. They had empty saddles of their own. This was not a horseman's battle, blundering through gullies with archers about.

According to Gilthas's map, the pass narrowed about a mile in. Kerian decided they would advance and make a stand there.

The noise of the enemy approaching from behind them grew louder. In close order, the elves rode straight down the center of the pass. Favaronas kept close to the Lioness. With luck and her tactical skill, he hoped they might yet escape the nomads' pursuit.

Adala took the loss of Gwarali in stride. Bilath, brother of Adala's dead husband, was leading the flanking riders now. Gwarali's nephew Bindas took his uncle's place at the head of the southern warband. Bolstered by the Weyadan's calm conviction, Weya-Lu warriors once more pushed forward, eager to close with the *laddad*.

On a rocky pinnacle three miles away, the sand beast raised its head and tasted the wind. Its prey was close by, and in great numbers. The itch in its iron claws soon would be salved by elf blood. It gathered itself to spring. There were humans in its path, but they posed no obstacle. One blinding rush and all the elves would die, then the burning in its heart would be extinguished. One rush, and it would all be over—

A new odor, propelled by the east wind, teased its nostrils. The sand beast froze. The scent was familiar, an ancient memory, one that caused the scales on its back to ripple in fear.

A strange warbling cry pierced the night. High overhead, a black object occluded the stars.

Kerian heard it over the thud and jingle of her troops in motion. Hardly believing her ears, she looked skyward.

"Eagle Eye!"

Favaronas, slightly ahead of her, tried to look back while maintaining his seat. "What?"

"My griffon! That's his cry! I know it as well as my own voice!"

She had no idea how Eagle Eye could be here, when she'd left him in Khurinost, but the griffon's call was unmistakable. Standing in her stirrups, she whistled shrilly. To her delight, Eagle Eye answered, sounding closer now.

When the warbling screech came a second time, the sand beast bolted. Strong as it was, the urge to hunt elves could not overcome the primal fear inspired by the sound of a natural enemy. Descending the hill in one great bound, the sand beast lowered its head, struck the opposite hillside, and immediately began burrowing. It tore through slabs of slate as easily as a child digs in sand. Before the shadow of the griffon crossed the hill where the sand beast had been, it was completely buried, lying still as the rock around it.

The Lioness stopped, and her warriors followed suit. They could now see the griffon's black shape moving in the sky. Kerian cupped her hands around her mouth and whistled again.

The griffon descended rapidly, flaring his wings and hovering over the elves. None of them could enjoy the sight; all were too busy trying to control their plunging horses. Kerian solved this dilemma for herself by vaulting from the saddle. Rising to her feet, she held up a hand to the griffon and called his name. Eagle Eye, utterly ignoring the chaos around him, landed next to her and lowered his hooked beak, tucking it under her arm like a pet songbird.

"You old monster," she said fondly. "I'm glad to see you, too. Your timing is excellent!"

A shout interrupted the reunion. Favaronas, engaged in a losing battle with his terrified horse, yelled, "The nomads are getting close!"

Two hundred yards away, the main body of nomads was in plain view. Their advance from the south had been halted temporarily as they, too, had to cope with frightened mounts. From the east, a second force of nomads was likewise delayed. Kerian estimated some four hundred Khurs remained.

"Form up! Form up!" she called, even as she leapt onto the griffon's back. She was airborne in the next heartbeat, Eagle Eye's muscular hindquarters sending them into the air with a breath-snatching rush. Kerian turned his head toward the larger (and closer) southern nomad band, shouting at her elves, "Into the valley—at a gallop! There's no time to waste!"

SANCTUARY

Her warriors sorted themselves into riding formation. Reins snapped and spurs dug in. They surged northward. On their right, the second party of Khurs was angling to cut them off. With the Lioness forced to concentrate first on the southern nomads, the eastern band was beginning to regain control of their horses.

Eagle Eye flew so low over the nomad horsemen that Kerian could have kicked their hats with her boot. Instead, she crouched low over her mount's neck. It wouldn't do to pick up an arrow from a sharp-eyed nomad archer. The griffon's screeching cries sent the horses into a frenzy. Their riders seemed scarcely more composed. Tribesmen in Eagle Eye's path flung themselves off their mounts.

Eagle Eye banked, flapped hard for altitude, and soared back over the hectic scene. Kerian aimed to rejoin her fleeing command. Her bird's-eye perspective showed a dire situation.

The flanking nomads, riding hard from the east, had succeeded in getting in front of her elves. She growled in frustration; the trap she feared had caught them. Nomads were ahead and, however disordered, also behind them. Their only hope of survival was the Inath-Wakenti, where they would have room to maneuver—and hide.

She reached her diminished band and hovered high above them. "Draw swords, all!" she cried. Three hundred-odd blades rose in unison. "Forward! Don't falter! If the humans get in your way, cut them down, but don't stop to fight. Go!"

Boot to boot, the wedge of elves hit the nomads head-on. The elves, highly trained veterans on taller, heavier horses, pushed through the loose nomad formation, trading sword cuts as they went. Bilath tried to hold his men as Adala had instructed, but the elves would not be denied. Bilath himself received a slash on the temple. A second cut might have finished him, but the elf warrior tore by without pause.

On the southern front, the Weya-Lu led by Bindas were coming up fast. Their desert ponies were a hardy lot, and the animals' fear had faded as they grew accustomed to the griffon's strange scent. Adala's stolid donkey had never given in to the terror. On beholding the griffon, Adala proclaimed the strange flying beast a sign. Monsters from the Abyss had been raised against them, she told her rapt followers. The wicked *laddad* thought to cow them, but Torghan the Avenger would strengthen Weya-Lu sword-arms and steel their hearts. The Weya-Lu shouted, "Adala maita!" Then they thundered forward at a gallop.

Riding near the Weyadan, Wapah stared uncertainly at the griffon. He recognized it as a creature associated with the Silvanesti and didn't quite understand how it could be both a sign from Those on High and a monster raised by the *laddad* for use against the people of the desert.

Shrugging, he decided this was just another example of what happened when a man strayed from the hard edges of the desert. Here, mountains pierced the sky, letting in confusion.

The griffon swooped in, hovering in front of the nomad band. Adala tugged Little Thorn's reins, halting the donkey. Her warriors stopped as well.

"Begone, monster!" Adala shouted to the griffon. "Return to the wicked land of your ancestors!"

"That's just what I plan to do!" said a voice from the creature's back, and a javelin came flying at Adala.

The mother of the Weya-Lu held her place. The javelin struck the ground a few feet in front of Little Thorn's hooves, burying its iron head six inches into the hard soil. The shaft vibrated with the force of the throw. The griffon wheeled and flew off into the night.

Etosh came riding back from the head of the nomad band.

"Weyadan, the *laddad* are entering the valley! We have failed!"

The anger Adala had felt on hearing the *laddad* voice subsided. Her face resumed its patient cast. "All is well, brother. They have gone into the sacred valley, but there they will perish."

The tribe, she said, would camp here, blocking the only pass out of the valley. When the *laddad* tried to escape, they would be destroyed. She urged Little Thorn forward, grasped the javelin, and worked it free of the soil. Wapah came up beside her as she was studying the weapon.

"We should not stay here, Weyadan," he said. "This land is not good. The hard edges are dulled. Unnatural things abide."

"We must stay. Our land and our honor demand it." She looked up at him, taller than she on his pony, and added, "I have seen a new vision of our path, cousin. It's not enough to expel the foreigners from the valley. When the *laddad* here have been dealt with, we will raise the tribes, all the tribes of Khur, and lead them to Khuri-Khan. We will deal with the *laddad* there, too."

She handed him the javelin, and turned her animal away. He touched the tip of the slender spear lightly; it was keen enough to make his thumb bleed. Had it hit the Weyadan, it easily would have pierced her back to front. Wrapping the sharp head in a length of protective cloth, Wapah lashed the javelin across the rear of his saddle. Nomads were never wasteful.

Six miles away, the Lioness brought Eagle Eye to ground far enough in front of her warriors that their horses wouldn't go wild. They reined up. Elves and horses alike were panting for breath. Her officers and Favaronas joined her on foot next to the griffon.

"They didn't follow us," she said. "I think they're afraid—of the valley or Eagle Eye, I'm not sure which."

Favaronas said, "Lucky your creature found us. I thought the time for such wonders was past!"

Kerian, too, had been marveling at the griffon's cleverness. With the rush of battle behind her she realized how odd it was that Eagle Eye had arrived fully saddled, with

175

weapons of battle, like the javelin quiver, in place. She certainly hadn't left him stabled that way.

The answer to the conundrum was tucked inside the javelin quiver. It was a folded parchment whose message convinced her that wonders were no match for the everyday power of love.

Thought you could use a friend, the note said. It was signed simply, "G."

8

Sa'ida, surrounded by chanting priestess-healers, stood by the bed of Prince Shobbat. She dipped a finger in the oil warming in a shallow copper pan and traced on his forehead the seal of Elir-Sana.

The high priestess was red-eyed and haggard from her efforts. This was the culmination of three days of work, weaving a great healing spell around the delirious prince. Lesser potions and cantrips had not restored Shobbat's shattered wits, nor healed his blindness, though his wild ravings had been soothed and he had stopped flailing uncontrollably. He was left lying rigid in his bed, eyes closed. Sa'ida had no choice but to perform the strongest, most arduous spell of healing known to her.

Acolytes and priestesses worked in shifts, new ones arriving at the palace every six hours to relieve their predecessors. The chant went on without a break for three days. Aromatics and incense were burned, and elaborate designs, in yellow paint, were drawn on the walls and floor of the prince's bedchamber. The design created a great invisible funnel through which the goddess's healing power could flow. Shobbat lay in the center of the vortex, a thick strip of leather between his clenched teeth to prevent them cracking under the strain.

The chanting priestesses came and went by a prescribed

schedule, but Sa'ida didn't budge. She alone was irreplaceable. For three days and nights she did not sleep. She had performed the great healing spell only once before, but none of the priestesses knew the circumstances; Sa'ida would never discuss it.

The chanting abruptly stopped.

"Shadows of sickness, leave this man!" she commanded solemnly. "Suffering one, be whole!"

For the space of three heartbeats no one moved. Time itself seemed to halt in the room. Then Shobbat sighed deeply, the sound echoing in the stillness. His rigid body went limp. His eyes opened. He blinked several times, looking around as though his surroundings were unfamiliar.

"Am I dead?" he rasped.

"Not yet."

Sa'ida moved away, to send word to Sahim-Khan that his son was healed.

On the bed, Shobbat lifted a hand to his face. Was he truly here? Was he at home in Khuri-Khan? The fire was gone from his mind, but the memory of what he'd seen in the Oracle's cave remained. Monsters—animals with the heads of humans and humans with the heads of animals—had come out of the shadows, and engulfed him. They'd called his name, said he was one of them. And suddenly he'd known it was true. His hands and feet changed to slender paws. Fur sprouted from his skin, and in his mouth he tasted carrion.

Jackal! the misshapen monsters had shouted at him. *You are one of us!*

Sahim-Khan entered. Clad in plain white geb, his dark head bare of crown, he looked like any worried father, attending the bedside of his sick child.

"My son," he said quietly. "Do you know me?"

"You are my lord, Sahim, Khan of All the Khurs," Shobbat murmured, a vast weariness dragging down his eyelids.

Sahim turned to Sa'ida, standing between two priestesses. It was obvious that she too was sorely spent.

"You have a father's gratitude, holy lady," he said. "Whatever price you name, I shall pay, gladly."

Shobbat's soft snores interrupted them, and Sahim-Khan held out a hand to the high priestess. She took his arm and accompanied him out the door that led to the prince's private sitting room. In silent ranks the priestesses of Elir-Sana departed by a different exit.

The sitting room was lush, the scene of many a princely revel. Sahim escorted the high priestess to a large chair and insisted she sit. Faint with weariness, Sa'ida complied. The austere white silk of her ceremonial gown stood out starkly against the chair's crimson, magenta, and gold wool brocade.

"Mighty Khan," she began, then had to clear her throat to begin anew. She was desperately thirsty, but other things must come first. "Mighty One, I believe it was no mortal illness that afflicted your son."

Sahim's brows lowered in a fearsome glare. "Poison? A curse?"

"No, sire. The sickness was self-inflicted." Sahim's mouth opened, but Sa'ida continued without pause. "Some deed of Prince Shobbat's provoked this bout of madness."

His surprise abated, and he looked dubious. "Shobbat is no ascetic, that is certain, but I doubt he would commit a deed foul enough to drive himself mad!"

"Not a foul deed, an impious one." The chair was deep and plush. Sa'ida forced herself to sit stiffly upright; the slightest relaxation of her vigilance, and she would lose her battle against the fatigue that encased her limbs like dense sand. The Khan had little use for gods Khurish or foreign, and he still looked unconvinced. She knew she must choose her words with great care.

"Prince Shobbat has looked upon things a mortal should not know," she said slowly. "What those may have been"—she shrugged her shoulders—"I cannot say, Mighty Khan."

Sahim waved these obscure matters aside, vowing to take

up the matter with Shobbat when he was stronger. If his heir was dabbling in magic, Sahim soon would cure him of such foolish curiosity.

He returned to the issue of payment, begging the holy priestess to name her reward. His coffers were full of steel and gold, courtesy of his *laddad* tenants. Alone with his cronies Sahim liked to boast that he was the best-paid landlord in the world.

"We do not crave wealth in our temple, Great Khan. But there is a boon you can grant us."

He grinned, opening his arms wide. "Tell me, beloved of the goddess."

"Put an end to the violence against the elves."

He blinked, taken aback. "How does the fate of the *laddad* concern you?"

She told him then of the Speaker's interest in the Valley of the Blue Sands and of the Lioness's mission to find out whether the fabled valley was habitable. When she finished, her voice was almost completely gone. She waited expectantly.

The Khan astonished her by bursting into laughter.

"The place where animals speak and stones grow like palm trees from the ground?" he sputtered, quoting the fables. "Excellent! Let them go there! It's a fitting place for them!"

His loud merriment caused Sa'ida to wince with pain. A prodigious headache was building behind her eyes. Closing them, she murmured, "Grant me this favor, Mighty Khan. Guard the *laddad* while they tarry here. Dark forces gather around you, seeking to destroy them. Have no commerce with these."

This time his laugh was sardonic. "The Knights you mean? Or the bull-men of the seas? Yes, all these 'dark forces' have sought me out. Each wishes to destroy the *laddad* for their own safety. I take their gifts if it pleases me." His black eyes grew hard, and no longer was he the grateful father. Robed and crowned or not, it was the Khan of All the Khurs who stood looking down at the priestess now. "But *I* rule in Khur, not these others. Gilthas's people can rely on my protection so long as it pleases me to guard them. Please concern yourself with your goddess, holy lady, and leave politics to me."

Sa'ida got to her feet stiffly, bowed, and departed.

The Khan watched her go, then took the chair she'd just vacated. Sa'ida was a great asset to Khur, and he was not a man to squander assets, but her request troubled him. Beyond a certain grudging admiration for the Speaker's tenacity, and an appreciation of elven style, Sahim cared little about the elves' ultimate fate. He was no friend of Neraka, nor the minotaurs. He knew well that once the elves were removed, his neighbors' appetites would quickly switch to Khur. For all its empty desert, Sahim's land bordered many vital areas. A navy with access to its coast could dominate the Bay of Balifor. Hundreds of miles of desert made a formidable barrier against minotaurs trying to enter Neraka from the north, or against Knights thrusting south to the fertile lands of minotaur-held Silvanesti.

The Speaker of the Sun and Stars was a temporary asset, a fine cat's-paw, distracting the troublesome Knights and holding the bull-men in check.

This Valley of the Blue Sands business worried him not at all. Yes, it would be easier to keep an eye on the elves if they were under the walls of Khuri-Khan, but if they chose to maroon themselves in a remote mountain valley, surrounded by the worst desert in the realm, then that would be perfectly acceptable. If the *laddad* waxed fat in the new location, so much the better. Fat sheep sheared thick wool, as the nomad saying went. Perhaps in time Sahim could make the Speaker of the Sun and Stars a true vassal of Khur. Hadn't he done that (for the most part) with the nomads? Elves couldn't be any more proud and arrogant than desert tribesmen. Then it would be Neraka and the minotaurs who must tread lightly! All would regard the name of Sahim-Khan with fear!

Thoughts of his nomadic subjects were like grains of sand in Sahim's cup of fine wine. Worthless fanatics, all of them! They'd been slipping into the city in larger numbers, conferring with the wretch Minok, and going out to harass and murder the *laddad* in the name of their brutal god. Or perhaps in the name of the Dark Order.

A servant appeared in the doorway to Prince Shobbat's bedchamber. He bore a tray laden with rosewater, fine linen, and sweet wine.

"Go away; I didn't summon you," Sahim said testily.

"No, Mighty Khan. Please forgive the intrusion. I was summoned to wait upon Prince Shobbat, but he isn't in his room. I thought perhaps—" The servant looked hopefully around the sitting room, empty but for the Khan.

Sahim shoved the lackey aside and entered the bedchamber. The hour was late, just past midnight, and the only candles burning were a trio on a stand by the bed—the empty bed. Shobbat's wrinkled, sweat-stained robe trailed off it onto the floor. The servant spoke truly: The prince was neither here nor in the water closet attached to his room.

The Khan perched his fists on his hips. He'd thought the boy would sleep for a week. Where in Kargath's name had he gone off to now?

* * * * *

The large man's shoulders nearly scraped the walls of the narrow alley. His four companions were hardly less imposing, yet despite their bulk, all five moved quietly, their soft leather boots silent on the timeworn pavement. At the intersection of two lanes, the leader stopped. He probed the corner of the wall in front of him, searching for three tell-tale notches scored in the brick. Finding them, he turned right and moved on. The others followed.

The lintel above the fifth door bore the same parallel notches. Leaving his four companions on watch in the alley, the leader entered without knocking and carefully closed the door behind himself. He turned back the hood of his cloak.

"I am here," Lord Hengriff said, his bass voice rumbling in the small room.

The room brightened as the thin red line of a lamp wick was adjusted. The light showed Prince Shobbat sitting at a table, his bare dagger gleaming next to the lamp. The ruddy lamplight also revealed the results of his encounter with the Oracle of the Tree. The Prince's face was the gray of wood ash. His eyebrows and beard were white, and white streaked the hair combed back from his forehead. His once soft features were drawn, and his eyes burned from deep, hollow sockets.

"I heard you were unwell, Highness," Hengriff said.

"I have recovered."

From what the Nerakan saw, this seemed a debatable conclusion. "This meeting is not wise."

"But necessary."

Shobbat's hand strayed to the dagger, caressing the wire-wrapped grip, but his eyes remained fixed on the Knight's face. "The time for talk is over. The time has come to act. My father must go."

He expected some reaction—at the very least, a nod of satisfaction—but Hengriff only stood there, immobile as stone. Shobbat demanded, "Will Neraka support me once I'm on the throne?"

"The Order always supports strong rulers friendly to its cause."

Shobbat's fingers closed on the dagger grip, and he slammed the weapon on the table, making the little lamp jump. "Why all the mystery?" he shouted. "Can't you just give me a simple 'yes' or 'no'?"

"Permit me to say, Highness, your timing is not the best. You have been out of circulation for some time, yes? And your father is very popular just now, thanks to his humiliation of the elves. How much money did he squeeze from Gilthas in the name of reparations?"

"Ten thousand steel."

A tidy sum, thought Hengriff. Sahim's little triumph over the Speaker would make him admired in the souks and taverns, even by those who knew him to be a bloody tyrant. He had executed eleven Torghanists captured during the rioting; even now, their heads gathered flies in the plaza before the Khuri yl Nor. Yet Hengriff knew the dead men were longtime criminals culled from the city dungeons. The real culprits had purchased their safety. Minok, high priest of Torghan, with the Khan's death sentence still hanging over him, had given Hengriff gold to buy freedom for himself and his followers.

After considering the possible repercussions of allowing the Torghanists to remain in prison (and perhaps talk under torture), the Knight paid the bribes. First, though, he swapped Minok's Khurish coins for Nerakan. He intended the released prisoners to associate their deliverance with the Order, and to spend that money in the souks. There was no better ambassador than money.

"—and slay him while he sleeps. What do you think?" Shobbat was saying.

"A very good plan," Hengriff replied, realizing with some amusement that while he was lost in thought the prince must have been outlining his plot to murder his father. "When will you strike?"

"Soon. There may not be time to warn you in advance."

"I understand."

Shobbat stood and tucked the dagger back into his sash—this one an unsettling mixture of cherry red and lime green stripes. Hengriff waited till he was done, then casually delivered the news he'd brought. "Your Highness, have you heard? The elves have found the Valley of the Blue Sands."

The effect was all he'd hoped. Shobbat gave a violent start, even faltering backward.

"How did this happen?" he gasped.

"Gilthas sent his bitch, Kerianseray, to seek the place. They reached the valley three days ago."

Shobbat sat back down with a thump. The Oracle's prediction rang in his ears.

"How . . ." The prince cleared his throat twice. "How do you know this?"

"I have many eyes and ears in Khuri-Khan, even in the elves' camp." He folded massive arms across his chest. "Why is this valley important, Highness? What does Gilthas expect to find there?"

Shobbat barely heard Hengriff, his thoughts were racing so. The chain of events foretold by the Oracle had begun. His future, his very life, was in the balance. He strove to master his emotions. He'd already given away too much to the Dark Knight.

"Who can say? The valley is uninhabited," he muttered. "It has some religious significance for the tribes who dwell nearby."

Hengriff studied Shobbat in silence. The prince's wan complexion was growing paler by the second, pale as the stain that had spread through his beard and hair. The man was a weakling, Hengriff thought. If he weren't so close to the throne of Khur the Knight would have washed his hands of him long ago. He'd been laughably easy to buy. Even more than his greedy father, Shobbat loved money, not only for the power it represented but for the luxuries it could buy. The Order had toyed with the idea of installing him as puppet ruler of Khur, but his behavior had become increasingly erratic and evasive. The elves' expedition to the Valley of the Blue Sands certainly disturbed the Prince deeply; it would probably disturb Hengriff's superiors as well. But they had an exaggerated opinion of Gilthas's shrewdness, and a positive mania about the Lioness. The latter Hengriff could understand much more than the former. Kerianseray had been a thorn in Knightly flesh for years.

Answering a question from Shobbat, Hengriff explained that the elves had crossed the High Plateau to reach the valley, avoiding the well-watched caravan route to Kortal.

"They fought several skirmishes with the Weya-Lu tribe. The last was a full-fledged battle, I gather. Having failed to stop the elves going into the valley, the nomads are camped at its entrance, and are trying to recruit other tribes to help destroy the intruders when they come out."

Shobbat tugged thoughtfully at his beard. Although he might wish the nomads every success in stopping the *laddad*, no would-be khan could be happy to hear the desert tribes were massing. Every time that happened, a khan lost his head.

Like the rising of the sun, but with much less warning, a smile spread across Shobbat's face. With his red-rimmed eyes and pallid lips, it was not a charming expression. And now it was Hengriff's turn to be surprised, though he was practiced enough not to show it.

"My lord," the prince asked, "are you able to communicate with these distant events, or do you only receive subsequent word of them?"

Aware of the import of what he was about to say, Hengriff replied, "The former, Your Highness."

"Good! I will compose a missive, and you will have it conveyed to the tribesmen you say have gathered to stop the elves."

Hengriff bowed slightly, thinking he would do what he pleased.

The prince snapped a command, and out of the shadows a lackey appeared, bearing a leather case. Shobbat pushed aside bottles of wine and perfume, a short sword, and a purse thick with coins, to pull out parchment, ink, and a pen-brush. The proclamation he composed was short and to the point, written in large, flowing script. Hengriff easily read the words upside-down. Again, he was surprised. This ambitious fool had more talent for intrigue than he had imagined. He might have to be more careful with the prince in the future.

Shobbat signed the document with a flourish, rolled it tightly, and sealed it with black wax. He pressed his signet into the wax and handed the scroll to Hengriff.

"You may be the savior of my country," said the prince earnestly.

"I'd rather be the destroyer of the elves," replied Hengriff.

Shobbat showed his eyeteeth. "It is the same thing."

"Your message will be in nomad hands in three days, Your Highness."

Shobbat extinguished the lamp, and the two men went their separate ways.

"Success, my lord?" asked Hengriff's lieutenant waiting outside.

Hengriff glanced at the closed door. How did one reckon success in this maelstrom of deceit and treachery? He was still alive, still working for the Order. That was one measure of success.

He grunted an affirmative and added, "I have another visit to pay. When we get there, you men can return to our quarters."

The five Knights slipped away, moving like a cluster of shadows. Out of the crowded Hameek district Hengriff led them to the northern part of the city, known as the Harbalah. Wrecked by Malys and her minions, it was still not rebuilt. The sights and smells of the vibrant, living sections of Khuri-Khan ended when they crossed Istra Street into the ruins. Hengriff halted by a broken dwelling and dismissed his men.

They hesitated. The lieutenant said, "My lord, we obey, but . . . our lives are pledged to safeguard yours. Shouldn't we accompany you?"

"Not this time. Go."

Reluctantly, they did. Hengriff remained where he was until the four loyal warriors turned a corner and were out of sight. When he was satisfied he was alone, he continued ahead. No torches or lamps burned here. There was only starlight to see by. Still, he made good progress through the rubble and shattered houses. He knew the way very well.

A tall tower stood out starkly against the night sky. Its upper floors had been toppled by the red dragon, but even truncated the tower was still many times higher than any other structure in the vicinity. Piled around its base were the ruins of a fine villa, once the home of the richest date merchant in Khur. His bones moldered beneath the toppled walls of his mansion.

Clouds drifting in from the sea passed over the stars, casting the ruins into deeper darkness. It was an eerie journey through the ruined grounds, cluttered with broken statuary, rubble, and blown trash, the gardens nowadays home to little more than thin, scraggly date palms. Roofless, the interior of the once fine home was open to the air. What remained of its gessoed walls was bright with painted scenes of desert life, the pictures cracked and peeling. The path through the trash was barely wide enough for Hengriff's feet. The one who'd made it was much smaller than he.

He passed the first sign—a six-inch square of parchment bearing markings in red and black ink. A warning. A panic-spell had been placed over the ruined house. Had Hengriff not been wearing a counter-charm, he would've been seized by unreasoning fear.

When he reached the atrium, with its dry fountain and garden of weeds, he passed the second sign. This one was a human skull, eye sockets packed with clay. A pebble of polished malachite had been pushed into each clay-filled socket, making grotesque eyes. That's exactly what they were. The occupant of the blighted villa could watch the path with these magical eyes. Interlopers were dealt with harshly.

The Knight came upon one such unlucky soul. A Khur lay sprawled by the fountain. His torso had been ripped open, his body left here as an extra warning to the unwary. By his clothes, Hengriff took him to be a beggar come to search for trinkets he could sell. He was past such needs now.

At the foot of the broken tower was the third sign. An ordinary copper plate, such as was used in taverns all around

188

the city, was nailed to the tower door with three iron nails. Lines were scratched into the copper. They formed the sigil of madness. Anyone passing through the door without proper protection would go immediately insane.

Hengriff snorted. Perhaps the villa's current resident had come home once without his protective amulets. That would explain much about him.

Despite the devastation all around, the great door swung smoothly inward, silent on well-oiled hinges. The interior smelled strongly of musk.

"Hello!" He tried to call softly, but his voice still boomed like a drumbeat.

Something stirred in the darkness. Something big. His hand went to his sword hilt.

"Faeterus! It's Hengriff," he said, feeling somewhat foolish. His voice could hardly be mistaken for any other's.

A square of light appeared overhead as a trap door opened. Hengriff held up a hand to block the sudden glare. The light showed him a strange beast curled against the far wall, several yards away. It had a lion's tawny body and limbs, but a long neck covered with small, bronze-colored scales. Its head was its most disturbing feature. Framed by a short, stiff mane of reddish hair, the head was round, like a human's, with human-looking icy blue eyes, a flat nose, and a very wide mouth.

The mouth split in a grin as Hengriff tightened his grip on his sword hilt. At least four rows of teeth, one behind the other, glittered like polished steel in the wide mouth. The large eyes gazed at him steadily, without blinking. The Knight knew then what had happened to the beggar lying dead outside.

A knotted rope unspooled from the open trap door, its end striking the floor at Hengriff's feet. The Knight began to climb, senses alert. A good place to ambush someone, he thought.

As his head and shoulders penetrated the room above, heat washed over him like a lowering weight. Oil lamps with silver reflectors lit the scene brightly, but the warmth came from two large fireplaces, opposite each other in the large, round room. Fires blazed high in each.

The room was decorated in an extreme of Khurish fashion that would have embarrassed a native-born Khur. Dark yellow carpets were layered six inches deep, helping to mask the warped floor. Every inch of wall space was covered by tapestries, depicting not only Khurish scenes of deserts and oases, but foreign sights as well—the barbaric splendor of Ergoth, the staid pageantry of old Solamnia, and geometric Tarsan designs shot through with spun gold thread.

There were no chairs or proper tables, only silk and velvet pillows, divans spread with plush wool and damask rugs, and low tables meant to be used by diners seated on the floor. Contributing to the suffocating atmosphere were jeweled incense burners hanging from the ceiling beams; they filled the air with the heavy reek of spice.

Hengriff's host had returned to his dinner after dropping the rope through the trap door. An etched silver tray was balanced on the divan cushions beside him. Hengriff glanced at its contents and quickly looked away. A bird of some sort, plucked clean, but still raw. Savage.

"Welcome, noble Hengriff," said Faeterus, waving a hand.

Gone was his bulky disguise. Shorn of the heavy, ragged robes and thick gray wig, Faeterus was revealed to be an elf of advanced years, with cottony white hair, eyebrows like flyaway wings over hazel eyes, and a chin sharp as the prow of a war galley. His hands were unusually large for an elf, with prominent joints and exceptionally long fingers, darkly stained by decades of mixing potions. He wore long, white cotton trousers and an abbreviated geb.

"That's quite a watchdog you have," Hengriff said, casting about for a decent place to sit.

"A rare creature indeed. A manticore from over the seas. It ensures my privacy."

Faeterus indicated the Knight could join him, but Hengriff settled himself on a low table nearby, after deeming it strong enough to take his weight. He would not recline on the cushioned divan with the mage, nor sit on the carpeted floor at his feet like a supplicant.

"A new development," he announced. "Prince Shobbat has regained his wits. As usual he's aflame to depose his father, but when I mentioned the elves had gone to the valley, he seemed ready to relapse. He's so frightened he's willing to stir up the desert wanderers to stop the elves." He held up Shobbat's letter. "He gave me this proclamation, in which he incites them to make righteous war on the elves."

"Shobbat is an idiot. Does it say anything more?" Faeterus bit delicately into the raw bird. Blood ran down his chin until he dabbed it with a napkin.

"He invites the nomads here to Khuri-Khan, to destroy the elves in their tent-city."

Faeterus froze, then put down his dinner. "Not an idiot—a madman!"

"Maybe. He says his father has betrayed Khur by allowing the elves to remain here, and by filling his coffers with elven steel."

"They'll have Sahim-Khan's head, too, in the bargain."

"I'm sure that's what Shobbat intends."

Faeterus picked up a narrow, conical goblet made of gilded glass and gulped wine like a sailor just back from a long voyage. His fingers left gory prints on the shiny stem. Hengriff wondered whether his nails were naturally that umber shade, or if he painted them.

"An idiot after all," Faeterus said, refilling his goblet. "Sahim is popular. The nomads won't unite against him, not now."

"Perhaps if they had more provocation," Hengriff suggested.

"That will take some thought. The wanderers aren't like ordinary people, elf or human. What pleases us offends them, and what angers them we would consider trivial." The mage leaned back against his cushions, and added, "What will you do for me if I do this favor for you?"

I won't wring your scrawny neck, Hengriff thought. "This isn't a souk, elf. I'm not here to bargain. Get to the point. What do you want?"

Faeterus reclined on the cushions, closing his eyes. "A trifle, really," he murmured.

Hengriff doubted that. The mage seemed immune to the standard temptations. As far as Hengriff could tell, he had only two guiding principles: hatred for his own race, and devotion to the pursuit of his magical arts. Whatever he wanted, it likely would be something extraordinary.

"I want what Gilthas wants: the Valley of the Blue Sands."

Hengriff frowned at this puzzling reply. He knew the nomads of the northern desert regarded the valley as sacred, belonging to the gods and forbidden by them at the same time. Most of the stories he'd heard, in the souks and various taverns, were improbable in the extreme. In one, the valley was said to house an army of stone soldiers, motionless for two thousand years, who would awaken on hearing a certain magical word. If the wrong word of power was voiced, they would animate only long enough to kill the one who'd said it, then resume their stony existence. Other tales said the valley contained a city of gold, a race of invisible dragons, or—oddest of all—the tombs of dead, foreign gods.

Why, all of a sudden, did Faeterus care about the Valley of the Blue Sands?

Hengriff stood stiffly. Over the years he'd acquired too many injuries, more than a few while chasing the Lioness, to remain hunkered down on the low table for very long.

"I'll convey your words to my masters," he said evenly. "Fables and legends aside, the valley represents an excellent defensive position. My Order certainly wouldn't want the elves to settle there."

He glanced at a carafe sitting on the rug near Faeterus. The mage had a penchant for a Delphonian vintage steeped with kuroba flowers, which imparted a narcotic effect. Hengriff wanted none of that; he would endure his thirst for a while longer.

"Oh, one thing more," he said casually. "Gilthas has an agent in the city looking for you."

The mage's hazel eyes opened quickly. "Really? An elf?"

"My spy on the Speaker's council did not specify. Could be a hired Khur."

"I hope not!" Faeterus rubbed his chin with his fingers, forgetting they were smeared with gore. The bloody streaks made his gaunt face seem savage indeed. "I need a full-blooded elf for my latest experiment. Maybe I should let Gilthas's ferret find me."

Hengriff had no desire to speculate on what experiments this loathsome creature might be planning. Duty discharged, he wanted only to be gone. He opened the trap door and held out his hand. He needed new paper amulets, so he could pass safely through the villa's magical defenses. Each set of warding amulets worked in a very specific fashion—once as Hengriff departed, and once more allowing him to reenter. Faeterus would not have it any other way.

Unfortunately, Faeterus was not ready to let him go. Instead of producing new amulets, the sorcerer brought up the valley again, asking for assurances it would be granted to him. Hengriff brusquely declined to make guarantees. "The decision is not mine to make," he growled, demanding the amulets.

Faeterus suddenly gave a very birdlike, warbling whistle. In the chamber below, the manticore sprang to its feet and came to stand below the opening. It looked up, and grinned. Hengriff had faced any number of horrors in his time, but the sight of that horrible, too-human face and its rows of steel-sharp teeth caused him to shudder. He thought of the disemboweled beggar outside.

193

He turned a furious look upon the sorcerer. Faeterus held the paper amulets in one long-fingered hand. "Of course you may leave if you really wish to," the mage assured him genially. "But perhaps we should discuss proper payment for my services first?"

* * * * *

Planchet set a covered dish before his master. Gilthas, dining alone, watched expectantly as the domed cover was whisked away. Chicken again, nestled on a bed of roasted vegetables. Planchet offered him a choice of wines, Goodlund red or Silvanesti white, but Gilthas told him to save the wine for Kerian's return.

The Speaker of the Sun and Stars drank water and ate in silence. Usually he dined with the members of his court, but for the past few days, since the audience with Sahim-Khan, his councilors had found various reasons not to attend. Everyone felt humiliated, the Qualinesti especially, as Gilthas was one of them. Lord Morillon had praised the Speaker's diplomacy, but even he made excuses to avoid dinner. So Gilthas had only Planchet for company, as the valet waited on him.

Ten thousand steel pieces had gone out of Gilthas's personal treasury. It wasn't all in steel, of course. Much of it was gold and silver plate rescued from the blazing halls of the palace in Qualinost. Some of the golden service dated back to the reign of Speaker Silveran. They knew how to make fine things in those days. The gold was hammered thin as paper, yet remained stiff and strong. No one today could duplicate the alloy Silveran's goldsmiths had used.

Golden plates and fine wines were extravagances they could live without. Sahim was a blackguard. Gilthas had always known that. Extortion at his hands was as much a part of the Speaker's life as the desert's incessant heat. Yet Gilthas would find a way to meet the Khan's greedy demands so long as it bought more time for his people. His proud councilors did not understand that. They clung to glittering memories of worldly glory. Those memories were all they had for comfort as they slept each night in their stifling tents, lying on itchy woolen pallets, and toiled each day just to stay alive.

Khuri-Khan had been quiet since Gilthas's visit. Armed patrols of Khurish soldiers tramped the back streets in strength, discouraging malefactors and maintaining an uneasy calm. Traffic in and out of the city had fallen off, although this was likely no more than a temporary condition. Traveling merchants were cautious folk. Having heard about the riot in the capital, many diverted to Delphon to peddle their wares. If the situation remained calm, if no more unrest developed, they would return. For now, though, the flow of Khurs in and out of Khuri-Khan had almost completely ceased.

Repairs on the city wall faltered as stone caravans from Kortal, in the Khalkist foothills, dwindled. Sahim was spending great sums to import hard stone from the far-away mountains to bolster his defenses. The route between Kortal and Khuri-Khan passed through the territory of the Weya-Lu tribe. For some reason, the Weya-Lu had abandoned their usual trade route. Without the nomads to man caravans, the flow of hard stone to the capital stopped.

Next to Gilthas's plate lay the dispatches from Kerian. A dusty, desiccated courier had arrived with the reports late last night. The Kagonesti had placed the leather pouch in the Speaker's own hands, then passed out, falling from the saddle into the arms of Taranath. The dispatches he brought contained wonderful news. The entrance to the Inath-Wakenti had been found.

However, Gilthas's elation was tempered by the other news in the dispatches. Kerian's troop had clashed several times with armed nomads. She reported this matter-of-factly, as if it was to be expected. She assured him they had nothing to fear from the nomads. The wanderers' weapons were poor and their tactics feeble. If necessary, she could defeat three or four times the number she'd faced thus far.

Her words, intended to reassure, had exactly the opposite effect. It was just this situation Gilthas had feared more than anything else. He understood Sahim-Khan, and that made working with the human possible. The nomads of the desert were another matter. Aloof, proud as a dozen Silvanesti lords, the nomads were motivated by a complex tangle of piety and honor. Their fierce conviction in their own virtue made dealing with them difficult at best. Should they decide to make war in earnest upon the elves, then life in Khur would become much, much harder. Perhaps even impossible.

The dark heart of the matter, Gilthas well knew, was Kerianseray's fiery nature. Could she control herself? She must not fight the desert folk. Defend herself, yes, but she could not hammer the nomads as she would Dark Knights or minotaurs. The fragile peace between Khurs and elves would not withstand wide bloodshed. Could the Lioness carry out her reconnaissance without starting a war?

His expression must have reflected his inner turmoil. Planchet, standing to one side, asked if he was unwell.

Gilthas smiled ruefully. "No, old friend. Just thinking instead of eating." He tried to pay attention to his dinner, but he'd lost his appetite. All he could think was, where was Kerian? What was happening to her now?

He didn't know whether the griffon had reached her safely, but already he was doubting the wisdom of sending the creature. He hoped she would use Eagle Eye wisely. He'd been second-guessing the mission for days now. The nomads were fighting to defend their land; he could understand that. An armed force of foreigners had entered their territory, and they were trying to drive them out. Perhaps he could have sent diplomats instead of scholars. Perhaps he should've tried to hire nomad guides. Perhaps he should not have put his hot-tempered wife in charge.

Yet, he knew he couldn't have done otherwise. Kerianseray was the general of his armies, his strong right arm.

SANCTUARY

Through the dark days of the terrible journey across the Plains of Dust and the Burning Lands, when thousands of their people had died, Kerian's strength had sustained him, had sustained all of them.

Planchet claimed his attention. Gilthas saw the valet was standing by the door flap, conversing with a servant. "Sire," Planchet said, "Lord Morillon wishes to see you. He says it is most urgent."

"Send him in." A few days earlier, Gilthas had informed his closest councilors, including Morillon, of Kerian's mission, that she was seeking the Inath-Wakenti, and that he hoped the legendary valley might become a new home for their people.

For once Morillon arrived without his usual corps of sycophants. He looked grave. "Great Speaker, I bring news."

"Of Kerianseray?"

"Partly, sire. The city is buzzing with the news of Lady Kerianseray's arrival at the valley."

"Already?" Planchet commented in amazement. "News travels fast."

"There is more," Morillon said. "There are rumors that a great massacre has occurred. Hundreds of Khurish women and children of the Weya-Lu tribe were slain in camp, many miles north of here. Some are saying that it was done by Lady Kerianseray's troops."

Gilthas stood so quickly his camp chair went over backward. "Filthy Torghanist lies!"

"I agree, Great Speaker, but the Khurs might choose to think otherwise."

This was undeniable. Unchecked, the massacre story could inflame Khur from one end to the other. Riots in the souks would be nothing compared to the Khurs' outrage over this.

Impatiently, Morillon asked, "Sire, what shall we do?

"I will go to Sahim-Khan, lay my thoughts before him. Once he sees we have nothing to hide, he will protect us."

"And if he won't?" Planchet asked bluntly.

"He must." Gilthas hesitated. "How many warriors are in camp?"

"About thirty thousand."

"Then have them stand ready, Planchet. No fanfare, though. Alert them quietly."

The valet hurried away to carry out his liege's order. Morillon's worry had only increased.

"Great Speaker, fighting isn't the answer," he said. "The Khan can field twice our numbers. More if he calls upon the desert tribes!"

Gilthas shook his head. "No, he won't summon the nomads. He fears them more than he fears us. And I agree: Fighting is not the answer. We must learn the truth about this massacre, if it actually occurred, and prove to the Khan and his people that we are not responsible."

"But what if—what we can't prove such a thing?"

Pressing a fist to his lips, Gilthas thought hard. He did not believe Kerian would kill innocent women and children, but who could say what might have occurred in the far desert. If a battle had taken place, if innocents had been killed, if proof of elven innocence was dubious. There were too many ifs!

"We must make preparations to leave."

The Speaker's pronouncement drained the color from Morillon's face. "Leave? To go where?"

"To where Lady Kerianseray is right now. Summon the council. I want an inventory made of all food and water on hand. I want emergency plans drawn up to evacuate Khuri-nost on a moment's notice."

He was talking of uprooting a hundred thousand souls. Stunned, Morillon could only nod as the Speaker continued to pepper him with orders.

"We'll need carts. Have as many made as possible. If there aren't enough animals to draw them, use people. If we can't make enough carts, use travois." The trip to the Inath-Wakenti would be very long, very harsh, he explained.

"Great Speaker, don't be hasty!" Morillon interjected. "Let us discuss this! Sahim-Khan is no friend of the desert tribes. With proper motivation, he would defend us if the nomads attacked!"

Gilthas's smile was bitter. "Perhaps. But what if you are wrong? What if he refuses to defend foreigners—*laddad* foreigners—against his own people? There's not enough money in the world to buy safety from the Khan, if too many of his own people rise up to threaten him." The smile vanished. "We must have a contingency plan. We can offer to pay more for his protection. That much steel will tempt him and buy us time. See to it, my lord. Personally. Arrange an audience at once. Today."

Morillon rushed to do Gilthas's bidding. Like a disturbed anthill, Khurinost stirred to frantic activity. Meager supplies were counted, weapons long stored taken out. If the exiles were forced to flee, every able-bodied elf would be required to take up arms to defend their lives and their freedom.

9

The Vale of Silence was aptly named. An hour after dawn, the Lioness and her warriors were riding across a flat, funnel-shaped valley that was utterly silent, with no breath of wind stirring or birds calling. The air was warm, but far from the blistering heat of the desert outside, and laden with moisture. The area's other name—Valley of the Blue Sands— also was appropriate. The soil beneath their horses' hooves was bright blue-green, a strange shade between malachite and verdigris. It also contributed to the quiet. The soft soil seemed to absorb the sound of their movements.

To spare the horses undue stress, Kerian had sent Eagle Eye aloft without her, then swung up behind Favaronas. The archivist would've exchanged places—after all, she was commander of the armies—but she waved away his offer. Balancing easily even without the benefit of stirrups or saddle, she studied their surroundings.

They rode past scattered stands of cedar and pine, and boulders half-buried in the sandy soil. The high mountains kept the valley floor in shade long after dawn, which probably accounted for the pockets of mist that clung to the low places.

"Well, librarian, what do you think?" the Lioness asked.

"Feels dead," Favaronas replied. "No birds, no insects, not even any flowers blooming."

SANCTUARY

He was right. A profound stillness lay heavily over the area. Only a few miles in, the effect was becoming unnerving. It was easy to imagine how the valley came to be shunned. Curious nomads, penetrating this far, would become spooked and flee, carrying with them tales of the eerie silence. Over the years, those stories would've grown with every telling.

If the atmosphere was unsettling, the scenery was increasingly beautiful, as the valley opened to them. The gray Khalkist peaks on the eastern side took on a slate-blue shade as the sun climbed over them, slanting into the valley and washing the facing western range with golden light. Islands of grass appeared, not the brown or gray flora of the desert, but familiar green shoots, the first they'd seen since leaving their homelands. The presence of grass was more than nostalgic. Where grass grew, livestock could live. Where livestock could live, elves could live.

With the sun above the eastern mountains, the temperature climbed, but never beyond a pleasant warmth. The Lioness and Favaronas came to a wide, shallow stream that wandered across the valley floor. It was shaded by two small willow trees, their slender branches motionless in the still air.

Kerian slid off the horse's rump and squatted on a flat boulder by the water's edge. Even as Favaronas called a warning, she dipped her hand in the stream and lifted it to her lips.

"To lead is to take risks," she said, smiling wryly, then swallowed.

He didn't have to ask if the water was good. His horse dropped its nose into the shimmering flow and drank noisily. In minutes, the entire command had followed suit. The fresh water was like a gift from the gods. The water they'd brought was warm, and tasted like the skins and gourds in which it was carried; the well water of Khuri-Khan was bland and flat. This water was ice-cold, with a distinct and pleasant mineral bite.

Eagle Eye alighted a dozen yards away, haunch-deep in the stream, and dipped his feathered head to drink. Thirst slaked, the beast stalked ashore on the east bank and lay down to sleep among cattails and tall grass. Before long his head was under his wing, and he was snoring like a boiling kettle.

Much refreshed, the Lioness allowed her warriors to linger by the stream, watering their horses and washing their gritty faces and feet. Favaronas sat on a gray rock overhanging the stream and sketched on a slip of parchment with a charcoal stick. The Lioness watched a map of the valley take shape beneath his skillful hands.

Drawing the long serpentine curve of the creek, he asked, "What shall we call this stream?"

"You're drawing the map. Call it whatever you like."

After a pause, he said, "Lioness Creek," writing as he spoke.

"Speaker's Creek would be more appropriate."

"You said I could call it whatever I like."

She shrugged and pulled off her boots. The chilly water was a blessing to hot, tired feet.

Less than a quarter of an hour later, their rest was abruptly interrupted. The air shuddered from some distant concussion. No sound of explosion followed; there was only a shock wave that made the air and ground vibrate once, very hard. The horses shied violently. Favaronas dropped his charcoal marker. Kerian jumped to her feet.

"The sand beast?" Favaronas quavered.

Kerian was dragging on her boots. "Curse it! Pleasant scenery, clean water, and we start acting like farmers at a fair!" They were in unknown territory, and she hadn't even posted pickets!

The elves quickly resumed their normal vigilance. Kerian ordered twenty riders to reconnoiter ahead. Another band of twenty she sent back toward the valley mouth, in case the nomads (or anyone else) overcame their fear and decided to follow them. Bow-armed flankers rode out from the main column to watch for danger.

With her warriors fully deployed, the Lioness felt more at ease. Favaronas, however, clutched his map in both hands and stared wildly, expecting any number of unnatural beasts to fall upon them.

"Calm yourself," she told the scholar. "I don't think it's the sand beast this time; look at Eagle Eye." The griffon was looking around, but didn't seem particularly excited.

She swung into the saddle of a fresh horse. "It's probably nothing more than echoes from an avalanche in the mountains."

He blinked at her in surprise, then nodded slowly. They were all so primed to find something otherworldly in the valley, he'd never considered a simpler explanation. Still, he was glad when she sent Eagle Eye skyward. It wouldn't hurt to have the griffon's sharp eyes watching over them.

They forded the newly named Lioness Creek. Scouts met them, reporting they'd found a clearly defined path beyond a field of half-buried boulders. Leaving the archivist with the main body of the army, Kerian trotted forward to see.

Beyond the boulders, three elves sat on horseback in the center of a wide lane thick with alluvial sand. A fourth was on his knees, digging with his hands. As the Lioness arrived, he announced, "Pavement!"

She swung a leg over her horse's neck and dropped to the ground. Sure enough, beneath four or five inches of blue-green soil, he'd found stone pavers. The ruler-straight joint between two blocks was clearly visible. Clearing a larger area revealed more pavers and something even more interesting—a deep groove worn into the road. They had seen such ruts before. The grooves were made by wheels, passing over pavement in the same line year after year. This groove followed the slight downslope back toward the creek they'd just forded.

"Someone has called this valley home," the Lioness said. Question was, was anyone still here?

She remounted and sent the scouts ahead. Her admonition to stay sharp wasn't really necessary; the very brief respite they'd enjoyed at the stream was over. All were alert. When Favaronas moved up with the main body, he made note of the pavement on his sketch map.

The paved path led northeast, into the heart of the Inath-Wakenti. The elves followed it slowly, cautiously, encountering nothing untoward until after midday, when a scout galloped back with news. They were approaching stone ruins, very old and very big stone ruins.

Ruins dotted the continent, from Balifor to Sancrist Isle. When Kerian was on the run from the Dark Knights who occupied her country, she often sheltered in ruins in the western Kharolis Mountains, relics of a time before the Great Cataclysm. Growing up in the wild, she'd had little knowledge of ancient history. Most of what she knew had been learned from tales traded around the campfire, of the beautiful, doomed Irda race, the twins Sithas and Kith-Kanan, the decadent human empire in Ergoth. Tales stranger still were told of the realm of Istar, where magic reigned until a fiery mountain fell from the sky and destroyed the city. Where glorious, doomed Istar once stood was now the whirling maelstrom of the Blood Sea, not so far away from this place.

The Lioness sent out more flankers to sweep either side of the road. She kept to the path, leading the main column forward. All the reports she received were negative. No quarry had been found, either of the two-legged or the four-legged variety. Not so much as a rabbit or a bird crossed their paths. The widely spaced cedars and pines seemed bare of all life.

Irritated by the lack of progress, the Lioness decided to try a loftier view. She dismounted and walked a few yards ahead, whistling for Eagle Eye. The griffon came skimming in over the low trees to land in front of her. She slipped a strung bow over her head and swung onto the tiny saddle pad.

"Continue down the road," she told her officers, then elf and griffon bolted skyward.

After years of Khurish heat, the rush of temperate air past her face was like a balm. The climate surely was better here than in Khurinost. Perhaps Gilthas was on to something.

Consternation flooded through her. What was she thinking? Trade her birthright for a little comfort? Never! Yes, this valley was more pleasant than the sweltering sandpit outside Khuri-Khan, but so what? It wasn't her homeland. Wasn't, and never would be.

She turned her attention to the terrain unrolling beneath her—clumps of trees, bramble thickets, broad stands of tall, fleshy aloe. No wonder the flankers hadn't seen anything. She'd forgotten how much real foliage limited sight.

The loftier elements of the ruins rose into view. At this distance they looked to be spires of white or gray stone, jutting above the trees. Not columns in the usual sense, they weren't fluted or faceted, only simple tapering spires. As she drew nearer, remnants of walls appeared, their dimensions amazing. Each stone block was at least ten feet long and tall as a mounted warrior. In some places the wall reared thirty feet high, massive block fitted neatly atop massive block. The cyclopean stones showed clear evidence of having been smoothed and shaped by intelligent hands.

Eagle Eye spiraled slowly down. He alighted alongside an impressively tall stretch of wall. Elf and griffon contemplated the ruins as the rest of the column arrived.

Conversation died. Everyone stared in awe at the mysterious monuments, wondering who built them, and how long ago. The lack of decoration gave the stones an air of great, indefinable age.

Favaronas noticed something else. The stones were completely free of lichen. All the boulders and rocky outcroppings they'd seen in the valley borne healthy coatings of lichen or moss. The ruins showed none. The stones stood stark and clean against the blue sky and blue-green soil.

"Have you ever seen stonework like this before?" Kerian asked.

Favaronas shook his head. "But judging by the size, perhaps it was the work of ogres."

She found that difficult to believe. Ogres built their dwellings in a rough fashion; they didn't waste effort carving or finishing the stones. None of the elves could think of any race, ogre or otherwise, which could move blocks as enormous as these. Two soldiers measured one of the largest stone blocks at the foot of the wall; it was twenty-nine feet long and eleven feet high.

Ahead and on the right, shouts and whistles arose, Qualinesti cattle calls. Many of Kerian's best scouts were former cow herders. She took flight, leaving Favaronas and the rest gawking at the ruins.

The griffon headed straight for a pair of huge standing stones still capped by a massive lintel. With Kerian leaning low over his neck, the creature sailed through, wingtips brushing the pillars on either side. He warbled low in his throat, sounding so smug she couldn't help but chuckle.

The road they'd followed to the ruins continued ahead, bound on both sides by a wall. Scouts wove in and out of the trees to Kerian's right. They were harrying something on foot. All she could see was a patch of pale brown darting through the brush.

The fleeing figure passed briefly into the clear. It was an antelope, the mountain breed with unbranched horns curving back over its head. She swooped down, shouting for it to halt, and it turned to look up. She glimpsed large brown eyes before the antelope's legs got tangled in the creeper and it went sprawling in the thick undergrowth. The Qualinesti giving chase converged on the spot.

By the time the Lioness landed and ran to where the beast had crashed, there was nothing but a rat's nest of torn vines. Two of the scouts, dismounted, were probing the foliage. The creature was gone. She helped them look, but it was obvious an animal that size couldn't be hiding here. Backtracking out of the bed of vines, they found its tiny hoofprints. Those at least were real.

Other scouts rode up and explained how they originally

had flushed the antelope. They'd been riding past a thin line of aloes and stunted pines when the creature suddenly bolted from behind them. Hungry for fresh meat, the elves had given chase.

"It came out *after* you passed?" Kerian said.

"Upon our oath," said one of the Kagonesti scouts, knowing it seemed illogical.

No wild creature, having secreted itself and avoided detection, would then squander its coup by dashing out before the hunters were gone. Just as difficult to believe was that savvy scouts would miss a full-grown antelope in the first place.

The Kagonesti scout put a hand to his heart and vowed, "It wasn't there, General. I rode right through the spot. There was no antelope there. I swear it."

"We were in the high desert a long time," she muttered, shaking her head. "Maybe the sun baked our brains."

They didn't laugh. The silent heaviness of the valley's atmosphere was affecting even the veteran Kagonesti. All were looking around warily, as though uncertain what else might suddenly spring up from beneath their feet. Kerian, who had knelt down to study the hoofprints, stood quickly and admonished them for their foolishness.

"We have enough problems to face without making up new ones. Next thing, you'll be telling me the creature was a spirit!"

They looked struck by what she had meant as a jest; Kerian could've bitten her tongue. The rest of the column was moving up, so she left the scouts and went to send Eagle Eye aloft.

Voices were hushed, as though the elves were passing through a holy place. When Favaronas arrived, on foot, Kerian was seated on a low section of wall. She gestured for him to join her. He touched the stone gingerly, as if expecting to find it hot. Satisfied, he sat down.

She told him of the quarry that had eluded them. "It appeared to be an antelope, but whatever it was, it disappeared right in front of us."

He didn't seem surprised to hear this. "The old chronicles speak of strange forces at work here. The manuscripts I've read don't mention clear dangers. Of course," he added wryly, "clarity is not their strong suit."

The two of them speculated on the odd lack of wildlife. But for the phantom antelope, they had seen no animals at all, not even insects. A day had passed since they'd drunk from Lioness Creek, and no one had reported any ill effects, so the water supply seemed fine. Was there something else in the Vale of Silence inimical to life?

Kerian knew Gilthas would be sorely unhappy should his scheme to transplant the elves fail. She was sorry for the disappointment he would feel, but at the same time she was freshly annoyed at him. He seemed convinced that the time had not yet come for them to liberate their ancestral lands. But if the valley proved unsuitable for their people, then what? Were they to continue in Khurinost forever, penned in their squalid tents, relying on the favor of the human khan?

"I wonder who could have built these great monuments?"

Favaronas's voice cut across her growing anger. The archivist had left his perch on the wall and was studying the wall further down the line.

"An excellent question, Master Archivist," she said, folding her arms across her chest. "How long would you need to find out?"

He looked across the vast meadow of stone ruins and shook his head vaguely. "I couldn't begin to say. It would depend on what we discover. I see no obvious hints of the builder's identity."

"But someone raised these standing stones, someone powerful. Long dead and long gone, I presume."

"The former, yes," he muttered. "The latter, perhaps not."

"What do you mean?"

"You touched on it yourself, speaking of the vanishing

antelope." She gave him a blank look, and he added, "Ghosts. Spirits of the dead may still walk the ruins."

Obviously her Wilder brothers weren't the only ones whose thoughts moved in that direction. They were all letting this weird valley and its massive stone sentinels play tricks on their minds. With a dismissive snort, she jumped down from the wall and gave the archivist a friendly slap on the shoulder.

"Try to figure out who built this, Favaronas. And don't worry; we can leave any time we need to."

She knew this last was probably a lie. An unknown number of armed nomads was likely poised outside the valley, just waiting for the elves to return. Getting out of the Inath-Wakenti might prove even more difficult than getting in had been.

Scouts returned. They reported the ruins went on for miles—there seemed no end to them—and still they'd found no signs of any living creatures.

It was late afternoon, and they'd kept going without stopping the night before, so the Lioness decided to make camp, here among the ruins. The warriors were glad enough of the rest, but Favaronas was distinctly nervous about the choice of campsite. Still, in this strange valley, one spot was likely as good (or worrisome) as the next.

Another courier, this one a Qualinesti, was dispatched to Khurinost. The Lioness knew he would need the cover of the coming night to slip past any nomads camped outside the valley, so there was no time to compose carefully detailed reports. The messenger carried a hastily written letter in which she thanked Gilthas for sending Eagle Eye, promised to put the griffon to good use against their enemies, and outlined the bare essentials of the valley's nature.

They made camp in the lee of a sarsen that reared forty feet high. While the warriors tended their horses, spread bedrolls, and gathered kindling for fires, Favaronas busied himself at the base of the towering monolith. He built a lean-to out of pine branches, then laid a small campfire. Fed with dry juniper twigs, the flames sent a sweet aroma into the cloudless sky. Equipped with fire and shelter, the archivist unpacked his case of manuscripts and began reading. He updated his sketch map and, on spare scraps of parchment, made notes for the Speaker about what they'd seen in the valley.

Kerian was pitching her own tent—a few yards from the archivist's fire, since she'd assigned herself the task of watching over him—when foragers returned. They brought only unwelcome news. There was no game to be had.

"You found nothing to eat? Nothing at all?" she asked.

"A few bitter roots and pine seeds, General," said one. Another added, "I haven't seen so much as a gnat or fly in this valley."

"Khur is the kingdom of flies and every other noxious insect. Why are there none here?"

"Something drove them out," Favaronas murmured.

Kerian turned. He was seated by his small fire, engrossed in his papers. She asked him to explain his comment. He looked up, blinking slightly as his eyes focused on her rather than the manuscript so close to his face. She asked again.

"I can't name what has no name," the archivist replied, unhelpfully, then returned to his studies.

He muttered to himself, too low for Kerian to catch the words. She gave up trying to make sense of his musings and went to walk among her warriors.

The place she'd chosen for their camp was at the intersection of two broad avenues, one aligned northeast-southwest, the other crossing at right angles and aligned northwest-southeast. Rain-washed dirt had filled in the slightly sunken roadbeds over the years, but a little digging revealed they were covered by the same large paving stones as the road that had led the elves here from Lioness Creek.

The high walls of the Khalkist meant sunset came early to the valley. Hours before the light would fade from the desert outside, dusk blanketed their camp. A chill seemed to spring out of the ground, and the elves could see their breath. Patches of mist coalesced in low-lying areas.

Kerian ordered a large bonfire built in the center of their camp, which was also the center of the crossroads. Foragers had found plenty of deadfall pine, cedar, and fir limbs, though no good hardwood, and by the time the first stars winked into sight, the blazing flames were sending sparks up to join them. The firelight only made the ruins around them seem more eerie, more strange. A rotation of mounted sentries was posted a goodly distance from camp. Each elf was given a horn to blow, and assigned a distinctive call. If anything untoward happened, the Lioness would know exactly which sentry raised the alarm.

She checked on the archivist. Whatever anxiety Favaronas felt about being in the valley, it hadn't prevented him from sleeping. He apparently had decided against sleeping in his lean-to, however, and was snoring away in the Lioness's tent.

She and her officers rebuilt the archivist's little campfire at the base of the great sarsen and settled down to have their supper.

"General, now we've found the Inath-Wakenti, how long will we stay?" asked a Qualinesti.

She shrugged, swallowing a mouthful of beans. "I see no reason to stay. We'll start back tomorrow."

Astonishment showed on every face. According to the information she'd given them (which she'd gotten from Gilthas's map), the valley was at least a dozen miles long. Shouldn't they explore further? There might be dangers they hadn't discovered or other ruins or—

"What of the nomads? On the honor of my sword, I'll wager they're waiting for us."

This came from Glanthon, one of the few remaining officers left from the royal Qualinesti army, and younger brother to Planchet, the Speaker's valet. Glanthon was as talkative as Planchet was taciturn, and Kerian had no doubt he would expound upon his theme, so she forestalled him.

"We'll slip out quietly, avoiding the nomads as much as possible."

A fighter by nature, the Lioness would've preferred to punch her way out, thrashing the fanatical tribesmen on the way. But her elves were too few. If a single battle went wrong the entire command could be lost, and she was determined to carry the truth of the valley back to Gilthas in person. The Inath-Wakenti was not a new homeland for their exiled people. A mild clime and scenic, yes, but something here was hostile to all animal life. She put no stock in the archivist's remark about ghosts, yet there was no denying the total absence of living creatures.

"We'll ride east, to the mountains, and look for another way out," she announced. "There's got to be something—goat track, deer trail, something." She smiled wryly over her beans. "All the animals had to go somewhere."

"There's no other way out."

Favaronas stood at the edge of the firelight, by the door flap of Kerian's tent. The Lioness and her officers stared at him.

"I studied the Speaker's map down to the smallest detail," he said, coming closer. "The ancient cartographer was very precise, and he shows no other way out."

Kerian asked, "Then where did all the animals go? Did they die out?"

Favaronas admitted he didn't know the answer to that question. He sat between her and Glanthon, accepting a plate of beans and a loaf of flat Khurish bread. Since he seemed to have nothing more to contribute, the warriors fell to talking about their clash with the nomads, dissecting the tactics and fighting skills of the Weya-Lu. All agreed that if the nomads had better weapons, they might not be sitting here now.

A horn sounded, far away. The discussion broke off, the officers alert and listening. The sound was a long, wavering note, the signal assigned to a Silvanesti scout named Camthantas. His patrol area was northeast, further along the same road they'd followed since crossing the creek.

Two more horns blew, and the Lioness was on her feet.

"Nomads?" said Favaronas, dropping his plate of beans.

"No," she said, her attention focused toward the sounds. "Northeast, from deeper in the valley. The other two signals are from the sentries on either side of Camthantas."

She pointed at two of her commanders, indicating they and their troops would accompany her. Glanthon would remain to defend the camp. The warriors scattered to their duties.

"You, too, Favaronas. You're with me."

He jumped to his feet, face ashen in the low light. "What? I'm no warrior! And I can't ride that beast of yours!"

"You don't have to. I'll go by horse." Eagle Eye was asleep, tethered inside an angle of stone wall. He'd spent many hours in the air today and had earned a good rest.

The Lioness took Favaronas's arm and pulled him along. "I'm sorry, but I may need your knowledge of the valley." When he continued to babble frightened protests, she whipped around and shouted into his face, "Favaronas! I need you! And I will protect you!"

In minutes forty elves, led by the Lioness, with her reluctant companion riding pillion, were cantering up the road toward Camthantas's position. The Vale of Silence was lit only by the stars, brilliant as a thousand diamonds on a bed of ebony silk. Off to Kerian's right, another alarm horn sounded, then another. In succession, the signals showed the source of the alarm was moving away from her and her small troop. She pressed ahead. When she reached Camthantas's assigned position, she knew something was very wrong. His horse was dead, its stomach slashed open.

"Draw swords!" Forty blades rose into the cool darkness. "First troop, deploy left; second, right! No one is to lose sight of his neighbor. At the walk, advance!"

She felt Favaronas trembling violently behind her, his hands lightly holding her waist. She was not without compassion. He was indeed no warrior. Despite this, and the deaths of his assistants, he'd not slowed them down on their difficult trek. Now he followed her into battle—perhaps not willingly, but without whining. Gruffly, she told him to stop worrying about protocol and hold on tight. His shaking hands clenched her waist.

They moved forward slowly. Her command to keep in sight of each other soon proved impossible to obey; the warriors were forced to ride around sections of walls or monoliths.

Something darted between two towering sarsens, and Favaronas let out a cry. He'd seen only a silhouette, but it was big—bigger than a horse. As he stuttered this warning, realization flooded through Kerian.

Wrenching her horse's head around, she shouted, "The sand beast! Retreat! Retreat!"

Her words were punctuated by a nearby chorus of shouts, followed by a veritable fanfare of horns. She kicked her horse into a gallop. Favaronas yelped as he was flung backward, but his grip never loosened.

"Rally to me, by the road! Rally to me!"

The forty elves converged on their general. Several confirmed her fears. They'd seen the reptilian monster. Arrows were nocked. The horses shied and snorted. They could smell the sand beast.

And then it was upon them, zigzagging through the ancient stones with unbelievable agility and speed. Bows creaked, strings sang, and arrows sped at the monster. Every one glanced off.

The Lioness drew a bead on the monster's eye, but it moved so fast her arrow flashed through empty air. The sand beast charged among the elves, throwing its horned head this way and that. The horses' mad panic made it hard for their riders to avoid the beast's rush. Horses and elves tumbled to the ground. It leaped upon one struggling pair, savaging them. All the while arrows bounced off its armored hide.

"How can we kill this thing?" Kerian shouted desperately.

One horse, braver than its fellows, lashed out at the blood-thirsty beast. With iron-shod hooves coming directly at its eyes, the monster backed up, bumping against a standing stone. The eighteen-foot monolith shifted.

Favaronas, clinging to Kerian's back, saw this, and it gave him an idea. "General, look!" he shouted, pounding her shoulder with the side of one hand. "The stone is loose! If we topple it—!"

She began issuing orders before he'd even finished. While most of the troop fought to keep the monster where it was, fourteen elves, dismounted, gathered on the other side of the stone to push.

The attackers charged, launching arrows at the sand beast's head. The creature was forced to blink every time an arrow flew at its eyes. Hips against the monolith, it shook its head from side to side and screeched with frustrated fury.

"Now!" Kerian cried.

Fourteen elves threw themselves on the tottering spire. It gave a little, and the sand beast obligingly stepped forward when it felt the cold stone nudge its back. The attackers pressed in, harder, and the sand beast fell back, rocking the stone backward and loosening it further.

"Again!"

Elves clambered up to their comrades' shoulders to get at the leaning stone. With groans, grunts, and more than a few curses, they shoved the monolith. At its base, the turquoise soil began to bulge and rise. The monument was breaking loose.

"Get back! Get back!"

Elves on foot and horseback scattered. Suddenly freed of the annoying rain of arrows, the sand beast lashed out with a foreclaw. With its double burden, the Lioness's horse lagged behind the rest. Iron claws snared the animal's flanks. Horse and riders went down in a heap.

The great stone continued its inexorable fall. The sand beast sensed the danger, but too late. The tapered spire crashed down on its hips, smashing it to the ground and pinning it beneath tons of stone. The beast let out a high-pitched howl.

Elves scrambled up the monolith, adding their weight to the burden on the creature's legs. As it roared and clawed at the stone, they stabbed furiously at the softer skin under its legs. Some swords snapped, but enough penetrated to make blood flow. Stirred by an agony it had never known, the sand beast arched its back with a mighty effort, shifting pillar and elves, and freeing itself. Crushed hindquarters dragging, it fled, mighty foreclaws propelling it several yards at a time. The lust to kill elves was subsumed beneath a more primal need—to live.

Her warriors found the Lioness, groggy but uninjured. Atop her sprawled Favaronas; the archivist was senseless.

"We beat it, General! It's running away!" they shouted, moving Favaronas aside and pulling her to her feet.

The words penetrated the fog in her battered brain. "What? Go after it! Don't let it escape!"

Mounted elves spurred away. Kerian called for a new horse. While one was being brought, she knelt by Favaronas. Blood trickled from his nose, but his eyes had opened. With her help, he sat up, holding his head in both hands.

"We aren't dead?" he muttered.

She grinned. "Didn't I tell you I'd protect you? I even let you land on me!"

The sour look froze on his face as his gaze went beyond her. "Look there!"

Issuing from the deep hole left by the uprooted monolith was a swarm of tiny lights. They drifted and darted in the night air: blue, white, red, and a smoky orange. The blue lights rose more quickly than the rest, and winked out one by one. White and red lights drifted to the ground and died like embers falling on wet grass. Only the orange wisps remained, circling and rising.

The Lioness had taken a few steps toward the lights, but Favaronas warned, "Stay back! Don't touch them!"

"What are they?"

"I don't know, but they were imprisoned by the standing pillar. They weren't meant to roam free!"

A horse arrived for Kerian. Wincing from her accumulated hurts, she swung onto its back, telling Favaronas, "Watch those things. Tell me what happens." She spurred hard after the sand beast.

The orbiting orange lights peeled off in groups of two and three, and followed her. Favaronas and the foot-bound warriors shouted warnings, but she was already too far away to hear.

Fiery pain kept the sand beast to a speed little better than a horse's best gallop. The bones broken in its left hip grated against each other. Sword cuts in the tender junction of its left hind leg burned.

Great as its agony was, even stronger was the fury blazing in its breast. The need for vengeance pushed it onward. It would visit this pain a hundredfold on the one who had sent it here. If necessary, it would cross the entire world to slay the one responsible for this agony.

Something snagged its right rear foot. Brought up short, the monster toppled forward, burying its chin in the turf. Before it could get up, more ropes whistled in, snagging its horned head and front limbs. Each loop drew tight, the one encircling its neck cinching so hard it couldn't draw breath. Then the creature found itself pulled in four directions at once.

Kerian galloped into the fantastic scene. The sand beast was down, thrashing against its bonds. Wounded and confused, it couldn't break the ropes holding it before more arrived. Its gyrations tore up clods of blue-green soil and widened its wounds. Blood flowed freely. Additional loops cinched its neck. Its eyes bulged as the pressure on its throat grew and grew.

As her horse skidded to a halt, she was amazed to see the orange lights sweep past her. They never paused, but flowed toward the tormented beast. They held off a few feet, sparkling like quartz in firelight, until all their number was gathered, then in unison they dropped. When they touched the sand beast's hard flesh the area was bathed in a silent flash of white light. A gust of cold wind stole Kerian's breath. The ropes abruptly went slack, causing the straining horses to surge forward and nearly unseating their riders.

To the amazement of all, the sand beast was gone.

* * * * *

Wapah halted at the flap of Adala's tent. "Weyadan, I have food for you."

"Enter, cousin."

He ducked under the ridge pole and knelt in front of her, taking care not to spill the contents of the tin plate he carried. Only ripe olives, bread, and rice, all cold, but she made no comment on the poor fare.

Two days had passed since the *laddad* had escaped into the Valley of the Blue Sands. Adala had pitched her tent where she stood, and the rest of the nomad warriors camped around her, tending their wounded and burying their dead. Here they would remain until the elves returned.

Trouble was, they were not equipped for a long stay. They had only the food and water they happened to be carrying at the time of the battle, and nothing more. It was their tradition to fight light and unencumbered; siege warfare was not their style. The bulk of their supplies had been lost when the family camp was attacked.

Shortages appeared immediately. In most Khurish camps, each tent had its own fire, but the nomads had so little fuel, campfires were rationed to one per five tents. Traditionally, they burned cow or goat droppings, but they were far from their herds. Water was precious, and food scarce.

Adala went without a fire, though any warrior in her host gladly would have given up his fuel to her. She sat in her tent and sewed on a project of her own, her only illumination the starshine she collected in a concave silver mirror set in the open door.

"There's no sign of the enemy," Wapah reported. She nodded, but didn't look up. Her fingertips were pricked and red with irritation, the inevitable consequence of sewing so long in such poor light.

He waited for her to stop sewing and eat. When several long minutes passed with no sign of this happening, he decided to go ahead and ask the question weighing on his mind. She would eat when she would eat.

"Maita, how long will we stay here?"

Lately, the tribesmen had added this to her titles. No longer speaking of "Adala's maita," they named her Fate itself.

"We will stay here until the *laddad* come out." She turned the heavy rectangle of cloth over and started stitching on the other side. "Or until we are told to go."

"Told by whom?"

"Those on High. I am but Their instrument."

Frowning, Wapah departed. It was a dark and somber camp he traversed back to the tent of Bindas, newly sworn war chief of the Weya-Lu. The tribe's warmasters had taken to congregating there, not least of all because Bindas's late uncle, Gwarali, never traveled anywhere without a generous supply of wheat beer. The leaders sat together in the hot darkness, sipping beer from tiny brass cups and speaking in low tones about their situation. Already there was talk of leaving the valley mouth. They didn't need to hover here, the dissidents said. All they need do was guard to route back to Khuri-Khan, and they would surely catch the *laddad* as they tried to return to their people. Food, water, medicine, and other supplies could be had by trading if only they left this place and kept on the move. That was their way. Sitting here in the shadow of the Pillars of Heaven was foreign, and dangerous.

"The Weyadan knows what she is doing," Wapah insisted. "Those on High have chosen her to cleanse our land. Do you doubt her?"

None would say so, but the beginning of that sentiment was plain in the black tent, as plain as the aroma of Gwarali's brew.

Talk turned to strategy. What was the best way to catch and defeat the elusive elves? Their long-legged horses were strong and fast, if not as hardy as desert ponies. *Laddad* armor resisted the nomads' favorite weapon, the bow. Even their swords had longer blades than the tribesmen's.

"In Estwilde, the Nerakans rode with lances," said Bindas. He'd served as a mercenary in the Knights' army during the recent great war. "They pierced any metal plate they rode at."

"You need hardwood to make lances," another mercenary veteran pointed out.

"We can trade for it."

"Before the *laddad* come out?"

And so it went. Voices rose and tempers flared as more beer was consumed and frustrations were voiced. A few of the warmasters who'd been to the world outside Khur offered to lead troops into the valley to find the elves.

The older chiefs were shocked. "Your crime would be as great as theirs!" one said.

"Where is it written we may not enter the valley?" said a young warmaster. "It is tradition, yes, but why? What makes this place so sacred?"

Wapah cleared his throat. Many rolled their eyes; the Weyadan's cousin was known as a talker.

"When Those on High made the world, each in turn pressed a hand on the new ground, leaving an impression. Each god said, 'This is my place. Let no one desecrate it.' Over time, the elements and various upheavals obscured most of these places. But the Valley of the Blue Sands remains, just as when the gods made it. It is their place, not ours, and not the *laddad's*."

Silence reigned for a time, broken only by the clink of brass cups and the splash of beer being poured. Bindas drained the last drops from his cup set it down. He was asking pardon of the group, preparing to suggest they all sleep, when a strange, metallic blast rang out over the camp. The men hurried outside, joining the rest of the camp, likewise turning out to see what was happening.

The sound came again, and they found its source. On the crest of a ridge sixty yards away, framed by the starry sky, a rider on a rearing horse was blowing a horn. Bows were strung, but Bindas put a stop to anyone loosing an arrow. An enemy would hardly announce his coming with a brass horn.

The rider galloped down the stony hillside, zigzagging around juniper bushes and large rocks, to the center of the camp. This put him outside Adala's tent. The Weyadan came out in time to receive the swirl of dust kicked up as the black horse skidded to a halt. Its rider was clothed in billowing robes, not light-colored like a traditional geb, but scarlet, turned nearly black by the starlight. His head was covered by the robe's hood. He was lean, with a pale foreign face. He seemed small, but perhaps that was only because his horse was so large, eighteen hands at least.

"Who commands here?" he asked. The voice was male, and young. "Do you understand me? Who is your leader?"

"I am." Adala stepped forward. "Who are you?"

"I bring you a message from Shobbat, Prince of Khur!" He paused, obviously expecting a response. When Adala gave none, he added, more loudly, "The prince calls upon the desert people of Khur to save their country!"

"That's what we're doing."

Adala lifted her hem and approached. She stopped quite close to the imposing horse and looked up at its crimson-clad rider. "I am Adala, Weyadan of the Weya-Lu, chosen leader of these people. This horse is not Khurish. Neither are you. Who are you?"

"A messenger, nothing more. I was born beyond the mountains. Now I serve in Khur. I have a proclamation from Prince Shobbat. Will you receive it?"

"Why does the Prince of Khur employ foreigners to do his bidding?" Adala asked.

The messenger had removed a small scroll from his belt. "My horse is powerful and swift. I came to Khuri-Khan to serve."

Adala shrugged one shoulder, and murmured an old proverb: "A rat in a palace is still a rat."

The rider flung the scroll at her feet. "There is Prince Shobbat's summons. Read it, and know the truth. Or do I need to read it for you?"

The slur went unchallenged. Adala picked up the scroll and handed it to Bindas, standing near her. The war chief broke the seal and read the message aloud.

" 'Be it known, I, Shobbat, rightful prince of Khur, do set my hand to this message.

" 'Beloved sons of Khur: the plague of foreigners we have long endured now threatens our ancient land. For five years, the *laddad* have dwelt among us, living their foreign lives and spreading their foreign ideas. In Khuri-Khan their steel buys hearts and their heresy clouds minds. My father, the Khan of All the Khurs, Sahim, has succumbed to the lure of *laddad* money.' "

The nomads already thought this was true. Hearing it from Sahim's heir was a revelation. There were murmurs and wide eyes all around.

" 'The temples of Khuri-Khan have become unclean. Sahim-Khan allows the *laddad* to go where they will and flaunt the laws and customs of Khur. As a loyal son of Khur' "—Bindas snorted at the irony of this phrase—" 'I cannot abide this treason any longer.' "

"Enough," Adala said. "What does he want?"

Bindas read silently for a moment, then related the kernel at the end of the flowery message. "'I therefore beseech all peoples of the desert, who hold in their hearts the true soul of Khur, to ride to Khuri-Khan and destroy the *laddad* pestilence there.'"

Wind made the flames of the oil lamps waver. The great horse, obviously disliking the large number of humans that enclosed it, snorted and stamped its hooves. No one spoke.

"Well, what is your answer?" the messenger finally asked.

Adala stared up at the horse, ignoring its rider's question. Bravely, the Weya-Lu woman held up her hand. Even with her arm extended, the horse's head, at the end of its proudly arched neck, was beyond her reach. The horse might have snapped off her fingers with one quick champ of its teeth. Instead, its nervous movements halted, and it lowered its head so the Weyadan could pat its cheek. Lowering it further, the horse nuzzled her hand.

The rider was surprised by his mount's docility. He jerked the reins, pulling his horse's head up again. "Are you going to answer?" he demanded.

Adala spoke, but not to him. She turned, black robes swirling around her feet and announced, "The foreign messenger and his great horse are signs. We will go to Khuri-Khan. We will raise the tribes. All the children of the desert will take up this cause. It falls to us to purify Khur."

Looking north, toward the blackness that was Torghan's Teeth and the mouth of the valley, she added, "Let the *laddad* perish in their vanity. Those on High will attend to the blasphemers."

Half a thousand Weya-Lu warriors raised their hands over their heads and shouted in unison. "*Adala maita! Adala maita!*"

The noise was so great the courier's horse reared in alarm. Only the rider's skill and quick thinking kept him in the saddle. His task was complete, and he had no desire to linger. He put spurs to his black horse and galloped away.

Filled with new spirit, the nomads heaped all the carefully hoarded fuel on their campfires. The flames blazed up, sending gouts of sparks into the air. The tribesmen's chant soared upward as well.

As he rode away, the Nerakan courier could see the glow of the nomad fires for a long time. He could hear their roaring chants even longer.

Hengriff, waiting on horseback in a draw a mile away, heard them, too. Sparks had fallen on the tinder. All that remained was to see how big a bonfire would result.

10

The gates of Khuri-Khan were closed and bolted. There was no warning, no flurry of horns or rushing of guards. The iron portcullises, which once defied the minions of Malystryx, simply dropped into place. The battlements, normally patrolled by the Khan's soldiers, emptied.

This was not a development Gilthas had expected. For a day and a half, since word arrived of the supposed massacre of the nomad camp, mobs of Khurs, armed with sticks, hand tools, and stones, had issued from the city to attack Khurinost several times. The largest of these groups comprised a thousand people, but each time, they were turned back without difficulty by Planchet, Hamaramis, and the elven host. Tents on the camp's periphery were torn down and burned, but the angry Khurs never penetrated far into Khurinost. Then the city gates had closed.

The Speaker and most of his advisors stood in the clear area in front of his royal tent. The spot was the highest point in Khurinost, though not by much. The late afternoon sun was behind them. Its orange light sparkled off the glazed tiles and yellow domes of Khuri-Khan, washing the scene in a deceptively pleasant and benign glow.

"What's Sahim-Khan playing at? Is he trying to protect us from his people, or what?" Gilthas muttered.

None of his advisors knew. Absent from the group was

Lord Morillon. He was in the city, seeking an audience with the Khan. Planchet, just returned from surveying the damage done to the outer ring of tents, removed his helmet and mopped his forehead with a rag.

"Could be he wants to cut off our water," he said.

He spoke out of his own thirst, but his suggestion was a logical one. Every drop of water in Khurinost had to be carried from the city. If Sahim-Khan refused them access, the next nearest wells were at Ving's Oasis, forty miles northeast, a journey of two or three days for elves on foot. The horrors of the march to Khur five years ago would be repeated, and on a daily basis. Gilthas needed alternatives. He recalled Hamaramis and, with Planchet, discussed how to repair the situation.

"We ought to storm the city," Hamaramis suggested. "The humans have left us ladders all around Khuri-Khan."

The scaffolding, erected for repair work on the walls, remained in many spots.

Planchet shook his head. "Sahim-Khan must know that. He's not a fool."

The Speaker studied Khuri-Khan through a brass spyglass. Its ruby lenses, polished by the gemcutters' guild of Qualinost, had allowed him to watch the streets of Qualinost from the heights of the palace. Now they brought Khurish defenses into sharp focus for the Speaker's tired, sun-scorched eyes. He hated the idea of attacking Khuri-Khan. They had dwelt here in relative peace and safety for five years. They had no real enmity with Khur. If they stormed the city now, they would have to go all out to win. Failure meant utter destruction. They were too few to overwhelm the humans quickly, so war in the desert kingdom would go on and on. If Neraka or the minotaurs intervened, catastrophe would engulf elves and Khurs alike.

"Perhaps it was not the Khan who closed the gates," Planchet said. He was worried about his young friend Hytanthas, who had not returned to the elves' camp. Perhaps Hytanthas had stumbled in his mission, and the gates had been closed at the instigation of the mage Faeterus.

Hamaramis reminded them about the fanatical followers of Torghan, and Planchet said they mustn't forget the Nerakan emissary they'd seen in the Khuri yl Nor. The Khurs had long-standing ties to the Dark Knights, and many of Sahim-Khan's soldiers had served as mercenaries in their hire.

"Are we prepared to move?" the Speaker asked, still gazing through the spyglass.

"We are short several hundred carts," Hamaramis replied. "There wasn't enough timber to build them, and no time to trade for the wood. So we're building travois."

Wilder elves often transported goods and possessions by this means. A simple travois required only two long poles and canvas or hide to stretch between them. It could be pulled by horse, donkey, or even a sturdy goat. The trailing runners would not bog down in the sea of sand outside Khuri-Khan.

Glumly, Hamaramis departed to continue the preparations. He was against leaving, and his opposition had grown more open over the past few days. He preferred to stay and attack. Seize the city, he had argued; negotiate with the Khurs from the safety of their own stone walls.

What this bold, forthright plan failed to consider was that once the city was theirs, the elves were trapped. The nomad tribes would gather and expend every last drop of blood to drive them out, and Neraka could not be ignored. The Knights would certainly intervene, storming into Khur as liberators. The last hope of the elven nations would be caught neatly in a stone prison of their own making.

The answer, Gilthas still felt certain, lay in finding a new place to live. The elves needed barriers of distance and inhospitable wastes to guard them from the sudden proliferation of enemies. Only then could they grow and rebuild their strength.

A shadow fell on him, and Gilthas looked up. Planchet had opened a linen parasol to shade him.

"I wonder where Lady Kerianseray is?" the valet said, offering him a damp cloth.

Gilthas pressed the cloth against his throat and brow. "Some place cool, I hope."

He'd received a very short dispatch from her, two days after the arrival of the first. Kerian and her warriors had entered the valley. The climate was mild and damp, but they'd found no signs of life. Strange stone ruins covered the valley as far as they could see. She intended to penetrate to the center of the valley, fulfilling her mission of exploration, then return.

Gilthas hardly knew what to make of the terse report. It contained no details from his archivist, Favaronas, and raised more questions than it answered. Was the Inath-Wakenti suitable for their people, or not? Was there a supply of fresh water? Any game? What was so strange about the ruins? Did they show evidence of having been built by ancient elves, as some of the legends had it?

The Lioness did thank him for sending Eagle Eye to her. But her promise to "put him to good use against our enemies" did not have a particularly diplomatic ring to it.

Of course she was under great stress, but did her reports have to be so vague and unhelpful? Was she allowing her personal feelings to color them? She was dead against his plan to migrate to the valley. Like the other warriors around the Speaker, Kerian preferred to decide her own fate by fighting. Even though he understood this, he could not allow war to overtake his people. He had to rule his own wife in that regard. The stakes were too high.

He mopped his brow again, glancing skyward. The sun was relentless. Khurinost would exhaust its ready water supply in a day if Khuri-Khan remained inaccessible.

"More to the point," he said, "where is Lord Morillon? We need those gates opened!"

* * * * *

SANCTUARY

Lord Morillon was saying those very words to Sahim-Khan, on the rooftop garden of the royal citadel. Enormous screens, woven of reeds and rushes, shaded the garden. In better times, fountains flowed among the ferns and willows, adding the music of falling water to the scene and allowing more tender plants to be grown. As yet, the water system had not been repaired, so the greenery was confined to smaller, potted bushes and flowers which servants carried indoors during the worst heat of the day. Despite its sparse look, the garden still afforded an excellent view of the city.

"If our people are shut out, Great Khan, they will be forced to storm the city for water."

"Attack Khuri-Khan?" Sahim thundered. "Blood will run down the walls of the city should that happen!"

The Silvanesti noble bowed, saying smoothly, "Your Majesty is wise. Blood indeed will flow, elven and human."

Honey-tongued Zunda stepped forward and intoned, "Great is the patience of my master, Sahim the Many-Blessed! His forbearance is like the gods' own! He has heard of the terrible atrocities wrought against his desert children, and still he is merciful. Still he stays his hand against the *laddad*, for he has pledged to maintain their safety. The word of Sahim-Khan is like a thunderbolt, implacable and unchanging!"

Suave, diplomatic Silvanesti never grind their teeth in frustration, but Lord Morillon was close to doing just that. He said—for the eighth time since arriving at the palace—that there was no proof a massacre had occurred, much less that it had been perpetrated by elves. "If the Mighty Khan would receive my king, the Speaker of the Sun and Stars, he would know this tale is false."

"Desert tribesmen are known throughout this land for their truth telling," said Zunda. "It is, for them, as essential as water and salt."

"I can only repeat: There is no proof Lady Kerianseray or any other elven warriors have harmed a single nomad. No one has offered the slightest evidence an atrocity has even occurred. If it has, the Great Khan should look elsewhere for culprits—Neraka, perhaps."

Lord Hengriff also was present on the rooftop. The representative of the Dark Knights stood a few steps away, among a crowd of other foreign dignitaries he overtopped by head and shoulders. His dark face was expressionless as a mask, even when the Silvanesti noble invoked his country's name.

"The truth will be known," Sahim declared. "I believe in the will of the gods."

In reality Sahim-Khan believed in nothing but Sahim-Khan. As always, his mind was busy considering how best to make use of the current situation. Morillon's threat to fight for water might prove a useful lever for prying more money out of Neraka. Sahim sought out Hengriff in the crowd, only to discover the bull-voiced warrior had slipped away unnoticed. Such discretion was remarkable in so large a man—remarkable and unnerving.

"Mighty Khan, the gates?" the Silvanesti lord was saying.

He was a persistent snake. Sahim had to credit him for that. Next to round, bewigged old Zunda, Morillon looked trim, cool, and elegant.

Sahim settled himself back in his throne—not the heavy, priceless Sapphire Throne, which never left the audience hall—and arranged his white and gold robes. Thus seated, he was a head taller than the standing elf. He made the most of his advantage, looking down his nose at Morillon.

"Zunda, how long till sunset?"

"One hour, Mighty Khan," the vizier replied promptly. He'd long ago learned to have a multitude of disparate facts to hand, even one which his master could easily know for himself, simply by looking over his shoulder at the lowering sun.

Sahim mulled the answer in silence for moment, then barked: "Commander of the Guard!"

The quick flash of surprise on Morillon's face was most gratifying. The *laddad* wasn't as sure of himself as he appeared.

SANCTUARY

General Hakkam came forward. Armor clanking, he knelt before his lord. "Commander, take what troops you need and clear the city gates of all malcontents," the Khan said. "If they resist, put them to the sword!"

Hakkam's weathered face showed even more surprise than the elf's, but he acknowledged the command immediately. Before he could rise to go, Sahim spoke again.

"However, the gates will remain closed."

It seemed all in the crowd were holding their breath. None could fathom what the Khan was up to. From the look on Morillon's face, it was obvious he, too, was at a loss.

"As you must certainly recall, my lord," Sahim said, "elves are not allowed within the city after nightfall. The Khan of Khur cannot allow his defenses to be compromised. The malcontents and rioters will be cleared from the gates at once, and the gates will open as usual—at sunrise tomorrow."

General Hakkam departed.

Morillon expressed his gratitude. His words carried no trace of irony.

"Justice is the cornerstone of khanship," Sahim said, allowing his amusement to show. It was not a pleasant expression. "The merchants in the souks must trade. I'm sure they miss their *laddad* customers." He put a hand to his lips, as if a thought had just occurred to him. "You had best warn your Speaker. Keeping sufficient troops on the gates to ward off rioters will be a drain on my treasury. I will of course be forced to institute a new tax."

An awed hush fell over the rooftop garden. Morillon's breathing seemed suddenly loud. All of his diplomatic training was required to keep him from shouting. "What tax, Mighty Khan?" he asked.

"Henceforth, all persons entering Khuri-Khan to trade must pay an entry tax." He glanced at Zunda. "One gold piece per head." The vizier lowered his eyes and nodded, ever so slightly.

The amount was ridiculous, exorbitant, and fell especially on the elves, who entered frequently for trade purposes. Morillon's Silvanesti aplomb failed him utterly. His mouth fell open. Sahim smilingly assured him the tax was only temporary, until the troops could be returned to their barracks.

Morillon bowed stiffly. "I will convey the Great Khan's words to the Speaker of the Sun and Stars. Will Your Mightiness receive the Speaker to discuss the matter of the alleged massacre?"

Sahim waved a hand magnanimously. "I need no reassurance, my lord. The word of the Speaker of the Sun and Stars is more than enough for me."

Pale, tight-lipped, Morillon swept out, ignoring the stares of Sahim's uncouth courtiers. Another so-called tax! This was the second time the Khan had insulted the Speaker to Morillon's face. The Silvanesti was a lifelong servant of the throne of the Stars and his patience was nearly at an end. Sahim-Khan didn't know it, but he'd made a lasting enemy of Lord Morillon this day.

Passing through the citadel courtyard, walking so rapidly his small entourage had to jog to keep up, Morillon noted two humans talking together. Lord Hengriff and Prince Shobbat were deep in conversation by a shadowed wall. That is to say, Shobbat was talking animatedly. Hengriff was listening, arms folded across his chest.

The Knight's eyes moved, crossing Morillon's gaze in passing, and his impassive countenance altered. The look on his face was so fleeting, Morillon found it difficult to categorize. Was it acknowledgment? A grudging respect? The Dark Order, for all its machinations, was a far more honorable opponent than the grasping, conniving Sahim. Perhaps in that brief moment Knight and elf shared the realization that both were heartily sick of Khur and its ruler. Change was coming. Whether it would be for Neraka or the elves was uncertain, but the current course could not continue.

A very eloquent glance. In a snap of sky-blue silk, Morillon was out the gate and gone. Hengriff continued to stare thoughtfully after him.

"—was delivered!" Shobbat was saying, voice rising. "Did your courier get through as I ordered?"

Hengriff nodded, and the prince demanded, "Well, has he returned? I would speak to him about the nomads' reaction."

The Knight didn't respond. He was still thinking about the Silvanesti noble. Lord Morillon was a chink in the Speaker's armor. Gilthas trusted him too much, relied too heavily on his counsel, but Hengriff recognized Morillon's type. He was of the class of elves who let their nation slide into ruin while they observed all the niceties of protocol and manners. Kerianseray and the Qualinesti were much more dangerous. They would have deduced long before now that they had a spy in their midst. Morillon was still in the dark.

"You're not listening!"

Hengriff fixed the impatient prince with a baleful eye. "No, I'm not. When you calm down and speak rationally, I'll listen, Your Highness."

Shobbat quivered. He wasn't used to such insolence, any more than he was used to standing in the heat. Sweat stood out on his forehead. Tiny red veins webbed the whites of his eyes. He had dyed his hair its usual dark shade, but in strong sunlight, the black carried a faint greenish tinge.

"I need to know what's happening," he said, striving for a calmer tone. "Are the nomads coming?"

"Who can say, Highness? Your desert folk are like wolves, fierce and wild. I've lived here two years and I don't begin to understand them."

Shobbat, Khur born and bred, didn't understand the nomads either, but he wasn't about to admit that to Hengriff.

Changing the subject, the Knight told him of his father's agreement to clear all the city gates of troublemakers.

"Really? All the gates, you say?" The prince pressed a fist to his lower lip. If soldiers of the Household Guard had been sent to all nine gates of Khuri-Khan, there couldn't be many left in the palace.

"Careful, Highness. Your thoughts leap from your face."

Shobbat forced a careless laugh and palmed sweat from his forehead. "I don't know what you mean. I'm simply suffering from the heat. I should retire indoors and escape the warmth."

Hengriff bowed to the heir of Khur. "To Your Highness's continued good health."

The prince withdrew. Once he had seemed a ridiculous figure but Hengriff was beginning to wonder if he had underestimated him. The situation was coming to a head, and quickly. Hengriff's dispatches to Jelek stressed this urgency. He felt the Order must be ready to move on a moment's notice. When the crisis came, the fate of the elves would fall not to him who struck first, but him who struck the most decisively.

Six lengthy dispatches, carefully enciphered, he had sent to Jelek via the border town of Kortal. Six dispatches in as many weeks, yet no answer had come back. If Hengriff had been the suspicious type, he might think his messages weren't getting through. Worse still, could Rennold be ignoring him?

Odd sounds reached the citadel courtyard. Distorted by the brick canyons of Khuri-Khan, the tumult sounded like the crash of waves on a rocky shore. Hengriff knew better. They were the sounds of conflict.

His four bodyguards arrived, already mounted, leading his horse. "My lord!" cried his man Goldorf. "There is fighting at the city gates!"

Hengriff swung into the saddle. "Sahim-Khan ordered his troops to clear the gates. Who are his guards fighting?"

"Torghanists."

Hengriff betrayed surprise. The priests of Torghan were taking Nerakan pay, and he hadn't asked them to blockade the city. So who had? His dark eyes narrowed. He suspected the meddling hand of Prince Shobbat in this development.

"Well, let's see how Sahim's men fight," he said, grasping his reins in one large fist.

He and his bodyguards galloped straight to the west gate, which faced the elves' camp. They scattered Khurs left and right. The Lesser Souk was emptying rapidly as the sound of swordplay rang over the market. The sight of the Nerakans on horseback only hastened the process.

This gate was known to city-dwellers as "Malys's Anvil" because the red dragon had crushed so many foes against the stout iron portcullises. When Sahim-Khan's guards arrived the gatehouse had appeared undefended, but as they broke ranks to open it, stones and timbers rained down, thrown by Khurs concealed inside. A squad was sent up each side of the battlement, to storm the gate in unison and trap the attackers inside. Unfortunately, the fanatics proved to be armed with more than brickbats; they produced swords and spears and, in the narrow confines of the parapet, Sahim's guards had a real fight on their hands. Soon the ground around the gatehouse was littered with bodies. Most wore nomad gebs, but more than a few wore the scale armor of the khan's royal guard.

Hengriff halted his horse some distance away to watch the unexpected fight. His men pulled up respectfully behind him. Silent at first, the bodyguards soon were offering a running commentary on the progress of the battle and bellowing advice to the outmaneuvered guards.

"Cut at their legs! Civilians are terrified of that—keeps 'em from running away!"

"Look at those shields, dangling from their wrists like a lady's nosegay. Get your shields *up*, you goatherds! Watch those spearpoints!"

"I'll bet you wish you had a score of archers just now, don't you?"

"Shut up," Hengriff growled and the bodyguards subsided, merely shaking their heads at the display before them.

Below, the guards breached the flimsy barricade around the gate. Leaping over baskets filled with brickbats, they quickly routed the Torghanists on the ground. In hours, the remaining eight portals were likewise free of "malcontents."

Long before that, Hengriff had led his men back into the city. The Knight had other falcons to fly during the coming night.

* * * * *

Hytanthas arched his back, stretching. He was tucked inside an angle of broken wall, on the grounds of a once-beautiful villa. Through a chink in the wall he'd been watching the ruined house for half a day. He'd begun to think he was on a kender's errand.

Disguised again as a human, he had lurked in wine shops and low inns seeking clues to the whereabouts of the elusive sorcerer Faeterus. He'd learned nothing of note until he overheard a merchant complaining to his fellows about a peculiar order he'd received.

"I am a poulterer," the merchant declaimed proudly, "not a trapper. Who orders a dozen live pigeons? Nobody eats those filthy birds!"

His colleagues mocked him mercilessly. Apparently this was not the first time he'd received such an order, nor the first time he'd complained about it.

"Then why didn't you refuse?" taunted one of his colleagues.

"Because of the money!" put in another.

There were guffaws around the table, and the poulterer joined in. The money was indeed good, good enough to convince him not only to procure the despised pigeons, but to deliver them to the city's ruined northern district. He'd stopped here for a refresher before venturing into that cursed area. His comrades agreed the Harbalah was home to ghosts—and worse.

SANCTUARY

At this point Hytanthas insinuated himself into the conversation. Posing as a Delphonian down on his luck, he offered to deliver the pigeons. The chicken merchant was eager to shift the duty to another. He paid Hytanthas two silvers—insulting wages, which the elf accepted with fawning gratitude—then gave him directions, and a warning.

"Remember, leave the cages outside the old garden wall. Don't go any closer to the house."

"Why so much fuss? It's a ruin, isn't it?"

"Just don't, if you value your life's blood!"

Hytanthas heeded the warning. He had placed the caged birds where he'd been told, then took up a position in one of the wrecked outbuildings to see who claimed them. He was certain it would be Faeterus. The shattered mansion was the perfect setting for a renegade mage. And Hytanthas had heard unsavory stories about dark magical rites involving the sacrifice of animals, like pigeons.

The land rose slightly from Hytanthas's position up to the villa proper. As the sun set, the shadows swelled like a dark sea, claiming first the grounds, then the decrepit house. Blocks warmed all day gave up their heat by night, so Hytanthas had a snug place from which to watch the pigeon basket. Too snug, in fact. After so many hours of inactivity, he began to nod.

The clatter of broken stones jerked him from sleep. Gripping his sword hilt, he peered through the chink in the wall. The wicker basket was where he'd left it, its avian cargo asleep.

He heard another small avalanche of disturbed masonry. Someone was moving in the ruins. A low, breathy growl penetrated his hiding place, then a voice, hoarse with age, pitched slightly high.

"What is it, Talon? Intruders?"

The voice was behind him, to the left of the villa's front door, in the ruined garden. With all the stealth imparted by heritage and training, Hytanthas rose up from his crouch and peeked over the low wall. There was Faeterus, not ten yards away. He was standing in profile, hooded, heavy robe draped over his hunched shoulders. One long-fingered hand held a thin, glittering leash. At the other end of the leash was a walking nightmare.

The monster stood on four feet, like a lion, and its body was covered by thick, tawny hair. It had a long neck coated in sleek, bronze-colored scales. Atop this, surrounded by a stiff red mane, its head was an awful parody of an elven or human face, with a flat nose and a mouth many times larger than a person's. Row upon row of silver metallic teeth filled the creature's fearsome smile. Its tail switched back and forth, like a cat's.

"This is what happens when I take down my wards to receive new birds; someone takes advantage," Faeterus said. "Very well, Talon. Find the intruder." He released the thin leash.

Hytanthas ducked down. He heard the monster's paws dig into loose rubble as it sprang away from its master.

"Whoever you are, you'd better run. When the manticore finds you, the meeting won't be pleasant."

Hytanthas gathered himself, took a deep breath, and leaped over the wall. He landed with feet wide apart and presented his blade to the robed mage. He looked around nervously. The manticore was not in sight.

"In the name of the Speaker of the Sun and Stars, surrender!"

Faeterus looked surprised, but only for an instant. "Ah, I see. An elf hiding in a human shell. That explains Talon's confusion. What's your name, Hermit Crab?"

Hytanthas told him, just as the manticore came bounding back down the path. Hytanthas rushed forward, laying the edge of his sword alongside Faeterus's neck.

"Keep that thing away, or I'll have your head!"

Faeterus snapped his fingers. The monster halted at once, as if arrested by an invisible tether. Dropping on its haunches, it stared at them with round, cold blue eyes, grinning with its insanely large mouth. Hot breath, stinking of carrion, washed over Hytanthas's face.

"I'm taking you to the Speaker to be judged for your crimes," he said.

"I don't think so." Hytanthas tapped him with the flat of his blade. Faeterus chuckled lightly, adding, "Yes, a good blade, and I'm sure you know how to use it. But it's not yet time for me to meet Gilthas Pathfinder."

With that, he simply went away. How or where, Hytanthas could not begin to guess, but one instant he was gripping the mage's bulky robe; in the next blink of an eye, his hand was empty. His sword, now resting on nothing, dropped to the dirt.

The manticore leaped.

Hytanthas got his blade up in time to ward off the monster. His point raked across the bright scales but did not pierce them. He backed rapidly, keeping his weapon pointed at the beast. Huffing, the manticore advanced slowly.

Hytanthas spotted Faeterus. The mage now stood on a veranda high on the side of the ruined villa. The basket of pigeons sat beside him. His face showed no excitement, merely calm curiosity. Apparently he wanted to see how his monstrous pet dealt with an armed and agile intruder.

Hytanthas cut at the manticore's eyes. The creature stood its ground, batting the tip away with one paw. Hytanthas reversed his motion and thrust at the paw. His keen point pierced it from furred top to padded sole. Dark blood flowed. The beast howled, opening its mouth so wide the elf feared its head would break at the hinge and fall off. Its voice was high and piping.

The manticore attacked again. Hytanthas pirouetted aside, but the beast's claws caught his Khurish robe. He was dragged down, landing on his back atop broken masonry, and the sword flew from his hand. The monster's claws slashed across his chest. The mail shirt he wore beneath his robe saved him from being gutted like a fish, but the blow still knocked the wind from his chest.

Furious at its failure to draw blood, the manticore swatted the elf like a housecat toying with a mouse. The blow sent Hytanthas rolling across the weedy ground until he fetched up against a sizable date palm. Shedding sun hat and shredded robe, the elf hefted several fist-sized stones and hurled them at the creature. They thumped against its chest, eliciting grunts, but barely slowed the manticore. Hytanthas turned and ran, Khurish sandals flapping.

He vaulted nimbly over ruined fences and broken walls, but was forced to detour around larger obstacles. His adversary simply bulled straight through everything in its path, thereby gaining steadily on him. As he leapt for the top of a stout pile of stone masonry, the creature was so close behind he felt the rush of air as it swiped at his legs. He hauled himself up and over the pile.

The manticore crashed into the pile, but the masonry was too thick for it to break through. With a human-sounding scream of frustration, the monster reared up, rested its paws atop the pile, and looked over. Frustration turned to unholy triumph, and it grinned. Its quarry was trapped!

Hytanthas stood with his back against the estate's outer wall, designed to enclose the villa like a miniature fortress. Whole sections had been toppled, but it was his misfortune that this portion, a good twenty yards long, was intact. Fifteen feet high, its surface was smoothly plastered, allowing for no handholds, even for a nimble and highly motivated elf.

With evident relish and terrifying slowness, the manticore scaled the masonry pile. Its pale blue eyes never left Hytanthas's face, and the elf stared back, afraid if he looked away it would pounce.

Suddenly, the manticore froze, right foreleg in the air. Hytanthas hadn't heard or felt anything, but the creature obviously had. It waited several long seconds, tail twitching, gaze flickering upward, then resumed its advance.

SANCTUARY

On the veranda, Faeterus felt something, too. He released the pigeon he'd been stroking, moved to the edge of the gallery, and stared out into the night.

A deep vibration suddenly shook ground and air. Gradually Hytanthas discerned a new sound: heavy footfalls, and the noise of something weighty being dragged. It was coming from his right, a part of the estate he hadn't explored.

As he tried to make sense of the noises, the manticore began behaving oddly. Attention fixed in the direction of the approaching footsteps, it shrank down, belly against the rubble pile, as if trying to make itself small. Its thin lips parted and it hissed like a frightened cat. The hair along its back stood up.

The heavy footfalls and dragging sound drew nearer, bringing with them the metallic reek of blood. The warm wind carried the stench of putrefaction, as of a large wound gone black with gangrene. The manticore howled loudly then rushed away, keeping itself close to the ground.

Cautiously, Hytanthas followed. He'd spotted his sword, glittering faintly in the rubble. It was a long way away and the manticore, departing or not, was between the weapon and him.

He was sizing up his chance of reaching it when something loomed up out of the darkness. At first he thought it was the manticore, but the sheer bulk of the thing was too great, at least three times the size of Faeterus's deadly pet. He made out a pair of green eyes, each at least ten inches across, with large vertical black pupils, and a huge face ringed by horns. Hytanthas screamed.

His cries were answered. Faeterus tossed a small globe into the air. It exploded, flooding the scene with brilliant white light. The light was painful to Hytanthas, but bearable. By its illumination, he finally realized what it was he faced, though he could hardly credit his eyes.

During his exile in Khur, the young elf had tried to learn all he could about the dangers his people might face here.

Never had he thought to see a sand beast. Especially not in the middle of a city.

Fortunately, the creature did not seem overly interested in him. Head lowered against the glare, the sand beast continued its advance toward the ruined villa. Someone had hurt it. It hauled itself forward by its forelimbs, its hindquarters dragging lifelessly behind. Where left hind leg joined sloping back, a great festering wound spread.

The elf never considered running away. His mission was to bring Faeterus before the Speaker; he could hardly do that if he left the mage at the mercy of this monster. Faeterus, hampered by his bulky disguise, was descending the stone steps from the veranda.

"Talon!" the sorcerer panted. "Attack!"

The manticore came galloping over the debris-strewn ground, its earlier fear of the sand beast overcome by the will of its master. In the last few yards its strides stretched to great bounds, and on the third leap it threw itself on the sand beast's back, wrapping its legs around the scaly hide. The greenish-gold scales covering the sand beast's throat resisted the manticore's teeth, but the mage's pet kept trying.

The sand beast shook its horned head from side to side, hoping to dislodge its attacker. The manticore climbed up and hooked its foreclaws on the beast's lower jaw. Mouth opening wide, the manticore worried the beast's throat. The sand beast gave up trying to remove its tormenter. Lowering its head, it ran itself against the nearest standing wall. Blocks burst apart, and the manticore finally was knocked loose. It rolled, got its feet beneath it, and sprang again. With lightning precision, the sand beast's head came around, its jaws opened, and it caught the manticore in mid-leap. The manticore yowled in high-pitched rage, but only for a moment. The sand beast's jaws closed on its neck. A sickening snap, and the human-looking head dropped to the ground.

Faeterus had reached the arena of battle. The mage extended his left hand toward the furious sand beast and uttered a string of mysterious syllables. An invisible concussion drove the beast backward a few feet, but that was all. Metallic lids narrowed over its eyes, a throaty growl rose from its throat, and the beast advanced again.

"You're only making it angry!" Hytanthas yelled. "Keep it busy, and I'll help you fight it!"

The mage's hooded head turned toward him. "Yes, perhaps you can be a help, at that."

Faeterus spoke a word, and the globe of light overhead went out. Hytanthas, his attention focused on getting to his sword, was suddenly astonished to find himself not only plunged into darkness, but dragged backward as if in the grip of an invisible hand. He protested, flailing futilely against the force that held him. Faeterus waited until he was nearly in range of the sand beast's claws, then released him. With the beast thus distracted, the mage made his escape. He vanished into the outer darkness.

Hytanthas wasted no time. As soon as the magical force let him go, he hurled himself to one side, rolled, and came up running. Clad only in mail shirt, leggings, and sandals, he was unarmed and helpless. Once determined to take Faeterus back to the Speaker, he would have to settle for bringing word of the mage's whereabouts. If he survived!

Behind him, he could hear the creature's advance. Chunks of masonry flew, date palms snapped, and broken walls burst apart as the sand beast kept coming. Its aim was uncanny. Either it could see very well in the dark or it had some other way of sensing Hytanthas's whereabouts.

The elf turned to see where it was. In that brief pause, the sand beast jumped at him.

Hampered by injury, the creature came up short, but one foreclaw swiped across his mail shirt. Once more his armor saved Hytanthas from death, but even the glancing touch of the metallic claws was enough to tear through the mail as though it was linen.

The sand beast was thrown off balance. It crashed to the

ground and rolled down a short slope.

While the monster floundered in a rocky, weed-choked area that once had been a stone-lined pond, Hytanthas made good his escape. He clambered up the shell of the gatehouse and dropped inside. Loose rubble shifted beneath his feet and he landed awkwardly, slicing his leg on a sharp limestone block.

Swallowing a groan of pain, he listened for sounds of the sand beast's pursuit. Instead he heard human voices, men's voices. A tiny ember of relief flickered inside of him. Perhaps Sahim-Khan's soldiers had heard the uproar in the Harbalah and come to investigate.

A new fire burned in the air over the villa grounds. No magical orb, it was a flaming arrow. Its light fell on the sand beast, dedicatedly gnawing off its own wounded leg, and something else: five mounted men. They cantered through an opening in the villa's outer wall. One had a long lance couched under his arm. The rest carried swords or bows. Their armor was Nerakan, not Khurish.

Hytanthas had no intention of cowering in safety while others battled that horror. He hunted through the debris in the gatehouse and found a length of lead pipe, corroded but heavy. With his makeshift weapon in hand, he slipped out to wait for the riders to reach him.

The sand beast gave up trying to sever its injured leg and dragged itself onto the cracked pavers of the road to wait for the oncoming riders. It was breathing hard, its nostrils sending clouds of white vapor into the cooling night air.

The five riders drew abreast of Hytanthas and rode on by. The one in the center, carrying the lance, was Lord Hengriff, the Dark Order's emissary to Khur. The five charged the wounded sand beast. Hengriff's lance pierced its broken hips. The monster roared in pain and whirled, snapping the lance shaft but leaving its head buried. One foreclaw raked through the air, and a horse went down. It and its rider had been shredded; neither rose again.

Circling away, Hengriff drew a two-handed sword. Hytanthas couldn't imagine wielding such a weapon with only one hand while on horseback, but the big Knight handled the sword with practiced ease. With his three surviving men guarding his flanks, he galloped straight at the sand beast. He rose in the stirrups and swung the sword, using all his size and strength to drive the blade in up to its hilt behind the monster's shoulders. His men loosed arrows at its head from only a few feet away. Two pierced its eyes before the beast shuddered and fell like a poleaxed steer. The ground shook from the impact, nearly knocking the approaching Hytanthas off his feet.

Hengriff, dismounted, leaning against the sand beast's ribs. He was slumped forward over the pommel of his sword, which he still gripped in both hands. His eyes were closed, his head bowed, and Hytanthas thought the breath had been driven from his lungs. The elf cleared his throat to speak.

"Shh," Hengriff said. "The heartbeat is fading."

Understanding came, and Hytanthas shuddered. The Knight wasn't recuperating from the mighty blow he'd landed, he was listening to the creature's life slip away. The young elf said nothing, conscious of the three other Dark Knights sitting on horseback around him.

"That's it." Grunting, Hengriff worked his sword free of the monster's carcass. Cleaning the blade on a scrap of leather, he angled a considering look at Hytanthas. "The kill would've been more satisfying had it been at full strength. How did you manage to wound it, elf?"

His disguise in tatters, wrung out by fear and fighting, Hytanthas had no strength left to fence with the Nerakan. "I didn't," he said bluntly. "It arrived like that."

An absent nod, then Hengriff spoke to one of his men. "Goldorf, that lance broke too easily."

"Time was short, my lord. I had to improvise."

"What of Faeterus?"

This question was directed at Hytanthas. The elf told the truth: The mage had disappeared when the sand beast arrived.

"I know you," Hengriff said, eyes narrowing. "I've seen you before. Ah, yes! You were in the Speaker's honor guard, when he had his audience with Sahim-Khan."

Hytanthas had been only one of fifty elves in the honor guard. Impressed by the Knight's memory, but striving not to show it, Hytanthas inclined his head, confirming his identity.

"So, you came here hunting Faeterus? You're triply lucky, elf. Lucky the mage's wards didn't get you, lucky his ugly pet didn't gut you, and lucky we came along to deal with the sand beast."

Hengriff sent his men on to the ruined villa. "I came hunting the mage, too," he said. "He was pursuing his own course, raising the nomads against the elves and the Khan, sending this creature out to kill that she-dragon Kerianseray. I wonder how it ended up back here." He shook his head. "Things have a habit of doing that around Faeterus. Appearing or disappearing without warning."

"Have your men been sent to kill the mage?"

Hengriff didn't answer, but he didn't really need to. Hytanthas doubted the Knights would have much luck. Faeterus didn't seem the sort to linger where danger threatened.

The elf was losing strength, swaying on his feet, exhausted, thirsty, and injured from his battles with manticore and sand beast. It seemed he was always tired or injured or thirsty, these days. Perhaps he'd been that way for years, for all the years of his exile. Stupid not to have planned better, brought food and water. He'd not expected to have to wait so long for Faeterus. Certainly hadn't expected to battle a human-headed manticore and a wounded, enraged sand beast.

Hytanthas realized Hengriff was speaking to him. He had no idea what the human had said. Worse, he'd completely forgotten the Nerakan was here, had forgotten everything but the miasma of fatigue and privation that enveloped him. He forced his slumping shoulders to straighten and gripped the lead pipe more tightly.

"I'm leaving," he announced. "Don't try to stop me."

A wolfish smile appeared on the Knight's face. "Go back to your people, elf, before you drop where you stand and another of Faeterus's creatures has you for dinner."

Before he departed, honor demanded one last thing of Hytanthas. "Lord Hengriff," he said with formal precision. "You saved my life. Thank you."

"That was today. Don't expect a like outcome next time."

Hengriff mounted his horse and cantered away, heading up the hill to the villa.

Hytanthas went in the opposite direction, beginning the long trek back to Khurinost. The world was indeed a crazy place, when a soldier in the Speaker's host was saved from death at the hands of a rogue elven wizard by a Dark Knight of Neraka.

11

Chanting to synchronize their efforts, a gang of elves hauled away on the ropes. A timber frame rose off the ground, wavered a bit, then climbed higher as the warriors continued to pull.

"Easy! Easy there!" Kerian called out. If they pulled too quickly, the frame would topple forward on them.

The early twilight had come to Inath-Wakenti. By torch-light the scene resembled a nightmarish dream. All the soldiers of the Lioness's command were mustered around the hole that had opened up when they pushed the monolith over on the sand beast. Some were on horseback, others on foot, but every one was armed and ready. The reason for their increased wariness could be found in their dwindling numbers.

Two nights had passed since the vanishing of the sand beast. The Lioness's original vow to leave the valley quickly was set aside after this event. She decided they would remain an extra day to search for the elusive monster. They hadn't found it. Instead, several of her warriors had gone missing. All were sentries, riding guard duty alone on the perimeter of the camp. Then, just past noon on this day, five more elves had vanished. The five were on foot, foraging for roots and nuts, no more than twenty yards from the site of the overturned monolith. When they didn't return, a search was conducted.

It turned up no signs of struggle, no torn ground, no dropped possessions. The elves were simply gone, together with everything they carried.

As Favaronas was the nearest thing to an expert on the valley, Kerian asked him what he thought was happening.

"I don't know, General," he said, shivering with the fear that had become his constant companion.

Glanthon said, "You've mentioned 'strange forces' at work in the valley. What do you mean?"

"Just that. Strange, unnatural things happen here. I myself have—" Favaronas broke off, coloring in embarrassment. Kerian had no time for niceties of feeling. She insisted he hold nothing back, and he admitted having seen apparitions himself, just the night before. He described them as white shapes, vaguely elven in form, drifting through the stone ruins.

"Patches of mist!" Glanthon scoffed.

"No, they moved against the wind," the archivist insisted.

The Lioness cut the air with an imperative hand. "We're not here to collect ghost stories, Favaronas! I want to know who's taking my people!"

"I don't know! Perhaps"—he gestured vaguely at the fallen monolith—"the same force that carried off the sand beast?"

After that discussion, with no other conjecture to test, Kerian decided to investigate the hole beneath the stone spire. Rocks dropped into it revealed the bottom to be at least twenty feet down. Their hollow-sounding impacts hinted at a chamber of some size.

As the sun lowered itself behind the western peaks, trees were felled, trimmed, and lashed into a frame to support ropes lowered into the hole. Kerian intended to descend herself, but her officers wouldn't hear of it. None doubted she was prepared to do anything she might ask of her warriors, but Glanthon reminded her she did not have the luxury of taking such risks. As General of the Speaker's Army, her life was too valuable to risk unnecessarily.

It finally was agreed that Glanthon would enter the hole. To Favaronas's dismay, he was tapped to accompany Glanthon.

"Me? Why me?" the archivist said, his face pale even in the firelight.

Kerian said, "You're the scholar. There may be things down there you can recognize."

Her phrasing was unfortunate. Favaronas blanched even whiter at the notion of "things down there." So, Kerian unbuckled her own sword and fastened the scabbard around his waist. "If you see any ghosts, give them steel. If they're flesh and blood, they'll feel it." She smiled. "And if they're not flesh and blood, they can't hurt you."

He did not look reassured.

A pair of stout ropes was tied to the handles of a small round shield that would serve as a platform. Glanthon and Favaronas climbed on, holding tight to the ropes. With the whole command looking on, they were lowered into the hole. The opening wasn't much wider than the shield on which they stood.

As their feet sank into the black aperture, Favaronas said, "Tell me again why we're doing this?"

"To find clues to our comrades' disappearance," said Glanthon stoutly. "And to carry out the Speaker's command to learn all we can about this valley. Aren't you curious?"

"Not any more."

Their heads disappeared below the surface. They entered a square shaft lined with stone. The air cooled rapidly. Only eight feet below the surface, their breath streamed out as white vapor.

"All right?" the Lioness called, sounding very far away.

"We could use a light!" Favaronas said, his voice rising.

Glanthon assured him torches would be dropped down the hole after they reached bottom.

"Seems backward to me."

"No sense announcing our coming."

"Announcing? Announcing to whom?" Favaronas's voice was a squeak now.

Their shield footrest, which had been lightly scraping the sides of the shaft, entered open air. They swung back and forth a few times, then bumped into a solid floor.

"Step back," Glanthon said. Cupping a hand to his mouth, he shouted, "Torch!"

A flaming brand crackled down the shaft. Where it caromed off the walls, showers of sparks fell on them. Favaronas yelped and leaped backward, but Glanthon caught the falling torch deftly in one hand. A second followed it. Favaronas didn't attempt to copy the warrior's action; the second torch hit the ground and went out.

The floor was ankle-deep in thick white mist. It was cold and damp, but caused them no apparent harm. Glanthon retrieved the second torch, lit it from his own, and handed it to the archivist.

"Merciful ancestors," Favaronas breathed, holding the brand high. "What is this place?"

Ahead and behind them stretched a tunnel, arrowing straight northwest and southeast. The ceiling had a slight arch to it and was high enough for both elves to stand erect. Favaronas's awed comment had been inspired by the walls of the passage.

The tunnel was covered, floor to ceiling, with the most beautiful painting either elf had ever seen. It depicted a landscape in such exquisite detail and realistic color they almost expected the trees to sway in the breeze, could almost smell the scent of the flowers, and hear the splash of the silvery river winding through the scene. The ceiling was a serene blue, with wispy white clouds. Who had painted this lovely vista? And why bury it under the ground?

Glanthon reached out to touch the wall, but Favaronas caught his arm.

"Don't," he whispered. "Don't touch anything!" Glanthon nodded in solemn agreement.

They walked slowly down the tunnel, the movement of their feet stirring the viscous fog. The hem of Favaronas's robe grew dark with damp. Dew glistened on Glanthon's boots.

As they marveled at the unfolding work of art, Glanthon noted an oddity. There were no living creatures depicted. The scenery was beautiful and varied, but contained no people, nor any animals.

"Like the valley above," Favaronas said. He frowned, staring at the right-hand wall. "It seems familiar somehow."

Not to Glanthon. Born and raised in Qualinesti, he knew its towns, forests, and farmlands well. This painted landscape resembled no place he'd ever seen.

"It looks older than Qualinesti somehow, and more . . ." Glanthon searched for the right word. "More formal. Like a lord's garden."

Favaronas stopped abruptly. "Are there any Silvanesti in our company?"

"Yes. Why?"

He pointed to the silver-blue river that serpentined through the landscape on the right-hand wall. "They should see this. I think that's the Thon-Thalas."

"Are you certain?"

"Not certain, no; I've never been to Silvanesti. But it matches descriptions I've read."

"Could this place have been made by ancient Silvanesti?"

Favaronas wasn't sure. The ruins above were without any identifying marks, yet they had none of the air of refinement associated with Silvanesti sites. The stonework was monumental but rather crude, much more reminiscent of human handiwork than elven. Yet if he was right, then whoever had painted this scene had at least visited the Silvanesti heartland.

Glanthon suddenly grabbed his companion's arm in a painful grip. Startled, the archivist yelped loudly. "What? Is there danger? Where?" He tried to draw the Lioness's sword with one hand.

The warrior's grip tightened further. "Quiet!" he hissed. "Look!"

Far down the tunnel, in the darkness beyond the reach of the torchlight, something stirred. Vaguely upright, it was coming toward them.

Glanthon's sword was already in his hand. Favaronas managed to free his borrowed blade from its scabbard, but Glanthon whispered, "Do nothing unless I say so."

Nodding vigorously, Favaronas stepped closer to the warrior.

The approaching figure was small, under five feet in height, and of indistinct shape. It resembled a person draped in diaphanous gray. Carrying no light, it came on assuredly, at a steady pace. A very faint glow, more attenuated than fox-fire, radiated from the figure and the pale aura was reflected by the mist, which remained undisturbed by its passage.

Sweat trickled down Favaronas's neck. He was shaking so hard he couldn't hold the sword steady. Never again, he vowed silently; never again would he leave his archive. Not even for the Speaker of the Sun and Stars would he abandon his beloved manuscripts again—if he lived to get back to them!

The apparition seemed heedless of the two elves. As it passed between them, head lowered, it brushed Glanthon's leg. He felt nothing. There was no sign of feet or legs; the apparition merged with the fog lining the tunnel.

A sound like a sigh rasped down the stone-lined passage. Alarmed, Glanthon thrust his torch at the specter. The flaming pine knot passed through it without resistance, but the ghost appeared to lift its head and turn. It looked back at the elves.

Both cried out in shock. Favaronas dropped his torch, and it went out. With that, the ghost disappeared.

"Extraordinary!" Favaronas exclaimed, as Glanthon relit his torch. "A cat! Or an ocelot perhaps, or—"

"What are you babbling about?"

"That thing! A long neck, pricked ears, white whiskers—yet feminine somehow! Unbelievable!"

Glanthon stared at the archivist with mouth agape for a few seconds then said flatly, "You're hallucinating. It looked nothing like that."

The warrior had seen a slight figure in loose robes, cowl hanging down its back. The head was wide and round like a human's, without the delicate bone structure of an elf. He had an impression of pale hair, a blank, unfinished face, and empty black eye sockets.

Despite his terror, Favaronas's scholarly instincts were engaged, and he seemed disposed to stand in the cold, dim tunnel, comparing and discussing their very different impressions of the ghost. Glanthon put a stop to this by taking his arm and hauling him forward.

"Wait! We're going on?" said Favaronas, wide-eyed.

"Not far. Fifty more steps, then we'll go back and report what we've seen."

Favaronas complained at the arbitrariness of his decision. "Why fifty? Why not twenty? Why not just turn around now? It isn't logical. What's the point?"

Glanthon ignored the mumbled commentary, deciding it was only Favaronas's method of coping with his fear. Although he kept muttering, the archivist also kept moving forward, sword held up, albeit in a very shaky hand.

They'd gone no more than thirty paces before the tunnel brought them to a chamber. About three times as wide as the tunnel and twice as high, its walls were barren of the painted reliefs. Along one side were a multitude of stone cylinders, each about a yard long and four or five inches thick, stacked on their sides like cordwood. The opposite wall was covered with peeling white plaster.

The strange cylinders drew Favaronas like a magnet. He lifted one. It was heavy, made of a soft, slippery stone like talc or gypsum. A hole was bored through its long axis.

SANCTUARY

The object looked for all the world like—

"A scroll?" asked Glanthon, holding his torch close.

"No one ever made books of stone," countered the archivist. Still, the resemblance was uncanny.

At his suggestion, they decided to take some of the cylinders back with them. Favaronas discarded his torch and laid two scrolls in the crook of each arm. Glanthon also took four, but bore all in one strong arm so he could keep his torch.

The elves were walking back down the long tunnel to the entrance when they heard alarm trumpets on the surface. Struggling under the burden they carried, warrior and scholar hastened to the waiting rope lift. The warriors above shouted for them to hurry. They stepped onto the shield platform and were hoisted back up. More horns sounded as they neared the surface.

Glanthon dumped his four cylinders on the ground as soon as he cleared the opening. "Where's the trouble?"

"We saw lights among the ruins, over there!" A Wilder elf pointed northeast. "The Lioness has gone to investigate."

She had left behind only enough elves to watch the hole and pull the two explorers out. The rest of her shrinking command had galloped off with her. Once Favaronas was safely out of the hole, Glanthon left a warrior behind with him and ordered the rest to horse.

Sitting on the ground, Favaronas watched them gallop away. The single elf with him also stared after his departing comrades, the look on his face eloquent of his desire.

"Go with them," Favaronas said, waving a hand. "I'll be fine."

The warrior shook his head. "You'd be alone."

The archivist sighed. "The trouble, whatever it is, is out there, not here."

With only a little more prompting, the elf rode away.

By the light of the torches that ringed the hole, Favaronas studied one of the cylinders. Glyphs were incised into the soft stone. In the uncertain light, his sensitive fingertips gave him a better idea of their shape than his eyes could. The writing was Elvish, or at least the characters were Elvish, the old writing used in Silvanost on monuments, palaces, temples, and public buildings. He sounded out the syllables his fingers detected.

"*Ba-Laf-Om-Thas, Hoc-Sem-Ath.*"

It made no sense. Perhaps this was some ancient dialect. But it seemed to confirm the notion that Silvanesti elves had inhabited this valley long ago. What of the apparition in the tunnel below? What was it, and why had it appeared to him as a catlike, female creature, and to Glanthon as a faceless human?

Less than a mile away, the Lioness galloped through the tall monoliths and cedar trees. Ahead was her quarry—a pair of glimmering green lights, flying at saddle height above the ground. Some of her warriors were strung out behind her, trying to keep up. Others had split off in smaller bands to chase different lights.

She was convinced these lights were flesh and blood riders, carrying hooded lanterns to lure the elves into an ambush. That must have been what happened to her missing warriors. A local tribe of humans was playing a deadly game, and she intended to put a stop to it tonight.

The twin green lights slowed. She reined back, not wanting to rush into a prepared trap, and waited for the soldiers trailing her. Once they caught up, she directed them to ride out wide on either side, then sent her horse ambling forward.

The green glimmers retreated, keeping the distance between themselves and her always the same. As she emerged from a copse of juniper trees, she glimpsed dark shapes close to the two lights.

Triumph sang through the Lioness. She was right! There were people out there!

She secured the reins to the pommel of her saddle and braced her bow. In seconds, she'd sent an arrow speeding toward the right-hand light. The missile flew true. The light shook violently, then was still. The left-hand light moved off swiftly, leaving its comrade behind. Crowing with satisfaction, she loosed her reins and cantered forward.

Her arrow was embedded in the trunk of a thin tree and one of the lights was impaled on the shaft. The fist-sized green glow was fading fast. By the time she'd freed the arrow and brought it close enough to study, the light was gone. Her gloved hands felt nothing foreign on the shaft.

Shouts from flanking riders told her the other light had been found. She rode toward them. A curving expanse of gray wall loomed. A band of mounted elves waited beside it. Kerian spotted Glanthon in the group.

She hailed him. "How was your crawl underground?" she asked.

"Like a sorcerer's nightmare, General, but right now, we seem to have an intruder trapped."

He gestured at the wall behind them. Massively thick, its top was at eye level to the mounted elves. No structures showed beyond it.

Kerian shook her feet free of the stirrups. Crouching on her saddle, she sprang atop the wall. Glanthon and eight other elves joined her on the broad stone barrier.

The wall was a perfect circle, enclosing a paved area forty yards across. In the center of the pavement was a raised platform ten yards across and four feet high. Great wedges of gray stone had been fitted together to make the round platform. Drifting over it, like leaves wafting on an autumn breeze, were four glittering lights: one each of green, red, yellow, and blue.

Kerian dropped to the pavement inside the wall.

"Our quarry has slipped away and left these will-o'-the-wisps to keep us busy," she said. "I intend to take one back to study."

"Wait! We don't know what they are!" Glanthon warned, gathering himself to leap down and follow her.

She told him to stay where he was, and kept going.

When she neared the center of the platform, the lights abandoned their aimless paths and began to circle her. Faster and faster, they whirled in ever-tightening circles. Remembering how the sand beast had disappeared when the lights touched it, Kerian didn't wait for the inevitable. She threw herself flat on her stomach. The lights crashed together above her and vanished in a silent burst of greenish light.

By the time Glanthon and the others arrived, she was sitting up. "Well, that's one mystery solved," she said, accepting Glanthon's hand to help her stand.

The Lioness thought it likely the lights were responsible for the mysterious disappearances among her warriors. Where the elves had been taken, and why, remained unknown, however, and she couldn't risk searching any further.

"We're getting out of this valley. Now."

* * * * *

The ride to Khuri-Khan would become legend. After Prince Shobbat's messenger departed, Adala's people hurriedly broke camp and began the journey south to the city of the Great Khan. Clouds, rarely seen over the high desert, blew in from the sea, piling up like brilliant white dunes in the sky. The heat of the wasteland caused the clouds to writhe and twist, forming fantastic patterns of light and shadow on the ground below. Shade was an experience few nomads ever had while crossing the burning sands. They rode with faces turned skyward, watching the spectacle with a mixture of fascination, awe, and not a little fear.

Adala swayed across the wind-driven wastes on the back of stolid, faithful Little Thorn, dozing when the glare of the sun became too intense. The frowning clouds were to her a portent of things to come. She saw in them the boiling anger and pride of the *laddad*, rising from their squatters' camp to try to frighten the children of the desert and turn them away from their holy purpose. Like the masses of clouds, the bluster of the *laddad* was impressive to behold but without substance.

Two days away from the Valley of the Blue Sands, just after sunrise, scouts brought word that a large mounted force was approaching from the west. Alarmed, the desert warriors unslung their bows and shields, forming themselves to receive an attack. Adala's warmasters and clan chiefs gathered around her, drawn swords resting on their shoulders.

Wapah, seated behind Bilath, speculated that the *laddad* had heard of the Weya-Lu approach and come out from Khuri-Khan to meet them, away from their vulnerable camp.

"Ten thousand pardons, O Weyadan!" said one of the scouts. "Those coming toward us are not *laddad*, but men."

Bilath shifted in his saddle. "Soldiers of Sahim-Khan?"

"They bear the banner of a scorpion on a field of yellow, with three notches in the wind's edge."

"The standard of the Mikku," Wapah supplied. He was widely traveled and knew the standard of every tribe and clan. The Mikku were far from their usual range, but they were nomads, too, brothers of the Weya-Lu, the Khur, the Tondoon, and the rest.

Zaralan, chief of the Black Horse Clan, voiced the prevailing opinion when he said, "They're invading our territory."

"We'll stand them off!" vowed Bindas, young and hot-tempered.

"No. We are not here to shed the blood of our own," said Adala. She addressed the scouts. "How far away are they?"

"Four miles when we first saw them. Less by now, Maita."

She lifted a mostly empty waterskin and wrung a warm trickle into her mouth. Their time at the Valley of the Blue Sands had left the Weya-Lu short of water, Adala most of all.

"I will meet them," she said.

The chiefs protested vigorously. If the Mikku had come to fight, the Weyadan could be captured or killed before the rest of her host could defend her. She shrugged off all their arguments.

"Brothers or enemies, the Mikku will not raise a hand against me."

Out of respect they did not contradict her. Zaralan suggested she take an escort, for protection. Even a small escort would be better than none.

Adala smiled a little. "I choose Wapah."

The garrulous philosopher, who even then was explaining in hushed tones the habits of dress and dining of the Mikku tribe to the clan chiefs beside him, heard his name and broke off his monologue.

"Weyadan? You want me?"

"Yes, cousin. Ride with me to meet the Mikku."

This was not what Zaralan had in mind. He said as much, assuring Wapah he meant no disrespect.

"No need to abase yourself," said Wapah as he guided his horse through the ranks of clan chiefs and warmasters. "I pledge my life to protect the Weyadan's."

He positioned his horse alongside Little Thorn. Adala noted the tears in his hat brim, made by *laddad* arrows, and frowned. Poor Wapah, unmarried and without mother or sisters, had no one to mend his clothes.

"Remind me to sew those up for you," she said, flicking a hand at his hat brim.

By her order, the nomad host was to remain hidden on the northern side of a high dune, so their great numbers would not startle the oncoming Mikku. Bowing to the wisdom of her logic, the warmasters rode back to their warriors. The clan chiefs remained.

"I don't like this," Bindas said. "The Mikku know the law of the desert. They should not enter our land unbidden."

"Honored Chief, be of strong heart. Whatever their purpose, the Mikku are just like us. The desert lives in their souls, and Those on High speak to their hearts. Believe in my maita. It leads me to a more distant place than this."

So saying, Adala tapped Little Thorn's flank with a cane switch. Ears flapping, the donkey shuffled over the crest of the dune with Wapah riding close behind.

Bindas turned to Bilath, Zaralan, and the other chiefs who had known Adala longer. "Does this woman think she holds fate in her hands?" he said.

"Permit me to say, Chief Bindas, you have it backward. It is not Adala Weyadan who holds fate, but Fate which holds Adala."

It was eloquence worthy of Wapah, but the words came from Bilath, brother of Adala's slain husband.

Adala and Wapah soon saw lines of darkly dressed Mikku riding across the sun-baked plain. Unlike the northern nomads, who rode in loose, time-tested formations, the Mikku were deployed cavalry-fashion in four exact lines, each a double horse-length apart. They wore a great deal of metal armor, signs of the favor shown them by the Khan. Wapah watched their slow, steady progress through the shimmering morning haze, early sunlight flashing off their brass and iron equipment. He commented on how heavy and hot their armor must be.

"When we reach the city, you may wish you were so burdened," Adala answered. She knew the *laddad* and Sahim-Khan's soldiers wore even more armor as a matter of course.

Between the lonely pair and the several hundred horsemen was a long, flat expanse swept by hot wind from the south. Adala tightened Little Thorn's reins, halting him on the lip of the sandy ridge above the plain. Wapah drew up beside her.

"Let's wait here."

Folding his hands across the pommel of his saddle, Wapah nodded, his pale eyes flicking skyward briefly.

"It is a good day," he said.

Even this early, the heat was devastating. Both of them had pulled the loosely woven dust veils over their faces, to protect their eyes from the parched south wind. The strange clouds towered above the land, rising so high their undersides were gray from lack of sunlight, while their tops were tinted orange by the dawn. Yet Wapah wasn't referring to the weather. He spoke of the feel of the day and his joy in their holy purpose. Adala's maita was running high. The broader world soon would feel its power.

They had been seen. The Mikku halted, studied the two mounted figures poised above them on the ridge, then came on. Four lines of horsemen became two as the Mikku spread themselves wide. Fifty yards away they halted.

"So many swords to take one man, one horse, one woman, and a donkey," Adala said. "What are they afraid of?"

The philosopher at her side said, "We all fear something. Those who wield swords are often the most frightened of all."

Nine riders from the center of the Mikku formation continued forward, while the remainder waited. The nine found their imposing display bedeviled by the loose sand on the face of the ridge. Horses sank up to their hocks, drawing their shod feet out with considerable effort. Wapah smiled, the expression hidden by the dust veil covering his face, as the full import of Adala's logic became clear to him. Stopping here had given them the moral advantage of meeting the Mikku on higher ground, but she had foreseen a tactical purpose, too. The Mikku lost momentum and dignity as they labored up the shifting slope.

Twenty yards away, the nine riders halted. In the center was a nomad with the tallest, brightest helmet the Weya-Lu had ever seen. Golden horns sprouted from the polished steel brow, curving up and back like a desert antelope's. From their tips fluttered squares of shiny gold silk. The sides and rear of the helmet were protected by heavy curtains of mail.

"I am Shaccan, warmaster of the Mikku," said the warrior in the horned helmet. "Who are you?"

SANCTUARY

Before speaking, Wapah glanced at his leader. Adala had shifted her dust veil, exposing her fiery eyes to the Mikku. She nodded slightly at Wapah.

"Greetings, brothers of the desert! Peace to you, and all your kin!" he called, then introduced himself and Adala.

"Are you alone, Weya-Lu?" Shaccan asked.

"Those who believe are never alone," Adala replied. "Is this not so?"

The warmaster plainly did not like having his question answered with a question. Gruffly, he said, "We were told the Weya-Lu had left their range. Is that so?"

"We went to the Valley of the Blue Sands, but we have returned. Why are you here?"

"With the Weya-Lu gone, we ride for Kortal, to hire as caravan escorts."

"You cannot."

Wapah flinched at the impoliteness of Adala's abrupt command. Shaccan's thick eyebrows rose.

"By what right do you stop us, woman?"

Adala lifted her eyes to the sky. "I claim the right of divine maita. Those on High have chosen me to lead all the people of the desert to Khuri-Khan, to cleanse our land of foreign corruption. You may join us."

After a moment of stunned silence, Shaccan put back his head and laughed. He laughed so long and hard, tears streaked his cheeks.

"You're either mad or the greatest woman in Khur," he said, dabbing at his eyes. "I like you! Are you married?"

For the first time in many years, Adala was nonplussed. As she regained her composure and admitted being a widow, six of Shaccan's men surrounded her and Wapah, and the other two rode off to confirm the presence of the rest of the Weya-Lu tribe.

Shaccan grinned. "I thought this was going to be a dull journey. When I heard the Weya-Lu had gone, I thought it must be because of plague or war. Now you speak of gods and corruption and maita. You've been out in the sun too long. Stand aside. It would be bad luck for me to harm one so insane."

Adala didn't move. "We're bound for Khuri-Khan. Join us, or share in the infamy of betraying your nation."

His affable manner evaporated. "You're in our hands now. Don't make trouble, or there will be bloodshed. The whole of the Mikku are at my back."

"You would take up arms against your sisters and brothers of the desert?"

"Anyone who threatens the Mikku is no brother—or sister—of mine."

A peal of thunder, startled the horses. Wapah looked up. The clouds had become heavy and dark. Lightning flickered among them. He was past fifty, and had seen rain only once before in his life, during a visit to Delphon twenty-two years ago.

Adala paid no heed to the gathering storm. "I am chosen by Those on High to do what must be done, Shaccan of the Mikku. I cannot refuse, nor can you oppose me without risking the wrath of the gods. This is my maita."

"You're mad as a mouse."

Shaccan ordered his warriors to take Adala in hand. Hardly had the words left his lips than a tremendously loud burst of thunder broke over them. Horses shied and bucked, and the men struggled to keep their animals calm. Only Little Thorn, his eyes protected from sand and sun by an embroidered cowl, stood placidly.

Rain began to fall, the fat droplets sending up tiny puffs of dust when they hit the ground. The Mikku, young men all, had never seen rain before. They began muttering among themselves. When he heard them use the word "maita," Shaccan angrily drew his sword.

"Idiots! Does a madwoman make the rain? Seize her! Immediately!"

Wind swept over them, driving warm rain into their faces. Wapah turned his horse's head away from the gusts.

A Mikku, thinking he was trying to flee, thrust his sword at Wapah. It would have pierced his side, had not Adala intervened. She caught the blade in her hand and shoved. Angry at being thwarted, the Mikku jerked his sword back, laying open Adala's palm. She hissed in pain.

Outraged, Wapah yelled. He pulled out a scarf and tied it tightly around her injured hand.

The rain fell even more heavily. Lightning flashed and thunder boomed directly overhead, blinding flash and ear-splitting noise coming almost simultaneously. This was too much for the Mikku's horses. The animals reared and fled, taking their riders back down the slope to the main body of warriors. Only Shaccan remained, his horned helmet gleaming dully in the gray light filtering through the thick clouds. He glared at the pair before him.

"Widow or not, your life is over!" he cried. "Here is your maita!"

He raised his blade high, to cleave the impassive Adala from head to waist. No sooner had the sword reached its apex than another bolt of lightning sliced down from the sky. It struck the Mikku's sword, searing down the steel blade and the warmaster's arm.

The blast knocked everyone down. Adala hit the sand and rolled to avoid being crushed by her falling donkey. When her head cleared, she crawled up the slope to Wapah. He was dazed but uninjured.

Where Shaccan had been was now a smoking pit in the sand. Adala crawled to its edge and looked down. What she found was ghastly. Horse and man were dead, horribly burned. Most of Shaccan's sword had melted and run down his arm like candle wax. His flesh, inside his armor, was charred black. His helmet was gone, for which Adala was profoundly sorry as it left bare the unbelievable ruin that had been his face.

She looked away from the grotesque visage and noticed the sand around Shaccan had changed. No longer filled with loose pale grains, the crater in which he lay resembled a bowl of crude glass, blue-green in color. Adala immediately was reminded of the hidden valley. Did its soil's blue-green tint come from the same source, the fire from heaven?

Raindrops sizzled and hissed into steam when they hit the blasted corpse and glassy crater. The other Mikku gathered slowly, dismounting and staring down into the crater. So great was the terror on their faces as they regarded Adala, Wapah was certain they would slay her forthwith. Disregarding the deeply ingrained stricture against touching the Weyadan, he crawled frantically to her and flung his body over hers.

"Away with all of you, lest Those on High strike you down as well!" he shouted at the sword-wielding Mikku.

Wapah had misread the warriors. They had no intention of lifting their weapons against Adala. Instead, all fell on their knees, calling to her to forgive them, pledging to serve her, affirming their belief in the power of Those on High.

Adala tried to rise. As she shifted beneath him, Wapah flushed in embarrassment and moved swiftly off. She sat up, straightening her black robes.

On her feet again, she looked around at the kneeling Mikku. "Will you believe in my maita?" she asked them. "Will you follow where I lead and fight only for the purity of Khur?"

To a man, they vowed they would.

Wapah went to round up his mount and Adala's donkey. The rain was easing, and as Wapah returned, it ceased altogether. He brought with him more than their mounts. Shaccan's helmet was cradled in his arm. The tall golden-horned helm had been flung many yards away. It appeared completely untouched by the lightning that had so utterly destroyed its owner.

While Wapah was marveling over this, and admiring the shining craftsmanship of the helmet, the scouts Shaccan had dispatched over the ridge came galloping back. They were pursued by Weya-Lu riders. Adala, leading Little Thorn, went to intercede. Mikku and Weya-Lu drew apart as the Weyadan stood between them.

"Judgment has been rendered upon Shaccan," she declared. "The Mikku have chosen to join us."

The warriors who already had pledged themselves to Adala's cause related the momentous events to their brethren. The scouts could hardly credit the tale, but the steaming crater and their dead warmaster brooked no argument.

The Weya-Lu raised a cheer, and the Mikku joined in. Adala acknowledged their support with a nod, then asked Wapah for his arm. He aided her in climbing back onto Little Thorn. Her face and hands were pink with flash burn, while her eyebrows and eyelashes were completely gone. Concerned, he asked if she was well.

The clouds had broken, allowing shafts of morning sunlight to slice through. The southern plain was dappled with these columns of golden light. Steam rose from the drying sand. Adala stared out at the view and said only, "Your hat is in sad shape, cousin. Take it off and I'll sew the tears quickly, before the sun returns."

And she did. A healer salved and bandaged her injured hand, then Adala worked steadily on the torn hat as she and Wapah rode down the ridge. The Weya-Lu streamed after them. The Mikku watched in awe until they fell in at the rear of the formation. Word of Shaccan's demise spread, and more and more of the Mikku joined the procession. The ranks of Adala's band had swelled from five hundred to more than five thousand.

12

When the sun rose on Khuri-Khan, the city gates opened as the Khan had promised. However, the soldiers on the western portal, having lifted the iron portcullises and swung the great wooden doors inward, gaped in consternation at what they faced on the other side.

The road, dusty and sand-scoured, sloped away from Malys's Anvil to the outer ring of elf tents. Many of these had been torn down during the recent rioting, but beyond them was the vast elven encampment. Elves stirred like hornets around a disturbed nest. Gathered on the road facing Khuri-Khan were ten thousand elf lancers and archers in well-used armor.

The Khurish soldiers had fought a bloody skirmish with wild fanatics the evening before, and now they stared across forty yards of desert at ranks of elven cavalry, poised to strike.

For a long time neither side moved. The sun lifted itself above the Khurman Sea. Lofty bales of clouds, blown in from the sea, maneuvered silently overhead, covering the ground with strange, ever-moving shadows. Word of the massed elven cavalry reached the Khuri yl Nor, and Sahim-Khan dispatched General Hakkam to find out the *laddad*'s intentions. Lord Morillon's warning about the elves storming the city was on everyone's mind, and no one's lips.

SANCTUARY

Hakkam, who as a boy had been shield-bearer to Sahim's father, was a burly, impatient man. His armor was too tight, and it chafed him unmercifully at the neck and waist. He was constantly being given impossible or contradictory tasks by Sahim-Khan, then receiving his master's ire when things did not turn out as he desired. Because of this, Hakkam was in a perpetually bad mood.

Facing the city wall with the morning sun in their eyes, the elves were hardly in better temper. Taranath commanded the ten thousand riders, sorted into squadrons of fifty, as in the old Silvanesti army. Under their battered helmets and sun-bleached mantles they were lean, spare, and ready to ride at any enemy they were commanded to destroy.

Word flashed back to the Speaker that the gates had opened. Throwing on an old robe of white silk (with most of the gold embroidery torn out, for it was too valuable to leave as mere decoration), Gilthas hurried to the eastern edge of Khurinost with Planchet at his heels.

"No word from Lord Morillon or Captain Ambrodel?" Gilthas asked.

Planchet shook his head. "No, sire. They may not have been able to reach us while the gates were closed."

The unexplained disappearance of one of the Speaker's councilors had only increased the tensions in the elven camp. Gilthas knew it would take very little for a confrontation to explode. The sight of numerous Khurish guards on the city gate was just the spark this volatile situation did not need.

They reached the closely packed ranks of riders, and Planchet bawled, "Make way for the Speaker! Make way!"

The riders chivvied their mounts to one side or the other to allow the Speaker to walk between them. Hair in disarray, sweat beading under his hollow eyes, the Speaker of the Sun and Stars made straight for the front line. When the last line of riders broke ranks for him, he found himself standing on the rubble-stone road before the city wall. Khurish pot helmets were thick on the battlements. As Gilthas looked on, their numbers increased.

"Has anyone come out, or spoken to you?" he asked the nearest rider.

"No one, Great Speaker."

Worried by his councilor's absence, Gilthas was nevertheless pleased to see the gate open. Perhaps Morillon had succeeded. Perhaps he would be coming out at any moment, unless the Khan had opened the portal for his own, possibly nefarious, reasons.

"What do you make of this?"

Planchet studied the city wall left and right before answering. "They look as surprised to see us as we are to see them."

Gilthas agreed. If Sahim-Khan meant to attack, his troops would have rushed out immediately, not gathered on the walls and gawked for half an hour.

"Find me a herald," he said. "Let's see if we can't find out what's happening, without bloodshed."

Planchet offered to go himself, and Gilthas agreed. Planchet's face was known to the Khurs and he carried the weight of the Speaker's favor. He was wearing a native geb, perfect attire for the task. No sense appearing as a warrior when a diplomat was needed.

A scrap of cloth tied to a lance made a serviceable white banner. Once Planchet was mounted, Gilthas took hold of his horse's halter.

"Find out their intentions, and stress that ours are peaceful," he said. "Make certain our people still have access to the city's wells." Already the grip of thirst was on the tent city. "Don't mention Morillon—not just yet."

Planchet nodded and started up the sloping road at a slow trot. Wind hissed over the northern dunes. As he reached the place where the road leveled out, he halted his horse. The clouds parted and a beam of sunlight fell on him. Gilthas was cheered. It was a good omen.

SANCTUARY

The mounted elf waited, exposed and alone, until the Khurs sent out riders of their own. After five long minutes, a quintet of armored soldiers came out the gate. A scarlet and gold pennant flew from one rider's stirrup-post.

The Khurs approached slowly, as though wary of treachery. At one point Planchet waved a biting fly away from his face, and the Khurs froze. He realized they were very frightened.

In the center of the quintet, flanked by imposing cavalrymen, rode a squat human with a thick neck and a beet-red face. As the Khurs drew nearer, Planchet recognized him.

"Hail, General Hakkam!" he called. "Peace be with you!"

"And with you, Planchet of Qualinost," rumbled the choleric general. "What in Kargath's name goes on here?"

"I was about to ask you the same question. The city gates have been closed to us since yesterday afternoon. Our only supply of water is what we carry from Khuri-Khan's wells. We were beginning to get thirsty."

"Is that why you called out your army?"

Why else? "Gangs have been assaulting us for the past two days, General. Tents have been burned and our people beaten, some quite badly. We didn't know what might come forth next from the city."

"The Sons of the Crimson Vulture have caused much trouble, for you and for the mighty Sahim-Khan. Consequently, many of them have been sent to meet their ancestors."

"Then the city is open to us?"

"I have no orders otherwise."

A fresh gust, smelling of the sea, swept over the parley. Planchet's truce banner snapped in the wind. Twisting in the saddle, he raised the banner high, and waved it at the horde of elven warriors who watched in silent concern. When Planchet turned back, Hakkam and his escort had their hands on their sword hilts.

"I was merely alerting our soldiers that all was well," Planchet said mildly.

"Who's that coming?"

Two elven riders emerged from the line of heavy cavalry and cantered to where Planchet and Hakkam waited. It didn't take long to recognize the Speaker and a single escorting warrior, General Taranath. When they arrived, Planchet explained the situation.

"Thank you, General," the Speaker said to Hakkam. He extended a lean hand. "Your duty has been well served."

With little enthusiasm the general shook the Speaker's hand. Gilthas assured him he would withdraw his warriors, then added, "One other matter. My councilor, Lord Morillon, did not return last night. Is he inside the city?"

"He had an audience with Sahim-Khan, then left the palace."

"Is he well?"

Hakkam frowned. "How would I know? He left the palace. That's all I know."

With a curt nod, Hakkam turned his horse around. Planchet was aghast at the human's rudeness, turning his back on a reigning Speaker without so much as a by-your-leave!

The shaft of sunlight, so long shining on Planchet and Gilthas, at last faded. Gilthas looked up at the roiling clouds. He frowned. A slender object, dark against the sky, seemed to hang in the air over the city. No, not hang. It was moving, falling.

"Arrow!" Planchet shouted.

He threw himself in front of the Speaker, but the missile was plummeting from such a height its path was almost straight down. The broadhead cut Gilthas's jaw and struck him in the hollow of the neck, on the right side.

Pandemonium erupted. Gilthas was saved from hitting the ground by Taranath, who caught him by the shoulders and bore him up. Hakkam's guards drew swords, whirling their horses in tight circles to see who had loosed the arrow.

A shout went up from the front rank of elven warriors. They had seen the arrow's fall and its awful termination. The shout was followed by a hedge of swords sprouting along the line. In ragged order, for the rear ranks did not yet know what had happened, the elves charged up the hill to their monarch's defense.

The thunder of the oncoming elves sent Hakkam's escort spurring for the city. The thick-necked general roared, "Come back, you wretches! Stand your ground!" One halted. The rest made straight for the city gate, now swinging shut.

"What treachery is this?" Planchet cried, kicking his feet free of the stirrups and leaping from his horse. The Speaker had collapsed over his horse's neck.

"It is not by my order!" Hakkam retorted, also dismounting.

He and Planchet took the Speaker from his horse and lowered him gently to the road. The arrow was still embedded in Gilthas's neck.

"That did not come from my men," said Hakkam. "It's not a Khurish war arrow."

"What is it, then?" Planchet demanded.

"A hunting arrow. My men aren't issued such."

It was fortunate for Gilthas the missile wasn't a war arrow. Stoutly shafted, with a square or triangular iron head and leather fletching, a war arrow would have driven deep into the elf's slender body. The hunting missile, lightly made, with a flat broadhead and white pigeon-feather fletching, had struck Gilthas's collar bone and stopped. The wound was nasty, but with prompt care it would not be fatal.

A wave of shouting elf warriors galloped by the figures kneeling on the road. A handful halted, but most kept going, charging the city gate.

Their angry shouts reached the weakened Gilthas. From somewhere deep within himself, he tapped an unknown source of strength. Face white, he struggled to rise. Planchet, holding him down, begged him to be still.

"Stop it," Gilthas said through clenched teeth.

Thinking he was hurting the Speaker, Planchet felt tears come to his eyes. He whispered, "I'm sorry, sire, but you must be still. Please don't move."

"No, Planchet. Stop the warriors! Don't let them fight! I command it!"

Taranath heard the Speaker's order. He snatched a trumpet from his saddle and blew "Recall." He had to repeat it four times before all the hard-riding warriors heard and heeded. The foremost ground to a halt only yards from the city wall.

In between trumpet blasts, Hakkam was shouting at his own soldiers. "Hold! If any man looses an arrow, I'll have his head!" he roared. None of the Khurish soldiers loosed arrows or threw spears at the elves. Men and elves looked at each other in mutual confusion and alarm until the elves turned and galloped back to Taranath.

Healers from Khurinost hastened through the press of warriors. When they arrived, the Speaker was sitting up, head bowed, his white geb covered with a spreading crimson stain. The first healer to reach him was a Kagonesti with callused hands and dark tattoos on her face and arms.

"Arrow's got to come out," she said immediately.

Planchet nodded once, face grim. "I'll do it."

"Someone must hold him still. If he moves too much, he could rupture an artery."

Hakkam, nearest, knelt behind the Speaker and gripped his shoulders. "I've got him."

The elves were nonplussed, but the Speaker murmured, "Thank you, General." Eyes flickering to Planchet's pale face, he whispered, "Proceed, my friend."

The valet wrapped his fingers around the blood-slick arrow shaft and whispered, "Forgive me."

SANCTUARY

With a single, mighty pull, he freed the arrow. The Kagonesti healer immediately sprinkled the wound with clotting powder and bound it tightly with linen. Too late, she realized she'd not offered the Speaker a leather pad to bite. She apologized, but he didn't respond.

"He's passed out," she said.

Gilthas raised his head. "Not yet." He smiled weakly at Planchet. "Wouldn't she be proud of me? I didn't faint."

Planchet understood who "she" was. He managed to return the brave smile. "Yes, sire. Yes, she would."

A litter was improvised, and the Speaker of the Sun and Stars carefully laid upon it. Four warriors hoisted the corners and headed back to Khurinost, leaving Planchet and Hakkam where they were.

"Taranath, disperse the warriors," Planchet said. The general began to protest, but Planchet cut him off. "Maintain your patrols, but stand down the cavalry!" Taranath saluted and rode away.

As the elves' cavalry began to disperse, Planchet handed Hakkam the bloody arrow. "This archer is Khur's enemy as much as ours," the elf said.

Hakkam gripped the arrow tightly. "Never fear. I'll see this returned to its owner." His meaning was abundantly clear; the arrow would likely be "returned" point first.

On a rooftop three miles away, Prince Shobbat lowered his bow. He could hardly believe his miraculous aim. No one could loft an arrow from so far, much less hit their intended target.

"Impossible," he whispered.

"Magic is the art of the impossible," replied the ragged, hooded figure behind him.

* * * * *

The Lioness withdrew her shrinking command across the creek Favaronas had given her name, and they camped for the night. Tomorrow they would depart Inath-Wakenti,

275

forever, she hoped. There were too many unknowns here—no animals (except those that seemed to vanish in front of them), strangely powerful lights, and unaccountable disappearances. This valley was no sanctuary for their exiled people. Gilthas would have to understand that.

The ride back to the creek, under a milky canopy of stars and clouds, was an eerie one. No crickets whirred in the underbrush; no whippoorwills or nightjars called from the trees; no frogs galumphed from the creeks. There was only the soft clop-clop of their horses' hooves. The more nervous among the warriors were for going on, not camping, but it was well past midnight and both horses and riders were tired. Better to start at dawn, especially if they might have to fight their way out through Khurish nomads.

Kerian felt it was safe enough to camp once they were beyond the stream. The massive stone ruins halted well short of the creek, and the weird phenomena had occurred only after they'd crossed the creek coming in.

They pitched a bivouac on the south bank, picketing the horses and dropping down to sleep on bedrolls, without putting up tents. Before turning in, Kerian toured the camp. She saw Favaronas had built a small fire (the only one in camp) and sat hunched before it. On his lap was one of the stone cylinders he and Glanthon had found in the tunnel.

Glanthon had told her of that strange expedition, but learning what Favaronas was doing with his prize could wait till morning. She was asleep on her feet. After a few words with the elves who'd drawn first watch, she unrolled her blanket beneath a juniper tree and lay down. In moments she was asleep.

Kerianseray did not dream much. At least, she didn't usually remember any dreams she might have. Her nights usually were battles between uneasy alertness and total exhaustion, with exhaustion often the victor. She'd once told Gilthas that living on the run from the Order had taught her to sleep with one eye open. He thought she was joking, but her old comrades could attest that the Lioness slept with one eyelid cracked open, balanced on the dagger's edge between sleep and wakefulness.

This was not the case tonight. Kerian fell deeply asleep. Then she began to dream. Vividly.

She was in a forest, a dense woodland, green and cool. Moss was thick underfoot, and gentle sunlight filtered through the canopy of leaves. The air was wondrous, full of the scents of growing things. A faint breeze teased her face. Reaching out, she felt the suppleness of the leaves. They were ash leaves, slender and pointed. Kerian was in a forest of ash, like the wild land along the Silvanesti border.

Into this idyllic setting came two figures. One was a goblin with a long, beaky nose, pointed chin, and sallow, gray-green complexion. The other she glimpsed only briefly through the foliage, but he appeared to be a Silvanesti elf, dressed in a silky green robe more suited to a city street than the deep forest.

The goblin said, "They's a nest in this one."

"Are you sure?" asked his companion.

"Oh, aye. I seen it come out last ev'ning."

With the illogical logic of dreams, Kerian was no longer standing in the forest, but was tucked into a hollow tree. She didn't mind the tight confines. This was home. Its walls were smooth and smelled strongly of musk. An opening overhead led outside, as did the hole in front of her.

Home trembled. The goblin's face appeared in the hole. He grinned, showing crooked yellow teeth.

"Careful," said the elf, below him. "I don't want it damaged."

The goblin's face went away from the hole and he reached one arm in, long, spidery fingers coming for Kerian's throat.

She didn't wait to be caught. Swift as a striking viper, she uncoiled and sprang at the intruder. She was slender, no more than two feet long, but her claws and teeth were sharp.

They tore into the goblin's cheek and left eye. With a shriek, he fell backward, taking Kerian with him.

They crashed to the ground. He jerked her loose and flung her hard against the trunk of her pine tree home. She lay on her back, stunned, four paws in the air.

The goblin would have killed her then, while she was helpless to defend herself. He lifted his hatchet high, but a hand grabbed his wrist from behind.

"That's not what I'm paying you for."

It was the elf. He had a long face, a sharp chin, and hazel eyes. A robe of pale green silk hung in pleated folds from his narrow shoulders. His blond hair was cut in an antique bowl-shaped style. His hands were large for an elf, with long fingers and knobby knuckles.

"Look what it did to me!" screeched the goblin. Blood ran from his ruined eye and cheek.

The elf merely took a small bag from his waist and shook it. The jangle of coins was unmistakable. He counted thirty steel pieces into the goblin's hand.

The goblin seized Kerian by the throat and thrust her into a dirty burlap bag. The effects of the blow were wearing off and she might have chewed her way out of the sack, but she didn't. The elf and goblin were talking about her, and the elf gave her a name: marten. With the word came a rush of memories.

Covered in brown fur, with a white neck and chest, she was more agile than a squirrel, swifter than lightning. She leaped from branch to branch, climbed up and down rough-barked trees, lay in wait among green boughs for an unwary squirrel. A dash, a pounce, teeth sinking into the rodent's throat. Blood. Delicious. Warm. She prowled the treetops, despoiling nests for eggs or hatchlings, and venturing to the ground to penetrate burrows in search of rabbits. She was mistress of the twilight woods. Not even the panther or the bear could compete with her in ferocity, in kills.

Kerianseray knew she was dreaming, but it was all so

rich and real, her own memories seemed to melt into those of the marten.

In the strange way of dreams, time began to telescope, passing rapidly yet with no sensation of speed. The Silvanesti was a mage. He'd been slaving for decades on a procedure that would transform a wild marten into a semblance of himself. He took the marten bitch to his hut on the edge of the forest and began the lengthy, laborious process. It seemed to go well. The marten became a young girl, flawlessly elven in appearance, with hazel eyes and sable hair. He taught her civilized ways, but she never quite lost her predatory instincts or animal appetites. These he indulged. He learned much from her associations with naturally-born elves and humans.

In her twentieth year, she began to change. Her pure Silvanesti features softened and thickened, giving her the look of a half-elf. When fur reappeared on her legs, the mage knew the transformation had failed again. So many times he had performed the spell, trying to find the perfect conjuration, but every one had failed, sooner or later.

One night soldiers from House Protector came and arrested the mage. Kerian found herself chained in a deep dungeon in the heart of Silvanost. There she met others like herself, creatures whose elven veneer had decayed. But although the mage's conjuration didn't make them fully elven, it kept them from returning fully to their animal state.

Such creatures could not be allowed to remain in Silvanesti, so they were exiled. Closed wagons transported them far from the land of their birth to the Silent Vale, where the half-creatures were turned loose to fend for themselves.

The night sky above Kerian's new home contained three moons—one white, one blood red, and a third, black moon she knew Two-Footers couldn't see with their feeble eyes. But she could see it.

She also could see something falling from the dark moon. Just as she recognized it as an arrow, it struck the base of her neck. She was knocked to the ground. Blood welled from her throat.

What treachery is this? cried a far-off voice. Then a multitude shouted, *The Speaker! The Speaker has been attacked!*

She jerked awake. She was lying on her bedroll, and the night sky above her was the one she recognized. She was Kerianseray, Wilder elf, warrior, wife of Gilthas, not some half-animal abomination.

Rolling to her feet, she caught sight of Favaronas. His back to her, he squatted at the water's edge a few yards away, sipping from his cupped hands. She rose and called his name.

He almost fell head-first into the creek. She covered the distance between them in two long strides, snagged the back of his robe, and pulled him to his feet.

"Favaronas, I had a terrible dream!" she said. "More than that! A premonition."

He was taken aback. The ever-sensible Lioness, talking of premonitions?

The earlier part of her dream, of being an animal made to look like an elf, was fading into a confusing jumble of sensations. Kerian skipped that part, describing only the end, the terrifyingly clear vision she'd had of Gilthas being hit with an arrow.

Favaronas, who had read much about historical presentiments of disaster, didn't think such things occurred nowadays. Doubt was plain on his face.

"It happened!" she insisted. "Or will happen. I don't know which. But I felt it!"

"So, what will you do?"

She raked her fingers through her matted, sweat-soaked hair. What could she do? Gilthas was her beloved husband. Even more than that, he was her Speaker, the king she had pledged to serve and defend. She wanted to fly to him, to make certain he was all right.

Fly!

"Eagle Eye! He can get me to Khurinost in half a day!"

The griffon was tethered twenty yards from the horses, further along on the path back to the mouth of the valley. Kerian turned to race off in that direction. Favaronas caught her arm.

"General, you can't abandon your warriors in the middle of the night because of a dream!"

She jerked her arm free and glared at him, but she knew he was right. Equally right was her conviction that Gilthas was grievously wounded, perhaps even dying while they stood here debating. A difficult quandary, but the Lioness was not known for being indecisive.

"Rouse the camp," she said. "Wake everyone!"

Favaronas hurried away, calling out to sleeping warriors, shaking their shoulders. Kerian did likewise. In minutes the entire band was awake, if not completely alert.

Glanthon, hair askew, rubbed his eyes and asked, "Has something happened?"

"Yes, I must return to Khurinost at once!"

"I'll have the riders mount up—"

"There's no time." Struggling for calm, she said, "I go alone, on Eagle Eye. The rest of you will proceed to Khurinost without me."

She explained her dream to them as she had to Favaronas. Her warriors knew her to be pragmatic, not given to flights of fancy. If the Lioness believed she'd been granted a premonition about the Speaker, they didn't question her conviction. They were, however, plainly disconcerted by the content of her dream and that she was leaving them.

She gripped Glanthon's shoulder. "I have no choice. You'll be fine. Avoid the High Plateau. Take the easier route down the caravan trail from Kortal." On the return journey, they had less to fear from spies. Still, she cautioned, "Tell no one where you've been."

To Favaronas, she said, "If I could, I would take you with me, but Eagle Eye won't tolerate anyone else on his back."

He assured her he was not offended at being left behind.

It was vital that he get his manuscripts, notes, and the odd stone cylinders home intact. He certainly couldn't have carried them all while hurtling across the sky on griffonback.

Kerian was not one to waste time. She filled two waterskins in the creek, took up a haversack with a bit of food, and said good-bye to all. The dazed warriors drew themselves up and saluted their leader.

Before jogging up the trail to Eagle Eye, she repeated her injunction to Glanthon that he and the rest were to get themselves home safely. If they were confronted by nomads, they were to try to slip away without fighting.

"And when you get back, I'll buy nectar for everyone!" she called, and then she was gone.

Favaronas and Glanthon stood side by side, watching long after she was swallowed by the darkness. The warrior was muttering to himself, speculating about the possibility of a nomad trick or weird dreams generated by the forces at work in the valley.

"This feels wrong," he said.

Favaronas was thinking the same thing, but they heard the cry of the airborne griffon and knew it was too late for misgivings.

*　*　*　*　*

Word raced through the streets of Khuri-Khan that the *laddad* king had been wounded, some said killed. The elves had withdrawn their soldiers, but for how long? Blood was sure to flow. Opinion was divided as to who should bear the blame. Many Khurs believed the Sons of the Crimson Vulture had tried to assassinate the Speaker. Others thought Sahim-Khan was involved.

Sahim had his own theory. The city gates, cleared by his soldiers, were kept open by entire companies of royal guards. The Khuri yl Nor was sealed tight as a tomb. Alarm flags were hoisted all over the city, recalling all soldiers to duty. General Hakkam brought the arrow, still stained with the

Speaker's blood, to the palace, and every bowyer and fletcher in the city was summoned. If the arrow's maker could be found, its owner soon would be known.

In the Nor-Khan, behind the thickest walls in Khur, Sahim-Khan raged. How had this come about? Who was trying to foment war with the *laddad*? His favorite suspects were the Torghanists, whom he castigated as insolent, ignorant savages.

His captains kept close around him. His current wife sat in her place behind the Sapphire Throne. Huddled around her were the Khan's seven youngest children, frightened but silent. Off to one side, Prince Shobbat leaned one hip on a sideboard, idly eating grapes from a silver bowl.

Zunda, who in moments of stress could speak as succinctly as any man, said, "An emissary must go to the *laddad*. With assurances of the Mighty Khan's goodwill."

"I'll show them goodwill! I'll decorate the city battlements with the corpse of every man who bears a red tattoo!"

"Mighty Khan, the situation may not call for such measures."

"You go to the *laddad*, Zunda! Take Sa'ida and all priestesses of Elir-Sana. If the Speaker can be saved, Holy Sa'ida can do it."

The old vizier bowed and obeyed. Any other action just now likely would cost him his head.

Once the vizier had departed, Sahim summoned one of his captains, a lean and wolfish fellow named Vatan.

"Collect a hundred men and go to the Temple of Torghan," Sahim said. "Arrest everyone—priests, acolytes, servants, all of them. If you find Minok, slay the wretch where he stands."

He turned away, then paused, a better idea coming to him. "No, Vatan. Bring Minok to me. Alive. His people might behave better if I hold their leader. I'll question him personally, and we'll learn who else is part of this conspiracy."

Vatan departed. For the first time since summoning this

emergency assembly, Sahim sat, dropping heavily onto the throne. His sun-yellow robes billowed around him. He spied Hengriff on the periphery of the crowd and waved the knight forward.

Hengriff's natural impassivity had been perfected by his time in Khur. When Sahim asked his opinion of the orders just given, Hengriff did not say, *I think you a crude and brutal fool*, but replied blandly, "The Mighty Khan thinks swiftly and acts even faster."

Sahim smiled. "I had good teachers. What does your Order do with rebels?"

"Hang the unrepentant and subvert the rest is our custom."

"The better policy would be to hang them all!"

Hengriff took Sahim's bloodthirsty admonition with outward good grace. The time had come for him to put into action a bold plan. He lifted the leather dispatch case in his hand and announced he had a confidential message from his Order.

In a better mood for having set Zunda and Vatan to their respective tasks, Sahim dismissed his frightened family, his captains, and his fawning courtiers. Only a handful of his personal guard remained. Prince Shobbat was among the last to leave, tossing aside an empty grape stem before going out the double doors.

"So, what does the Lord of the Night have to say?"

After weeks of hearing nothing from the Order, Hengriff had decided on a dangerous deception. He had forged a set of instructions, ostensibly from Rennold to himself. If he guessed right, all would be well. If he chose a faulty course, his head would certainly be forfeit. His masters might forgive failure, but not one committed in their own names.

He opened the leather flap and pulled out a sheaf of papers. He made a show of glancing over the papers before clearing his throat and booming, " 'To his Mightiness, Sahim, Khan of All the Khurs, greetings—' "

SANCTUARY

A loud noise halted Hengriff's recitation. Shobbat suddenly reentered the hall at the head of twenty guards.

"What's the meaning of this?" Sahim demanded. "Are the *laddad*—"

"I have news, Mighty Khan. I have learned the identity of the traitor in our city, the author of all our troubles, the one who conspired to slay the king of the *laddad*."

Pleased, Sahim said, "Excellent, my son! Excellent! Who is it?"

Shobbat advanced until he was standing abreast of the Dark Knight. The soldiers halted two steps behind the prince. "The traitor, sire, is Lord Hengriff."

For a moment no one moved. No one seemed even to breathe. Brief as a heartbeat, as long as forever. Then nearly everyone was in motion.

The papers fell from Hengriff's hand. The Khan's eight guards drew swords and rushed at him. So did Shobbat's escort. Because he was at court, Hengriff was armed only with a dagger, but he drew it without hesitation and lunged at Shobbat. The prince backed away, groping for his own blade.

Only the Khan was still. He sat on his golden throne, watching.

Hengriff slashed overhand at Shobbat. The prince clumsily warded off the strike, his feet slipping on the polished floor. Much white showed around his eyes. The soldiers who would have intervened were waved off by Sahim. He wanted to see how his son would fare against the formidable Hengriff.

The answer was, he quickly realized, not well. Shobbat was no duelist. His father, a redoubtable warrior in his own right, had required him to serve eight years in the army of Khur. Shobbat spent the time learning archery and dice, not swordplay.

The Knight made a series of wide, circular cuts. Shobbat backed away until his heel caught the hem of his robe. He fell. The Knight stood over him, sneering.

"Even this you bungle!" he said.

A sword point, bright with blood, suddenly protruded from his chest. Hengriff's sneer froze. He looked back at the guard who'd stabbed him.

"Now!" Shobbat cried. "Everyone, strike home!"

The guard withdrew his blade. In spite of his wound, Hengriff whirled, flinging his dispatch case at the man's face, but nine more blades thrust home. The Knight thrust his dagger into the belly of another guard and wrenched the sword from his hand. At last Hengriff had a real weapon.

He caught two blades in a bind and whipped them aside. Thrusting, he took the closest Khur in the throat; the man went down. A blade passed under Hengriff's outthrust arm, cutting deeply into his armpit. Cursing the pain, he recovered and slashed at the guard who'd cut him, severing the man's jaw from the rest of his face.

The Knight avoided cuts and stabs from three sides as the Khurs tried to hem him in. He dispatched a fourth attacker when the man lunged too far and Hengriff caught him by the wrist. Bringing his blade down, he all but severed the man's arm at the elbow. The guard dropped to the floor, screaming and clutching his savaged arm. He rolled away.

The doors of the throne room burst open. More soldiers appeared. They didn't charge in, but stood transfixed by the appalling scene that met their eyes. Teeth bared in a hiss of pain, drenched in his own blood and that of his attackers, the towering Hengriff was the very picture of an assassin.

Shobbat shouted at the newcomers to surround the Nerakan and kill him. The prince's voice broke through their shock. They attacked.

Hengriff was a master warrior, but there was no escape for him. Still, he put his back to one wall and fought on. Two more Khurs fell to his sword. The tiled floor around him grew slick with blood. His wounds burned, and his right arm was weak from loss of blood. With one particularly effective counterthrust, he drove half a dozen soldiers back against that many more. In this temporary lull, Hengriff sagged against the wall. He turned his burning obsidian gaze on Shobbat. The prince stood next to his father's throne, both of them protected by a wall of outraged soldiers.

"You think you've won?" Hengriff panted, his voice still deep and carrying. "You forget who you're dealing with. You'll not outlive me long, traitor!"

Shobbat sneered. "I don't fear your Order. Loyal Khurs will protect the throne."

"Not my Order, fool! Fear the *laddad!*"

Paling, Shobbat shouted, "Finish him!"

Like a bear bayed by a pack of wolves, Hengriff fought with the desperate ferocity of the doomed. He maimed three more attackers before two Khurs with pole arms speared him from opposite sides. Their surviving comrades joined in, pushing the halberd shafts, and Hengriff was driven back against the wall and pinned there.

His life drained away. He slumped forward, still held upright by the spearpoints piercing his body. His eyes glazed. The sword dropped from his lifeless fingers.

The guards gave a victory cry. They sorted themselves into proper formation before their monarch.

"Shall we take his head, Great Khan?" asked one.

Throughout the bloody battle, Sahim-Khan had sat on his throne with apparent calm, taking in every aspect of the fight. He was not convinced Hengriff was a traitor, but this was not the place to question his son's accusation. The Khan rose, straightened his yellow robes, and stepped forward to examine the dead Knight.

"No," he said. "Drag his body to the square before the palace. Placard it, so all will know of his treachery."

The soldiers dragged Hengriff out by the heels and dumped him in the courtyard before the palace gate. One scrounged materials to make the sign Sahim required. The others stared up at the sky, crowded with slow-moving, billowing clouds. They'd never seen such a display before.

"What does it mean?" asked one.

Another, secretly a worshiper of Torghan, said, "Those on High are angry! They would see this land purged of evil."

A loud gargling screech gave emphasis to the soldier's prediction. It sounded like no bird known in Khur. Deep and powerful, the cry was halfway between a lion's roar and an eagle's scream. A second screech was followed by a freshening of the wind. The gust traveled through the streets of the city. The soldiers at the palace could follow its progress by the dust clouds it raised. They turned away and covered their faces as it whirled through the square from west to east, scouring the pavement and rocking the spindly scaffolding still attached to the palace walls. Uprights gave way, and planks tumbled. Then as quickly as it had come, the wind was gone.

* * * * *

In Khurinost, the odd screeching noise drew the elves out from under the woven grass mats that shaded the encampment's narrow lane. Unlike the Khurs, many elves recognized that cry. It had come from a Silvanesti griffon.

Planchet emerged from the Speaker's tent. He certainly knew the cry, although he could hardly credit hearing it now. Its author was so high, silhouetted against roiling white clouds, that Planchet's keen eyes could not discern whether or not the griffon bore a rider.

Across the square, an elf woman tried to comfort her crying child, both of them frightened by the commotion overhead. Planchet went and spoke kindly to her.

"Don't be afraid," he said. "It's only a griffon."

"I thought the Khurs were coming to kill us," whispered the elf woman.

"They aren't our enemies," Planchet assured her. He squeezed her hand and chucked the chin of the crying child. "Our Speaker will not allow us to come to harm."

The elf woman obviously had not seen Gilthas carried

into his tent earlier, barely conscious. His wound had festered and a fever had erupted in his slender frame. Just now he had little ability to guarantee anything, but the Throne of the Sun and Stars had a power that went far beyond the mortal elf who held it. Like a potent talisman against evil, Planchet's invocation of the Speaker's name calmed mother and child, and he was able to leave them in much better spirits.

He had lost sight of the griffon. He hurried back to the Speaker's tent to tell him of the sighting.

In Gilthas's bedchamber, healers, courtiers, and captains stood by, poised to do whatever was required of them.

"Great Speaker!" Planchet said, kneeling by the bed. "Did you hear the call of the griffon?"

Blue eyes hazed by fever turned slowly to the valet's face. "You heard it? I thought I was delirious," Gilthas whispered.

"No, sire. It was real."

"Is she here?"

"I don't know. I lost sight of the creature, but we will find out soon."

Gilthas licked dry lips, and Planchet held a small cup of water to his mouth. Once Gilthas had swallowed a few drops, he asked about Lord Morillon.

Unfortunately the Silvanesti had not been found. Planchet was forced to report they feared the worst.

An elven healer bent and whispered in his ear. The valet nodded. "Sire, Vizier Zunda has come, with priestesses from the Temple of Elir-Sana."

"Holy Lady Sa'ida? She is said to be wise in her craft. Admit them."

Planchet turned to relay the order but a bizarre interruption occurred. The air suddenly rushed out of the tent, drawing the roof down violently. The tired canvas split, opening a great rent to the sky. The attendants cried out in alarm.

Directly over the Speaker's tent, a neat round hole had been bored through the towering clouds. It looked as though a giant finger had poked through the overcast sky and into the center of Khurinost. A whirlwind spun down from the hole, drawing streams of cloud vapor with it as it descended on the Speaker's tent.

As the wind screamed, Planchet shouted orders. Healers knelt around the Speaker's bed, covering him with their bodies. Warriors formed a square, facing outward with swords drawn.

Only seconds after it was first sighted, the vortex touched down on the Speaker's tent, tearing it apart. Walls and ceilings collapsed. Elves were buried under masses of fabric. Hands over their heads, the Speaker's loyal guards kept the roof off him and the healers covering him.

Suffocating in the thick canvas, Planchet could not see but only hear the chaos. Elves were shouting, footsteps pounding. Carefully, he thrust the tip of his sword through the canvas and made a small opening. No one protested, so he widened the hole.

"My ancestors!" Planchet breathed.

"What is it?" demanded Gilthas, pushing away the healers covering him.

"Not what, Great Speaker—who!"

The Lioness was bounding over the wreckage of the tent. Eagle Eye hadn't even touched ground before she was off his back and running toward her husband. She wore only the tattered remains of her smallclothes, and was soaked from head to toe. She cleaved through the astonished guards and healers, dropped to her knees, and took her husband in her arms.

Gilthas said her name, over and over, as Planchet propped him up from behind. Despite the fresh blood that seeped from his cheek and neck, his voice was joyous with relief.

"Kerianseray, how? How in the names of all the ancient gods did you get here?"

"I flew. You sent Eagle Eye, so I returned him." Her voice quavered nearly as much as his. "All the way from the Valley of the Blue Sands, I came."

She eased him back against the strong shoulder of Planchet. "An arrow!" she said, studying his wound with a practiced eye. "I knew it!"

"How did you know, lady?"

Kerian shook her head at Planchet's question. "Never mind. Who did it. Was it Khurs? Nerakans?"

The valet admitted they didn't know yet.

With Kerian's help, Planchet settled the Speaker on his bed, then went to round up food and drink for her. And clothes, though he did not say as much to her.

While they were moderately private, Gilthas took her hand. "You look wonderful," he whispered, his tear-filled eyes looking her up and down.

She grimaced, suddenly self-conscious. "We ran into a storm aloft, a tornado. I'm lucky it left me any clothing at all!"

"Only the Lioness could ride home on the back of a whirlwind," he teased. "Are your warriors near?"

She shook her head, embarrassment hardening into grim lines. "No, they were just leaving Inath-Wakenti when I had to leave them."

Briefly, for her throat was truly parched, she described their experiences in the valley—the phantom lights, the stone ruins, the disappearance of the sand beast and many of her warriors, and the utter lack of any animal life.

"Not so much as a fly lives there, Gil. Leave it to the ghosts and will-o'-the-wisps."

During her recitation, however succinct, Gilthas began to succumb to the effects of his wound and fever, as well as the shock of her arrival. He was barely conscious.

"Can't be done," he murmured, and she had to bend close to hear what he said next. "We must leave this place."

His eyelids closed, and he slept.

Planchet returned with a jug of palm wine in each hand. The guards and servants began working to rig new supports for the tent roof. Kerian took a jug of wine and put it to her lips.

Planchet informed her of the disappearance of Lord Morillon. She replied with a flippant comment, but his careworn face was very somber. "He's been found, lady," he continued. "In the desert outside the north city gate. His throat was cut from ear to ear."

13

Daybreak came, with the nomads nowhere in sight. Glanthon had riders scour the pass for signs, but the Weya-Lu appeared to be gone. The pine copses and juniper thickets on the hillsides overlooking the pass were empty. On the floor of the pass, a distinct trail of hoofprints led due south. The way out of Inath-Wakenti was free and clear.

As the Lioness had commanded, the company of elves would bear west, not south, the direction from which they had come. This eventually would put them on the caravan road from Kortal to Khuri-Khan. Since that road bypassed the cauldron of the High Plateau, it was a safer route in some respects, but for several days they would be riding further away from their comrades in Khurinost and closer to the border with Neraka. Still, Glanthon agreed with his commander's reasoning that this was the best way to go. Feeling a bit naked without the encircling mountains, trees, and ghostly ruins, the elves rode forth into the open desert again.

One of the last tasks they'd completed before leaving Inath-Wakenti was to make a small lap table for Favaronas. Thin planks of yellow pine were pegged together into a surface that allowed the archivist to write and read while on horseback. A hole near the top center of the board fitted over his saddle pommel. This stabilized the lapboard and kept it from sliding off the moving horse. Favaronas shortened his stirrups and balanced the lapboard across his drawn up knees. In this way, he could work on his report to the Speaker even as they were on the move.

Without nomads to fight, Glanthon soon grew bored and came back to ride alongside Favaronas and distract him with a discussion of the valley. Glanthon believed a system of tunnels underlay the ruins. He was certain the secret of the ruins lay underground. Had time permitted, he would have sought permission from the Lioness to search further in the tunnels they'd found, looking for signs of their missing comrades and more evidence of previous civilizations.

"You think our missing warriors are in the tunnels?" Favaronas said.

"Where else?" Glanthon reasoned.

"With magic involved, there's no limit to where they might have been taken. The next valley over, or even to the stars themselves."

Favaronas's testy response silenced the talkative warrior, but only briefly. Glanthon changed the subject, asking whether Favaronas had learned anything about the odd stone artifacts they'd removed from the underground chamber.

The archivist sighed. "Not very much," he admitted. Each of the eight stone cylinders bore a brief inscription engraved on one side. Favaronas was convinced they'd once been real books, but had been changed to solid stone.

"I have deciphered the labels, at least partly. They are not, as I first thought, a forgotten dialect of Old Silvanesti. Instead, each syllable is an abbreviation of a longer word or phrase. The first is marked *Ba-Laf-Om-Thas*, which means 'Balif, Lord of the Thon-Thalas,' and *Hoc-Sem-Ath*. which I believe translates as 'Halfway Between Lives.' "

"What does that mean?"

"I wish I knew." The archivist recalled the discussion at the Speaker's dinner, the night before they'd begun this journey. The cartographer Sithelbathan had said the furthest outpost of the ancient elven kingdom, Balif's Gate, was supposed to have been located in or near the valley.

Glanthon looked over his shoulder at the three mountains, Torghan's Teeth, receding behind them. "You think those stones are the ruins of that outpost? You think Silvanesti made them?"

"Not necessarily." The imprecision of it all plainly made the archivist unhappy. "But I'm beginning to think the valley was visited by followers of General Balif, probably after the First Dragon War, thirty-five hundred years ago. We know from ancient tradition that Balif left Silvanesti under a cloud, or a curse, and eventually helped found the kender nation of Balifor. Some authorities claim he became a kender himself, but there's no evidence for that theory." He sighed. "Many relevant records are still in the temples of Silvanost, closely guarded. Others were lost in the First Cataclysm."

"Perhaps these cylinders contain the *true* history of Balif!" Glanthon exclaimed.

Favaronas drew his geb close around him as if feeling a chill despite the desert heat. "Perhaps. One other possibility has occurred to me, but it's really too frightful to contemplate."

Glanthon had to prompt the scholar, reminding him of his duty to the Speaker, before he would continue. Even then, Favaronas looked around furtively, making certain no one was eavesdropping.

"Do you know much about the history of our race?" he asked.

Glanthon's education didn't extend much beyond reading, writing, and simple mathematics. He admitted his lack of scholarship.

Briefly, Favaronas described the founding of the first elven nation under Silvanos Goldeneye, first Speaker of the Stars. The land claimed by the elves, the land that would one day be Silvanesti, was then occupied by powerful dragons. Conflict ensued, the First Dragon War, in which Balif led his griffon riders to victory. The triumph was not Balif's alone. The gods of magic sent a trio of mages to aid the elves. The mages were armed with five powerful dragonstones. Balif and the mages set a trap for the dragons, luring them into a final battle, then capturing their souls within the dragonstones. The dragons' empty bodies were transformed to ridges of stone, and became part of the Khalkist range; they were part of that mountain range still.

Like all elves, Glanthon knew Silvanos had founded the nation that bore his name. But hearing the story, thrilling even in abbreviated form, left him open-mouthed.

"What happened to the dragonstones?" he asked.

"Let me quote the *Chronicle of Silvanos*." This was the book all aspiring archivists were required to learn by heart. " 'Victorious, the Cloud-Legion of Lord Balif carried the captive dragon spirits away, north to the deepest range of the mountains. Here was the Pit of Nemith-Otham, the deepest cleft in the world, and into it Lord Balif cast the souls of one hundred dragons.' "

In case Glanthon didn't follow him fully, Favaronas added, "The exact location of Nemith-Otham is not known today, but I suspect—I fear!—Inath-Wakenti was once the Pit of Nemith-Otham."

Glanthon was amazed. If Favaronas was correct, beneath the surface of the valley lay the greatest concentration of magical force in the world, the captive souls of one hundred dragons, and the nomads' fearful respect of the place was entirely justified.

One dragon, just one, the formidable green dragon Beryl, had destroyed an army comprising thousands of elves. Even in death she had murdered elves. Plummeting from the sky, she had crushed the city of Qualinost so badly that the land collapsed and the White-Rage River rushed in. Nearly all the survivors of the battle drowned. The Speaker's own mother, Queen Mother Laurana, had been killed, and the .

site remained flooded to this day, as far as anyone knew. The dragon's rotting corpse was still at the bottom of the lake, giving it the well-deserved name *Nalis Aren*, the Lake of Death.

Glanthon was a survivor of that battle. Hardly a month went by that he didn't relive in dreams the horror and gallantry he'd witnessed. Knowing well the havoc one green dragon had wreaked, he could scarcely comprehend the destruction a hundred creatures could do.

Seeing his stricken face, Favaronas reminded him it was only a theory, and it didn't explain the ruins, the disappearing antelope the Lioness had seen, or the strange ghost that had passed Glanthon and Favaronas in the tunnel. The only hard facts the archivist had wrung from the scrolls thus far was that someone, in sizable numbers, had occupied the valley, and they had a connection to the valiant, doomed Balif. The titles of the other seven cylinders were as cryptic as that of the first. He had puzzled them out as "Counting of the Tribe," "Halfway Order of the Breeding," "Raising of the Pillars," and "Sleeping of the First One."

He thought it odd the labels of two of the eight randomly chosen cylinders mentioned "halfway". Judging from the way the word was used, he felt it referred to a group of people, not a location.

"Whatever it means," he said, "I confess I am glad to be out of that peculiar valley for good."

Glanthon shook his head. "It may not be for good. The Speaker hopes the valley will be our new homeland." Ignoring Favaronas's shocked expression, the warrior added that he thought the valley, with its hidden entrance, abundance of water, and tunnel system, would make a fine haven for them.

"We must simply solve its various mysteries," he finished stoutly.

Favaronas said, "The humans may be right about the place. There may be mysteries there we should not disturb."

"What about our people? Not only the thousands languishing in that filthy camp outside Khuri-Khan, but the hundreds of thousands who bear the yoke of foreign conquerors? Do we forget them and take the easy path to everlasting exile?"

Favaronas had no answer. Glanthon was a dedicated warrior. He found virtue in hardship and nobility in war. How could an archivist at least twice his age tell the proud soldier that his ideals were wrong?

He couldn't. Instead, he silently vowed to continue his study of the cylinders. There had to be a way to get at the interior text, if any.

The westward ride progressed without incident. As dusk fell, the warriors camped just below the summit of a broad, gravelly hill. They'd come across no signs of nomads. The desert west of the mountains seemed as devoid of people as the Vale of Silence had been.

They had plenty of water from the valley, but rations were growing short. Only pine nuts and berries had been found during their foraging trips in the valley. This sterility caused much comment among the elves. Many were former herdsmen or farmers, and a few had been gardeners in the great city of Qualinost. In elven lands a gardener was no menial laborer, but an artist comparable to a sculptor, poet, or painter. They could come up with no obvious reason for the valley's lack of game and edible plants. No two-legged hunters prowled its paths; it contained plenty of water; its climate was mild. The soil was sandy and poor in many places, not to mention having that odd color, but nearer the highlands there should be better minerals in the earth. Common sense dictated the valley should be teeming with life. Why, then, was it so silent and empty?

Favaronas had formulated an answer, but he did not share it with the others, not wishing to be drawn into a long discussion. The ghostly lights in the ruins were attracted to horses, riders, and even the murderous sand beast. He believed that, over time, the will-o'-the-wisps had cleared the valley of animal life, right down to the flies. Where the creatures had been taken he could not say, but the Speaker must consider this danger before bringing the entire nation to dwell there.

Clouds appeared in the east, high and solid looking. The desert air usually was so dry no clouds could penetrate this far from the sea, so their appearance caused much comment as the elves settled into camp. When flickers of lightning flashed beneath the clouds, the elves knew they were seeing something extraordinary, but not even that could keep the weary warriors awake long.

Favaronas labored far into the night, trying to unlock the secret of the stone cylinders. He gathered dry desert grasses and built a small fire by a stand of saltbush, whose grayish-green leaves had served as his dinner. He laid one of the cylinders in the flames, but fire had no effect on it. He tried pouring water, then oil, on the cylinders, to soften them, but again met with failure. The ends of the cylinders bore tight spiral patterns. They looked like nothing so much as ordinary vellum scrolls turned to stone, perhaps by age or magic. If the former, it might be possible to separate the books using mechanical means, but if magic was involved, his efforts were pointless. The Speaker would have to find skilled mages to unravel the guarded cylinders.

Sometime past midnight Favaronas fell asleep, the cylinders arranged before him. His fire had died to a bed of shimmering coals.

The soft crunch of footfalls woke him. He had spent too many fearful days and nights in the valley to ignore such noises.

"Who's there?" he hissed. Likely the noise was innocent, caused by one of Glanthon's soldiers. Favaronas called out again, by turns nervous and angry. The fellow could have the courtesy to answer!

He tossed a handful of dry grass on the coals of his fire. Flames blossomed. To his heart-thudding shock, they illuminated a cloaked figure standing a few feet away. The figure moved back, seeking the darkness.

Favaronas shouted, getting quickly to his feet. Glanthon had given him a Weya-Lu mace because it required little skill to wield. He clutched it now. He was terrified, but certain his cry would rouse the warriors and they would protect him.

Strangely, none came. The warriors around him remained still. Despite his continued shouts, he heard snores and deep inhalations as they slept on, undisturbed.

The cloaked intruder joined several similarly clad figures at the foot of the hill. Favaronas could make out four distinct forms, and in the night's deep folds, he spied the movement of many more. Instead of fleeing, the four came closer and surrounded him.

He waved the mace, shouting at them to stay back. With an enemy at each point of the compass, he found himself whirling in a circle, trying desperately to keep them all in view.

"Stranger."

The whisper brought him around to face one of the four.

"Give back what you have taken."

He knew immediately what was meant: the stone cylinders. "Who are you?" he demanded.

Slender hands turned back the dark hood. A lovely face appeared, that of a young female elf with eyes and hair the color of sunlit gold.

The other three uncovered their heads, revealing themselves to be elf maidens, too. One had hair and eyes of darkest onyx; another was copper hued, and the fourth silvery white. All four were beautiful, with flawless, milky skin and crimson lips, but their expressions were somber.

"Give back what you have taken," repeated the golden-haired maid.

Favaronas lowered the mace. "These relics are important to us," he replied. "Can't you spare them?"

SANCTUARY

In unison, the four advanced a step toward him. Golden Hair once more repeated her command, with the others echoing it.

These weren't phantoms. Unlike the translucent ghost he'd encountered in the tunnel, these elves were flesh and blood. Even in the poor light he could see the tracks left in their hair by combs, hear the rustle of their robes, see how their thin sandals pressed into the gravelly sand.

"Please, we didn't mean to steal anything," he said, addressing Golden Hair. "I'm an archivist, an expert on documents. These cylinders are very old, and I'd like to read them. You're elves; you must know how important these cylinders could be to our people. Do you know how to open them?"

She unclasped her cloak and let it fall, exposing bare flesh. The others followed suit. Before Favaronas could digest this development, one of the maidens sprang on him from behind. Another snatched the mace from his hand, and a third struck the backs of his knees, toppling him to the ground.

His head hit the ground with such force that the stars overhead vanished in a sunrise of pain. A terrible weight settled on his chest. When his head finally cleared, he saw the golden-haired elf sitting on his chest. Although she looked so slight a strong breeze would sway her, she was extremely heavy. He could hardly draw breath against the crushing weight of her body. He pleaded for air.

She leaned down, grasping his head between her hands. As she moved closer, her lovely face shattered. Instead of a radiantly fair elf maid, Favaronas found himself eye to eye with a wolf, one with golden eyes and matching pelt.

"Give back what you have stolen!" the wolf snarled.

He couldn't understand why the creatures didn't just take the stone cylinders and go. They had certainly defeated him. He couldn't move, could barely breathe.

"Take them!" he wheezed. "Why don't you . . . just take them?"

"You shall have no rest until you return what you have taken!"

So saying, the wolf lifted one paw high. Favaronas couldn't draw breath to scream before the claws slashed across his throat.

* * * * *

The uneasy calm continued at Khuri-Khan. Slate-colored clouds piled higher and higher over the city until they no longer flowed with the wind. For the first time in living memory, the desert sun vanished completely. Khurs and elves sweltered despite the unexpected shade. No breath of wind stirred, and the heat was stifling. Brief, unpredictable showers of rain fell, keeping everyone sodden, steamy, and uncomfortable.

The murder of Lord Morillon fanned the flames of fear and distrust already smoldering from the attempt on the Speaker's life. There were no clues to his death. No evidence pointed to anyone in particular, but the view in Khurinost was that Morillon had been slain by fanatical Torghanists.

Sahim-Khan agreed. His fierce captain Vatan and one hundred elite palace guards cleared the Temple of Torghan. The entire college of priests was dragged away in chains, along with two dozen scruffy nomads hiding in the temple grounds, and a handful of terrified servants. High priest Minok could not be found.

The elves kept close to their tents. They saw conspiracies every time more than two Khurs appeared on the city streets. Planchet and Taranath quickly organized water collection for the entire colony. Warriors, rather than ordinary citizens, were sent to purchase the life-giving liquid. Even without their chargers, and dressed in regular attire, the warriors cut an unmistakable profile as they stood watch over their comrades.

During one of these expeditions Hytanthas Ambrodel learned of the death of Lord Hengriff. He sought out Planchet on his return from the city. The Speaker's guard commander, Hamaramis, was with the valet.

"Hengriff's corpse lies in the palace yard," Hytanthas announced grimly. "Wearing a placard that says 'Traitor.' "

"A suitable end for a Dark Knight," Hamaramis opined.

"He saved my life that night at the ruined villa," the captain insisted. "He may have had a nefarious purpose in mind, but the truth is, he saved me. He seemed an honorable man." Hamaramis snorted, and Hytanthas added stubbornly, "He deserves better than to feed the flies!"

Planchet understood. He went to a chest standing against the wall of the Speaker's tent and removed a small sack from one of its drawers. He tossed it to Hytanthas.

"Bribe the guards and secure the Knight's remains. See to it he gets an honorable burial."

Head held high under Hamaramis's disapproval, Hytanthas departed to repay his debt to the Dark Knight of Neraka.

"That money could be better spent."

The two elves turned to see the Lioness standing in the doorway leading to the Speaker's bedchamber. Dark circles shadowed her eyes. She'd been up all night, nursing her injured husband.

"It could be used to find Morillon's killer, or the spineless fiend who tried to kill the Speaker," she said.

Planchet poured a cup of raw wine and handed it to the Lioness. "They might be the same person," he said evenly. "Barring a new player, the roster of our foes is shrinking. Sahim-Khan, for all his grasping ways, has shown he's not our true enemy, and Lord Hengriff is dead."

"Who does that leave?" she asked.

"The mage Faeterus, for one. We don't know much about him, but he tried to kill Captain Ambrodel, evaded the Nerakans, and is still at large."

"What about the Torghanist high priest?"

Planchet shook his head. "A pawn in the game, not a player, I think. Sahim-Khan's been hunting him for days. He dares not show his face anywhere in Khuri-Khan."

"Prince Shobbat?" Hamaramis suggested.

Here, Planchet frowned without replying. The heir to the throne of Khur was a cipher to the elves. He had little to do with the running of the country and spent most of his time overseeing repairs to the palace or pursuing his personal pleasures. It was rumored he was involved in Hengriff's fall, but the elves found this hard to credit. No one in Khuri-Khan took the spoiled, pleasure-loving prince seriously as a threat.

Kerian held out her empty cup and Planchet refilled it.

"How fares the Speaker, lady?" Hamaramis asked quietly.

"He sleeps. His fever waxes each night and wanes by day."

Planchet said, "An entire corps of healers from Khuri-Khan waits to attend him."

"Humans have done enough for the Speaker!" she snapped. Her furious expression lasted only seconds, then settled back into its usual stolid exhaustion. "Our people can take care of him."

Although she had no grudge against Sa'ida or the Temple of Elir-Sana, Kerian had been so shaken by the treacherous attack on Gilthas that she wouldn't allow any humans near him. Elven sages, lacking the resources of their native lands, were having difficulty controlling his fever, but Kerian insisted only elves treat the Speaker.

She finished her drink, then returned to the dim room where Gilthas slept. The temperature was warm but bearable, the heat kept at bay by the palm fan that rotated slowly next to his bed. It was powered by the strong arms of boys who turned the crank located in an adjacent room. So great was their desire to aid their Speaker, most had to be forced to rest and allow another to take his place.

Around the room's shadowed periphery, healers consulted each other in whispers. Irritated by their murmuring, Kerian ordered the room cleared.

SANCTUARY

She sat on her side of the rope-framed bed, careful not to block the breeze from the fan. In the low light she could see sweat on Gilthas's forehead and along his jaw. His breath was slow and steady, but a little raspy. His eyes were closed. When she touched his cheek, she felt the fever burning inside him.

"I found the valley, Gil," she said softly. "It's just where your librarian said it would be, but I fear it's no place for us. There's something wrong with it, some kind of curse"—she grimaced at the ignorant word, but could think of no other—"on the place. A force snatches away living creatures, including our people. We never discovered where they went. The Inath-Wakenti holds no animal life at all, not so much as a lizard or a fly. I know the place fascinates you, and we can certainly send other explorers to study it, but that valley is no sanctuary for our beleaguered nation."

He never stirred. She took his hand. Despite the sweat on his face, his hand was dry, and hot as the sands outside. She put her face close to his, willing him to waken, to be well, to hear.

"You must give up the foolish idea that we can find a new homeland. We have a home. Two homes, in fact. It's our sacred duty and our destiny to return and take them back. That's what we should do, what we *must* do!"

She realized she was squeezing his hand. Releasing it, she stood and paced across the room like a caged version of her namesake.

"There's talk about me in the tents, you know. They say I abandoned my warriors to come home to you. I can't deny it, but I won't apologize for it. I flew here to be by your side."

She halted her restless movement.

"We have to get out of here, Gil. Once Sahim-Khan drains us of all our treasure, he'll sell us to the Knights or the bull-men or any of the other half-dozen groups that would like to see us exterminated. Or the nomads and Torghanists will unite against us and save him the trouble. Then what will we do?"

He didn't answer, only lay breathing slowly. Six feet away, yet he might as well have been across the continent. Her husband wasn't here. He'd gone somewhere she couldn't reach. Fear, frustration, and worry squeezed her heart. She could no longer simply sit and stare at him.

Picking up her helmet and sword-belt from a chair by the bed, she departed. When she reached the audience room, she sent the healers back in again.

"Heal the Speaker," she said curtly.

Past Hamaramis and Planchet, past the courtiers waiting in hushed circles, past her husband's loyal servants she strode in unyielding silence. In the square outside the sprawling tent she found the company she'd summoned. One warrior held the reins of her horse. She swung into the saddle without benefit of stirrup.

The Lioness rode away toward Khuri-Khan with forty armed and armored warriors behind her.

Gilthas inhaled sharply and opened his eyes.

"My heart," he gasped. Healers rushed to his side, thinking the Speaker was complaining about the organ in his chest, but he was not. "I heard you," he panted. "Come back, my heart!"

But Kerian was already gone.

* * * * *

Water from the recent rains stained the ruined villa's white limestone walls. Opportunistic seeds, long dormant in the soil, had sprouted, covering the pebbled paths and former gardens in a profusion of hairy, green shoots.

The Lioness had heard a full account from Hytanthas of his adventure with Faeterus and the mage's monsters. When she and her riders reached the villa ruins clustered around the broken tower, she sent twenty elves to find the carcasses of the sand beast and manticore, while she and the remaining twenty scoured the grounds for clues to the mage's whereabouts.

SANCTUARY

The clouds above were still, and no air stirred through the rubble piles and toppled columns. The atmosphere carried the heavy, expectant feeling of an impending storm. It was unnerving to the elves and their horses.

The dead monsters were easy enough to find. The headless manticore was draped over a pile of rubble. Closer to the villa, the sand beast was likewise yielding to corruption. The elves were forced to tie kerchiefs over their noses just to approach its body.

Kerian entered the mansion's front doorway. Scraps of parchment blew over her feet. She speared one on her sword tip and brought it up to read. It looked scorched. Every line of ink on the vellum was charred. Her reading skills were limited, but she recognized the curls and tracery of a magical sigil. The weakened parchment broke apart. The fragments fluttered to the floor.

A warrior hailed her. He had found the sorcerer's sanctum in the broken tower. She entered the tower through a large door that swung inward on silent hinges. The interior was lit only by the faint daylight from an open trap door overhead. She mounted a ladder they'd knocked together from house timbers, and entered Faeterus's former residence.

The round room was filled with carpets, tapestries, and numerous pillows. Daylight penetrated through hairline cracks in the tower walls. Aside from the overblown furnishings, all they found were more pieces of disintegrating parchment, a collar and leash for the manticore, and an empty wicker cage.

One of the elves bent down, peering into the shadows. He stood up abruptly, cursing.

Kerian came over. "What is it?"

"Dead birds!" Six common pigeons, the bane of soukats all over Khuri-Khan, lay dead on the rug. Their headless bodies were arranged in a neat line.

Kerian spied a squat brass urn in the corner. Recognizing it as a Khurish oil pot, she picked it up and shook it. It was half full. She sent her warriors out. As they went back down the ladder, she began pouring mutton oil on the thick carpet. Tossing aside the empty urn, she swept parchment fragments into a heap on the oil-soaked carpet. With flint and steel, she showered sparks on the little pile of tinder. Soon, the first red flame crept forth. Smoke was puffing from the trap door opening as she joined her elves.

Outside, Kerian saw the first flames erupt from the windows of the villa proper and knew the job was done. Not only was she taking away an enemy's fortress, she was sending him a clear message: The Lioness had taken the field against him, and there would be no quarter.

In the gardens, the other half of her company had gotten a dozen ropes around the sand beast's carcass. The gangrenous wound on its hip gave Kerian great satisfaction. Hengriff may have slain the beast, but she and her warriors had slowed it down so he could do the job. Had he encountered the sand beast as they first had, she had no doubt it would have killed the Knight as easily as it had her brave warriors.

Having roped the stinking carcass to their protesting horses, the elves awaited her next order.

"Follow me," she told them.

The company rode out of the Harbalah and into Khuri-Khan proper. At the rear of the procession, six riders dragged the lifeless body of the sand beast behind their mounts. From windows and doorways Khurs reacted with horror as the putrefying remains were dragged past their houses, shedding blood and flesh as it went. Some screamed, and many cursed the *laddad* as they passed.

The warrior riding nearest the Lioness said, "General, why are we—?"

"It's a gift for Sahim-Khan," she said calmly.

The elves held their formation, but all wondered whether they were on a suicide ride. The human Khan had been known to kill for insults far less than this.

The bulk of the carcass forced them to keep to the wide

thoroughfares. These took them through the heart of Khuri-Khan. By the time they skirted the Grand Souks, a crowd had gathered behind them. The Lioness ignored the hostile, angry Khurs and rode steadily on.

Word of their approach sped ahead, and they arrived to find the gates of the Khuri yl Nor solidly shut against them. Kerian directed her troopers to drag the decaying sand beast up to the gate and cut it loose.

From the battlements above, a Khurish officer yelled, "What are you doing, *laddad*? You can't leave that there!"

She removed her helmet. Despite the clouded sky, her golden head shone like a land-bound sun.

"I am Kerianseray, consort of the Speaker of the Sun and Stars," she proclaimed in her best command voice. "This is a gift for Sahim-Khan with my compliments. Summon him."

The officer laughed harshly. "No one summons the Khan of All the Khurs!"

"Tell him it has to do with the massacre of the nomad camp, and with his pet sorcerer, Faeterus."

Mention of the atrocity stirred the mob behind the elves. Angry shouts and denunciations flew. The elven warriors, tense already, fingered sword hilts and worked to control their restive mounts. Only Kerian remained calm. She sat tall on her bay horse, back straight, eyes never leaving the Khurish officer.

Perhaps it was her calm insistence, or the growling mob behind her, that convinced him, but the officer disappeared from the battlement. For a time nothing happened. Distant thunder rumbled. Flies, drawn by the carrion, tormented everyone. "Unclean!" cried the mob. "Drive the killers out!"

At last the double gates parted. The crowd fell silent. Thunder murmured again.

A double line of Khurish soldiers, twenty in all, marched out the gate. Behind them walked, not Sahim-Khan, but Hakkam, commander of the Khan's army. The soldiers halted and Hakkam strode between their lines, approaching the Lioness.

309

"Lady Kerianseray," he said. He grimaced at the carcass. "You've been hunting, I see."

"No, General. Like a vulture, I only picked up what was already dead. Is Sahim-Khan coming?"

"Of course not. Say what must be said to me."

Sensing that she had gotten as far as she could, she crossed her wrists on the pommel of her saddle and leaned forward over them.

"This stinking carcass is all that remains of a sand beast. I believe they are native to your remote desert." Hakkam conceded they were. "It was slain a few nights ago by Lord Hengriff. You know the man?" Kerian said sarcastically.

Matching her tone, Hakkam replied, "A warrior of considerable prowess. Not the best intriguer."

"This beast was slain in the Harbalah, on the grounds of a villa destroyed by Malys. The beast traveled there from the Valley of the Blue Sands, where it tried to kill me and my entire company."

Her words set the mob surging and muttering again. Kerian raised her voice to be heard above them. "At first I thought it had come across us by accident, but after its first attack, it tracked us across fifty miles of open desert. We passed by the peaceful camp of the Weya-Lu tribe one night on our way to the valley. We did them no harm. The sand beast, on our trail, must have slaughtered them after we passed on."

A profound silence descended. The buzzing of the flies sounded very loud.

"When we fought the beast a final time, we wounded it, and it escaped." Wisely, she didn't cloud the issue with talk of will-o'-the-wisps and the instantaneous transference of the one-ton sand beast from Inath-Wakenti to Khuri-Khan.

"Ask yourself, General Hakkam, ask yourself as I have done, why did this creature, wounded and in agony, turn up on the grounds of a wrecked mansion in your city?"

He folded sinewy arms across his chest and obligingly said, "Why?"

"It was returning to its master, the sorcerer Faeterus, who lived in the ruined mansion. Maddened with pain, it attacked one of my warriors who was keeping an eye on the mage. The fortunate arrival of Lord Hengriff put an end to its murderous rampage."

Hakkam stared at her for a moment longer, eyes narrowed in thought, then slowly approached the dead beast. Its rotting hide was nearly invisible beneath a writhing coat of blowflies. Hakkam was a hardened desert fighter and did not flinch.

"What proof have you?" he called out over the buzz and whir of busy insects.

"The proof of my word, and the proof of logic. I do not kill innocents. A sand beast will, and did."

"And this sorcerer you speak of?"

"At large in your city, perhaps in the palace of the Khan even now. Find him, General. Put your questions to him."

She raised a gloved hand, and in unison her escort wheeled their horses. A crowd of nearly one thousand Khurs packed the back of the square. The Lioness rode back through her warriors and continued unhesitatingly toward the wall of humanity. When the Khurs realized she was not going to turn aside, they scrambled out of her way. The rest of the elves followed her.

An irritated Hakkam spat on the pavement and glanced back at the Khuri yl Nor. He hoped his sovereign had gotten a good whiff of the Lioness's gift. After ordering the rotten carcass hauled away, he went to report to the Khan.

Sahim-Khan was waiting in the inner courtyard. He demanded an explanation. The general gave a brief account of the Lioness's reasons for bringing the dead monster to the palace.

The Khan's expression was odd, unreadable even to his long-time general, but his voice was firm as he replied, "This is a grave affront to the throne of Khur. I will complain to the Speaker."

"Mighty Khan, the Speaker lies gravely wounded in his tent," Hakkam reminded him. "While he is laid low, Kerianseray rules the *laddad*."

The general saluted and was dismissed. He departed quickly so as to hide the faint smile on his face. This also caused him to miss his khan's low, bemused chuckle.

Sahim was intrigued by Kerianseray's argument. The *laddad* had neatly escaped the massacre charge. Thickheaded nomads might still believe the elves had done it, but word would circle the city within hours and the cityfolk would think otherwise. Sand beasts were nearly legendary nowadays, so rarely were they seen, but every Khur knew the stories of their savagery. In olden times, a single sand beast had been known to rip through a herd of two hundred cattle or sheep in a single night. In the territories where the monsters once dwelt in numbers, nomad bands had to erect timber fences to defend their night camps. Even then, many tribesmen still were slain. To have one turn up here, within the city's wall, was indeed a wonder.

Neatly done, lady, Sahim thought, as he reentered the citadel.

Unfortunately, his thoughts turned to Faeterus, and all trace of amusement vanished. He was rapidly losing patience with the wretched mage. Faeterus's machinations were costing the throne of Khur far more than his services were worth. Something would have to be done about that. Soon.

Some distance away, atop the citadel, near where he'd loosed the amazing arrow, Shobbat watched the elves depart and Khurish soldiers drag the dead sand beast away. The smell of corruption reached him even at this height. He turned away, holding a perfumed cloth over his nose.

"Potent smell, isn't it?"

Shobbat flinched. Faeterus was there, where he had not been an instant before.

"I didn't send for you!" the prince gasped.

"I wanted a good vantage point for the spectacle." The hooded mage went to the edge of the balcony and peered down, resting his long fingers on the parapet. "Ugly creature. I wonder how it got from the desert to the city? Surely someone ought to have noticed it wandering through an open gate."

"It appears to have come here from the Valley of the Blue Sands in a single night," Shobbat said, rubbing his hands together. They were unaccountably cold. "It came straight to you. Did you summon it?"

"Certainly not. The stupid creature wanted to kill me. This incident will bear some study."

"Don't come here again, Faeterus. It's too dangerous for me."

The hood turned away from the distant view. "Yes, it is," Faeterus agreed, and then was gone.

Shobbat's legs were trembling. He sat abruptly on the sandstone bench at his back. The mage was out of control, coming and going from the palace at will. Something would have to be done about that. Soon.

Still, he had every reason to feel confident. The elves had made it to the valley, but they'd not stayed. Surely this would overturn the Oracle's prophecy. He had rid himself of Hengriff, who first bribed him, then blackmailed him about the bribery.

The memory of Hengriff's death brought a small smile. In some ways that had been a trial run for the removal of his father. Murder behind closed doors was no good. It aroused opponents, and gave traitors the mantle of pursuing justice. The best assassinations were carried out in public, with loyal supporters standing by. Many of Sahim-Khan's guards were already in Shobbat's pay. More would follow. Then Shobbat would strike.

Soon.

14

Favaronas awoke with a start.

The monstrous creatures of his nightmare were still vivid in his mind, and he ached as if he'd been wrestling a legion of attackers. Three hundred sixteen years he had lived, and here he was sleeping in the desert, dodging murderous nomads, and prowling haunted tunnels. The lovingly shaped halls of Qualinost were far away, in time and distance. How he missed his old life there! The measured pace of the royal library, the smell of venerable parchment, the dust of time collected on the wisdom of the ages. He feared all of that was lost forever.

Profoundly thirsty, he sat up slowly and reached for a handy waterskin. The collar securing the spout was a ring of polished tin. It made a small but perfect mirror. In its mirrored surface he glimpsed something on his reflection that brought a gasp of shock.

Across his neck were four deep, parallel scratches.

He cried out, dropping the leather waterskin and clutching his throat. The wounds did not hurt, but he could feel the beads of clotted blood clinging to them. It had not been a dream! The bloodthirsty shapechangers were real. He had to tell Glanthon at once.

The sun was just peering over the featureless horizon. Its light was faint, as the sky was layered with dull white clouds.

SANCTUARY

Scrambling up the hill to Glanthon's tent, Favaronas found himself caught by the sight. He'd not seen an overcast sky since coming to Khur. It actually looked as though rain was possible. He glanced back at his bedroll, to make certain his parchments were covered.

One of the stone cylinders had unfurled.

Favaronas hurled himself back down the slope, his need to find Glanthon forgotten. Muted sunlight dappled the book. He touched the page. It was cold, stiffer than natural parchment, but no longer stone. It felt like heavy vellum, the sort usually reserved for covers, not text pages. With great care, he unrolled the curled page. It was covered in writing, a neat scribal hand, the ink copper-brown against the yellow vellum. The words were the same abbreviated Elvish as the labels on each cylinder. He couldn't simply read off the contents but would have to decode the abbreviations.

He ransacked his meager supplies for ink, pen, and paper. He must transcribe the writing, get it all down, and worry about deciphering it later.

While he was engrossed, the sun continued its slow rise, the filtered orange light traveling across his bedroll. When the light fell upon the second and third cylinders, they also softened into readable scrolls, the tightly furled pages loosening with a soft *whish*. Favaronas's heart thudded in his chest. What was happening here? The cylinders had been exposed to sunlight before and had not opened. Was it because the clouds were screening the normally harsh sunlight? Was it the first light of dawn? Could it have something to do with his dream that was not a dream?

Just now it did not matter. The mysterious books were open!

Around him, the warriors stirred. A sparse meal was prepared and eaten. Horses were watered and fed. Whenever a warrior passed by, the archivist found himself shielding the open scrolls from view. Without knowing why, he felt a need to keep this development to himself.

When the sun was more fully up, beams of stronger light reached out through gaps in the clouds and fell upon the scrolls. One by one, they curled up again, turning white and hard, becoming stone once more. Favaronas tried to stop the process by shading the books, but the transformation was inexorable. Barely an hour after he noticed the first book opening, all were stone again. He'd managed to copy out only a third of the first tome.

"Good morning!"

The archivist convulsed like a guilty lover. Glanthon had arrived, bearing his gear on one shoulder. "What?" Favaronas said, looking up. "Oh, yes. Good morning."

Glanthon squinted at him. "Are you hurt? What are those marks on your neck?"

Favaronas's hand went to his throat. "This? Nothing. I rolled over on a stone while sleeping and scratched myself."

Glanthon could see no such stones in the immediate area of Favaronas's bedroll, but if the Speaker's archivist didn't want to parade his problems Glanthon would not press the matter.

"We'll be moving out soon. It's two days to the caravan road. I want to keep clear of Kortal itself. Too many Nerakan spies."

Favaronas nodded. What he wanted most right now was for Glanthon to go about his business, so he could begin translating the writing he'd taken down from the first open scroll. He feigned a headache and asked to be left alone until the company actually departed. Unsuspecting, Glanthon wished him better health and left.

The camp grew noisier as the warriors curried their horses, saddled them, and stowed their gear. Favaronas broke his fast with a bag of dried vegetable chips and a cup of water, and tried to make sense of what he'd written.

The writing was like the labels, line after line of abbreviations, without break, punctuation, or capitalization, and only a small tic of the scribe's pen separating each syllable.

Who would record valuable records in such a difficult fashion? Still, if each syllable represented a word in Old Elvish, he should be able to read the entire document. But it would take time. The first line was *nat.hat.om.bar.sem.hoc.ved*. *Nat* could stand for many things, from the word for rooster (*nathi*) to the verb meaning "to behead" (*natcar*).

By the time the company was ready to depart Favaronas had translated four lines, and those only roughly. The book on which he was working was apparently volume three of a longer work. It began in mid-sentence, not unusual in documents from ancient times: ". . . he commanded [us?] to raise the stones as part of the sacred star [or pattern?] that the powers of heaven had buried. [?] might be enhanced in this place. . . ." There followed several words he could not puzzle out, then: "Many were weak and reverted [or changed] by this time. The work went slowly. Many died, and their spirits walked by night, confined by the power [or place?] they sought to control."

Now Favaronas really did feel a headache coming on. The thicket of ambiguous syllables yielded their secrets so slowly he knew translating the cylinders would require weeks of continuous labor. He would never be able to keep their secrets for that long in the confines of Khurinost.

Why keep them a secret at all? He raised the cup of water to his lips with a trembling hand. The answer was terribly clear. Power. A frightening theory was growing in his mind: that the fabled dragonstones were buried under the ruins, that a secret colony had grown up in the valley centuries after the dragonstones were buried, a colony devoted to harnessing their forbidden power. He imagined the ruins were all that remained of an enormous magical operation, intended to allow the colonists to tap the dragonstones as a water-wheel and mill and utilize the power of a flowing stream.

Was the design finished? History did not record the rise of a great city of magic in the Inath-Wakenti. The few lines Favaronas had read implied the colonists died off faster than their work could be completed. Who were they, and why did they die? The fact that their chronicles were written in truncated Silvanesti lent weight to the theory they were elves, but no Speaker of the Stars would have tolerated such an illicit enterprise. Maybe that was the final answer to the mystery of Inath-Wakenti. The builders of the ruins had been rounded up, and perhaps exterminated, by the Speaker of the Stars.

Oh, how he longed for access to the ancient archives of Silvanost. What mysteries they must contain!

He regretted saying as much as he had to Glanthon. Glanthon was a good soldier, but the scope of this revelation was beyond him. He might spread the word to the other warriors, and he would want to turn over anything they found to the Lioness. The Vale of Silence was no place for swords and soldiers. It ought to be quarantined, with access strictly controlled and only the wisest sages and mages allowed inside.

Of course, Favaronas himself did not qualify as either. But wasn't this exactly the task of an archivist, to recover lost records while searching for evidence in the annals of two ancient kingdoms? Who better than he to unravel the secrets of Inath-Wakenti?

Favaronas had learned much from the hardships of this journey. No longer was he merely a beer-loving librarian. His time with the Lioness had taught him the necessity of decisive action. Thus inspired, he moved swiftly now. He wrapped the cylinders in his bedroll, added his notes and the few provisions he had, and tied the resulting bundle with cords. He placed the precious bundle at the foot of the hill, on a large area of soft sand. He swept his footprints away, then dug a hole large enough to contain the bundle and himself if he drew his knees to his chin. Wrapping his belt sash around his face, to protect eyes, nose, and mouth, he lay in the hole and buried himself completely.

For a moment, the weight of the warm sand pressing down on him brought panic. With his head turned to the side, he discovered he could breathe well enough. The sash

filtered the sand from the air. Concentrating on the marvel-
ous knowledge contained in the cylinders he clutched to his
chest, he forced himself to be calm. This was the right thing
to do. He must have time to decode the knowledge contained
in the cylinders. He waited.

"Favaronas! Fa-va-ro-nas!"

Glanthon and other soldiers could be heard calling him.
He felt the vibration of hooves pounding nearby. Sweat pooled
in the hollow of his neck, but he did not answer.

Eventually the calls died away, though it took longer than
he had imagined. Guilt stabbed him. Glanthon sounded very
worried. He kept his soldiers searching for what seemed like
hours, but although the archivist's legs twitched once or
twice with the urge to put an end to his scheme, he did not.
He stayed where he was.

The sand grew warmer as the day wore on, but the unusual layer of clouds kept it from becoming too hot to bear.
Favaronas dozed, waking in terror several times, dreaming
he'd been buried alive or was sharing his hole with those
horrible leaping spiders.

At long last, the heat in the ground abated. He had heard
nothing outside for hours and decided it was safe to emerge.
When he tried to unbend his knees, he found them locked
in place. His arms and hands worked, so he clawed his way
to freedom.

The sun was still up, but sunset was only an hour or
so away. Pain like knife-thrusts gripped both of his legs. It
took an age but finally he was able to straighten them and to
stand.

The walk back to Inath-Wakenti would be a long one, but
night was the best time to cross the desert on foot, if any time
was right. He took up the bundle of cylinders and supplies.

Abruptly, loneliness swamped him, a sense of his own
insignificance in the vastness of the desert. He felt fear bubble
up too. Very little would be required to cause his fear to bloom
into panic, and panic would kill him. He must think clearly

and carefully. He squeezed the bundle in his arms, reveling in the weight of the scrolls.

"I will know all!" he declared. "I will learn all that they can teach me!"

Courage bolstered, he put the lowering orb of the sun at his left hand and set out north across the rocky sand and windblown dunes.

* * * * *

Wind gusted through the sea of tents, flapping roofs, and shivering taut anchor lines. A hard rain had lashed Khurinost just after sunset, and the sodden tents steamed in the cool night air. No one slept. Elves clustered in the narrow lanes or sat in groups before fires in open squares. Talk was of the growing dangers around them—the attempt on the Speaker's life, the murder of Lord Morillon, the attack on the city gates by Khurish fanatics. Morillon was respected by many, the Speaker loved by all, yet no one in Khurinost would survive if the water supply was cut off.

The gates had reopened, but talk turned inevitably to the fact that it could so easily happen again. Half the elves believed it would be necessary to storm Khuri-Khan and secure the wells. The other half felt it was time to leave. Exactly where they would go was a subject of great debate.

With Gilthas sleeping, Kerian took some time for herself. General Hamaramis, a fastidious fellow, owned one of the best bathtubs in Khurinost. His tent was currently unoccupied, as he was with his troops keeping watch on the Khurs, so she stole away for a much-needed bath. Long days in the desert had left her feeling dry, dirty, and wrung out like a washcloth. Worse, the stench of her encounter with the sand beast's carcass could not be overcome by her usual quick ablutions in a basin of water. The odor of decay had permeated every part of her, right down to the roots of her hair. If she didn't clean up soon, she thought it might never come off.

SANCTUARY

Hamaramis's tub was a homemade contraption comprising tent stakes supporting heavy canvas sides, but just now it seemed more luxurious to Kerian than the gold, silver, and porcelain fixtures in the palace of Qualinost. She hauled her own water from a brass tank outside the general's tent, and she didn't bother heating it. It was nearly the warmth of blood anyway, thanks to the Khurish climate.

Long hunted by enemies, the Lioness was too wary to strip to the skin and chose to retain her underclothes. Before stepping into the tub, she carefully combed the thick, grit-encrusted mass of her hair. Sand and tiny gravel cascaded to the floor with every stroke.

The tub wasn't long enough for her to stretch out full-length. Once in, she pulled up her knees and leaned back, submerging head and hair. The clear water turned gray.

The old general disdained soap as an effete affectation, preferring to scrub himself with a sponge. Kerian eyed the creamy brown sponge, which hung on a peg inside the tent, decided it looked rough enough to plane wood; and made do with a scrap of linen for a washcloth.

She straightened her legs, leaning against the back of the tub, and closed her eyes. The tent was quiet, save for intermittent gusts of wind outside and the tapping of some metal object, stirred by the breeze. With effort, she cleared her mind and let the quiet and blessed moisture work their soothing magic. She dozed.

"That looks wonderful."

She didn't start, since she'd heard him coming and recognized his halting gait, but she was surprised to see him.

Looking more than frail, Gilthas leaned against the wooden doorframe. He'd donned a geb, the sleeveless garment hanging loosely without benefit of belt. It bulged over the bandages on his right shoulder. A dressing gown was draped over his shoulders. The stump of a spade handle served him as a cane.

"I can't believe you're up and about," she said.

"It's a shock to me too," he replied, smiling faintly. Without warning, he began to slide off the jamb. Kerian was out of the tub in a flash, catching him before he hit the floor.

Hamaramis's furniture, like the general himself, was rather spare. Kerian eased Gilthas onto a short, unpadded bench and stood looking down at him, hands on hips, dripping on the carpet.

"You shouldn't be out of bed. You'll aggravate your wound."

"It's healed." She looked surprised, and he added, "High Priestess Sa'ida is quite skilled."

"I gave orders she wasn't to be admitted!"

He was taken aback. "Why?"

"It was a human who wounded you. We've had quite enough favors from them!"

Gilthas coughed, wincing. "You wouldn't say that if it was your shoulder," he rasped. But she would, of course.

Annoyed, yet unwilling to berate him while he was so weak, she decided to finish her bath. Taking up Hamaramis's rough sea sponge and stepping back into the tub, she dedicated herself to scrubbing feet and legs while her husband watched.

Finally, the heavy silence and his grim expression were too much. "Whatever it is, just say it!" she said, tossing the sponge into the bath with a splash.

"I'm trying to find the words." His voice was calm, but concern laced every syllable. "You left your command in the Valley of the Blue Sands?"

"Yes."

"Kerian, this is a grave matter."

She nodded. "It wasn't a decision I made lightly. But Glanthon is a competent officer. He'll get his warriors, and Favaronas, home."

"That isn't the point." He paused, then spoke, the words seemingly wrenched from him. "A commander shouldn't abandon her soldiers!"

"I thought you were dead or dying! And I don't need you to school me in how to be a commander!"

"Apparently, you do! My health was totally irrelevant. Your first duty was to your warriors. Leaving them to fend for themselves could be construed as cowardice."

That brought the Lioness to her feet, sending waves of water over the sides of the tub. "How dare you! No one calls me a coward, not even you!"

He leaned back, panting slightly, exertion and emotion taking their toll.

"You're no coward, Kerian. I know that. But your behavior of late has been reckless and dangerous. I'm told you dragged the rotting corpse of a sand beast to Sahim-Khan's door."

With a grim nod, she admitted it.

"Why?" he asked.

She flung out her hands. "To make a point, of course! I was accused of slaughtering unarmed women and children. I realized the sand beast was probably responsible, maybe at the direction of that traitor, Faeterus. If I had simply told the story to Sahim-Khan, he might not have believed me, or he might've ignored me. By putting my case to the people of Khuri-Khan, I ended the lie at once!"

"You have sorely offended Sahim-Khan's dignity."

"I don't care about his dignity!"

She wrung water from her hair and stepped out of the tub. When she looked at her husband again, his face was utterly still, the lines on it seemingly etched twice as deep as before, his gaze fixed on the floor. Concerned, she held out a hand to him, meaning to help him back to bed.

"Do you care about my dignity? You have disobeyed my strictest orders."

The hand dropped to her side. "What orders?" she asked, genuinely confused.

"Not to fight with the Khurish nomads."

"What in Chaos's name are you talking about? *They* attacked us!"

"Then you should have evaded them." He thumped the carpet with his cane.

"They knew where we were going! I couldn't very well evade them and carry out your pointless expedition at the same time!"

He pushed himself upright. His eyes held no anger, only a deep sadness.

"Kerianseray, I love you more than my life," he whispered. Her towering rage drained away. "But I must do what's best for the elven nation," he added. "Your actions continue to provoke our enemies and aggravate our allies. You have consistently made impulsive, reckless choices at a time when the slightest nuances of our deeds can mean life or death."

His posture straightened, and in that instant, her husband was gone. It was the Speaker who addressed her now. "You are removed as commander of my armies."

Had he pulled out a blade and thrust it home, he could not have astonished her more. She stared at him in shock as he went on.

"In time, I trust, you will appreciate why I must make this decision, will understand what an increasingly difficult political situation we're in. Taranath will take command of the cavalry. Hamaramis retains command of my personal guard. You may serve in any company you wish, or you may retire from service."

With that he turned ponderously and, leaning heavily on his makeshift cane, limped out.

Several yards away, in the corridor leading to the tent's main room, Planchet waited. When the Speaker appeared, Planchet covered the distance between them in three long strides.

Many unhappy tasks were required of a monarch. The one he'd just performed had been the very worst. Gilthas turned a gray, sweating face to Planchet and whispered, "It is done. Take me home."

SANCTUARY

* * * * *

Water dried on Kerian's skin. How much time passed, she didn't know, but when she finally came to herself, she was sitting on the rug, her back against the bathtub. Her small-clothes were stiff and dry.

Dismissed. She was dismissed. By her husband!

How many years had she borne arms against the enemies of her people? How long had she shed blood and fought foes more numerous, more powerful, more ruthless than she? She had won and she had lost, many times over, but always she fought on. Never had she quit. And now she was dismissed, cast aside, disparaged.

Gilthas was wrong. She had made mistakes, she admitted that, but her course wasn't reckless, it was *right*. If their people were to survive, they needed bold and vigorous action, not soft words and evasion. Inath-Wakenti was a dead end, as dangerous to the elves as the desert heat and marauding nomads. Perhaps their people weren't yet strong enough to retake Silvanesti and Qualinesti, but they would hardly grow any stronger in this dreary field of tents, living off the charity of barbarous humans. Nor could they grow stronger by crossing the murderous cauldron of the High Plateau only then to face the deadly mysteries in the Valley of the Blue Sands.

No. Elves must take control of elven destiny once more. If Gilthas and his soft advisors couldn't see this, someone would have to show them the way. They clung to an imaginary life, thinking protocol and precedence mattered, thinking politeness and accommodation would keep their people safe. Someone would have to make them understand reality.

The first step to saving the elven race was right here. They must take Khuri-Khan, and use it as their base for striking outward from Khur. Gilthas always had been reluctant to confront Sahim because the human khan had offered the elves sanctuary during their time of trouble, but that sanctuary had come to have much too high a price—and Kerian wasn't

325

thinking only of steel and silver. The life they'd been forced to live, begging humans for every scrap they received, was draining the heart and soul from her people. Sahim-Khan was a liar, a schemer, and a greedy bandit. He deserved no consideration, and less mercy.

With Khuri-Khan in their hands, the elves would have access to the sea. Ships could be commandeered or built, and the Lioness and her fighters would harry the coasts of Silvanesti and Qualinesti. Ships of their former conquerors could be taken, and raids mounted on coastal towns. There were islands with temperate climates in the Southern and Eastern Courrain that would fall to a determined attack. The new elven nation would be a seafaring nation, building their wealth and power against the day they would take back their ancestral lands.

That day would come. Fists clenched, Kerian swore to herself it would come, and not in some dim, distant future, but soon. Very soon.

She got to her feet, dressing quickly in her dirty garments. It was obvious that talking to Gilthas and his advisors would be pointless. She would make her case to the warriors. Like herself, they understood the realities of life. With them behind her, Gilthas would be forced to listen to her. He could be made to see the logical perfection of her plan.

It was fully dark outside, and the wind rushed through the lanes, first one way, then back the other. Rosy haloes glowed inside the clouds overhead. The strange sight halted Kerian, despite the fervor of purpose burning in her breast. Lightning was white or bluish. Even in the gods-blasted wastes of Khur, lightning wasn't red.

As she navigated the twisting byways on her way to the warriors' quarter, she encountered no one. However, she quickly knew she was not alone. A hundred yards from Hamaramis's tent she glimpsed shadows moving behind her. Senses honed by years on the run warned her. The next time there was a flash of scarlet lightning, Kerian whirled

SANCTUARY

abruptly. She saw no one, but had no doubt she was being followed—and by more than one person.

She shucked the scabbard from her sword.

Cooking smoke drifted through the lane. Small black shapes flitted overhead, making faint chirping noises. She'd seen bats in Khur just one other time, the night the ash leaves had fallen on her. Recent events had driven the omen from her mind. Now that memory returned full force.

She continued her march up the alley, making as much noise as she could without being too obvious. Reaching a three-way intersection, she sprang to her right and sprinted down the winding path, taking long strides and landing only on her toes. An old Kagonesti trick, to foil trackers.

She ran far enough to lose her breath, then ducked behind a cloth merchant's stall, its flaps closed for the night. The bats still flickered overhead, dodging between the canvas rooftops. When they had passed, silence descended. No sounds of pursuit reached her ears. She stepped out of hiding to continue on her way, and her bare feet trod on soft, green leaves.

Without looking, she knew they were ash leaves.

Fresh air teased her back. Turning, she glanced back along the twisting lane. The overlapping edges of the fabric roofs flapped lazily, then settled again. Wind puffed down the path, making the tents belly in and out like the breathing of enormous animals. All but one. One tent didn't flex—because someone was pressed against it.

Kerian set her feet firmly and gripped her sword hilt in both hands. She didn't have long to wait.

Four figures dashed into view. The leader held a hooded lamp, and when he saw Kerian he opened the shutter wide. Bright light dazzled her, so she lunged forward and swatted the brass lamp away. It landed in the sand, flickered, and kept burning, but less brightly.

Recovering from her lunge, she heard her attackers draw swords, one after the other. The first, the one who'd held the lamp, thrust at her, throwing himself off balance in his zeal to reach her. She bound up his blade in a parry and drove him back with a punch to his nose. A second attacker came at her, point first. She swung up at him in a wide arc. Their blades met, and the force of her swing sent his sword flying. Completing the circle, she beat aside the blade of the first attacker and repaid him in full, shoving the tip of her sword through his collar bone, deep into his chest. Blood welled.

Her attackers were strong and fast. Dressed in gebs, they wore gray cloth masks that completely covered their heads. They carried Silvanesti-style swords, but that meant little. Local artisans had taken to making such blades to peddle to the elves, who did not care for the guardless Khurish swords. The craftsmen's ingenuity had sparked a fad for laddad-style weapons among the youths of Khuri-Khan.

As she held them off, she shouted for help. No one answered. This part of Khurinost seemed deserted. The Lioness was on her own.

She snatched up the fallen lamp and used it like a shield, fending off sword points. One of her three remaining foes got too close, and she clouted him with the lamp. He went down, but his hard head broke the oil reservoir off. The lamp died. She dropped it, and a blade found her empty hand. It scored a deep cut along the back of her left wrist.

Rapid footfalls told her that at last someone was coming. Her hope of assistance died quickly when she saw the new arrivals wore gray hoods. Having whittled her attackers to two, they now swelled to eight.

She flung herself at a tent wall, sword outthrust. She sawed the stiff canvas and dove headfirst through the opening.

The tent was used for storage. Only baskets and sacks greeted Kerian's eyes. She dodged around them, slashed through the opposite wall, and found herself back outside, in a parallel street.

Scarlet lightning danced above her, and the wind played down the lanes in gusty waves. Tents flapped. Somewhere nearby a metal bucket got loose and clanged end over end, driven by the freakish wind.

From the noise they were making, Kerian knew her attackers had split up. Some were coming through the holes she'd made in the tent while others were circling the tent to try and cut her off. She saw no glory or purpose in dying just now, so she took to her heels. Her hand was bleeding, leaving a distinct trail in the sand. Even a goblin could track her now.

A single set of rapid footfalls closed in behind her. When they got close enough, she threw herself on her face and let the assassin overrun her. In a flash she was up, and had run him through. He dropped to his knees. She dodged in front of him and tore the hood from his head.

He was an elf, a Silvanesti!

Placing her bare foot on his chest, she shoved him onto his back. With her sword tip at his throat, she cried, "Why are you doing this? Who put you up to it?"

He writhed in agony. His comrades were coming fast behind them. Kerian repeated her question, letting her blade draw blood.

"The prince!" he rasped. "The prince of Khur!"

Thunderstruck, she dropped to the sand beside the dying elf. She took hold of his geb and dragged him up till they were nose to nose.

"Why? Why does Shobbat want me dead?"

"For the throne of his father."

That made no sense, but he was past answering any other questions.

The rest of the murderous band was upon her. She snatched up the dead elf's sword. In the weird light of wind-blown torches and red lightning, the Lioness went through the remaining assassins like a reaper through hay. One of her early teachers was a master of two-sword fighting, which he always claimed was superior to any other type. The secret, he said, was to let your opponent parry, then counterstrike while his blade was engaged. On this night, she put his teachings to the ultimate test.

The assassins were nimble and capable fighters, but they had never faced a warrior like the Lioness. One by one they fell, stabbed or slashed by one of her whirling blades. None fled. Their orders were clear.

The last fellow fought best against her, slicing a bloody line on her right arm and another on her left cheek, before she broke through and impaled him with both her swords at once.

He collapsed, and she released her blades, allowing his dead body to carry them to the ground. For a moment she stood, covered in their blood and her own, breath coming in gasping gulps, then the strength left her legs. She dropped to her knees, then fell facedown onto the bloody, hard-packed ground.

15

The cavalry spent fruitless hours sweeping the dunes for Favaronas. Worried, but unable to delay further, Glanthon resumed the trek southwest.

The sun was touching the western dunes, painting the broad desert in shades of gold, when Glanthon rode to the top of a sand ridge overlooking the caravan trail to Kortal. It was always a busy trail, thick with long trains of plodding donkeys burdened by panniers of goods, or herds of goats and shaggy desert sheep. Hundreds of Khurish nomads plied the caravan route every day, carrying goods from south to north and back. Trade had never ceased, even during the most terrifying days of the late war.

The trail was empty today. As far as Glanthon could see in both directions, nothing stirred but the wind, carrying streams of sand across the packed roadbed.

Inath-Wakenti had seemed the most isolated spot in the world. After its emptiness, Glanthon would have welcomed the company even of scruffy humans. Instead, he found their isolation persisting.

He descended the ridge to the road. Years of traffic had left it sunken a foot deep. From horseback, he could tell that not only had no one passed by today, no one had passed by in several days. The desert wind, constant as breath, had erased all but a few prints. In another day there'd be no marks left at all.

Had some calamity overtaken Kortal? War, plague, sand-storms—many possibilities sprang to mind.

The rest of the expedition appeared on the ridge. Glan-thon whistled and waved them down. Of the five hundred riders (and three scholars) who'd left Khurinost with Keri-anseray, just under three hundred remained. To be honest, Glanthon found the most recent loss, of Favaronas, cut him the deepest, because the archivist had vanished while he himself was in charge.

His second-in-command, a Qualinesti named Arimathan, rode up. Glanthon hailed him. "We seem to be alone in the world. What do you make of this strange situation?"

"The nomads are gone," said the laconic Arimathan.

"Yes, but where have they gone?" No sooner had Glan-thon said this, than an awful answer entered his mind.

"Form up two lines!" he barked. "All who have bows, string them! Keep them braced and ready!"

The elves obeyed, but questioned him with puzzled looks.

"The nomads have left their territory! They'd only do that in the direst circumstances. And where would they go? Khuri-Khan! They must have gone to Khuri-Khan!"

He chivvied his elves until all were ready. The entire command set out at a trot, down the caravan road.

Anxiety knotted Glanthon's chest. He could be wrong, but he didn't think so. It all made terrible sense. The nomads, having decided to drive the foreigners from their land, were no longer satisfied to fight the Lioness's small band of explor-ers. They had gathered their people together and ridden to Khuri-Khan, to strike at the source of the *laddad* contagion, to destroy Khurinost.

* * * * *

Shobbat sat in a heavy mahogany chair regarding an elegant goblet. The silver had been hammered paper-thin. The bowl was small as a child's fist and, from certain angles, translucent, allowing the delicate amber nectar inside to shine through. The utmost care and concentration were required to handle and drink from such an ethereal cup. Each one was unique, made by an elf artisan enjoined by law to create only a single such vessel every ten years. Since the coming of the *laddad* to Khur, Shobbat had acquired sixteen of these precious vessels. He'd ruined four before learning how to hold them. These so-called cloud cups were among his most treasured possessions, relics of a vanishing culture that would not rise again if he had his way.

Not one of his hand-picked assassins had returned. He found this very unsettling. So much so, he'd had to set the cloud cup on the table at his elbow. In his current state of agitation, he would surely snap the slender stem and crush the airy fineness of the bowl. Since the laddad soon would be extinct, he must preserve those of their arts he found attractive.

Surely enough time had passed for his hirelings to carry out their mission. How hard was it to kill one female?

Even as he posed the question to himself, he knew the answer: In the case of the Lioness, very hard indeed.

The resources of the Knights of Neraka been devoted to capturing or killing her for many ineffective years. That's why Shobbat had hired Silvanesti for the task. These particular elves had no attachment to Kerianseray. They didn't revere her past deeds, as the Qualinesti did, and like most who had once lived in luxury, they had not adapted well to their current poverty. Shobbat merely added plenty of steel to their own sense of noble purpose. As elves, they had the stealth and senses to reach the Lioness. He thought it a neat solution to a thorny problem. Every hunter knows that the best way to trap a jackal is with a trained jackal.

Shobbat didn't like elves. Even in exile they reeked of smug superiority and condescension. On the other hand, he didn't hate them. Hate was a failing only the lowly could afford. A king must be above such petty sensations, lest they cloud his mind. No, the destruction of the elves was simply a necessary action if he was to circumvent the Oracle's prophecy. They had to go, and that was that.

It wasn't murder, but an act of statesmanship. Monarchs—and monarchs-to-be—did not commit crimes. The elves represented an obstacle to his attaining the throne of Khur. He'd overcome so many others: the meddling Hengriff who was nearly as smug as the *laddad,* the high priest Minok (no one would ever find him), and the smooth *laddad* schemer, Morillon. Removing him had been a spur of the moment decision. Shobbat realized Morillon had too much of the Khan's ear to be allowed to live. Too often his clever tongue unhinged Shobbat's carefully arranged plans.

He'd made certain the *laddad* noble was found. His death sowed doubt about Sahim-Khan's authority and confusion about his loyalties. Shobbat had failed to kill the *laddad* king, but even wounding him had been very helpful. The *laddad* blamed Torghanists for the crime, just as the Sons of the Crimson Vulture blamed Sahim-Khan for the disappearance of their high priest. Everyone was in a proper turmoil and, at the right moment, Shobbat would step forward to restore order and bring glory to Khur once again.

Only two more needed to die before Shobbat moved against his father. One was the *laddad* queen, and the other, the slippery sorcerer, Faeterus. Shobbat knew he would have the most trouble with the mage. Faeterus came and went like smoke through a chimney, making him difficult to poison or stab. Perhaps the best way to get rid of a mage was to use magic.

The night crept by like a craven cur, fearful of being noticed. Shobbat's servants had long since retired, leaving their master alone in his sitting room on the east side of the royal citadel. He passed the time by considering how he would redecorate the private quarters of the khan, once he held that position. His father reveled in the acquisition of wealth, a trait Shobbat shared, but Sahim had no taste, no sense of style. His quarters were a jumble of possessions, thrown together without any regard for arrangement or aesthetics.

Why didn't even one of his hired blades return with news of success or failure? Perhaps Kerianseray had managed to evade death. Shobbat considered the worst possible case, that she had discovered her masked assailants were elves and forced one to reveal who hired him. What would she do then? She would go to her husband—not for protection but to get her liege's sanction for her vengeance. But Gilthas was still very ill. Kerianseray had forbidden Holy Sa'ida even to see him.

Shobbat was in the most secure place in Khur. He had already destroyed an important Knight of Neraka. He had little to fear from one laddad female, even one so fierce as the Lioness. Except for her barbaric ploy with the sand beast, Kerianseray hadn't stirred from the elven camp since her husband was wounded.

He put out his hand and let the weight of the goblet rest on his fingertips. He brought it to his mouth. One never touched a cloud cup with one's lips. Instead, he held it a hair's breadth above his open mouth and allowed a slender stream of nectar to pour from the cup and down his throat.

* * * * *

Kerian did not return to the Speaker's tent. Wounded, she continued on to her original destination, the one place she felt she belonged. The warriors' enclave. Almost half the army was in the field, patrolling the desert outside Khurinost. The rest were astonished when she staggered in amongst them, wan and bleeding. They settled her on a stool and put a clay cup of raisin wine in her hand. An elf knelt by her and began to dress her sword cuts.

"The Khurs are plotting against us!" she declared, describing her narrow escape from assassins. She did not mention her attackers were Silvanesti; more important was the one who had hired them. "They killed Lord Morillon, tried to kill the Speaker, and they've tried to slay me twice!"

"What shall we do, Commander?" asked a Qualinesti veteran.

She opened her mouth to give orders, then closed it with a snap. She gulped sweet raisin wine then said, "I am no longer commander of the army. The Speaker has relieved me."

Surprise did not rob them of their voices. Numerous warriors demanded to know why.

"I was told that my transgressions were these: I left my company in the field to fly to my husband's side. I fought nomads who attacked me first." She lifted her head and stared at the elves around her. "I who have fought with all my strength to save the elven race from destruction! I continue to fight! If you'll follow me, we can save our people!"

Her appeal met with a mixed reaction. The warriors of long service, whether Silvanesti or Qualinesti, found the idea of flouting the Speaker's authority deeply troubling. Others, younger fighters who'd known no other leader than the Lioness, were not so hesitant. Two stood, then six, then ten, vowing to follow the Lioness wherever she led. In moments, nearly half the warriors present had declared for her.

It was to the rest that she addressed herself. "I know you wish to keep faith with the Speaker. That is your choice. But know this: He is consumed by a dream to transplant the elven nation to a hidden valley in the Khalkist Mountains, the place from which I have just returned. I tell you now, that valley is no place for us. It is rife with strange magic, which cost our band a dozen warriors. And there is no game; no deer, no rabbits, not even insects or birds live in the valley."

She paused to watch the elf work on her hand, then added, "There's only one true home for us, the home in which we were born! I swear I will dedicate my life to freeing those homes from the foreign oppressors who hold them now. The Speaker"—she swallowed hard—"has given the homeland up. He thinks we can live happily in a tiny foreign valley, kept safe only by the good graces of the Khan of Khur and our neighbors beyond the mountains, the Knights of Neraka!"

Her stirring, heartfelt speech moved many of the holdouts to declare for her, but a number of warriors still remained silent. They stood and made to leave the warriors' communal tent. A few younger elves moved to stop them, but Kerian waved them off.

"Let them go," she said. "They're honorable warriors. They must follow their own hearts."

"They'll go to the Speaker!" one of her supporters protested.

"They should. He needs to know where we stand."

The officers dispersed to rouse their sleeping troops. Even should some of the troops switch sides, Kerian reckoned she would have seven to eight thousand elves pledged to her. That would give Gilthas pause. It was one thing to consider arresting a few malcontents, quite another to restrain eight thousand seasoned warriors.

By the time Kerian's loyalists assembled on the north side of Khurinost dawn was breaking. A column of riders appeared from the south, heading straight for them. This was the night patrol led by Taranath. He'd mistaken Kerian's band for his morning relief.

As economically as she could, Kerian explained she had broken with Gilthas. She didn't try to minimize her own failings, but laid out the whole tale.

Taranath listened in silence and when she was done said, "This is the wrong course, Commander. You're splitting the army, and a divided host is a weakened host."

The most ardent among her supporters began to shout challenges at Taranath, demanding to know whether he believed it was their destiny to regain their lost lands.

Before he could answer, a third column of riders emerged from Khurinost and rode steadily toward them. At their head was old Hamaramis, in full martial splendor. With him were the officers who had first declined to stand with Kerian.

When Hamaramis drew near he called, "Lady, give over your sword to me at once! Those are the Speaker's orders!"

His use of her title rather than her rank caused her to flinch slightly. Some of the older elves tended to prefer her title as a matter of course, but the difference had taken on a new significance now that Gilthas had dismissed her.

Recovering, she smiled a dark and dangerous smile. "If the Speaker wants my sword, he'll have to ask for it in person."

"Please don't provoke a fight, lady," Taranath pleaded quietly.

"Then don't fight me, Taran. Join me."

The sky above was still cloudy, but a narrow band of clear air lay on the eastern horizon. The disk of the rising sun shone through that clear band, flooding the desert with roseate light. The brilliance only made the clouds appear even darker by contrast.

"What will it be?" she asked. "Our swords together, hilt to hilt, or opposed, point to point?"

An elf in Taranath's company interrupted, drawing their attention to the city. The battlements of Khuri-Khan bristled with signal flags. Even as the elves turned to look, the deep blat of rams' horns rang out from the city, sounding a general alarm.

"The Khurs think we're going to attack!" growled Hamaramis.

"And so we should," Kerian retorted. "Take the city. Make it the base from which our campaign begins!"

The old general, twice her age, stared at her from under his dented, gilded helmet. "You've gone mad, lady," he said soberly. "Utterly mad."

SANCTUARY

The conclave was interrupted again. A trio of elven scouts came galloping across the western desert, bent low over their racing steeds. Before they reached the mass of cavalry, one rider slid from his horse. His back bristled with arrows. The other two kept coming.

They rode straight into the center of the three forces gathered on the slight rise west of Khuri-Khan. Somewhat confused by the presence of three senior commanders, they saluted the Lioness.

"Commander! An army of nomads approaches!"

Hamaramis was all set to inform them that he, not the Lioness, was in command, but their news drove the words from his lips. Consternation was general and loud. Only the Lioness seemed unfazed.

"How many, and where?" she snapped.

Some ten thousand nomads were approaching from the west, one scout reported. They were no more than six miles away.

Recollecting himself, Hamaramis called for couriers. One he sent to carry the news to the Speaker. Three others were to ride through Khurinost, alerting the people in general.

"What are the people to do then?" Kerian demanded. Her horse began to prance, sensing her agitation. "Follow me, and we'll stop the nomads before they reach the tents!"

"They may not be hostile," said Hamaramis, though even he did not believe this. The last time so great a concentration of nomads had assembled in Khur was to aid Salah-Khan against the hordes of Malys. Khurish tribes didn't congregate in such numbers for any purpose but war.

From the ranks of Hamaramis's escort emerged Hytanthas Ambrodel. The captain was still bandaged from his encounters with the manticore and sand beast.

"Commander, shall I fetch Eagle Eye?" he said, raising his voice to be heard over the ceaseless bleating of the horns in Khuri-Khan.

"No time for that." Kerian looked west, from whence ten thousands nomads approached. "Just cut his tether," she added. "He'll seek me out."

He hurried away as she wrenched her horse around. "General Hamaramis, an enemy is near. You can arrest me later. Right now we have a battle to fight."

She spurred forward, with her loyalists streaming after her. Without being ordered, the elves from the night patrol behind Taranath broke ranks and followed as well. Hamaramis's two hundred warriors stirred, anxious to join their comrades. Some called for permission to ride after the Lioness.

Hamaramis said, "The Speaker of the Sun and Stars earnestly wishes to avoid war. Those are his orders. I obey my Speaker."

Turning his horse, Hamaramis started back down the low dune for Khurinost, now alive with alarm. The first two rows of his warriors followed him, but the rest remained rooted where they were, dividing desperate glances between the disappearing Lioness and their valiant old leader. Someone finally snapped reins with a loud crack and bolted after the Lioness. Most others joined in, leaving Taranath, Hamaramis, and a couple dozen or so riders behind.

Dawn's light washed Taranath's agonized expression. "I want to go, too," he whispered.

"So do I." Hamaramis unbuckled his helmet and pried it off. Barely sunup, and already he was sweating. "But being a soldier means more than lusting for battle. It means you obey the orders of your lawful superiors. If you don't, you're no more than a barbarian."

He replaced his helmet. Proudly, the old warrior returned to his Speaker. With him went fourteen warriors. General Taranath fought his conscience for a few seconds more, then rode off with a handful of others to join the Lioness. For today, he was a barbarian.

* * * * *

SANCTUARY

From a ridge northwest of the city, Adala scrutinized Khuri-Khan. By the muted light of the cloudy new day, the place was little more than a brown smudge above the desert sands, but it was the first true city she'd ever seen. For days in advance of her arrival she'd sent spies into Khuri-Khan to learn what Sahim-Khan and the laddad were doing. The news they brought was very troubling. The laddad came and went as they pleased, while the Khan's soldiers had violated the Temple of Torghan and arrested his holy priests. The holy ones were being blamed for an attack upon two laddad, an attack most likely done by thieves or beggars. To the chiefs and warmasters gathered with Adala it sounded as though the foreigners had Sahim-Khan doing their bidding.

"What shall we do, Weyadan?" asked Hagath, chief of the Mikku.

In the still air, the bearded men were sweating profusely. Even lifelong desert-dwellers needed a breeze. Adala gathered the long braid of her hair and pulled it forward over her shoulder. This helped cool her neck only a little.

"I will speak to the khan of the laddad," she announced.

The men were shocked. What purpose could there be in talking to the foreign invaders?

"Their necks are on the block. If the laddad swear to leave our homeland, I would let them go."

"What about the massacre of our parents, wives, and children?" cried Bindas.

With her eyebrows and eyelashes singed off, Adala's face looked stark and fearless. "The guilty will not escape. Their lives are part of our price. If the laddad khan gives over the killers of our people, then his nation may depart in peace, but they must go out from Khur!"

Bindas asked who should go with her to meet the elves. Adala proposed they all go. She felt it would be best for the chiefs and warmasters of the tribes to hear what the foreigners said, and how she answered them.

The party rode out, flanked by riders carrying spears with inverted water jugs on their points, the traditional nomad symbol of truce. At Adala's command the men kept their swords sheathed and bows unstrung. She herself went unarmed, as always.

During their discussions, thunder had rumbled. As they crested a long ridge, a fork of lightning flashed directly over Adala's party, and thunder cracked immediately. The horses shied, but the anxious horde of nomads let out a cheer. Those on High were signifying their favor again! Anyone could see it. The fire from on high followed the Weyadan and did not harm her.

A small patrol of elven cavalry saw the party of nomads come trotting out of the desert. The patrol had not yet heard of the nomad horde's approach, but they were wary of the small band in front of them. One of the elves recognized the truce sign and explained to his captain the meaning of the upside-down pots on the escorts' spears.

"Send a message to Lord Planchet," the captain said calmly. "Tell him some nomads are paying us a friendly visit." He turned to the courier. "Emphasize *friendly*."

The sun had risen beyond the clear air on the eastern horizon and was once more sheathed in clouds. The courier galloped in and out of uncharacteristic sprinkles of rain. By the time they entered Khurinost, horse and rider were trailing wisps of steam.

The Speaker and his closest advisors were assembled in the circular audience hall in his repaired tent. One by one various couriers relayed their news. Word of Kerianseray's revolt set the councilors humming. When this was paired with notice of the arrival of ten thousand nomads, the conversation grew heated indeed. Gilthas had sent orders for Kerian to halt her advance on the nomads and return to Khurinost, but he had no confidence she would heed his command.

The sodden courier delivered his news, that nomad leaders wished to meet with the Speaker of the Sun and

Stars, and that they carried the nomad symbol for a friendly parley.

With that, the room fell still. Gilthas said, "I will meet them."

"Great Speaker, no!" Planchet burst out. "It's not wise or safe. Let me go in your stead." Healed of his fever and wound, the Speaker still was weak and found it difficult to walk or stand for extended periods. Seeing the leader of the elves in such a state might embolden the nomads.

Reluctantly, Gilthas was forced to agree with his old friend's assessment.

* * * * *

There was no time to organize an awe-inspiring procession of elven strength. From his days in masquerade, Hytanthas Ambrodel had learned enough about the nomads to tell the Speaker they would not respect Planchet if he showed up alone or in too ragged a fashion. So a fine white horse was secured for the Speaker's valet. With a retinue that included a hundred mounted warriors and Captain Ambrodel, Planchet rode out of Khurinost. First, he must head off the Lioness. The parley would be pointless if she launched an attack.

He found her leading eighteen thousand warriors, over half the elven army, along the ridge northwest of Khuri-Khan. Her headlong charge had slowed to a walk as her well-honed tactical sense took over. She'd sent out numerous scouts, and was awaiting their return when Planchet's delegation overtook her.

"Lady, in the name of the Speaker of the Sun and Stars, I command you to return to Khurinost with all your riders!" Planchet said.

"I answer to a higher power than the Speaker now," she replied, reining up. "The elven people."

"The nomads have asked for a parley. Are you so bent on war you won't let me talk to them?"

She shrugged. "Talk all you want, it won't change a thing. The Khurs want our blood."

Time was short. Amid echoing thunder, Planchet put his white horse next to Kerian's bay.

"Stay your hand, lady," he urged. "For one hour, I beg of you."

Like the ardent young officers at her back, he held his breath. He could watch the thoughts progress across her face, like the play of sun and shadows on the desert sands. Despite the shared years that lay between them, he had no certainty she would give him the time he needed.

At last, she nodded. "For an old friend, one hour. Less, if the nomads move against Khurinost."

Planchet nodded and dug in his spurs. His entourage bolted down the dune after him. Relief at the Lioness's agreement quickly faded, swallowed by new worry. The valet felt like an impostor. For all his gifts, he did not have the regal bearing or poise that came naturally to his liege. His physique was long, but slightly stooped, his hair bleached dead white by the Khurish sun. He was no one's idea of a king—or khan, for that matter.

The chiefs of the nomads heard the horn blasts and saw dust trails rising into the leaden sky.

Adala was bent forward on Little Thorn's back, hands busily working. Wapah saw she had a small rattan basket. The binding on the rim had become frayed, and she was replacing it with a fresh strand of grass.

"The khan of the *laddad*," Wapah whispered. She nodded.

"I will be done before he arrives."

As the elves drew closer, the nomad chiefs and warmasters sat up straighter on their sturdy ponies. The elves were mounted on long-legged horses, making them seem taller. Seated as she was on her faithful donkey, Adala was the lowest person in the entire group. She was also, as always, the only woman present, She gave no sign of noticing any of this. Instead, she finished her repair of the basket, working the ends of the new rim into place, then hung the container from the short horn on her saddle.

The elf on the white horse leading the others stopped. Looking up and down the line of nomad chiefs, he announced, "I am Planchet, councilor to the Speaker of the Sun and Stars, monarch of all the elves."

Mild surprise rippled through the human assembly. He had spoken in Khur.

Adala seemed unimpressed. She replied in the Common tongue, "I am Adala Fahim, Saran di Kyre, Weyadan of the Weya-Lu, and keeper of the maita. I would speak to your khan."

Now the elves were caught off guard. Planchet regarded the black-draped, motherly woman with surprise. Clearly, he had expected to be dealing with one of the fierce-looking men. "Our Speaker is engaged. I represent him," he said.

"And I speak for the Weya-Lu, the Mikku, the Tondoon, and the Mayakhur."

"You are the leader of all those tribes?"

"In this cause, by the will of Those on High, I am."

"I am honored to meet you. How shall I address you?"

"She is Weyadan or Maita," Wapah offered. Some of the chiefs glowered at him for speaking out of turn.

Planchet recognized the second word as meaning something like "destiny" or "luck." He chose the other, less emotional, title. "I am honored to meet you, Weyadan. There are many swords here today. How can we keep them in their scabbards?"

"Many transgressions have been committed against our people by the *laddad*. I tell you only two: You are foreigners, and you are invaders."

"We have the permission of Sahim-Khan to dwell in his country," Planchet countered.

"Sahim-Khan will answer to Those on High for his venality."

"So shall we all, Weyadan."

Adala's dark eyes hardened. "You send spies to measure our land. You have entered a valley sacred to Those on High. This is sacrilege."

"Our Speaker meant no blasphemy," Planchet replied evenly. "We need a place to live where the climate is not so harsh. He heard the Valley of the Blue Sands was such a place. We had never heard it was sacred. We thought only that there we would be out of your desert and away from your cities. Desecration was not our intention."

A snort of disbelief came from one of the younger warmasters. The chiefs around him, although plainly just as skeptical, glowered at him for his breech of manners.

Adala never took her eyes from Planchet. "What's done is done, and you must answer for it."

"We must dwell some place, Weyadan. It is the right of every living being to have a home."

"You had homes and lost them. The gods have turned their backs on you, *laddad*."

From his place behind Planchet, Hytanthas listened to the exchange with growing annoyance. He had expected the nomads' leader to be a simple, uncouth fanatic. This woman was neither. There was strength in her, strength even the young Qualinesti recognized, but while Planchet was mindful of the diplomatic niceties, she persisted in hurling insults and epithets.

Planchet tried to reason around Adala, saying dark forces had conspired to deprive the elves of their homelands and they sought only to take their fate in their own hands and find a new sanctuary. If some customs of the desert folk had been transgressed, he regretted it, but the survival of the elven race required bold measures.

"What of the customs of war?" Adala asked, her entire demeanor suddenly eloquent of barely suppressed fury. "The custom that one does not murder wives and mothers, children and the aged, those who cannot fight!"

The tenor of the meeting changed instantly. Hatred emanated from the nomads, like the heat of the desert. Planchet was taken aback. After the Lioness's ill-conceived but undeniably dramatic gesture with the dead sand beast, he'd put the rumored massacre out of his mind. Like the city-dwelling Khurs, the elves now believed that if the deaths had happened, they were the work of a wild beast.

Unfortunately, the nomads knew nothing about that or about the possible involvement of the rogue Faeterus. They still blamed the Lioness's troops for the deaths of their families.

Hoping her answer would help him formulate a response, Planchet asked Adala to explain her accusations.

"Hundreds of Weya-Lu were murdered near the entrance to the Valley of the Blue Sands. No warriors were present, only children, women, old people; yet every one was cruelly slain. Not simply put to the sword, but ripped to pieces, then set afire!"

"Why do you think we are responsible?" he asked.

"We found tracks of *laddad* horses, of a *laddad* army, nearby. The Khan's soldiers were in the city, and no foreign soldiers have come over the mountains since the red beast perished. The only killers in the area were the *laddad* army and its female warmaster!"

Hytanthas could remain silent no longer. Before Planchet could speak, the younger elf burst out, "General Kerianseray didn't slaughter anyone! It was a sand beast controlled by the will of an evil sorcerer! It nearly killed me, too!"

His outburst provoked the nomads. The younger warmasters actually drew swords. Planchet, alarmed, raised a placating hand. At his back, he heard the concerted creak of a hundred elven bows being drawn, all because of this simple gesture. If his arm fell, the nomads would die.

"Stay your hands!" Planchet said sharply, realizing his error.

Adala spoke with equal harshness to her nomads. Swords were grudgingly sheathed. Bowstrings relaxed. Adala's gaze skewered Hytanthas.

"The Speaker's woman led the *laddad* in the desert," she said. "That I know. Who is this sorcerer you speak of?"

At Planchet's nod, Hytanthas told her what they had learned of Faeterus, that he was in the Khan's pay, was perhaps an elf, but certainly a criminal, and had caused the massacre with one of his nefarious creatures.

The nomad delegation muttered among themselves. Adala appeared to weigh something in her mind, found an answer, then folded her hands across her donkey's neck.

"Very well. Planchet of the *laddad*, tell your Speaker this: Those on High teach us mercy is the gift of the strong, so I grant you mercy. You may go in peace."

The elven warriors were astonished, Planchet less so. "Go where, Weyadan?" he asked.

"Anywhere beyond the borders of Khur."

"And if we refuse?"

Eye to eye, Adala stared at her opponent. In her black matron's robes, the Weya-Lu woman did not look much like the loyal bodyguard of the elven Speaker, but inside, their hearts were made of the same stern stuff. Both knew it.

"Then there will be war. Terrible war, with no conclusion but annihilation."

Adala's words sent a chill through everyone present. An instant later, a cold breeze swept over the dunes, carrying heavy droplets of rain and more than a little sand.

Members of both delegations were shifting on their mounts, eyeing each other, muttering to their comrades. Planchet did not move. He kept his attention on the Weyadan. She had not moved either, and something told him she was not done yet. He was right.

"In exchange for this mercy," she said, "you must give us the slayers of our families, both of them. We will do them justice."

SANCTUARY

At that Hytanthas jostled forward. Planchet snagged his reins, stopping him well short of the nomads, but Bilath, Bindas, and Hagath of the Mikku interposed themselves between their leader and the furious young elf.

"Our commander is not a murderer!" Hytanthas shouted. "As for the mage, we want him too. You cannot charge his crimes to us! Savages! You're the ones who murdered Lord Morillon, aren't you? What mercy did you show him? He was left to rot in the desert with his throat slashed!"

"Be silent!" Planchet cried in as great a voice as anyone had ever heard him use. "Go back to camp! Now!"

Snatching his reins free, Hytanthas galloped back through the lines of the escort. He did not return to the city as ordered, but galloped directly over the intervening sand hills to where the Lioness was poised with her army. Only his wound had kept him from joining her in the first place; not even that would stop him now.

Adala looked to the dark sky. Would her maita come forth again? Would the fire from on high strike down the *laddad*? Or would the sun break free of its shroud and shine on her, highlighting her righteous cause?

Neither happened. Instead, a squall of tepid rain lashed the motionless parties. Adala drew her veil close around her face and pointed an accusing finger at Planchet.

"It is on your head!" she intoned. "The choice of life or death, war or peace, is yours. Give over the Speaker's woman and the *laddad* sorcerer. You have until the next sunrise. Ever after, we are enemies!"

He made no reply, only sat stiffly in the saddle as the rain poured down. Adala turned Little Thorn's head and trotted away. Her warmasters and chiefs filed behind her, watching the elves warily for signs of treachery.

Rain fell harder. Finally, Planchet tilted his head back, to let the rain wash down his sorrowful face.

"Save us all from true believers," he muttered.

PAUL B. THOMPSON & TONYA C. COOK

* * * * *

Sahim-Khan strode briskly through the corridors of his citadel while horns blasted outside. Every living soul in the Khuri yl Nor was in motion, running hither and yon, carrying arms or foodstuffs or valuables deeper into the fortress. Sahim parted the chaos as he went. Even in their terror of a nomad attack, servants moved nimbly out of his way. In the citadel courtyard, he found General Hakkam and Prince Shobbat.

"Why are the nomads here?" Sahim demanded.

Hakkam said, "We don't know, Mighty Khan. The city gates have been shut, and the garrison mustered on the walls."

Shobbat put a soft fist to his lips and coughed discreetly. His father roughly bade him speak up.

"Mighty Khan, the nomads obviously have come to make war on the *laddad*. Perhaps the Torghanists stirred them up." Shobbat paused, assuming a thoughtful air. "The *laddad* Speaker sent an armed company to the Khalkist Mountains on a mysterious errand. They violated Weya-Lu territory, and it's said they massacred two thousand women and children in their beds."

The Khan snorted. "A lie. Only two hundred were killed, and it appears a sand beast committed that crime." He turned to his general. "Hakkam, how many riders can you field?"

"Five thousand on short notice, Mighty Khan. More, given time."

"Gather your troops. You are to drive the nomads back into the desert. How dare they bear arms before my city! When I'm done with them, they'll think the sand beast a gentle pet!"

Hakkam bowed and was about to go when Shobbat laid a hand on his father's arm, saying, "Wait, Mighty Khan!" Hakkam paused, and Sahim looked at his son as if he'd lost his mind. Shobbat released him, adding quickly, "Sire, don't be too hasty! Perhaps this dire situation can yield a great harvest for Khur! Let the fight go forward. Whoever wins, Khur will be a better place for the loser's absence."

Sahim made a fist and knocked his son to the ground with a single blow.

"Idiot! Dolt! Fool! What are you thinking? I have given the *laddad* my protection! How strong will our neighbors think me if I allow the elves to be destroyed beneath the very walls of my capital, by those I am supposed to rule?"

When Shobbat was felled, activity in the courtyard and in the gatehouse ceased. Everyone halted to stare at the prince, sitting on the ground, his lips bleeding, his scarlet-clad father standing over him like an avenging demon. The powerful voice of Sahim-Khan filled the courtyard.

"And consider this, wastrel! If the nomads lose, more will come to avenge them. If the *laddad* lose, there will be no one left to pay for our repairs and your pleasures!"

Goaded beyond reason, the Khan drove the toe of his slippered foot into Shobbat's ribs. "Don't presume to offer guidance to me again! Get out of my sight!"

Doubled over in real pain, Shobbat got to his feet and slunk away. No one, not Sahim or Hakkam or those in the courtyard, saw the strange look of triumph that passed quickly over his face.

"Go, General! Take your soldiers and drive the nomads back into the wastes!"

"At once, Mighty Khan!"

Sahim was still shaking with fury when he stalked into his private rooms. His son's foolish words had given him an outlet for his fears but hadn't erased them from his mind. His worry over the sudden appearance of the desert tribes so disturbed him that he didn't notice the figure standing by the wall in the seam of two great hanging tapestries. Only when it spoke did he whirl, drawing the short sword concealed in his flowing robes. When he saw who accosted him, he uttered several choice curses.

"Such language!" said his visitor. "And from a king!"

"I'm in no mood for your tricks, Keth," Sahim said testily. He tossed his sword onto a tiled tabletop and ran fingers through his beard.

Keth-Amesh was a distant cousin, a member of the same tribe as Sahim, and his private woman-of-all-work. While he dropped heavily into a chair, Keth poured herself a cup of his best wine. She lowered the dust veil from her face to drink. Long ago she'd lost an eye, and wore a tan leather patch over the empty socket. Her skin was tawny brown, like that of many nomads, but she had fair hair, wisps of which escaped from her headdress. She was a so-called 'Yellow Khur,' from the coastal lands of the extreme eastern part of Sahim's realm.

"I found the mage, but not the priest," she reported. She drained her cup then refilled it.

Sahim had set her to find Faeterus and Minok when his legion of soldiers, informers, and spies failed in that task.

"Where is he?"

"Below," she answered, tapping a foot on the stone floor. She meant the system of caverns, natural and man-made, under the city. They had been enlarged by Sahim's grandfather for use as cisterns, but the water proved brackish and undrinkable. The empty, noisome caverns were a perfect retreat for the hunted Faeterus.

"If you know where he is, go get him."

Keth shook her head. "There's not enough money in the world to get me down there." When he said he would order her to go, she did something no one else in Khuri-Khan would dare do: She laughed at him. "I'm not one of your soldiers. You can't order me anywhere."

Sahim changed tack. "What of Minok?"

"No trace at all. He must be dead."

"You haven't earned your pay," Sahim told her sourly. "I hired you to find both and bring them to me!"

She tossed a heavy purse on the rug at his feet. "Your

money. Farewell, cousin. Call me again if you need anything—if you're still khan, that is."

Replacing her veil, she went back to the secret door behind the tapestry. Sahim called for her to wait, and she paused, one sinewy hand on the fringed tapestry.

"How can I get to the mage? I can't leave him down there, hatching plots unhindered," he said.

"You know assassins. Send some."

Sahim's laugh was bitter. "Cutthroats will never take Faeterus's measure. I need someone better."

Keth lowered her dust veil again. "There is a man, or rather, not a man. A *laddad* bounty hunter called Robien. I worked with him once."

"Well, bring him to me, right away!"

"You'll find him hard to work with."

"Why? Is he a drunkard?"

"Worse." She grinned. "He's honest and true. Not like you at all."

Tired of her insolence, he snapped, "Just get him! I'll overlook his honesty if he can bring Faeterus before me."

She bowed and went out the hidden door.

Sahim listened to the horns still blowing outside. The whole palace was quivering with marching soldiers and scurrying servants.

Damn all the foreigners! he fumed. *They're as bad as those desert savages.*

* * * * *

While the Khan was surrounded by boiling excitement, the Speaker sat alone in his silent tent. Planchet and Hamaramis were out tending to his business. The servants had been given leave to be with their families.

Gilthas had never felt so alone. In all the years of separation from Kerianseray, while she lived and fought in the greenwood and he played the Puppet King in Qualinost, he always had felt close to her. They shared a connection that went beyond love, beyond proximity. During the terrible march into exile, they were apart for weeks at a time, each knowing the other might be killed at any moment, but still they had been connected. Now she was gone, in every sense of the word. Gone from his house, gone from his city, gone from his life.

He knew he had done his duty by removing her. She had no vision, no understanding of the delicate, dangerous path they must tread if their race was to survive. Her way would lead to total destruction. Yet duty was small comfort to him.

It was a good thing to be alone. No one should see the Speaker of the Sun and Stars weep.

* * * * *

Hytanthas brought the Lioness the news from the parley. The nomads were demanding her and the sorcerer Faeterus as their price for peace. The assembled warriors greeted this broadside with shouts of derision.

"Sounds like a good bargain," Kerian remarked.

"Commander!" Hytanthas cried.

She stared out over the rolling dunes and at the dust raised by the nomad host on the move. A great deal of dust, from a great many horses. "It would be a fair bargain," she said, "if they meant it."

Unfortunately, she was certain they did not mean it. Nomads wouldn't have come all this way just to avenge the camp massacre. That was nothing more than a convenient excuse, a wedge to pry apart the elves and Sahim-Khan. The nomads had no intention of giving up everything for the heads of two elves. They were on a mission to destroy every elf in Khur.

Still, it sparked an idea. She was confident her warriors could defeat the nomad host, but the war thus started wouldn't end with this single battle. More and more tribesmen would join the fight, until the elves found themselves swamped by fanatics. Her dreams of retaking the elven home-lands would founder beneath a horde of unshod hooves.

She studied the officers clustered around her horse. The longest serving among them was a Qualinesti named Rama-canalas. "Take command, Ramac," she said. "I'm going to the nomads."

Shouts erupted, and Hytanthas seized her horse's bridle to keep her from riding away. She broke his grip and silenced them all with a hard-eyed glare.

"I'm going. Remain here. If the nomads move toward Khurinost, hit them as hard as you can with everything we've got."

"They'll kill you!" Hytanthas exclaimed.

The Lioness favored him with an ironic smile. "Not today."

16

Eight men abreast, the Khurish royal cavalry rumbled out the city's north gate. Their armor was a mix of native and Nerakan style, with pointed helmets, angular breastplates, and spiky knobs at every bend of knee, elbow, and ankle. Their favored weapon was a very heavy saber, its blade shaped like a crescent moon. Their mantles had started out royal blue, but long exposure to the harsh sun had faded them to the color of the spring sky over Khuri-Khan. The Khurs were among the best soldiers hired by the Dark Knights, but since the arrival of the elves Sahim-Khan had allowed the longstanding contract with Neraka to lapse. He had ample compensation from taxes, fees, and other official extortions to replace the money paid by the Order.

General Hakkam rode at the head of the column, flanked by standard bearers and heralds. Once the tail of the column cleared the city gate, he halted his men and sent out flankers on both sides and well ahead to scout the situation. The cavalry moved forward at a walk, alert for ambushes. In his long career, Hakkam had fought nomads before. They were fearless, hardy, and addicted to surprise attacks. He had no intention of losing men to (or being humiliated by) a rabble of tribesmen, especially with the *laddad* as witness.

The scouts soon returned with strange news. A sizable force of mounted *laddad* were on the north ridge, watching the nomads. The tribesmen were massed in the Lake of Dreams. This dry depression, six miles from Khuri-Khan, had earned its name because travelers commonly saw mirages of water in the broad hollow between dunes. Like the *laddad*, the nomads were motionless, waiting.

Hakkam uttered an oath. His lieutenants thought he was cursing the nomads or the *laddad*, but in fact he was abusing the name of Sahim-Khan. What had the master of Khur sent him into?

"Forward," he said, facing his horse west. At a leisurely walk, five thousand Khurish horsemen followed their general into the unknown. Shafts of sunlight pierced the clouds, casting beams down on the glittering, clanking procession. Unlike Adala, Hakkam didn't take the light as a sign of godly favor. It was shining in his men's eyes.

* * * * *

Alone of all the nomads gathered on the dune ridge overlooking Khuri-Khan, Adala slept. After returning from the tense meeting with the *laddad* lord, she finished some mending, then lay down in her small tent and went to sleep. Rain and thunder did not disturb her, nor did the presence of eighteen thousand armed *laddad*.

After midday, the sky grew dark and swollen, as if the heavy clouds would burst of their own weight, soaking the land below. Sentinels galloped back to the nomad camp with peculiar news. A single *laddad* rider was approaching. Bilath had sent a band of bow-armed Weya-Lu to the high sandhill on the north side of the Lake of Dreams. From there they could pick off anyone daring to enter the camp. They might have dealt thus with the rider had not the sharp-eyed warmaster of the Tondoon, Haradi, recognized her. Haradi had been with Adala at the parley and had heard talk of the female *laddad* warmaster, Kerianseray, also called the Lioness. This rider had burnished gold hair, which fell unbound past her shoulders. It must be the Lioness.

Etosh dispatched Wapah to waken the Weyadan.

Wapah knelt outside the closed door flap of Adala's tent and called softly. She bade him enter. He put his head inside, keeping his eyes respectfully on the ground.

"Weyadan, the female *laddad* warmaster comes. Alone!"

She lay with her back to him. Without moving, she said, "Summon the chiefs and warmasters. They will sit in judgment of the criminal."

"It is maita," he said sagely, and then withdrew.

Adala sat up slowly. Her head still ached, as it had ached for the past three days. The sky was responsible. The clouds hung over the desert like a gravid beast. She'd never known air this ponderous. It weighed on her so heavily she felt her skull would crack from the pressure. The usual cure for headache, chewing a leaf of the makadar bush, had provided no relief at all.

She poured tepid water in a copper pan and washed her hands, face, neck, and feet. During her ablutions, she blessed the names of her ancestors and called upon Those on High to judge her deeds this day. If she was found wanting in virtue or truth, she begged the gods to strike her down.

A bundle lay just inside the entrance to her tent. It proved to be a beautiful new robe of red linen, handsomely embroidered in white. The style and skill of the needlework marked it as having come from the women of the Mayakhur tribe. The collar and matching headdress were silk, hand-dyed, and fit for the khan's consort, but as much as Adala respected the sentiment behind the gift, she couldn't wear the beautiful robe. This was not a feast day, nor a day of celebration. Justice was to be done, harsh justice. It was not a time for festive clothes.

She put the new clothes aside and retied the sash of the much-mended black robe she wore every day, and slept in as well. Taking up an ivory comb—a gift from her late husband, Kasamir, and one of her few fine possessions—Adala mastered her unruly hair. Lately, she had noticed that some of the hairs the comb pulled out were not black, but gray.

Once her hair was smoothly braided, she emerged from her tent. Every chief and warmaster awaited her. They stood in a double line, facing inward, with Adala at the apex. Small patches of daylight speckled the ground, shining through rents in the ceiling of clouds.

Turning to the Weya-Lu on her right, Adala greeted Bilath and Etosh. Wapah stood a few steps behind them, as he was neither chief nor warmaster. Then came Yannash of the Tondoon and his warmaster Haradi, then Hagath of the Mikku, and so on down one line and up the other, ending with the Mayakhur leaders on Adala's left. She took an extra moment with Wassim, thanking the chief of the Mayakhur for the embroidered robe given her by his women and explaining why she could not wear it today. Then she addressed herself to the entire gathering.

"The day is coming," she said. "For our land, for justice. We must be strong." She spread her arms. "This land was granted us by Those on High, but only so long as we remain pure enough to hold it. Let the foreigners, the killers of our children, be purged from Khur."

She spoke calmly, but her last declaration brought a cheer from the assembly. They raised their swords high and shouted, "Maita! Maita! Maita!"

Beyond them, the warriors of Khur heard their chiefs and warmasters proclaiming their loyalty to Adala's fate, and they echoed it even more loudly. Again and again they roared, voices soaring to the turbulent heavens and rolling out in all directions. People for miles around could hear them.

Raising his voice to be heard over the shouts, Bilath said, "Weyadan, what of the sorcerer and Sahim-Khan? We came to impose justice on them, too."

"Sahim will meet his fate, but not today. As for the supposed sorcerer, I do not know him. If he is guilty, the gods will bring him to us." Adala frowned. She could have forgiven Sahim-Khan his past transgressions if he had sent his soldiers to fight alongside her people, but he had not. He continued to cower behind his stone walls. In time, Adala had no doubt her maita would deal with him, too.

Wapah brought Little Thorn forward and helped her climb onto the donkey.

"Let this day be long remembered," she said. "It is the day justice was reborn in Khur!"

With these words and the acclaim of ten thousand voices, Adala rode to the lip of the Lake of Dreams, trailed by her loyal chiefs and warmasters in their varying martial finery. The Mikku were the best armed, but the Tondoon were the most numerous. They wore no metal at all, reserving what iron and brass they had for their swords and daggers. Tondoon weaponry was highly prized.

At the top of the depression, she halted Little Thorn. The donkey lowered his head to munch on a clump of saltbush.

Through the haze and warping heat rising from the sand, she saw a single rider approaching on a tall bay horse. Archers on the hilltop followed her every move with arrows nocked. With utter nonchalance, the *laddad* woman came onward.

Someone behind Adala remarked on the elf's bravery. Adala shook her head. "It is not courage, but arrogance. She does not believe we can harm her."

Haradi moved forward. "Maita, let me slay her! I will do it for you, for all the tribes of Khur!"

Men, no matter their tribe, were united by a childish love of glory. "Be still," she said, as to an impatient youngster.

The Weyadan was wrong about one thing; it wasn't arrogance that fueled Kerian's bravery, but calm acceptance. The archers on the hill didn't concern her because she knew the nomads wanted revenge, not simply to kill her. She knew she wouldn't die today, knew it might be days before she died. Maybe longer. On the other hand, there was a possibility, however slim, that she would get out of this alive. If she did, then nothing would stop her goal to restore the fortunes of the elven nation.

After announcing her intention to turn herself over to the nomads, she took the time to write several letters to her comrades and friends. The last, and shortest, was to her husband.

Save our people. Take them home, she wrote. That was all. Words didn't seem to matter anymore, but maybe by this gesture she could restore Gilthas's will to do the right thing for their race.

Twenty yards from the line of bedecked barbarian chieftains, Kerian halted her horse. She wished Eagle Eye was here. Nothing made a grander or more frightening impression than a rampant Silvanesti war griffon.

"I hear you wanted to see me," she called.

Bilath shouted, "Come closer! It is not seemly to bellow at such a distance!"

Kerian made no move to comply, so some of the warmasters started toward her. She drew her sword in one fluid motion, feeble daylight flashing off the elf-forged blade. The nomads stopped.

"Did you come to fight or surrender?" Adala called.

"Fight! The Lioness never surrenders!"

So saying, she dug in her spurs and shot ahead, leaning low over the horse's neck. Arrows hissed into the sand behind her as she charged. In moments she was among the nomad chiefs, thrusting and slashing. This ended the threat from the archers who couldn't loose at her without hitting their own leaders.

Adala steered her donkey out of reach as Kerian laid about on all sides. She lopped the hand off a chief in a bright green geb, then booted another in the ribs with her iron-shod foot. The nomads' swords were keen, but close in their lack of handguards was a grave disadvantage. Kerian cut off fingers of two warmasters who tried to flank her, her blade hissing down their swords, finding no crossguard to halt its run, and biting into their hands.

Unable to cope with this whirlwind up close, the nomads

flew apart like grains of sand before a storm gust. Shouts rang as the chiefs called for support. Then one nomad cried, louder than the rest, "No, I will take her! For maita!"

Kerian now faced a single opponent, Haradi of the Tondoon. Only twenty, already he was warmaster of the most populous of the seven tribes. He was handsome, with olive skin, green eyes, and a closely trimmed beard. He also had the only sword with a handguard in the nomad army. The weapon was a relic of his father's days as a Nerakan mercenary.

The two combatants went round and round, slashing, probing, finding no openings. Kerian had to keep one eye on the other nomads swirling close around her in case they tried to intervene. None did.

With his blade inverted, Haradi stabbed at her face. She diverted his sword enough to spare her eyes but not her left ear. The tip of his sword tore through the shell of her ear, an ugly, painful wound. She promptly repaid him with a thrust under his outstretched arm, which pierced his armpit. He gasped, slumped forward, and dropped his sword.

She would have finished him, but the world around her exploded. Lightning flared and thunder crashed all of a sudden, pitching Kerian to the ground. Had any nomad come upon the Lioness then, he would have found her an easy kill.

The flash seared her eyes so severely she couldn't see. All was white glare and roaring noise. She couldn't have been hit directly by lightning; she'd be dead. But the strike must have come very close.

In the midst of the intense, dazzling light she saw a flicker of darkness. Gradually it grew more distinct, became darker and more defined. She heard the flutter of wings.

For a moment she thought it was Eagle Eye. But it was not the majestic griffon that flashed past her bleeding face, but a large bat. Why did she keep seeing bats? she wondered, though the question did not much trouble her. She was floating in a strange, disconnected netherworld.

SANCTUARY

A torrent of cold rain jerked her back to reality. She found herself lying close behind her fallen horse. The poor bay was dead, its neck broken, and her left leg was caught beneath its weight. Nearby was the nomad warrior's mount, also dead. Of the warrior himself, she saw no sign.

Men on horseback surged past her. Shaking off confusion and streaming rain, she realized they were Sahim's royal cavalry, not nomads or elves. The heavily armored Khurish horsemen had charged into the Lake of Dreams, smashing the larger but disorganized nomad host and driving it back. Flying above the hard-riding Khurs were five balls of blue fire.

She rubbed her eyes and shook her head hard, thinking her vision had been affected by the blast, but the lights remained. Larger than the will-o'-the-wisps at Inath-Wakenti, they flew more purposefully, turning in a stately, slow dance some thirty feet above the battlefield. Neither Khurish cavalry nor Khurish nomads seemed to notice them.

Kerian wrenched her leg from under the dead horse and stood. Immediately, the blue globes angled toward her. They moved so swiftly, she had no chance to dodge. At their touch, the world exploded once again in a crack of thunder and blaze of light.

*　*　*　*　*

The storm clouds dispersed quickly after the battle. Like a forge-hammer, the sun returned to beat down on the scene. The Lake of Dreams was littered with the remnants of the flight. Hakkam's cavalry, reinforced by fresh contingents from the city, had driven the nomads back so hard and fast, their camp was overrun and abandoned to the Khan's men. Hakkam ordered the camp burned. While the elves watched from Khurinost, a tent city not unlike their own was ruthlessly destroyed.

Hakkam broke off his pursuit of the beaten nomads. He and his men rode back to Khuri-Khan, to be greeted by the cheers of their people. In the wake of the cavalry's departure came scavengers from Khuri-Khan to poke in the ashes of the nomad camp. By the Khan's law, robbing those who had fallen in battle meant death. Despite this, desperately poor (or boldly greedy) Khurs stripped fallen warriors on both sides. In the Grand Souks, so much iron and brass turned up in the days following the battle, the price of scrap metal fell by two-thirds.

Late in the day, scroungers quartering the Lake of Dreams found a big bay horse, quite unlike the usual nomad ponies. The bay was trapped in the *laddad* fashion, with a heavy war saddle and mail aprons protecting neck and hindquarters. It lay dead at the edge of a six-foot-wide hole in the sand. The crater was lined with blackish-green glass, remnants of a lightning strike. No rider's body was found nearby.

Thorough if not reverent, the Khurs stripped the horse of its trappings. To do so, they had to heave the dead animal up. Beneath it they found a thick pile of leaves, still green, though crisp and dry. It seemed a weird discovery, but none of the Khurish scavengers recognized the leaves. They had never seen the ash trees of more temperate climes. Exposed by the removal of the fallen horse, the desiccated leaves whirled away on the wind.

* * * * *

"And the dead?"

The Tondoon chief consulted the tally in his hand. "Four thousand one hundred and sixteen slain or rendered incapable of further fighting," he said solemnly. Adala thanked him.

She and her champions rode near the head of their warbands, making for the safety of the deep desert. Iron-fisted Hakkam had finally ceased his pursuit, not wanting to risk his cavalry in the deeper sands, but still the nomads kept going, west toward the lowering sun, into the fastness of the desert.

SANCTUARY

The faces of the chiefs around her were grim. Practical as ever, Adala was noting the cuts and tears in their robes. She'd need an army of seamstresses to mend them all.

"What now, Weyadan?" asked her kinsman Bilath, trying not to sound dispirited.

"We continue the fight," she answered simply. "This war isn't finished until one side or the other is undone. We still live. Those who live can continue the fight."

"But can we defeat the Khan and the *laddad?*" The new chief of the Tondoon, Othdan, scowled and clenched the reins of his pony. Like Bindas of the Weya-Lu, Othdan was young, only twenty-six. Many of the old faces were gone. Othdan was succeeding two chiefs who had died fighting; one had been forty-four, the next, thirty-seven.

He reminded them of the scouts' reports. The *laddad* had at least ten thousand cavalry that had not entered the fray. There were nods and murmurs of agreement. The Weya-Lu fighters remembered how fiercely even a small force of *laddad* cavalry had fought during the journey to the Valley of the Blue Sands.

"How can we stop such troops?" Othdan said. "They're too powerful!"

"Too powerful to fight in open battle, yes," Adala agreed. "But as ants devour the panther, so can we overcome the *laddad*. It will take patience and skill. We must bind up our wounds and wait for our opportunity." Her stare burned into each of them, like the blazing sun in the west. "None of us must forget the debt we owe our dishonored dead, to avenge their murders and purify the land of Khur of its foreign taint!"

Wearily the chiefs agreed and turned their mounts to gallop off and see to their men. Only Wapah remained.

Adala was silent for a long time, so long that Wapah thought she dozed. But she wasn't sleeping. She was thinking hard thoughts.

"Do you still believe in my maita?" she asked. "Many

think our defeat by the Khan's troops means Those on High have abandoned us."

"I believe," he said simply. Then, because he was Wapah the philosopher, he added, "Does the herd know the mind of the shepherd, Adala Weyadan? Virtue will triumph. Your maita will triumph."

For a moment a smile played over one corner of her mouth. Good old Wapah. "How can you be so sure?"

"Your maita must triumph. If we are given the choice between good and evil, it follows there is value to making the choice. Evil means chaos and the end of our lives. Since sane people do not willingly end their lives, we choose good so we may survive. For the world to survive, good must triumph."

In the face of such confidence, Adala did not mention her own doubts. Sheer power had saved the laddad this time. Such force was itself neither good nor bad. The morality lay in how it was used, as a sword could kill an innocent child or a fiendish enemy. If Adala and her people were to prove victorious, they needed power of their own before they faced the laddad in open battle.

* * * * *

Striding the halls of the Khuri yl Nor, Prince Shobbat stopped every so often and looked back into the shadowed recesses behind him. He kept hearing noises—rustlings and soft scrapings, like the scrabbling of rats. It was not rodents but assassins he feared. Hengriff's death might stir trouble with the Dark Knights, but the Order had no patience with bunglers. They might blame Hengriff for his own death, for mingling too intimately in Khurish affairs. Either way, their next emissary would have to be a far more clever plotter to get the better of Shobbat.

He smiled at the thought. The expression ended in a wince of pain. His father had a hard fist; Shobbat's jaw was well bruised.

SANCTUARY

The stone walls jealously hoarded every sound inside them. As Shobbat entered his private quarters, again he heard a soft rustling sound, as of padded feet. Turning quickly, he saw them. Half a dozen monstrosities, like the ones the Oracle of the Tree had shown him, lurked in the shadows along the far wall of his sitting room. Animals with human heads, and humans with animal heads.

Terror ran its icy fingers through his gut, but he refused to give in to his fear. The creatures weren't real, they were only hallucinations, a product of his weariness and the ache in his head. He'd had a very trying day. He closed his eyes tight, then opened them.

It worked. The monstrosities were gone.

He laughed in relief. In answer, six inhuman voices chuckled and growled.

* * * * *

The elves who'd chosen to follow the Lioness returned to Khurinost somber and chastened. Their leader was gone, and shortly after she rode away to give herself to the nomads, Sahim-Khan's warriors fell on the unsuspecting tribes like a thunderbolt. The elven warriors had accomplished little this day. The nomads were in headlong flight for the safety of the deep desert. The body of Lady Kerianseray had not been found. None knew whether she was dead or alive.

The Speaker of the Sun and Stars awaited the return of his prodigal warriors in a small pavilion pitched just outside the northern edge of Khurinost. With him were Planchet and Hamaramis. He leaned on a cane crafted from a spear shaft. Decorating the front of its wooden handle was a square-cut amethyst, the gift he'd received from the old gemcutter weeks before.

Hytanthas Ambrodel was among the returning riders. The young Qualinesti broke ranks and approached. He dismounted before the Speaker.

"Captain Ambrodel. What word do you bring me?"

367

"A sad one, Great Speaker. There is still no sign of Lady Kerianseray."

Gilthas had feared as much. He'd ordered the Lake of Dreams searched for any trace of his consort. The captain had led the search himself.

The Speaker sent him back to the returning riders. Hamaramis cleared his throat. "Great Speaker, what of the warriors who mutinied? They disobeyed their commanders and followed Lady Kerianseray against your orders. They must be punished."

From their faces, Gilthas thought they'd been punished already. The old general obviously did not. "Discipline must be maintained, sire," Hamaramis added.

"Punish over half the army? What would that do to morale?" Gilthas said gloomily.

Planchet intervened. "Certain zealots can be singled out, Great Speaker."

After a pause, Gilthas nodded. "Don't treat them too harshly," he said. "Their loss is my loss."

He swayed a little, despite his cane. Smoothly, Planchet eased a stool behind him and he sat. The valet hid his own worry, but he'd begun to wonder whether the Speaker would ever be whole again. The Khurish priestesses had cured him, yet he was still so weak, the silver in his hair more pronounced. Gilthas was not much older than Captain Ambrodel, but he seemed a generation removed.

"Sahim-Khan has done us a great service today," the valet suggested. The nomads had been repulsed without the loss of elven life—save one, perhaps.

"I wonder how much he'll charge us for the service," Hamaramis muttered sourly.

Gilthas gazed over the dunes that filled the landscape around the tent city. The tan hills seemed to him the body of a vast sleeping giant, lying on its side.

"Sahim will not get another copper from us. This incident proves the time has come for us to go." Hands cupped over the head of his cane, Gilthas looked up at his loyal friends, first Hamaramis, then Planchet. "To Inath-Wakenti, the Valley of the Blue Sands."

"Is the place hospitable?" asked Planchet. "What of the dangers Lady Kerianseray mentioned?"

"We have many scholars and sages among us. They will unravel the mysteries. Besides—" Gilthas frowned. "There are dangers here too, and they will grow greater if we stay."

The nomads had been driven back, but only temporarily. They would recover and return, using the desert as a shield against Sahim's powerful but ponderous army. Plots in the city would continue so long as the Sons of the Crimson Vulture agitated against the elves. The rogue sorcerer Faeterus was still at large. Compared to these pressing ills, how terrible could Inath-Wakenti be?

Gilthas saw his retinue watching him, and he knew their troubled thoughts. He, too, sometimes wondered whether he had become obsessed with a spot on an old map. Was it sanctuary or delusion? The only way to know the truth was to go there.

As inevitable as drawing breath, his thoughts returned to Kerian. He refused to count her as dead. He would know in his heart if her life had ended. More likely, she had been carried off by the nomads, to whom she'd so valiantly surrendered herself. He already had resolved to send a small band of warriors to determine her fate and rescue her if possible. He would put Hytanthas Ambrodel in charge. However far the nomads went, however long it took, the dedicated captain would follow. If Kerian had been slain, Gilthas must know. If she was Adala's prisoner, he must get her back. The one thing he could not do was remain any longer in Khuri-Khan. Sahim's resources would be invaluable in the search for Kerianseray, but the elves must leave him on good terms. If they tarried, Gilthas risked losing the entire elven nation. The survival of his people must outweigh the welfare of his wife.

Dreams were murky things. As the sun settled low between the western dunes and the hot blue sky cooled to the colors of fire, Gilthas closed his eyes and let his chin rest on his hands. They were all such a long way from home. Like children, they were trying to find their place in the world. But children, he mused, didn't usually have half a continent trying to kill them.

Trying. Many had tried, and failed. The ancient race of elves, firstborn of the world, would not be swept into oblivion without a mighty struggle. They would call on every scrap of strength, talent, and enterprise to save themselves. A hundred thousand had followed their Speaker into exile after the dual destructions of their homelands. From this core of strength, this seed, a new elven nation would grow. All that was needed was a sanctuary to allow the seedling to take root.

Dreams were awake. Gilthas opened his eyes to the dying sun.

A KHURISH GLOSSARY OF
WORDS AND PHRASES

affre — A hooded, ankle-length robe worn over the *geb*; especially favored by nomads of the high desert.

Fabazz (a.k.a. Lesser Souk) — An outdoor market in Khuri-Khan, for spices, incense, and foodstuffs.

geb — A sleeveless robe that hangs straight from the shoulders unless tied at the waist with the *ghuffran*; especially favored by nomads.

geel — One of the eleven civic precincts of Khuri-Khan.

geel-khana — The guard commander of one of Khuri-Khan's eleven *geel*.

ghuffran — A leather cord used as a belt on the *geb*.

Grand Souks — The main outdoor market in Khuri-Khan and the largest market in all of Ansalon.

Harbalah — The northern district of Khuri-Khan, ruined by Malystryx and not repaired.

Khuri-Khan — The capital city of Khur; historically, the seat of the Khur tribe.

Khuri yl Nor ("Palace of the Setting Sun") — The palace of the khan in Khuri-Khan.

laddad — (ancient) Literally, "those who walk on air," referring to griffon riders. (modern) Elves, encompassing Qualinesti, Silvanesti, and Kagonesti, since Khurs make no distinction.

Laddad-ihar ("Elves' Anthill") — The Khurish name for the elven tent settlement outside Khuri-Khan.

Lesser Souk — see *Fabazz*.

maita — Fate, carrying connotations of inevitability, an outcome predestined by the gods which no mortal can escape.

Malsh-mekkek ("Malys's Tooth") — A boulder buried in the *Nak-Safal*, hurled by Malystryx in an unsuccessful attempt to destroy Khuri-Khan's great well.

Malsh-sakhar ("Malys's Anvil") — The western gate into Khuri-Khan; so called because Malystryx crushed many foes against its iron portcullises.

Mazin yl Sadaf ("Lake of Dreams") — A dry depression six miles from Khuri-Khan; so called because travelers commonly see mirages of water in it.

Nak-Safal ("Bottomless Pool") — The great artesian well in the center of Khuri-Khan.

Nor-Khan — The central citadel in the *Khuri yl Nor*.

soukat — A merchant in the Khurish *souk*.

souk — Outdoor market.

Weyadan ("mother of the Weya-Lu") — A title of the widow of the Weya-Lu chief.

Zacca-Khur ("Father of Khur") — One of the khan's many titles (i.e., Sahim Zacca-Khur).

SEVEN TRIBES OF KHUR

Fin-Maskar — Coastal tribe. Herders and fishermen, one of the wealthiest of Khurish tribes.

Hachakee — Their territory lies south of Khuri-Khan. Highly-skilled horse-breeders.

Khur — Tribe of the royal house of Khur. Native territory, the eastern desert to the sea.

Mayakhur — From the far south of Khur. Smallest of the tribes, renowned for their tracking skills.

Mikku — Their territory is north of Khuri-Khan. Frequent suppliers of mercenaries to Neraka and the Khan's army.

Tondoon — Their territory is west of Khuri-Khan. Largest tribe in Khur.

Weya-Lu — Their territory is in northwest Khur, between Khuri-Khan and Kortal.

GODS OF KHUR

Khurs worship a legion of gods and demi-gods only vaguely familiar to outsiders, and nomad deities vary from those worshiped by city dwellers. The following seem to be the most frequently mentioned:

Eldin the Judge — High god of nomads.

Elir-Sana — The divine healer, bringer of plenty; may equate to Mishakal.

Torghan, the Avenger — God of vengeance; may equate to Sargonnas.

Kargath the Warrior — May equate to Kiri-Jolith.

Rakaris the Hunter — Patron deity of hunters and predators; may equate to Chislev.

Anthor the Hermit — God scholars, poets, and dreamers; usually equated with Majere.

Hab'rar the Messenger — Carrier of the winds; thought to be Habbakuk.

Soro the Firemaker — God hearth and home. May
  equate to Sirrion.

Ayyan the Deceiver — Goddess of darkness.

RICHARD A. KNAAK
THE OGRE TITANS

The Grand Lord Golgren has been savagely crushing
all opposition to his control of the harsh ogre lands of
Kern and Blöde, first sweeping away rival chieftains, then
rebuilding the capital in his image. For this he has had to
deal with the ogre titans, dark, sorcerous giants who have
contempt for his leadership.

VOLUME ONE
THE BLACK TALON
Among the ogres, where every ritual demands blood and every ally can
become a deadly foe, Golgren seeks whatever advantage he can obtain,
even if it means a possible alliance with the Knights of Solamnia, a
questionable pact with a mysterious wizard, and trusting an elven slave
who might wish him dead.

December 2007

VOLUME TWO
THE FIRE ROSE
With his other enemies beginning to converge on him from all sides,
Golgren, now Grand Khan of all his kind, must battle with the
Ogre Titans for mastery of a mysterious artifact capable of ultimate
transformation and power.

December 2008

VOLUME THREE
THE GARGOYLE KING
Forced from the throne he has so long coveted, Golgren makes a final
stand for control of the ogre lands against the Titans . . . against an
enemy as ancient and powerful as a god.

December 2009

COLLECT THE TALES OF THE
HEROES OF THE LANCE!
NEW EDITIONS AVAILABLE!

THE MAGIC OF KRYNN
Volume One

In these ten tales of adventure and daring, the original
companions of the War of the Lance are together again. The
tales tell of sea monsters, dark elves, ice bears and loathsome
draconian troops.

KENDER, GULLY DWARVES, AND GNOMES
Volume Two

Nine short stories by superlative writers tell the tales of the
well-loved companions as they confront danger, beauty, magic,
friendship, and their destinies.

LOVE AND WAR
Volume Three

Finally, the legend of Raistlin's daughter is revealed. This story,
in addition to ten other compelling stories of chivalry, heroism,
and villainy fill the pages of this stirring addition to the
DRAGONLANCE canon.